Just because you have a shit start in life, doesn't mean it'll be that way forever...

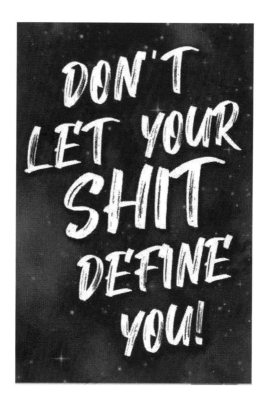

By Hadley C

1 THE STAIRWELL

It's gone 2 a.m and the night bus slows to a stop at the side of the road, pulling in next to a row of tatty old shop fronts. Metal shutters cover the windows, each one padlocked at the bottom in an attempt to protect the shops' contents so that only the dirty old signs at the top of each shop give away what each one sells.

A man - too sober for a night out (a night worker maybe?) - steps off the bus and onto the pavement, leaving a single passenger alone on the bottom deck, lit brightly for security. The man throws his rucksack onto his back and walks off with a swagger, but his bravado slips, just briefly, as he glances back quickly over his shoulder before disappearing down a side street and out of sight.

The bus pulls off. The lone passenger, a young man in his 20s, slumps against the window, drunk. Staring out into the street with a blank expression, exhausted from his boozy night out.

Across the road, a 1970s tower block looms over the road, it's pebble-dash fascia an attempt by some well-meaning architect in a climate-controlled office somewhere to bring something a little more 'creative' to the cold, dark slabs of concrete that make up the body of the tower. Cascading upwards, rows after rows of balconies, each one lit as brightly as possible for security. Except that everyone who lives there knows there's no such thing as security. If trouble comes, it comes. And if anything happens - which it does on a regular basis - all it means is it's there for all to see. But just because it's seen, doesn't mean it's reported.

Hurtling full pelt - *UP*- the stairwell of the tower is Flash, his name a reference to the speed at which he moves. Sixteen, dressed in light grey trackies and a hoodie, he takes the steps two at a time, skidding on the damp, gritty surface as he hits each level with a sliding thud where the stairs open up. There's nothing distinguishing about him other than what he's wearing, and a flash of black skin. In his hand, he carries a shoebox, with a picture of some trainers on the side. The pristine white of the box glows in the hazy dankness of the tower block.

Flash hurtles up the stairs, faster and faster - his face completely focused, relaxing only when he reaches his flat. He pulls his key from his back pocket and unlocks his front door as quietly as he can. Placing the cardboard box down on the floor in front of him, he kicks off his old trainers, and reaches for the new pair inside the box. He pulls them out, lifting them up in front of his face to inspect them more closely. Just for a second, a look flashes across his face. But it was there. Definitely. Categorically… A look of pure and utter love. This is a guy who *loves* his trainers. The trainers are pure white - and give off a throbbing glow in the dark. Flash admires them for a second longer before placing them back on the ground. Carefully, he slides his feet into them so as not to damage the heels, places his old pair back in the box and shuts the lid. "Thanks for the times," he mutters quietly, in a thick, London accent, straight off the street. Kissing the lid for old times' sake, he balances the box under his chin, using his spare hand to open his front door before heading outside.

Locking his front door behind him, he heads back out into the night. But instead of heading for the stairwell at the side of the building, he races to the end of the balcony, stopping to peer over the edge to examine the skips about a hundred feet below. His eyes rest on the one with the open top, and he fist bumps the air. "Yes!" Holding the shoe box out in front of him, he focuses for a second before letting go - watching as his old trainers fall out of the box and hurtle towards the skip, landing with a thud at the bottom, followed closely by the shoe box. Flash punches the air in victory and laughs, muttering to himself under his breath. "Not sure they're recyclable, but hey..."

And with that, he's off. Hurtling back down the stairwell, into the night. On his way... somewhere.

2 A TINY, CRAMPED SPACE

Boom huddles inside the tiny, cramped space. Light filters through a slit at the bottom of a door; just enough to mark the outline of his body, but nothing else; his face and expression hidden.

He sits in the dark, knees drawn tight to his chest, foetal like a baby; his body in self-protect mode, hiding from something we can't see. He buries his head in his knees and presses his headphones tight to his ears, until the sinews in his hands strain with the pressure.

Garage music pumps at a deafening volume inside his head; the sheer noise of it causing him to wince as it crashes through his delicate nervous system. The heavy sounds of DJ Luck and Mc Neat's 'Little Bit of Luck' play over and over in his head.

> *"With a little bit of luck,*
> *We can make it through the night."*

The same line plays over and over in his head as he stays hunched up, cramped and uncomfortable. Releasing a hand from one ear, Boom reaches down to pull something out from under him. It's a trainer.

As he moves, his head brushes against something soft and floaty, inches from his head. It's a piece of material - the bottom of a shirt that dangles from a hanger just above his head.

4

Boom is hidden inside a wardrobe.

As he shifts his weight around in an attempt to get more comfortable, his headphones slip from his head and the sound of a man's voice kicks in, harsh and abusive.

"Who's gonna believe *you*?! You sad, FUCKING CUNT!"

Venom lines his voice, the words falling out of his mouth like acid, burning everything in its pathway.

Boom covers his mouth with his hands, stifling a noise. The sound of a wounded, frightened animal, expressing only what it knows in that moment: the raw emotion of fear. Hands trembling, he tugs at his headphones and shoves them back on his head, pushing them tight to his ears to block out the shouting from somewhere inside the flat. Burying himself down deeper and deeper into a tight ball at the bottom of the wardrobe; the same line of the song repeating over and over in his head, like a personal mantra.

Boom struggles to breathe, his breath laboured. He shuts his eyes tight, talking to himself in an attempt to keep himself calm. "Just keep breathing, really slow. In. Out. You can do this."

There's a heavy THUD, as a body hits a wall, and the music cuts dead. Then--

Silence.

Boom pulls off his headphones, allowing them

to slip down to rest on his neck. His hands hover over them though, so that at any given moment should he need to, he can pull them back over his ears at even a hint of a noise. Boom stays there, huddled in the dark; motionless in the tiny, cramped space and waits. The slightest creak of a floorboard, or groan of a water pipe, enough to send him spiralling straight back into a state of heightened anxiety, his sensors on hyper alert as he sits poised in the dark.

After a minute of no sound, Boom reaches forward in the dark. He slides open the wardrobe door and falls out onto the bedroom carpet in front of him, burying his head deep into the worn threads of the carpet; his body a crumpled mess, falling in a heap like the haphazard outline of a murder victim.

He's tall, but at 16 not yet an adult. He sits there, resting his head on the carpet, stuck in child's pose with his arms stretched out either side of his body. Surrounded by an eerie silence, Boom focusses on his breathing until he brings it under control and is calm enough to sit up.

Boom's eyes are large and expressive, his pupils pumped wide with fear.

His body remains taut like a tightly-coiled spring as his eyes scan the room. Slowly, Boom brings himself back into his surroundings; his body starting to shake as he takes in the familiarity of his room. A duvet that lies in a crumpled heap at the bottom of his bed and the blue glow of his computer pulsing in the otherwise black cave of his room.

He glances at the clock on his desk. It's 2:20 a.m.

Boom gets up slowly, as if coming out of a daze.

He ruffles his jeans back down his legs to cover his ankles and reaching underneath his bed, pulls out a black rucksack. The bag clinks loudly as he picks it up, causing him to freeze for a second. He keeps his eyes fixed on his bedroom door... waiting for something. Some kind of noise or movement, from beyond. But there's nothing.

Boom opens his bedroom door and creeps out into a dark, unlit corridor, freezing as he hears a loud thud. His pupils dilate and his gaze shifts to a door at the end of the corridor. It's shut, but light pools out from underneath the slit at the bottom. Boom stands there for a second, frozen with fear, until he comes back round, visibly gaining consciousness as he allows himself to enter back into the world of reality once more.

Quickly - quietly - he walks into the kitchen, making sure not to turn the light on as he manoeuvres his way around the room in the dark. Running his hands along the curve of a small, round table, he passes a chair and heads for a door at the side of the kitchen. He opens it, stepping out into another corridor; this time a tiny, narrow corridor where a row of coats hang from the wall. Beneath them, rows and rows of shoes line up next to each other. A pair of large, steel-capped boots dominate the pile, crushing the pair of worn, pink slippers beneath them.

Boom opens a door off the side of the corridor which leads straight into a tiny toilet where there's barely enough space for him to turn around and shut the door. Keeping the light turned off, Boom pulls the toilet seat down and climbs on top, reaching for the tiny window above the windowsill. He opens the window and stands on tiptoe on top of the toilet, peering out onto the balcony outside. He checks the coast is clear before lifting up his rucksack and lowering it out of the window as slowly as he can before letting it drop the final few feet below. But no matter how gently he tries to lower it, the bag lands with a loud clink on the balcony below.

Visibly stressed, Boom lets out a slow, controlled breath, and waits.

Hearing nothing, he pulls himself up onto the tiny, narrow ledge below the window, balancing precariously for a second as he positions his arms like a diver before twisting them through the tiny window. He sucks his breath in as he scrapes the sides of his arms before turning himself into some kind of crazy contortionist, twisting his body through the window, arms first, followed by his head, then body. His waist follows, then his hips, and lastly his feet as he lowers himself onto the balcony below, as quietly and as slowly as he can.

He lands in an awkward heap next to his bag, but shoots back upright, glancing in both directions before grabbing his rucksack and heading off as fast as he can, past his front door. The heavy, wooden door is painted a bright, angry red and a rusty number - '201' - hangs upside down from a screw halfway down the frame. Boom pauses in front of the number and slides it back up, holding it level with a finger for a second or two before letting it go again, leaving the number to swing there for a few seconds as he slips off into the night, heading down the stairwell next to his front door.

3 THE MEET

Boom reaches the last balcony before the ground floor and stops, heading over to a railing overlooking the semi-deserted street below. Next to him, the silent doors of two broken lifts are jammed open, each one plastered with a poster warning residents that the lifts are out of order.

Boom reaches into his pocket and pulls out a packet of fags, or 'bogies' as he and his mates jokingly call them, after Humphrey Bogart, the actor from the days of the black and white movies who smoked his way through all his films. He slides a fag out of the pack but his hands are shaking - he's clearly still shaken by what happened earlier. Boom tries to light the fag but fails several times before, finally, managing to light it. He takes a slow, deep drag on the fag and reaches for the railing, gripping it tightly with his spare hand. Boom's body is taught and rigid as he stands there inhaling the smoke deep into his lungs, gripping the railing painfully tight as he stares out across the City streets below.

Above him, several floors up, Flash hurtles down the stairwell, closer and closer until he passes Boom's dilapidated front door with the red paint and its rusty door number. *Except that he doesn't know it's Boom's flat.* As he passes, the full force of a body slams into the door from the inside, and a woman lets out a painful moan.

Flash jumps sideways in shock. "Fuck!"

Shaken, Flash stares at the door, where the rusty 201 swings from its hook, vibrating from the force of the hit. A neighbour, a wiry, anxious-looking man in his 30s, stands outside his front door, glancing nervously at Boom's front door. He spots Flash and looks away quickly. His wife steps out onto the balcony beside him; a two-year-old balanced on her hips, his hair ruffled and messy, his face stunned, like he's woken suddenly from a deep sleep. The boy looks terrified. The woman spots Flash staring at them and pulls her husband back inside their flat, shutting the door quickly behind them.

Flash shakes his head in shock and heads back down the stairwell.

Back on the level below, Boom grips the handrail, his hands moulded to the metal like they've been welded on. Boom sucks his fag down to the filter before throwing it on the floor and stubbing it out with his foot. Immediately, he lights up a second one, breathing in a deep lungful of smoke and holding it in. But before he gets the chance to breathe it back out, he's rushed from behind and someone grabs his arm. Boom chokes - coughing and spluttering and struggling to catch his breath. Someone tackles him from behind and play punches him in the sides, making him drop his fag.

Boom swings round to confront his attacker, only to see Flash standing opposite him with a big grin on his face.

"Fucking *twat*!" Boom tells him, shaken and pissed off, all in one.

Flash throws his head back in delight, talking in excitable, but hushed tones. "Waiting long, bro?"

Boom picks his fag up off the dirty floor, his

hands still shaking. Flash looks at him.

"What? I scare you?!" He's taking the piss, but Boom doesn't smile. Flash looks at his mate and frowns. "You ok, G?"

Everything about Flash is rushed. His speech clipped… the first word missing off the start of each sentence. He's fidgety too. Clumsy and all limbs, like a newborn colt.

Boom looks at him. "Just tired, that's all."

"Two a.m. ain't good for no-one bro," Flash replies. "Still don't get why we don't just meet at yours though. Fucking freezing out here."

Booms shrugs. Flash tips his head towards Boom's fag.

"Got a spare bogie?"

Boom hands him one from his pack and leans forward, covering his so Flash can use it to light his one off the back of it. Boom's hands are still shaking though and he drops his cigarette, narrowly missing Flash's new white trainers by inches. Flash jumps back several feet.

"Yo! Watch my pearlies, will ya?!"

And then Boom grins. "Serves you right for picking such a gay colour!"

Flash grins, pleased to see his friend 'back'. He glances down at Boom's bag. "You ready?" he asks. Boom nods. Moving in sync, they pull their hoods up over their faces before heading out onto the deserted streets below.

4 DA CREW

Flash and Boom walk next to each other in silence, through an empty industrial estate, the gates at the front of each unit heavily chained and padlocked for the night. Their bodies move in sync, like two old friends who've known each other all their lives (which they pretty much have). Their length of step the same, even their pace; completely unaware they're even doing it. Weirdly, for this nighttime mission, they walk with their hoods down and their faces completely exposed, leaving their eyes free to scan their surroundings. They stalk their way through the estate, which runs alongside a canal lit by powerful street lights. They walk in the middle of the road, not the edge; their eyes scanning the road ahead. Every now and then Boom spins round, walking backwards alongside Flash, his eyes checking the streets behind them. Cameras face the street, positioned on the corner of every building as they pass. Flash keeps veering back towards the pavement but Boom keeps pulling him back into the road each time, tipping his head in the direction of the cameras to warn him away.

Then--

The tiniest of frowns touches Boom's face and without having to say a word, both he and Flash pull their hoods up over their heads and slip down a side street and into the shadows. They push their bodies up tight against the exterior wall of a building as a police car appears from nowhere. The car can't be doing more than ten, fifteen miles an hour. Silently, they watch it pass with two cops in the front, their faces as clear as day under the bright white light of the streetlights, both edged forward in their seats, their eyes scanning the estate looking for any sign of illegal activity.

Flash and Boom wait for the cops to pass before turning to face each other. Without saying a word, Boom tips his head in the direction of the canal, its dark, still waters visible between a gap between two buildings; its icy air making its presence felt. They head off down some steps, towards the black, velvety waters of the canal.

Boom struggles to keep up as Flash races ahead, moving at his normal frenetic pace. Shaking his head in frustration, Boom whispers ahead to Flash. "Slow down, will ya?" But Flash is already at the bottom of the steps by this point, waiting for Boom to catch up. Keeping their hoods up, they head towards some bushes close to the water's edge. When they get there, they stand and wait; shoving their hands deep into their pockets, their eyes scanning the dark. Watching and waiting.

Back in the street above, two teenagers step out of the shadows, following the same route that Boom and Flash took minutes earlier. It's The Watcher, 16, and Curl-i-Cue, also 16. They reach the top of the steps leading down to the canal and The Watcher takes one look at Curl, gives him a mischievous grin, and signals to where Boom and Flash are standing, close to the canal. He puts his finger over his mouth and tips his head for Curl to follow.

Down by the canal, Boom and Flash wait in silence, lit only by the hazy glow of the street lamp several feet away, its light softer than that of those on the Industrial Estate.

A hooded teenager, the same age, slinks out of the shadows next to them. It's The Cat. Lithe and athletic like a cat, his body moves in graceful, fluid movements. The three of them fist bump in the usual Crew greeting, but no-one speaks.

The Cat pulls a bottle of whisky from his pocket, takes a swig and passes it to Flash. Flash tips his head back, takes a large swig-- and chokes. Boom and The Cat slap him, exaggeratedly, on the back, pissing themselves laughing.

Flash shakes his head at them. "Piss off, you twats!" But despite how animated they all are, their words are weirdly muted. They work mainly, instead, with hand signals, talking only in hushed tones.

Boom passes the bottle back to The Cat who takes another swig before passing it on. He then flips onto both hands, before raising one of them off the ground to perform what looks like an effortless, one-handed handstand next to Flash. Head pointing at the floor, he clocks Flash's trainers.

"What's with the glow whites?"

"Cool, no? Sell for eighty in the shops," Flash replies.

The Cat flips back onto his feet, grinning. "Save up for them, did ya?" He gives Flash a pointed look, implying something totally different, before adding:

"Bet you could buy 'em for a tenner off the market."

Flash looks offended, making Boom and The Cat laugh. "These 'aint no market shoes! These are S-T-Y-L-E-Y, just like Cyrus M-I-L-E-Y!"

"Don't know about styley. Damn HOT'S what she is," The Cat whispers back, using both his hands to mark out the shape of a curvy silhouette, stopping to squeeze a pair of imaginary tits in front of him, making the others laugh.

Boom looks relaxed now and is stood with his head tipped back, staring at the stars, smiling at the banter.

"Besides," The Cat continues, "It 'aint the style I'd be worried 'bout, 'bro. It's you. Odds on they'll be covered in paint or at the bottom of the canal by the end of tonight."

All three of them laugh, acutely aware of how accident-prone Flash is, before falling into a comfortable silence. The Cat glances at Boom, still staring up at the stars.

"What's up G?"

"Just making the most of blurry hour, my friend," Boom replies.

"What the fuck's blurry hour?" The Cat asks him.

"Blurry hour is now my friend," Boom replies, pulling his hands from his pockets and using them to express himself. "The time when normal people are asleep. 'Our' time."

Flash jumps in. "Watchit. Boom's getting all poetic again."

Boom laughs. "Shut it. Or I'll set me dog on those poncey white trainers of yours."

"You aint got no dog." Flash thinks for a second, then frowns. "Have you?!"

They laugh but stop immediately as a twig cracks underfoot. They freeze, falling into a breathless silence as they get ready to run. The Cat looks at Boom and Flash. "What was that?" he mouths.

They stand there, poised, and silent. There's another crack and Flash loses it. "Run!"

Before they can move, though, they're grabbed from behind. They let out a terrified yelp as pairs of arms clamp them from behind, pinning their own arms to their sides. A second later, they're released, and they spin round to find The Watcher standing in front of them, in hoodie and tracks, laughing quietly to himself. Next to him, unsure quite how to react, is newcomer Curl - a little bit more hip and designer than the rest of them. The Cat turns to The Watcher and gives him a hard shove.

"You dick! I thought you were the feds!"

He shakes his head at The Watcher and catches his eye before both of them break out laughing. Relieved, the others laugh too, punching The Watcher on the arm in retaliation. The Watcher - ever the joker - does a triumphant dance in front of them all.

"We did good, right Curl?"

The group turn towards Curl, as The Watcher introduces him.

"Everyone, meet the newest member of Da Crew, Curl-i-Cue. Curl for short. Curl, meet--"

Flash leans forward and fist bumps Curl. "Flash.

'Cause I is as fast as lightning."

The Cat follows. "The Cat. Cat for short. 'Cause I *always* land on my feet."

The Watcher introduces Boom as he leans forward. "And, finally. The other writer in the group..."

"Boomshakalaka," Boom says. "Boom for short." Slipping into Jamaican patois, he tells Curl - "Mean joy and 'appiness. An onomatopoeic 'in your face.'

"Onomata-what?!" Flash asks, lost.

"Never mind," Boom replies. He turns to Curl, continuing in Patois, "You're da one wit da fancy writin then?' He catches Flash's confused face and tries to explain. "Curlicue. Means lots of curls and 'tings." Boom fist bumps Curl's balled up hand. "Good to meet you, bro. You got tonight's piece?"

Curl nods. Boom turns to The Watcher. "Signal?"

The Watcher starts to whistle The Octonauts tune, from The BBC's underwater kid's adventure show.

"What the fuck?!" Flash laughs.

The Watcher falls back from the rest of the group, positioning himself at the top of a hill, giving himself a clear, 360-degree view of his surroundings. The rest of the group then gravitate, telepathically and en masse, towards a bridge further down the pathway. Torch beams flicker across the path in the dark before Flash's voice penetrates the silence.

"No way!"

Someone shines a torch on Flash's face. "Got shit all over me brand new white trainers!"

Torch beams travel down his legs to his feet. The Crew laugh as Flash rants quietly to himself in the dark.

"What idiot lets their dog *poo* in the middle of the path and not pick it up?!"

The group howl at the use of poo, their voices reverberating in the dark as the sound bounces off the railway bridge just ahead of them. Flash tries to wipe the dog poo off his trainers but it's really runny so his trainers get more and more smeared with shit.

"Fucking stinks man!" he says, screwing his face up in disgust. "Whatever dog did that needs to wipe his arse somewhere else next time."

The Cat laughs, humming a couple of beats of music out loud before breaking into Queen's "Another one bites the dust!" He laughs, throwing his arms up at Flash, "What d'I tell you?!"

Laughing, Boom drapes his arm affectionately around Flash as they reach the bridge. "I love you, G!"

5 FEISTY GIRL

Someone shines a torch beam onto the bridge. Without warning, The Cat takes a running jump and hits the wall hard, scrambling up the side using only his feet. Grabbing the top of the bridge, he pulls himself up several times, doing makeshift press-ups, before letting go and landing agilely on both feet on the ground below. The urban equivalent of a gymnastics display.

"Save the gymnastics for later, will ya?" Flash says.

"Ooo!" The Cat walks away, giving Flash some attitude, before turning to the others. "Don't worry about Flash. Must be his time of the month!"

"Fuck you!" Flash replies as the others laugh, but he's smiling. It's friendly banter.

Boom walks over to where Curl's dumped his bag. It's a regular shopping bag from The Co-op, plastic with two handles - the least likely looking graffiti bag ever.

"Wanna hand?" Boom asks him.

Curl nods. "Sure."

Curl opens the bag to reveal a stack of graffiti cans, paint dripped down the sides of them, and a stack of blue latex gloves. He pulls out a pair of gloves and chucks them at Boom, before grabbing a pair for himself.

Standing in front of the bridge, they take in how it looks now. The word FUCK is scrawled across the bricks in bright, pink graffiti letters, the 'fluffiness' of the colour at complete odds with the harsh brutality of the word.

"Guess they were at least creative enough to use some pink," says Boom sarcastically, making Curl laugh. "Shall we?"

Curl nods, "With pleasure." Working next to each other in silence, the others stand behind them, shining their torches onto the wall to light it up for them. Boom pulls a can of paint from the bag and gives it a shake. The bearings rattle loudly and the Crew fall silent. Boom glances nervously up at the embankment where The Watcher is stood. He gives Boom the thumbs up before Boom pops the lid of the can, covering the wall from top to bottom in plain brown paint. Keeping his hand close to the wall, Boom works in short, sweeping movements, making sure he covers every last inch of the old graffiti as well as the wall.

Curl grabs a can, pops the lid and swaps the existing cap with one at the bottom of the bag. The jet of paint comes out finer this time, as Curl traces the outline of a word in black. He picks up a second can and injects a burst of yellow onto the wall, filling a letter. He grabs another can, gives it a shake. Except this one's half-empty, making the bearings rattle even louder. The Crew shift nervously in their spots, looking round warily to make sure the coast is clear before a burst of luminous pink hits the brick. Curl doesn't stop, moving quickly, can after can, until he's done. Stepping back to admire his work, his once clean blue gloves are covered in a myriad of colour.

In front of him, in bold, bright letters, is the phrase, 'Shit happens'. But instead of the typical, geometric look of graffiti, Curl's letters are a dedication to his name. Curly and elaborate. *Fancy* almost, and beautiful despite their meaning.

The Cat stands next to him, balancing on one leg like a flamingo, admiring Curl's work.

"*Posh* graffiti! I like it."

There's a muffled shout from the top of the hill and The Watcher whistles the Octonauts tune.

And in a second, the friends splinter like a bomb.

Reaching down, Booms grabs a brick from the floor, shoves it into his gloves before hurling them into the canal. He grabs his bag and starts to run. Curl shoves his gloves into a prickly bush next to him, spiking his fingers as he pushes them deep into the bush. "Fuck!" He grabs his bag, shoving the loose cans into it before hurling it into the water and sprinting away, up the embankment--

Crashing headlong into someone coming down in the opposite direction.

"Watch it, dickhead!"

It's a girl's voice. Curl makes a lunge for her in the dark, just as The Watcher sprints up behind them. Boom's there too, and pulls Curl back, shining a torch right in the girl's face to check her out.

"Get that fucking light out my face, will ya?"

The girl's their age; 16, short, with a tiny frame. Despite the cold, she's dressed only in t-shirt and jeans.

Curl glares at her. The girl looks back at him with disdain.

"What's your fucking problem?!"

He leans towards her. "You. My paints are in the fucking canal now because of you. And they 'aint cheap!"

Boom steps between them, pushing them apart. His eyebrows raised at Curl.

"What?" Curl looks at him defensively.

"Go get your paints," Boom tips his head towards the canal and watches Curl head straight for the water, followed by The Cat. The rest of the crew gravitate back towards the bridge as Boom turns towards the girl, who's still mouthing off. "Keep it down will ya?"

"Why should I?" she replies with attitude.

"Because you'll get us busted if not, that's why," Boom says, fixing her with a pointed look.

The girl laughs sarcastically, before replying, "What exactly is it you do here then *boys?*" Her emphasis is on the word boys, delivered in a mocking tone at normal volume, which now sounds ridiculously loud in the dark - only going to emphasise just how quiet they've all been till she showed up.

The Watcher's had enough. Not as patient as Boom, he takes a step towards her but the girl runs off to the top of the hill where she eyeballs them all from a distance, a face full of attitude.

Boom looks at the others. "Probably just got a load of shit in her life. Like us," he adds, with more than a hint of wryness in his voice.

His words have the effect of pacifying them in an instant. Situation now under control, Boom tenses up all of a sudden. Pulling his headphones out of his pocket, he pushes the buds deep into his ears, cranking up the tunes before walking off to stand by the water's edge by himself. Flash is about to follow but thinks twice about it and spins round to join the girl instead.

Away from the rest of the Crew, Boom stares into the inky black of the water as music pumps loudly in his ears. So loud it's deafening. He stares across the water, in a trance. His mouth shut, he chews at the skin on the inside of his cheeks, unaware he's even doing it.

Back at the top of the hill, Flash sits down next to the girl, who's sat on the edge of the group, moody as fuck - glaring at them, but refusing to leave. Flash tips his head in greeting. "Flash."

The girl glares back at him. "Mercedes."

She's got a young face. Innocent almost, if only she'd drop the attitude. She stares down at Boom, his body silhouetted in the dark.

"What's his problem?"

"He doesn't do confrontation."

"Hmm," she turns to face Flash. "What are you anyway? Some kind of gang?"

Flash laughs. "Nah. We're writers." He catches the confused expression on her face. "Graffiti artists. Writers. Whatever you wanna call us."

Down below them, Boom takes a step back from his precarious position where the tips of his feet hang over the edge of the canal. Spinning round, he heads back up the embankment to where Flash is sat next to Mercedes. He stops in front of them, music blasting from his headphones; loud enough for everyone around him to hear the words. Flash looks up at him, raising his voice. "Yo, Boom! My mum just called to say she can hear your music from ours!"

Boom flips him the bird, but reaches down to

turn the music off, pulling his buds out of his ears.

Flash looks over at Mercedes. "Boom, meet…

He trails off, thinking for a second and grins. "Feisty Girl. Feisty for short."

Mercedes glares at him. "Go fuck yourself."

Flash grins. "My point exactly. Feisty, meet Boom."

The Cat, who's just walked back over to the group, has been watching it all unfold. He sits down next to Flash and pulls him to one side.

"What you playing at?" he asks him.

Flash lowers his voice. "She's gobby. But she's ok."

The Cat gives him a knowing look, like he's asking for trouble, but shrugs, before getting back up on his feet. He gives Flash a slap on the arm to show there's no hard feeling. Feisty, who's been watching them both, looks at Boom.

"What was all that about?"

Boom looks at her before replying. "Never had a female member of 'Da Crew before, that's all. Or a stranger." He pauses for a second, before adding, "So. How d'you fancy it?"

Feisty shrugs. "Got nothing betta to do."

They should be annoyed, but instead The Crew let out a laugh. Feisty scowls at them. She grabs her phone from by her leg and is about to shove it in her bag when Boom grabs her arm, gripping it tight. For the first time that night, she drops the facade and actually looks scared.

"What you looking at me like that for?! I'm not gonna fucking hurt you!" Boom tells her, indignantly.

The Watcher intervenes. "Yo. Chill, bro."

He turns to Feisty. "Rule number one. Never put your phone in your bag. That way if you need to dump it, the feds - cops," he says explaining, "don't have your numbers. Rule number two. Always scout a joint out first so you know all the good hiding places." He pauses. Glances over at Flash and grins. "And rule number three. *Never* wear white trainers. Not unless you want them covered in 'poo' by the end of the night."

The Crew laugh, Flash too. Feisty looks at Flash's feet in disgust. "I thought I could smell something. That's disgusting!"

The Watcher whistles from the top of the hill, a reminder that it's time to leave. Flash gets up. "Been here too long already." He walks over to where Curl is dredging the last of his cans from the water and stuffing them back in his carrier bag. Ever restless, The Cat starts to climb the wall of the bridge next to them, leaving Feisty on her own with Boom. She turns towards him.

"Have you ever used it to get back at someone?"

Boom looks at her. "Graffiti? What for?"

"For being a cunt!"

Boom looks shocked. He wasn't expecting it to come out of her mouth.

At the bridge, The Cat drops to the floor, landing on both feet. Glancing back over his shoulder, he shakes his head at Feisty, letting her know he heard.

"What?! You never heard the word cunt before?" Feisty asks them sarcastically, glaring at them both.

"Just wasn't expecting it from you, that's all," Boom says.

"Yeah well," she says, staring at a patch of grass ahead of her.

As Curl walks back over to them, accompanied by Flash, a SIREN hits the air and flashing blue lights light up the bridge, bouncing off it as the colour revolves and spins. The Watcher shouts down from the top of the embankment. "Feds! Run!"

6 THE CHASE

Boom, Flash and Feisty race onto the deserted streets of the industrial estate, above the canal. They spot the police cars, lights flashing, just feet away. Feisty stops for a nanosecond to catch her breath, but Boom yanks her arm, pulling her away from the cars before they're spotted. "No time for that." Boom pulls her out of the road, whispering, "Stay in the shadows."

Back down by the canal there's blind panic and a flurry of feet. Torch beams zigzag over the path and sky as the Crew that are left start to panic, unsure which way to run. There's a splash as the torches are thrown into the canal, and the lights go out. There's people running everywhere, and the sound of a police dog barking.

Up on the road, Flash, Boom and Feisty have made it as far as a residential street. Flash is up ahead, as usual. As he turns to look back at the others, his jacket catches on a bush next to him and he yanks himself free, ripping a hole in his jacket. "Fuck it!"

Behind them, a police dog rounds the corner, followed by two police officers. Flash waits for Boom and Feisty to catch up, pulls a bottle of booze from his bag and pours it over his head, pouring alcohol into one of his eyes by mistake. "Shit!"

Boom looks at him in horror. "What the fuck you do that for?"

Flash winces in pain, covering the eye with one hand. "Faster than you, remember."

"The alcohol, I meant," Boom tells him.

"Gives the furry fucker a scent to follow," Flash grins.

"You've just fucking blinded yourself," replies Boom.

"I'm fine. Now fuck off before they catch us up."

Feisty looks at Boom, not sure what the hell's going on. Boom grabs her by her sleeve and pulls her off the road and down a side street. She glances back, just in time to see Flash hurl his empty booze bottle onto the ground, smashing it into a hundred pieces in order to grab the attention of the cops.

They look up, spot Flash standing there, and give chase. But they're heavy and overweight and are already struggling to catch a breath.

Flash sprints away, focused entirely on the dog as he looks back over his shoulder to size him up as he gives chase. Weirdly, Flash is much better - less clumsy - when he's moving fast, almost like it's the speed he's built to go at. No longer having to worry about catching up with his limbs when he's going fast.

Sprinting down the street, Flash enters residential territory - passing row after row of identical town houses. Terraced houses from the twenties, poky on the outside but opening up like a Tardis on the inside. Managing to leave the cops - and the dog - far behind him, Flash carries on running; making it look effortless like an Olympian sprinter.

He races past a row of wheelie bins, lined up in front of a house, before spinning back round, his arms flailing to slow himself down. Glancing behind him to make sure the cops are nowhere in sight, he slips behind the bins, peering down the street to look for them through a misty, alcohol-soaked eye; steely still and focusing only on the street ahead.

Something catches his eye and he looks down to see his trainers glowing white in the dark. Struggling to find enough space behind the bins to kick off his shoes, Flash wriggles around in an attempt to kick them off, but there's barely enough room to move. Suddenly, he hears a dog bark and he peers out from behind the bins, just an inch or so until he spots them. The two cops have caught up now and are at the end of the street, panting heavily, the dog racing several hundred feet ahead of them.

Still out of breath, Flash keeps his mouth open to silence any noise from his breathing. He pushes himself back against the wall of the house and watches as the cops hurtle past, the dog running ahead of them, hunting him like a pack animal.

Flash lets out a sigh of relief as they pass, but seconds later the dog's back, circling the gate in front of the house a couple of times before racing up the path towards the bins. He stops in front of the bins, barking loudly. A light turns on in one of the upstairs windows of the house and a face pops out from behind the curtains. But whoever it is takes one look at the cops below and darts back behind the curtain before turning the light back off again.

The officers catch up; both breathless, with a middle-aged paunch. They follow the dog up the path and stop in front of the bins. Bending over to catch their breath, they lean forward, resting their hands on their legs. One of them looks at the other and tips his head over to where a pair of white trainers stick out from underneath one of the bins. They take one look at the trainers and roll their eyes at each other. Officer Matthews, the older of the two, puts on a loud but cheery voice.

"Trainer boy! Haven't seen you for err, let me see, couple of days at least."

He waits, staring at the bins. Then tries again.

"Are you gonna come out, or do you seriously want us to squeeze in there after you?"

There's something good-natured about the exchange, if there's such a thing as a good-natured police exchange. It's silent for a second, then one of the bins starts to move and shift. Flash lets out a groan as he shoves himself free, sending the bin crashing to the floor in the process. Rubbish scatters everywhere. Officer Matthews shakes his head, just about managing to hide a smile before telling Flash, "Pick it up." Next to him, Officer Wilson pulls his radio out of his belt and radios control.

"How d'you know it was me?" Flash asks Officer Matthews, as he works his way across the path, picking up the litter and shoving it back in the bin.

Matthews replies in a droll voice. "Nasa."

Flash doesn't get it. Matthews spells it out for him. "North American Space Agency. Picked up the glow from your trainers from outta space."

Flash looks down at his trainers. "Good aren't they? D'you like 'em?"

Matthews raises his eyebrows as if to say, 'did you really just ask me that?!'

Flash resigns himself to the inevitable and walks over to Matthews, hands outstretched. Matthews grabs a pair of handcuffs but stops in his tracks, screwing up his face.

"You stink of booze! And -- something else. What IS that smell?!" he asks Flash, screwing up his face.

Securing the handcuffs around Flash's wrists, he walks him over to the police van but the police dog won't leave Flash alone, and keeps sniffing his feet. Officer Matthews takes one look at Flash's trainers and screws his face up in disgust.

"Off! Now!"

Flash kicks his trainers off as Matthews opens the back of the van. Officer Wilson holds open the door of the van for him, but just as Flash reaches them his radio crackles back into life.

"All cars. Blue light. Domestic at two zero one, Falcon Towers. I repeat. Two zero one, Falcon Towers. Roger."

Officer Matthews turns to Flash, unlocking the handcuffs.

"Looks like someone else's bad luck is your good fortune, Trainer Boy."

Flash watches from the side of the road as Officer Matthews jumps into the front seat, next to Officer Wilson. They drive off at speed, blue lights flashing.

7 MY DAD CAN GO FUCK HIMSELF! HIM AND HIS BITCH OF A NEW GIRLFRIEND!

Back in another residential part of town, Boom and Feisty walk side by side, heading for home. Everything about Feisty's body language is defensive and guarded. They walk in silence as they pass row after row of rundown houses, junk and rubbish dumped in all of the gardens. Boom's lent Feisty his hoodie, but it's way too big for her and drowns her tiny frame, emphasizing just how small and vulnerable she really is underneath all her bravado.

Boom glances over at her, and a grin lights up his face. Teasing her, he asks, "So does your dad know you're out this late with a strange guy?"

She spins round angrily.

"My dad can go fuck himself! Him and his bitch of a new girlfriend!"

"Woah! Take it that's who the graffiti's for then?" Boom replies, a little taken aback by the aggression in Feisty's voice.

Feisty stares at the ground, stony-faced and nods. They reach a house on the corner of the road, and Feisty slows to a stop.

"This is me."

Boom pulls a graffiti pen from his pocket and tags the street lamp outside her house. She rolls her eyes at him.

"Is that so I don't forget you?"

He looks at her and gives her a sweet smile. He's a good guy, underneath all the shit that coats his exterior. Feisty unzips his hoodie and hands it back.

"Thanks."

Boom puts it on, wrapping it around himself and clinging to the warmth.

Feisty looks at him.

"Where are you?"

Boom tips his head to a cluster of tower blocks on the City skyline, about a mile away.

"See that big shiny metropolis in the distance? That's me." He's about to walk away but turns back to ask her something. "D'you wanna come bombing with us tomorrow?"

Feisty looks shocked.

Booms shakes his head at her, laughing.

"It's a graffiti term. It just means do some graffiti."

Feisty shrugs. "Sure."

She heads up her path to her front door, opens it and slips inside, shutting the door silently behind her.

8 THE ESCAPE

Boom reaches the top of the stairwell by his flat and stops, his hands shaking. Pupils dilated with fear, he approaches his front door with care. He hangs back from the kitchen window, peering round just about far enough to look inside without being spotted.

His mum, Lorraine, is sat at the kitchen table, head bent, nursing a cup of tea. She senses movement from outside and looks up.

The front door opens and Boom's mum stands there, waiting to let him in. A large red swelling covers the left side of her face. Still only 38, her whole demeanour, however, is that of a much older woman - her spirit, soul... *everything*, completely crushed. Even her clothes look downtrodden. Everything from her large, shapeless brown cardie that's too big for her to her worn out jeans and tatty pink slippers. She looks at Boom but he glances away quickly, unable to look her in the face. He walks in, head down, following the tiles on the floor with his eyes. He walks over to the kettle, fills it with water, and turns it on. He leans back against the counter, facing his mum, still unable to look her in the eye.

"Where've you been?" she asks, her words slow, and slightly slurred; her swollen face making it hard to talk.

Boom shrugs.

"Out."

His voice is flat. He glances over to where the kitchen door leads into the corridor, towards the lounge.

"Where is he?"

"Out."

Boom's mum smiles at the repetition. It's a weary smile, but it's a smile nonetheless. But Boom still can't bring himself to look at her though.

"Don't know how he can go out after doing that to you."

"Neighbours called the police," she replies.

His mum turns her shoulder to pick up her cup of tea and winces in pain.

Boom glances up, concerned, but looks away again quickly.

His mum starts to sob. Silent tears cascade down her face and into her tea, but still Boom refuses to look at her.

"I'm sorry." His voice is drenched with guilt.

"For what?" she replies.

"For letting him do it to you." There's a pause, before he adds: "For not being there to protect you."

It's why he can't quite bring himself to look at her. It's the guilt of the helpless, eating away at him and gnawing at his insides.

"It's me that's sorry, Jamie. Sorry I ever brought him into your life. Sorry I've not walked away. I should have thrown him out the first sign of any trouble."

Boom scuffs his feet, staring at the patterns on the floor tiles. Anything not to look at his mum's beaten-up face.

"I keep thinking, one day I'll do it," he tells her. "Stand up to him. Give him a piece of his own medicine. Beat the shit outta him. But every time I try, I just freeze."

He breaks off, his voice cracking with emotion.

His mum walks over to Boom and stops a feet away. "Look at me."

Boom still can't bring himself to look at her. She says it again, even more gently this time. "Jamie. Look at me."

She reaches her hand out, gently tipping his chin up until he's looking her right in the eyes. Boom takes in the bruises and the swelling around her cheeks and his mouth starts to wobble at the edges. He's close to tears. His mum takes on a kind of strength in her voice as she tells him,

"I *know* how scary he is, Jamie. And I don't want you anywhere near him, do you hear me? Promise me. Promise me you won't say anything to annoy him. Do anything. Look at him even. Just get yourself through school, then you can leave. Start again somewhere new. Till then, please just promise me you'll just leave the evil bastard alone."

Boom looks at her. "I'm not leaving you with him."

His mum shrugs. "I don't think you've got a lot of say in it, Jamie. One of us has got to do the right thing. And it's much better that it's you." Even now, she's determined to try and protect her son from all the shit.

Boom glances at the clock. "When *is* the arsehole back?" he asks. Boom emphasizes the word arsehole, relishing the only chance he gets to truly display how he feels about his stepdad.

"Not till the morning."

Boom lets it sink in for a second before a sudden

energy surges through him, kick-starting him into action.

"He's staying out for the night? The whole night? Are you sure? He's never done that before."

His mum nods, "That's what he said."

Boom grabs his mum's arm. His speech urgent and frenetic.

"We've gotta go. Now!"

Boom's mum looks at him, unable to take in what he's trying to say to her.

"Listen to me mum! We need to go, NOW!"

"But he'll find us."

"No he won't. Not if we go now." He picks up her hand and holds it tight. "We can escape. Get away. Never see him again, ever."

His mum's still floundering, but Boom carries on. His voice strong.

"We can do this, mum. But we've *got* to go now."

His mum gets up out of her chair. Boom rushes towards the front door and stands guard at the kitchen window, making sure the coast is clear. He waits for his mum to grab her coat but instead she starts heading towards the hallway.

"What you doing?!" Boom's starting to panic.

"I need to pack." Her movements are slow compared to Boom's, his body filled with a sense of urgency compared to the haze his mum seems to be in.

Boom grabs her arm.

"Just leave everything, there's no time. He could be back any minute. We need to go. Now."

His mum stops in the middle of the kitchen as

she remembers something. She walks over to one of the kitchen cupboards and opens the door. Reaching down, she peels a photo from the underside of a shelf. It's a photo of her on her wedding day, blissfully happy with Boom's dad, a huge smile plastered all over her face.

Boom clocks the photo and grabs his mum's hand and gives it a tight squeeze as they leave the flat, pulling the door shut behind them. As they walk along the balcony towards the stairwell, Boom glances down into the car park below. A habit he's never grown out of. He spots his stepdad's Oli's blue car pulling up in the car park below and ducks back behind the balcony.

"I thought he wasn't back till the morning!"

Boom stands there panicking, head spinning in every direction, trying desperately to figure out what to do next. Decision made, he moves quickly, pulling his mum towards his neighbour's house. She looks at him like he's mad.

"It's four in the morning!"

Boom steers his mum back to the balcony. "Tell me when he's in the building."

Boom's mum walks over to the balcony and hangs over the edge, watching the car park below; her body shaking violently with fear.

Boom hammers on his neighbour's door with the base of his fist; quietly, but with enough power to wake them up. He shuts his eyes, muttering to himself, over and over. "Come on, come on!"

The front door opens and Boom's neighbour, the anxious-looking bald man with the young son, stands there in his pyjamas, looking at Boom. Boom's on the hop now, his body unable to stay still with the sense of impending danger, his voice rushed and urgent.

"Can we come in? Please!"

His neighbour looks down at the ground. "I dunno. My son..."

Boom's mum steps forward. "Please. Just take my son."

The man looks up. He glances back at his wife, who's stood the other side of the kitchen in her dressing gown.

"Let them in," she whispers.

Boom grabs his neighbour's hand, clasping it tightly. "Thank you."

Boom and his mum step inside, shutting the front door silently behind them.

9 OLI

Boom's stepdad, Oli, reaches the top of the stairs, just in time to see his neighbour's front door shut. Forty-two, with an angry face, he's a dark-haired man of mixed race. He has a closely-shaved head and large, ugly features with large ears and a nose that's splayed across his face, like the product of some long ago fight.

Oli reaches inside his pocket, pulls out his key and lets himself into his flat.

Entering the kitchen, he throws his coat over the chair and frowns. The lights are on and two mugs of tea sit undrunk on the kitchen table.

And he instinctively knows...

Stepping towards the kitchen table, Oli wraps his hand around one of the cups. It's still warm. He looks up, standing still for a second to listen. His cool, calculating manner both frightening and disturbing.

Keeping his heavy, steel-capped work boots on, Oli walks down the corridor, opening each door in turn, until he reaches the door at the end. It's the lounge. He peers inside, sees that it's empty and shuts the door. He turns back around and heads out his front door, leaving it wide open, and walking straight next door to his neighbour's house.

He stands in front of the door and listens for a minute or two before hammering on the door.

No-one answers.

It's dark inside the neighbour's flat. Boom and his mum are huddled together behind the dividing door between the hallway and the kitchen, out of sight from the front door. Just behind them, further down the corridor, his neighbour's wife is standing in one of the bedroom doorways. Behind her, Boom can see her tiny two-year-old lying in his cot bed, sleepy but awake after being woken by the hammering on the door. Boom watches him suck his thumb, keeping his eyes trained on his mum's face as she walks back into the room to stroke his head, whispering words of reassurance in his ear.

Back in the kitchen, Boom's male neighbour stays silent - hidden behind the closed shutters of the kitchen windows.

Oli hammers even louder this time.

"I know you're in there! I saw the door close. So you better let me in before I break your fucking door down!" he shouts.

Boom glances at the little boy's face, his eyes widening with fear... desperately searching for reassurance from his mum. He looks up as the kitchen light goes on. Boom and his mum look at each other in fear.

Oli's neighbour opens the door. He stands there, in his pyjamas, facing Oli. He's terrified but is desperately trying to look like he's not hiding anything. Behind him, Boom watches as his neighbour's wife leaves her son's bedside for a minute and walks closer to the hallway to listen to what's happening.

"Where are they? And you better not lie or you'll have this to fucking answer to!"

Oli raises his fist. But before his dad can answer, the little boy jumps down off of his bed and rushes out into the corridor, pushing past his mum as well as Boom and his mum to get to his dad. "Daddy!"

He flings his arms around his dad's legs and clings on to them for dear life. It's too late now though, Oli's knows there's someone behind the kitchen door.

The boy's mum rushes past Boom and his mum and scoops her son back up in her arms, holding his tiny frame close to hers. Nervously, she glances back to where Boom and his mum are hiding behind the dividing door. She looks up to catch Oli staring straight at her, their eyes locking before all hell lets loose.

Oli drags her husband out onto the balcony. He starts pummeling him with his fists, knocking him to the ground in seconds.

Inside the kitchen, the man's wife places her son on a chair in the corner.

"Don't move!"

The boy starts to wail, making a grab for his mum, but she takes his hands and places them onto his lap.

"You'll be ok, I promise. Just stay there!"

She runs out onto the balcony and tries to pull Oli off of her husband, who's lying on the ground, groaning, as he's attacked by Oli. Oli shoves her away, with barely any effort. As the boy wails loudly from inside the flat, Boom's mum steps out onto the balcony behind them. Her eyes dead, she walks slowly towards Oli, her voice flat.

"Leave him alone."

Oli gives her a derisive sneer. He grabs his neighbour by the shirt of his collar. His face is covered in cuts and he's got blood pouring from his nose, the man so obviously unaccustomed to violence he doesn't stand a chance against Oli. Oli raises his neighbour's head off the ground until his mouth is level with his ear, and in a low, threatening voice whispers slowly to him.

"Stay out of it."

Oli lets go of his neighbour's head and it hits the concrete floor with a sickening thud. He walks away but a second later turns back round. He swings his leg back as far as it can go before aiming his steel-capped boot full force at his neighbour's ribs, leaving him writhing on the floor in acute pain.

Grabbing Boom's mum by her neck, Oli drags her back inside their flat. Boom rushes after them and as they enter the flat, Oli slams the door behind them.

10 I'LL DIE BEFORE I LET YOU LEAVE ME

Oli stands in the kitchen facing Boom and his mum. Without warning, he slugs Boom's mum hard in the stomach, knocking her to the floor. Boom spins round, jittery and panicky, tearing at his hair as he watches Oli squat down next to his mum.

The photo of her wedding day pokes out from the top of her cardigan pocket. Boom shuts his eyes and reopens them a second later just in time to see Oli pulling the picture from his mum's pocket. He stares at it for a few seconds before turning to face his wife, who's still on the floor, too scared to move.

"Love's young dream. Aint that sweet."

He lowers his face until he's level with hers, and in an icy, emotionless voice asks her, "Where have you been hiding it?"

Boom's mum's too scared to answer. Oli turns to Boom.

"You knew about this, did you?"

Frozen to the spot in fear - waiting for what he knows is about to come - Boom just about manages to shake his head.

Oli walks over to the cooker and ignites a gas ring. Turning to face his wife, he holds the photo over the flame and destroys it. Chemical-laced smoke billows from the picture, setting off the smoke alarm. Boom makes a move to stop the alarm, but Oli bellows at him.

"Did I say you could move?!"

He drops the photo into the flame as the smoke

alarm's high-pitched beeping deafens them all. Oli squats back down next to Boom's mum and lowers his face until it's level with hers. He puts his lips close to her ear, and in a calm, controlled voice, tells her: "I'll die before I let you leave me." Walking calmly away, he heads for the lounge, shutting the kitchen door behind him.

Boom dives into action, pulling what's left of the photo out of the flame. The only thumbnail-sized reminder of his dad, and happier times.

11 PLEASE TELL ME THAT DIDN'T JUST HAPPEN!

Teenagers pile through the gates of a grubby, Inner City Secondary School. Two overly-made up blondes wait for a friend by the entrance; their hair bleached peroxide blonde, their make-up thick and eyebrows heavily plucked and drawn over. Their skirts stop just below their bottom and their shirts are unbuttoned as far as their chests, revealing the top, fleshy part of their breasts and below that a hint of lacy, black underwear. They drape themselves provocatively over the brick wall leading into the playground, laughing as groups of teenage boys pass by, staring hopelessly in their direction. But as one group approaches, led by ringleader Yusef Ali, the girls' faces harden and they climb down off the wall covering their chests with their arms. Ali says something to them as he passes, accompanied by a lewd gesture. The girls look at Ali and his gang in disgust.

As the boys walk away laughing, there's a gap for a second when no-one passes. Hovering by the gate is Boom, his eyes fixed on the road ahead, looking for someone. Bleary-eyed and still shell-shocked from the night before, his body language says he's still on high alert. Twitchy, nervous, but trying as hard as fuck to hide it.

His eyes scan the pavement. Recognition darts across his face as a young girl approaches. Caught up in a group of students much older than her, she looks tiny in comparison - no more than 11 years old, a first year for sure. She wears her long, dark hair in an impressively tidy French plait and holds a plastic bag stuffed full of clothes in one hand. Keeping her head down as she approaches, she levels with Boom, and, without looking up, chucks him the bag. He catches it and she carries on walking like nothing just happened. It's Flash's sister, Rachel.

Just behind her comes The Cat, with a group of his friends, and behind them, The Watcher and Curl, walking side by side. Pale and tired all of them, they yawn, mouths wide, as they enter school. They throw Boom a quick wink as they pass but no-one speaks. Instead, they walk into school like they don't know each other.

Boom pulls his phone out of his pocket and checks the time.

"Come on Flash, where are you?" he mutters to himself, as behind him the playground starts to thin out as the students start piling into school.

The bell goes, and teacher Mr Britton, 40s, white, with an air of utter weariness about him, starts to walk towards Boom, who's already spotted him approaching from the corner of his eye.

"That's all I need," he mutters to himself, under his breath.

Britton reaches Boom, just as Flash arrives - at a sprint - from the opposite direction. Breathless, he's dressed in the same clothes he was in last night. Standing with his hands in his pockets, Boom's shoulders twitch slightly, in a kind of unseen question. Much more subtle than Britton, who takes one look at

Flash and raises his eyebrows.

"Forgotten something have you, Mr Pritchard?"

Flash doesn't get it.

"Something called school, maybe?!" Britton adds, with a hint of sarcasm.

Britton looks down at Flash's feet and pulls a face.

"Where d'you sleep last night? A cow shed?"

Boom smothers a smile as Flash bends down to sniff his trainers, wincing at the smell. Flash kicks his trainers off and stands on the pavement in a pair of holey socks. Boom chucks him the bag from Rachel and Flash pulls out a pair of black school shoes, sticking them on his feet to protect them from the dirty pavement.

Britton watches, fascinated. Curious to see how this is going to play out.

Flash takes one look at Britton and mutters, "Fuck it", before peeling off his hoodie and t-shirt. He's ripped, nothing to him but pure, lean muscle. Britton and Boom keep watching, amused, waiting to see what Flash will do next. Boom's mouth turns up at the sides as he stifles a grin as Flash rummages in the carrier bag and pulls out a plain white polo shirt. He slips it over his head before pulling out a pair of trousers. Britton takes one look at the trousers and says with a wry smile, "Don't think I need to stay for any more Mr Pritchard, do you?"

He walks off, spinning back round to address them both.

"Five minutes. Otherwise you'll be marked as absent and your parents will be notified you're late."

He walks off, leaving Flash panicking. Standing in front of Boom, Flash yanks his jeans down as far as his ankles to reveal a pair of Daffy Duck boxers.

"What the fuck, bro?!" Boom's laughing now.

"You heard Britton," Flash says, defending himself. "Last thing I need is the social round just 'cause I'm late into registration. *Again*."

"You not go home last night?" Boom asks him.

Flash shakes his head.

"Didn't want the feds following me. Had me handcuffed at one point but they got a call out. Let me go. Domestic. In our block. Thank fuck for them, that's what I say, otherwise I'd still be in the clinker this morning."

Boom's face clouds over with a dark, troubled look. Knowing only too well the domestic was at his house.

Flash's jeans, meanwhile, have got tangled around his shoes. Flash yanks at them, but they're stuck. The pair of them crack up as Flash struggles to untangle them, hopping about the pavement in his boxers. A car drives past and honks, the driver shouting out the window at Flash as he passes. Flash gives them the bird but loses his balance and lands on Boom - just as a stunning schoolgirl walks past, with a smirk on her face.

Unable to hide her laughter, the girl eyes Flash's boxers in horror before commenting, "Nice boxers!" before disappearing through the school gates and into the playground. Mortified, Flash hops about even more frantically, as Boom doubles up with laughter.

"Please tell me that didn't just happen!" Flash

says, mortified. "Nicole Folsey! Of all people, why her, man?"

Flash gives his jeans an extra yank, pulling them over his ankles, to the sound of Boom mimicking Nicole's "Nice Boxers!" in a high-pitched, piss-take voice. Laughing, Flash gives his mate the bird as he pulls on his grey school trousers, throws his shit-covered trainers into the bag with the rest of his clothes, and legs it into school with Boom hot on his heels. Flash tears ahead, laughing, shouting back at Boom, "Now who's laughing, pussy boy?!"

12 NOW YOU'RE AWAKE, JAMIE, PERHAPS YOU COULD EXPLAIN TO THE CLASS THE MEANING OF A DOUBLE NEGATIVE

Mr Britton is stood at the front of the class, staring at the sea of bored faces in front of him. On the whiteboard behind him are the lyrics to RIZZLE KICK'S hip hop song: **Dreamers**.

"Poems don't have to be boring. Nor do they have to rhyme in order to be a poem. Who knows this one by Rizzle…?"

Britton trails off, staring at Flash as he tips further and further back on his chair until he's almost horizontal. He gives Flash a pointed look.

"How many legs does your chair have, Mr Pritchard?"

"Four," Flash replies.

"And how many are you balancing on right now?" Mr Britton replies.

Flash tips his chair back onto four legs, but almost immediately, without even realising, he starts to tip himself back again, unable to sit still for more than a few seconds at a time. This time, Britton gives up. Firing a question at Flash instead.

"What did I just say about poems, Mr Pritchard?"

"Er--"

Britton raises an eyebrow, expectantly, as Flash continues, "You said poems don't need to be boring.

They don't need to rhyme. And then--"

"That's fine. Thank you, Mr Pritchard."

Mr Britton spins round, his back to the class, heading for the white board. But before he gets there, there's a loud crash from behind. Without even needing to turn back round, Britton quips, "Up off the floor please, Mr Pritchard," delivering it in a calm, dry manner.

The class crack up, pissing themselves laughing.

Britton reaches the front and spins back round just in time to see Flash standing his chair back on four legs and sitting back down. Britton gives him a droll look.

Asleep on the desk next to him, head on his hands, is Boom. Britton clocks it but doesn't say anything, prompting a comment from Yusef Ali in the back row.

"How comes you never say nuffin' to Jamie? He's always sleepin' and you never say nuffin."

Mr Britton peers at Ali over the top of his glasses, unimpressed.

"First of all, Mr Ali, please refer to me as 'Sir' when you address me in class. Or come to think of it, anywhere else in school. Secondly, if you must insist on questioning me and what I do, please don't offend me with your use of bad grammar. The correct phrase is not 'how comes you never say nothing?' but 'Why do you never say anything?"

Ali makes a lewd hand gesture at Britton from under his desk, muttering some kind of expletive under his breath at the same time, prompting a snigger from the boy sat next to him.

Mr Britton turns to face the class.

"Can anyone tell me why Mr Ali here got it wrong?"

Ali scowls, pissed off at being the butt of Britton's focus. The whole class stare at the floor. Sighing, Britton walks over to Boom and gives him a gentle nudge to wake him up. Boom stirs, wiping his bleary eyes before sitting upright in his seat.

"Nice of you to join us, Jamie," Britton says, to more sniggers. "Now you're awake, Jamie, perhaps you could explain to the class the meaning of a double negative."

Boom, still bleary-eyed and in a bit of a daze, looks at Flash for inspiration.

"A double negative is actually a positive because one negative cancels out the other. So if you say someone's funny, they're funny. And if you say they're not funny, they're not funny. But if you say they're never NOT funny - it means they're always funny." Boom grins at his mate.

Mr Britton nods his head, and turns to Ali in sheer, gloating delight.

"And therein lies your answer Mr Ali. When - and only when - you can hand in straight As for all your assignments - despite the fact you've slept through the whole class - then and only then will I leave you alone. Till then, you can suck it up like the rest of them."

More sniggers.

The bell goes, signalling the end of class. Mr Britton takes a step back, sighing as he watches the students bolt out of the classroom, unable to escape fast enough. He gives the classroom his usual obligatory scan, searching the desks for any student debris left behind - anything from a notebook to pens or jumpers, even the odd phone. He spots a homework book Boom left behind, and grabs it, making his way out into the corridor to find him.

13 DO ME A FAVOUR, WILL YOU? STAY AWAY FROM HER. SHE'S NOTHING BUT TROUBLE

Flash and Boom are jostled out into the school corridor, packed with kids. Feisty spots them from the other end of the corridor and makes a beeline straight for them. She reaches them just as Britton steps out of his classroom, waving Boom's book at him.

"Jamie! You forgot your book."

Boom takes it from him. "Thanks, Sir."

Britton clocks Feisty, standing there taunting Boom, with a raised eyebrow, outwardly amused.

"Jamie, huh? Had you down more as a Stephen or a Patrick. Definitely not a Jamie."

She laughs, clocking Britton as he takes in the exchange.

"See you later, boys," she says, smirking at Flash and Boom as she walks away.

Britton looks at the boys, frowning. "How d'you know Mercedes?"

Boom gives Flash a quick look, as if to say 'I've got this one.'

"We don't Sir. She was just giving us some verbal the other day, that's all."

"Hmm," Britton replies. "Sounds about right. Do me a favour, will you? Stay away from her. She's nothing but trouble."

He watches Flash and Boom as they walk away, a worried look on his face.

14 THINK I'VE LEFT IT IN MY LOCKER

Boom and Flash are walking home together at the end of the school day, passing tower block after tower block on their estate. They reach their own block of flats and Flash pulls open the entrance door, holding it for Boom to go through first. But as he gets there, Boom hangs back, making a real thing of searching for something he can't find in his rucksack.

Flash rolls his eyes, waiting for it. The same old familiar problem.

"Where have you left it this time?"

"Think I've left it in my locker," Boom says sheepishly.

"Every fucking day, G. Serious. Put a fuckin' chain on it, or something."

Boom looks up. "I've gotta go back. Mum'll kill me if I've lost it."

Flash replies, thinking for a second. "Do you know, all the time I've known you, I don't even know where you live, bro. 'Aint that a bit weird?"

Boom deflects him with a smile. "Very. You're right. Catch you laters. Usual place, right?"

Flash nods. Shaking his head, he fist bumps Boom before heading inside.

Boom watches from the pavement outside, waiting until he can see Flash making his way up the stairway, two at a time; usual Flash pace, hitting each level at a dizzying speed. He waits until he reaches his floor, and disappears, before reaching into his pocket and pulling out his front door key.

Boom heads inside. Walking slowly to the top of the stairwell on his floor, he looks over to his front door and freezes. He can hear his mum's screams from where he's standing. He turns straight back round and heads back out. Destination unknown, just anywhere but home.

15 HIS NAME IS MAX!

It's dark and Flash, Curl, The Watcher and The Cat are sat huddled under a lamp-post inside a children's playground. They're all in hoodies, studying a piece of paper resting in Curl's lap. The Watcher looks up and has a quick look around before bending back down to look at whatever it is in Curl's lap.

All of a sudden, the silence is broken by shouts from the end of the street. They look up to see Feisty, screaming at her dad, whose car has pulled up several hundred metres away at the side of the road.

Mr Havara, late 40s, is dressed in a nondescript jacket, stood by his car, driver door open. Whatever he's said to Feisty, it's made her rage. She stands there, totally oblivious of anyone else around them, screaming abuse at him.

Inside the car, a blonde woman, in her mid 20s, sits in the passenger seat, shaking her head as she stretches over to the back seat to try and calm a baby that's screaming loudly from its car seat.

Feisty rams her dad hard in the chest with her finger, before throwing her arms back to point at the woman in the car.

"It's all about her, and what *she* wants, isn't it? Well, what about *me* and *Summer*?!"

The Watcher raises an eyebrow, nudging the others to alert them to drama ahead, but they're already on it. They sit there mesmerised, watching from the safety of the playground. But all of a sudden The Watcher spots Boom at the corner of an intersection, headphones on, pounding the pavement towards Feisty and her dad - totally oblivious to the drama that's playing out in front of him.

"This oughta be interesting," he says.

Scuffing the ground as he walks, Boom's music pounds in his head, drowning out everything else around him. He's still in his school uniform from earlier, his school bag slung over his shoulder. He gets to within about six feet of Feisty and her dad and looks up. Finally, they've broken the sound barrier. He slips off his headphones, and watches Feisty tear into her dad.

"Are you _ever_ gonna see us again?"

"It's not that easy, love. I do want to but it's difficult. Max is--"

"What d'you mean it's _difficult_? What kind of fucking response is that?! You're our dad for fuck's sake. For what it's fucking worth."

The baby's cries ramp up a notch, forcing the blonde woman out of the car. She walks over to Feisty's dad. Ignoring Feisty, she tries to pull him back inside the car. "We need to go. Max won't stop screaming."

Feisty grabs the woman by her shoulders. Swings her round to face her.

"What? Can't look at me? I wouldn't be able to look at me either if I was you. Fucking homewrecker!"

The woman turns round, ignoring Feisty, which only incenses her even more.

Feisty gets within inches of her face and forcing herself suddenly calm, gives her a smirk before addressing her in a cool, calm voice.

"What you worried about? That dad'll finally

come to his senses and dump you along with that *annoying* little baby of yours?"

"His name is Max!"

The woman's anger gets the better of her and she bites. Feisty claiming her sad little victory, replying with a dismissive, "Whatever!"

The woman shoots Feisty's dad a warning look. "We need to go. Now."

The two of them climb back into the car, and it speeds off but before they disappear, Feisty jumps into the road behind them. Facing the rearview window, she flips them the bird, shouting: "FUCK YOU, MOTHER FUCKERS!"

Back in the playground, The Watcher and the rest of The Crew smile. "Give her her due. She's got balls," The Watcher says.

16 WELCOME ANGRY BIRD

Feisty crashes through the gate of the kids' playground and slams herself down on the edge of the group. Boom follows behind, agitated and jumpy from the argument. He takes one look at Feisty, and storms over to her, pointing his finger in her face, spoiling for a fight.

"Don't *ever* do that, again!"

"What? You scared of a fucking fight? Just grow a pair will ya?!"

The Watcher walks over, standing between them, before turning to Feisty. "Calm down, will ya?"

The Cat shakes his head at all the drama. It's new for the Crew and has only ever happened since Feisty joined them. He throws her a pissed off look.

"Keep it down, will ya? Curl's got his sketches on him."

Boom leans over to Feisty.

"I wasn't talking about you and your dad. I'm talking about when we're at school. You don't let on you know us, alright? In case you hadn't noticed, we don't all hang about together at school. For obvious reasons."

Flash looks at Boom, music still blaring from his headphones. "Turn your tunes down, bro!"

Boom turns his music off, and suddenly the air is calmer. "Don't know how you hear yourself think," Flash tells him.

"That's kinda the point. I can't." Boom replies drily.

Flash clocks Boom's school uniform. "Why you

still in uniform?"

"Couldn't find my key," Boom replies.

Flash screws up his face. "What's wrong with your doorbell?"

Boom lies. "No-one in."

He leans forward to peer at the piece of paper in Curl's lap in an attempt to distract Flash. Sketched on Curl's piece of paper is a picture of all the crew, all dancing their different moves next to a stereo, with the words: **"Dance To Your Own Beat."**

"Like it bro!" Boom slaps Curl on the back appreciatively. Guilty, he glances over at Feisty, who's sat there, sad and subdued. He follows her face closely with his eyes, but is disturbed by Curl, leaning towards him, asking to see his sketch.

"Let's see yours then."

Boom pulls a balled-up piece of paper from his bag and lays it out on the floor, flattening it out with both hands.

His sketch is of two aliens standing at the top of a ramp leading down from a spaceship to a red bird below. It's Red, the red bird from the animated computer game, Angry Birds. Except this one has a pair of tits and the word Feisty written on its chest. Lit by a luminous green glow, the aliens' balled up hands form the familiar fist bump greet of the Crew. Just below them are the words: "Welcome, Angry Bird."

The Crew look at Feisty and laugh. "Feisty, come check this out!", The Cat shouts over to her. Feisty walks over, takes one look at the picture and says to Boom, "Fuck you!", making the Crew laugh even more.

The Watcher turns to the group. "All those with

Curl, say 'Ay!' All those with Boom, say 'sick!"

The Crew shout 'sick' in unison. It's unanimous. Boom's design wins. His is the graffiti piece they'll do tonight once blurry hour kicks in and your average person is wrapped up safe and sound - and asleep - in bed.

Boom gives Curl a casual bro hug. "You cool with that?"

Curl smiles at him. "Like I said, your piece is sick!"

Boom pulls out a pencil. "Just need to sketch you lot in now."

He looks up, just in time to spot a young lad in his early twenties walking along the road towards them. He's dressed in a parka, the hood pulled tight to his face. As he crosses the road, Boom jumps up, running the length of the fence to talk to him.

"I know you from somewhere, right?"

The boy pulls his hood close to his face, crossing back over to the other side of the road without a word and keeping his eyes trained to the ground. He speeds up, rounding the corner, before disappearing out of sight.

Boom sits back down next to the Crew.

"Tell me that wasn't weird. He didn't even look at me. Didn't even speak."

He sits down next to The Watcher, grabs his chin and turns his face sideways, copying the profile onto his paper as part of the sketch.

"Make sure you get my best side!" The Watcher jokes.

Flash gets in there quick. "You 'aint got no 'best' side, bro. They're both as bad as each other!"

"Fuck you!" The Watcher laughs, scanning Flash for something to take the piss out of him for. He catches Flash's feet. Another new pair of trainers. This time a bright luminous yellow.

"Subtle as the last pair I see!" he laughs. "Which establishment did you 'buy' these ones from then, G?" The Watcher asks, putting speech marks in the air with his fingers, around the word 'buy'.

"The - I can run faster than you can - shop," Flash replies.

The Crew laugh, knowing full well Flash is permanently broke. He doesn't even have enough money to buy food for him and Rachel, much less a pair of brand new trainers.

The Watcher continues his ribbing. "Don't worry 'bout it Flash, we don't care that you're colour blind. We just think of you as our 'special' friend.' And with that, all of the Crew (except Feisty) bundle on top of him, wrestling each other to the ground while Feisty looks at them like they're a bunch of idiots. A drop of rain hits their heads. Then another. Heavy drops that come thick and fast once they start. The group breaks up, checking the skies before they leave.

"Time to go," Boom says, quickly stuffing his sketch back into his bag before it gets wet. Then to The Watcher, "What time, W? And where?"

"Sycamore Industrial Estate. Unit 19," The Watcher replies. "2.a.m," shouting back to them as he races off with Curl and The Cat, "Bright and early gents, bright and early", before adding just for Feisty's sake,

"And Feisty." She flips him the bird in response.

Only Boom, Flash and Feisty remain, diving under a slide to escape the rain. Boom looks at Flash. "Can I finish my sketch at yours?"

Flash rolls his eyes at him. "How about yours for a change, G? 'Bout time you made me a cuppa instead of nicking all me biscuits for once!"

Boom grins, but doesn't offer up an invite.

"Suppose you wanna borrow some clothes too," Flash adds, shaking his head. Boom nods, and Flash replies, "I want them all back tomorrow, ok? You could kit out a fucking baseball team, twice over, with all the shit I've lent you this year."

And with that, they pull their hoods over their heads and sprint out from under the slide, into the pouring rain, heading for Flash's flat.

17 COME TO MINE IF YOU WANT, YOU JUST CAN'T GO UPSTAIRS, ALRIGHT?

Feisty, Flash and Boom race along a dark street, Flash at the front as usual. His phone rings and he stops to answer it.

He waits a second, listening to whatever's being said the other end, before replying in a worried tone, "I'll come now."

Boom looks at him. "Rach?"

Flash nods. "Sorry Boom. You'll have to go somewhere else."

There's an awkward silence as Feisty waits for Boom to step in and offer his place but he doesn't. Reluctantly, she tells him, "Come to mine if you want. You just can't go upstairs, alright?"

"Why, what's upstairs? The bogeyman?" Flash laughs, taking the piss, wiggling his fingers and moaning like a ghost.

Feisty glares at him. "Are you always such a dick?"

Flash laughs. "Are you always such a moody cow?"

Boom steps in, telling Flash. "Thought you were going."

Feisty and Flash are glaring at each other in a face off, making Boom laugh. "Fuck me, it really is like having kids around with you two."

Flash is about to leave but Boom stops him just before he goes. "Can you bring me some clothes later?"

"Yes!" Flash replies, frustrated but not able to

say no, having promised Boom some earlier. Crossing the road, he spins back round to shout at Boom. "I meant what I said. I want them back tomorrow, ok?" And with that, he heads off and out of sight.

Feisty's gaze follows Flash as he disappears out of sight. "What's his deal?"

"Let's just say his mum likes a drink or two," Boom tells her. "Super cool lady. Or she was, until Flash's dad died a couple of years ago. You can tell she loves them. But she's only really good for stuff before 10 a.m. Any time after that she starts drinking again, and then she's no use to anyone."

"Is that why he left?" Feisty asks.

"Yeah. Think he feels responsible for Rach. He got to grow up normal. But Rach… She's had to figure a lot of stuff out on her own. I guess he's just trying to make up for some of that. Be like a parent to her 'cause his mum can't be."

"What's he do?" Feisty asks, curious.

Boom shrugs. "Helps Rach with her homework. Pretty hot on that believe it or not. Cooks dinner. Does all the washing. Shit like that."

"Wow," Feisty replies, going quiet.

"See him in a different light now, right?" Boom says smiling, adding: "He's a good guy, Adam. One of the best." Feisty, unusually sombre, doesn't reply.

Boom breaks the spell, nudging Feisty to remind her they're heading back to hers. They set off at a walk in the direction of her house but then the rain kicks in with a vengeance, flooding the sides of the roads in seconds as the old city sewers struggle to hold the excess of water. They break into a sprint, reaching Feisty's house a few minutes later, drenched and out of breath.

It's 9 p.m. but the house lies in virtual darkness. Just a single light coming from the kitchen at the side of the house where a small lamp throws a muted light across the room.

As they step inside, Feisty shuts the door silently behind them, signalling for Boom to stay quiet. Feisty glances up the stairs quickly as they pass but keeps the lights off; Boom stubbing his toe on a skirting board as they head down the passageway in the dark.

They walk into the kitchen to find Feisty's sister, Summer, 12, sat at the kitchen table with homework spread out in front of her. She looks up, telling Feisty: "I haven't started cooking yet, sorry. I've gotta finish this for the morning but I haven't got a clue how to do it."

Boom leans over Summer to check out the complicated maths equation in front of her.

"I can help you with that if you want. It's easy once you know the method."

His drenched hair and body drips a puddle of water onto her work.

"Watch it! It's in pencil!" she says.

"Sorry," he replies, aware he's dripped even more water onto her book. Without a word, he peels off his blazer, followed by his polo shirt, revealing a taut six-pack and strong, muscly arms. He's hot, but totally unaware of the fact... even more unaware of the effect he's having on Feisty, as well as Summer. Reaching inside his bag, he pulls out a school sweater and pulls it over his head. Glad, finally, to be dry.

"Got somewhere I can hang these?" he asks,

holding his clothes up as they drip all over the kitchen floor.

Feisty stands there, mute, for a minute, thinking about Boom's ripped body, until Summer coughs, breaking Feisty out of her trance and smirking at her. Summer holds her hand out to introduce herself to Boom.

"Summer," she says.

Boom grins at her. "Boom."

"Boom?! What kind of name is that?!"

Boom laughs but doesn't expand further. "Can I use your loo?" he asks, turning to look at Feisty.

Feisty and Summer exchange a look. Feisty stands up and Boom laughs.

"Think I'm old enough to get there by myself thanks."

Ignoring him, Feisty leads the way, climbing the stairs ahead of him - keeping the lights off. Boom runs his hand along the side of the wall in order to feel his way in the dark, already an expert at this from living with Oli and having to make a silent getaway every night.

They pass a bedroom door with the name Summer on it, and then a second bedroom, its door slightly ajar, light spooling out from between the gap. Feisty looks at Boom and whispers. "I'll wait here."

She pulls the bedroom door to behind her and waits on the landing as Boom enters the toilet. Seconds later, he's out and she leads him back downstairs in the dark and into the kitchen.

As Boom sits down next to Summer, Feisty pulls a frying pan out of a cupboard. Lightly covering the bottom of it with a layer of oil, she lights the stove and places the pan over the flame. She watches Boom for a second as he patiently takes Summer through the equation. Feisty smiles at him, forgetting about the oil heating up in the pan... oblivious to the smoke that's starting to form over the oil. Then, she smells it; spinning back round to pull the pan off the flame just as the smoke alarm is set off. "Shit! Shit! Shit!" she says, turning the gas off and throwing Summer a tea towel as she races into the hallway to flap at the alarm to stop it from beeping.

"It's all right, it'll stop in a minute," Boom tells her. "Just open a window."

"You don't get it," a stressed Feisty tells him, as the stairs creak and a woman appears at the kitchen door.

It's Feisty's mum, a dark-haired lady in a dressing gown, pale and exhausted, her hair a tangled mess. Summer mouths 'sorry' at Feisty from behind her mum's back. She's stopped flapping at the alarm now, even though it's still going off.

"I'll get that shall I?" Boom says, grabbing the towel off Summer and flapping at the alarm until it stops.

Feisty's mum hasn't even registered Boom's presence. Her face, or more precisely, her eyes are completely dead. She speaks to Feisty in a quiet, barely audible voice.

"Everything ok?"

"Everything's fine, mum. Go back to bed. I've got this."

Feisty's mum gives her a weary smile and heads

back upstairs, but her appearance has left Feisty in a foul mood. She slams the frying pan and plates onto the surface of the counter as she returns to cooking.

She fries some eggs and stirs a pan of baked beans next to it but just as she turns the gas off and is about to serve up, her phone rings. She glances at the screen and mutters an expletive under her breath before picking up.

"What?!"

Summer watches her sister's face closely. Feisty's only too aware of Summer reading every miniscule movement in her face and looks away quickly. There's a pause, before she tells whoever's on the phone, "Shall I tell her then, or will you?"

Whatever the person's said, Feisty's not impressed. She holds the phone several inches from her head before pressing end, finishing the call before they've finished speaking.

"Idiot!" she mutters under her breath, before looking up to catch Summer's expectant look. "He's cancelled. Max is ill again," she says, adding, "apparently."

Summer gets up, slamming the chair against the wall and storms out without a word, leaving her homework spread all over the kitchen table. Still in a foul mood, Feisty scoops it all up and slams it down at the side of the counter before shoving the plates to one side, telling Boom, "I've gotta go!"

"I'll be there in a minute," Boom replies, pulling his sketch from his bag and adding some last-minute touches as Feisty turns her back to him.

"I'll be outside when you're done," she tells him. "Make sure you shut the front door behind you."

After she's gone, Boom - who's starving - shovels a slippery fried egg up in his hand and stuffs it into his mouth, being careful not to burst the egg as he does. Oil drips down the front of his mouth but Boom wipes it off with the sleeve of his jumper.

Reaching over to the radiator to collect his damp clothes, Boom stuffs them into a side pocket of his bag before placing his sketch into the main part to keep it dry. He's about to leave when a thought enters his head. Grabbing a fresh sheet of paper from his bag, Boom scribbles down a note, watching the kitchen door for any signs of movement as he writes.

When he's done, he peers out the window to check Feisty is still outside. He spots her pacing under the lamppost opposite. Quickly, he heads out of the kitchen and up the stairs, making sure to keep the lights off. He ducks past Summer's bedroom so as not to disturb her, and spots her lying on her bed listening to music on her headphones. He carries on, stopping at the second door and nervously pushes it open. Lying on the bed in her dressing gown, facing the wall, is Feisty's mum; the room lit only by one of those tiny night lights you plug into the wall when toddlers are little, giving the room an ethereal feel.

Boom clears his voice nervously, speaking softly as he breaks the silence. "I've left something for you. By the door." He bends down and places his letter by the door as he leaves.

18 THE KISS

Stepping out of Feisty's house, Boom pulls the front door shut behind him, being careful not to slam it. He crosses over the road to where Feisty's stood waiting, underneath the street light; head bent and kicking at the lamp-post with her foot.

"You ok?" Boom asks.

She nods, refusing to look up.

Boom watches her for a second, then in a soft voice tells her, "Come here."

He pulls her close for a hug, and without warning she drops her guard, letting out a loud sob she's been stifling for the last 10 minutes. Or more to the point, the last few months.

Boom wraps his arms around her protectively and despite how wet their clothes are, she allows herself to relax enough to wrap her arms around his waist, leaning into his chest and allowing him to stroke the top of her head until she calms down and the sobbing stops. She looks up, a little shocked; her eyes swollen from crying. She gives him a soft smile, grateful for the hug. She's about to say something when a police car rounds the corner. Boom spots the car - with a number 63 on its roof - over the top of Feisty's head and swears.

"Shit, feds."

Feisty tries to wriggle free but Boom pulls her closer instead. "What you doing?" she asks, struggling to break free from his grip.

Burying his head in her hair, his voice muffled,

Boom replies: "Teenager, hoodie. I'm fucked if they stop. Gotta make it look like we're boyfriend and girlfriend."

Peeking over the top of Feisty's head with one, half-opened eye, Boom watches as the police car slows down in front of them, and the cop in the passenger seat leans forward to take a look at him and Feisty. Boom looks up, pretending he's only just spotted them, and gives the cops a friendly nod, his arms tightening around Feisty's back as he does. The cop says something to the other one before deciding they're not a threat and they drive off up the road before turning down a side street.

Boom releases Feisty. "That was close."

They start walking. A couple of minutes pass in comfortable silence before Boom looks across at Feisty.

"How long's she been like that for?"

Feisty stares at the floor as she answers.

"About a year. Ever since dad left. He had an affair with someone at work. Such a cliche. Got her pregnant, moved in two months later, and now he doesn't want anything to do with me or Summer. It's all about Max. Max this, Max that."

"The lady in the park the other day?" Boom asks her.

Feisty nods, and in a mocking voice - obviously meant to be her dad - she says: "He's only little, Mercedes. You don't understand. He needs me right now. You and Summer are old enough to look after yourselves but Max isn't. You must know I'm always there for you if you need me." Her voice returns to normal, but her tone is angry and bitter, "Except he's not is he? Seen him twice for fuck's sake. Twice since he moved out. Dickshit!"

"Were you close?" Boom asks, sensitive to how he asks the question. "Before it happened."

"I thought we were. Shows you can't trust anyone though, not even your dad."

There's a break, before she continues, "It's the stupid cow's fault. Carla, the blonde from the park. Guilt trips him every time into cancelling."

They continue in silence for a bit, before Boom asks: "Have you thought about getting her help?"

Confused, Feisty bites back angrily. "That fucking bitch?! What would I want to help her for?!"

"No!" Boom replies, shaking his head. "Your mum."

Now it's Feisty's turn to shake her head.

"Yeah, right. Social Services would have a fucking field day with us. We'd be in a home by next week."

In that second, her walls go back up and Feisty returns to her angry, agitated self.

"What's it to you anyway, Mr 'I never talk about my feelings ever?' You don't *ever* talk about anything. You just draw pretty pictures all night with your mates. Doesn't solve a thing."

Boom laughs, ironically. "What, and talking does?"

He spins round, walking backwards, surveying the street as he talks.

"Guys just do things differently that's all. When girls shut their front door, all they wanna do is talk about it. All I wanna do is forget. Me and my mates. The 'pretty pictures' as you call them. They're what keep me sane."

Feisty shrugs in response.

Turning into a side street, they spot the same police car up ahead, doing a U-Turn and heading back towards them.

"That's not good," Boom says.

Without warning, he grabs Feisty's arm and pulls her up the nearest garden path.

"What you doing?!"

Feisty tries to shake him off but Boom's got a firm grip. He watches as the police car starts to slow as it approaches and before Feisty has a chance to protest, Boom leans in and gives her a full-on kiss, his tongue deep inside her mouth, his hands ruffling her hair at the back of her neck, like two lovers who know each other really well. Feisty struggles for a second before her body softens and her tongue responds.

Careful not to be seen doing it, Boom opens one eye, just enough to watch the cop car from a sideways gaze. As the car slows to a stop at the bottom of the path, Boom ramps up the pash with Feisty, pushing his tongue further into her mouth whilst wrapping his arms around the sides of her head, and clasping a clump of her hair in what looks to an outsider like the height of passion. The officer in the passenger seat looks away awkwardly, muttering something to the driver before putting his seat belt back on, and pulling away.

Feisty's still responding to Boom's kiss, her eyes closed and her body pulled into him, as he watches the cops round the bend. He pulls away sharply, like nothing happened.

"That was lucky!" Boom gives her a cheeky grin, before adding: "Hope you were ok with that. Had to find a way to get rid of them." He picks up his paints and heads back down the path and onto the street where he carries on walking, oblivious to the fact that Feisty's frozen to the spot, her hand lingering over her lips where Boom's just kissed her.

Realising she's not there, he spins back round.

"Come on. The others'll be waiting for us."

Feisty follows him, still in a bit of a daze - with Boom completely unaware of the feelings he's just stirred up in her.

19 THE PIECE

Boom and the rest of the Crew squat down low in front of a ten-foot wall surrounding a business. Leaning back against the wall, away from the prying eye of the security camera, The Watcher whispers to his mates.

"Behind me, at the front of the building, is the security camera. To the right, the light. Make sure you climb the wall to the left of the building to avoid setting off the light. Got that?"

The Crew nod. Feisty looks at the ten-foot wall in front of her, the heavy metal gates, and the security camera, and her face says it all.

"How the fuck are we gonna get up there?"

"You're not," Boom replies. "The Cat is. Watch and learn, sister. Watch and learn."

She watches as The Cat takes a running jump at the wall, scrambling up by just his feet. Spiderman style, no arms required.

"What the fuck?" She sounds seriously impressed.

"Told you he was good," Boom replies, taking himself away from the rest of the Crew to change into Flash's clothes.

Feisty watches closely as Boom strips down to just his school trousers. She can't help herself. Her eyes are locked on Boom's body again, checking out his six pack and his strong, broad shoulders and muscly arms as he reaches into a bag for Flash's t-shirt. He pulls the t-shirt over his head, a dark grey t-shirt with a policeman on it, giving someone the bird. Unknown to

Feisty, however, Flash has spotted her watching Boom. His eyes flit between the pair of them, checking to see if Boom is giving her the eye back, but Boom's totally oblivious to the effect he's having on Feisty, who is unable to look away until he's fully dressed.

Flash watches Feisty as her eyes travel the length of Boom's body, as he steps out of his trousers, her eyes lingering on his boxers and the way they cling to the cheeks of his behind. She carries on watching until he's slipped into a pair of Flash's trousers and he's done.

"Hmm," Flash mutters to himself, as next to him The Cat runs the length of the wall in front of the Unit, taking a running jump at the security camera above his head. Swinging on the camera arm by just one hand, The Cat uses his spare hand to knock the lens towards the wall - giving the Crew a clear path to the back of the building. Mission complete, The Cat starts to swing back and forth, building up momentum like a gymnast on the bars, until he's swinging himself with enough force to launch himself away from the camera, back up onto the wall, where he returns to the rest of the Crew.

Stepping forward to where everyone else is standing, Boom whispers to Flash as he passes.

"Cool t-shirt. Very apt" - then off Flash's confused face. "The policeman."

"Just keep the paint off it alright?" Flash replies in response.

Boom beckons to The Watcher to come to the front of the wall, where The Cat is pacing back and forth impatiently. Boom pulls each of the Crew over, one by one, where between them The Cat and The Watcher hoist each of them up onto the wall in turn. Boom helps The Watcher hoist Feisty up, where she waits at the top of the wall, visibly nervous. Once everyone's up, The Watcher stays put, using hand signals to tell the others to follow The Cat to the back of the building, avoiding the security light and keeping an eye on the security camera on the way past.

The Crew reach the back of the building where The Cat holds his hand out to stop them from moving. Motioning to them in the dark, he points towards a second security camera, angled into the compound below where vans and electrical equipment are stored. Signalling for them to wait, The Cat runs ahead, sprinting to the end of the wall where he throws himself at the camera, knocking it to face the wall, before landing agilely in the compound below, on both feet.

There's a quiet round of applause from the rest of The Crew before everyone jumps down and positions themselves in front of the wall to watch as Boom and some of the others work their magic with their cans of paint.

Feisty meanwhile is pacing back and forth at the back of the compound, unable to relax. Boom whistles to her, signalling for her to move away from a street light that filters into the compound from the street the other side. Feisty walks over to him, visibly stressed.

"I don't think I can run faster than that dog."

Boom grins, pulling a pair of latex gloves from a bag. "You won't have to, don't worry. The Watcher's already staked it out. Forty minutes is more than enough time to get this done."

"You gonna do all that in forty minutes?!" she

replies, looking down at Boom's sketch on the floor in front of him.

"I won't. We will though," Boom replies, nodding at the wall where the piece is already underway. Curl has covered the wall in a black background and is standing there awaiting Boom's instructions. This time, The Cat's got stuck in too, and has sketched a block of grey which is beginning to take the shape of the spaceship.

Boom picks up a can of luminous green paint and sprays an unearthly glow around the edge of it as Feisty takes a deep breath in. "I love that smell."

Flash comes to stand next to her as Boom finishes the outline of the spaceship and is now starting on the two aliens, and Red. Feisty is properly impressed and can't help herself.

"Wow!"

"Like what you see, do you?" Flash asks her, pointedly. Enough to make her turn and give him a quizzical look. But before she can respond, Boom turns round, laughing, telling Feisty: "I do believe that's the nicest thing you've said to me since I've known you. Must be turning soft in your old age."

"I'd say so," Flash adds, making it impossible for Feisty not to respond this time.

"What's that supposed to mean?!" she scowls.

Flash shrugs, but his body language says it all.

"Say it!" Feisty confronts him.

"Just that you seem very interested in everything Boom does, that's all," he replies. But before she gets a chance to respond, Flash adds: "He's one of the best. Just not really into relationships, if you catch my drift."

"What the fuck you going on about?!" she replies testily, trying to detract any implication away from her and Boom.

Flash laughs. "You're still in there then. Thought you'd gone all soft on me earlier. Being nice to me and all that," he says, before adding, "Just don't want to see you get hurt, that's all."

The Cat walks over to them and pokes them hard in the ribs. "In case you hadn't noticed, you're the only two making any noise right now. Can you just stop fucking arguing for half an hour," he says, before tipping his head towards the wall to show them the job's nearly done; the finishing touches being added as they speak.

Boom's drawn Red, the Angry Bird - aka Feisty - with a pair of boobs, standing at the bottom of the spaceship, surrounded by the hooded outlines of all the Crew members. He's managed to capture their stance and personality perfectly just by outline alone and it's properly impressive... The Cat, lithe and athletic, swinging from a bar at the top of the spaceship; The Watcher, calm and alert, standing guard; then Curl and Boom with their cans of paint in hand, and last but not least, Flash... tripping up and stumbling down the steps of the spaceship, seconds away from landing on top of Feisty.

Flash laughs. "When did that get changed?" he asks Boom.

Boom smiles. "It came to me. A second ago."

The Crew watch as Boom initials the finished piece with the letters, DC - short for Da Crew. He throws his can back into his bag and without speaking, the Crew haul themselves back up onto the wall and race back to the front of the building, in single file, where The Watcher is waiting for them.

As they reach the front, however, they hear a warning whistle. Feisty panics, following suit as the Crew jump back down into the compound, her heart racing. Boom peers over the wall, looking for The Watcher but he can't spot him anywhere. He signals to the rest of the crew to stay low.

A car approaches, pulling over at exactly the place where they were due to jump down into the road just seconds earlier. They hear a second whistle and The Cat looks down the line to Boom, who throws his arms up in confusion. He doesn't have a clue what's going on either.

Without speaking, The Cat grabs the top of the wall and carefully raises his head an inch or so over the top and has a look around to try and work out what's going on. There's a car pulled over at the side of the road, directly in front of them. Sensing movement at the other side of the road, he spots The Watcher, signalling for The Cat and the rest of the Crew to ignore the car and keep going. Unsure, however, The Cat lingers there for a second, checking the car out, until the passenger window slides down and a thick fog of aromatic smoke billows out, along with loud stoner's music. Below him, Boom takes a deep breath in.

"Nice," he says, breathing in the potent smell of cannabis.

The Cat drops back down and signals to the rest

of The Crew to keep going, miming a pair of stoner's the other side, making them laugh.

One by one, The Cat and Boom hoists everyone up onto the wall, where they jump back down into the road unnoticed. The Watcher, last one over, can't help it though. Stopping to lean into the driver side of the mystery car, he yells 'Boo!' through the open window, making the teenage boy inside drop his spliff, burning a hole in his jeans. "Fuck!"

"Sorry, couldn't resist!" The Watcher laughs, before sprinting off to join the others.

20 DON'T YOU GET TIRED OF BEING SHITTY ALL THE TIME?

Tired from the late night and suffering an energy dip from the adrenalin come down, the Crew wander home in dribs and drabs, walking together in small, splintered groups, with Boom, Feisty and Flash at the back. Exhausted, no-one speaks for a while, until Flash glances over at Boom, and checks out his T-shirt. He takes one look at it and shoves Boom in the chest.

"For fuck's sake. There's paint all over it!"

Boom looks down. Grey and luminous green paint is splattered all over the front of Flash's T-shirt, obscuring some of the body of the policeman, but not his face - or his gesture.

"I'll get you another one."

"That was my favourite t-shirt, G. Probably don't even sell it no more," Flash says, annoyed.

"I've gotta go into town tomorrow to buy some paints. I'll look then," Boom says, reaching behind his back to try and find the label. "Where's it from?"

Flash gives Boom a look. "Dunno, do I? Cut the label out!."

Boom gets it, trying to pacify Flash by telling him, "I'll find it, don't worry." There's a beat, before he adds: "You gonna come with me?"

"Can't. Promised Rach I'd help her put her desk up tomorrow."

Boom turns to Feisty instead. "Fancy coming

paint shopping with me tomorrow?"

She gives Boom a shy smile before replying. "Sure."

Flash raises his eyebrows at Feisty. She scowls at him, making sure Boom isn't looking.

Ahead of them the rest of The Crew have reached a crossroads and are standing there, waiting for the three stragglers to catch up. They fist bump and exchange quick hugs before slinking off into the dark in different directions, leaving Feisty, Boom and Flash stood on the pavement.

Feisty watches as Flash lights a fag, scuffing the ground with her feet, her face dark and intense. Boom looks over. "You ok?"

"I'll pay," she says, without a word of explanation.

Boom and Flash look at her, puzzled.

"The revenge graffiti," Feisty says, rolling her eyes, like she expected them to know exactly what she meant this time.

Flash shakes his head at her. "Don't you get tired of being shitty all the time?"

Feisty gives him a sarcastic look in return. "Don't you get tired of being happy all the time?"

Flash rolls his eyes at her. "That's the point. I'm not. Life sucks sometimes. Quite a lot of the time as it goes. But when I'm with my mates I just wanna chill. Have a good time. It's that simple."

"Well, good for you," Feisty replies sarcastically, squaring up to him.

Flash pushes her away. Winding her up, he turns to Boom.

"Just think, bro. Feisty here could turn you into the Robin Hood of the graffiti world."

Pointing a fake arrow into the sky, he mimes pulling back the string and fires, singing - loudly, and not very in tune - the theme tune to Robin Hood, but with his own words mixed in.

"Feared by the bad, loved by the good. It's Boom the Hood. Boom the Hood. Boom the Hood."

Feisty glowers at him. "Go fuck yourself, Flash."

Boom's had enough. He turns to Feisty.

"I get it. You've got a lot on. But graffiti's not about revenge. Not for me. It's about expression. The one place where I can truly say what's on my mind. Be myself. Speak - and for once be heard. You start fucking round, doing it for all the wrong reasons, no good's ever gonna come out of it. You just need to chill out."

Flash looks at her, softening a little. "He's right."

Feisty glares at Flash for spoiling her plan. But any bad feeling is broken by Boom and a cold hard reality check.

"We need to get home," Boom says. "School in three hours."

And with that they pick up their pace, and head home.

21 ALL THE GIRLS ARE WEARING THEIR HAIR LIKE IT. AND GETTING BRAS.

Flash's sister Rachel is in the kitchen, blazer on, ready for school. Two bits of toast pop out of the toaster and she grabs them, adding them to an already large stack of toast piled up on a plate in front of her. She whacks two more pieces in the toaster and while she waits, butters the slices that have just popped out, glancing up as a bleary-eyed Flash walks into the kitchen, rubbing his eyes.

"You look knackered," she says.

"Didn't sleep that well last night," he mumbles, grabbing a piece of buttered toast and shoving it in his mouth, giving her hair an affectionate ruffle as he passes.

She looks at him.

"What?!" He knows that look.

"Can you do my hair? Pleeease?" she asks, with a sweet smile.

Flash rolls his eyes, checking the time.

"You're fucking kidding me. Five minutes Rach! Even I'm not that fast."

"I've done the toast. We're ready to go. Apart from my hair..." she replies, giving him another sweet smile.

Flash relents, shaking his head at being suckered in again, even though he doesn't really mind. "Just as long as you don't want triple braids with ribbons and all that shit," he says, raising an eyebrow at her.

"French plait, top to bottom," she replies.

"Seriously?!"

"Yeah. All the girls are wearing their hair like it."

"You could do this yourself you know. Look it up on YouTube and give it a go."

Rach doesn't answer but falls silent for a second or two. Something clearly on her mind, before replying, "And getting bras."

"Jesus, Rach. Can't you go with a friend?"

He knows from her face it's a no. "I need someone to pay for it for me."

"Ok, we'll talk about it. Not now though," he replies, signalling for her to sit down on the chair in front of him. Grabbing a brush and two hair bands from the side, he gives her hair a quick couple of brushes, before expertly parting it straight down the middle with his fingernail. Starting at the top of her head, he parts the hair into three, weaving it quickly between his fingers, until a French braid starts to take shape one side.

"You're getting good at this, bruv," she teases, stuffing a piece of toast in his mouth as he carries on braiding. Unable to use his hands, he chews his way through the piece of toast, speaking with his mouth full. "Seriously, Rach, it would be nice to eat my breakfast with my hands next time."

She laughs. "Sorry, won't do it again." Adding, "You could start a hairdressers."

"Like I want to hang out with a load of girls all day," Flash laughs, his mouth still full of toast.

"You is opening up a hairdressers soon as you finish sch-ool," Rachel teases, giving him a playful punch in the stomach, making him drop his toast.

Flash gives her hair a playful yank in retaliation. "Stop pissing about will ya? Otherwise it's bunches for you next time."

Rach grabs a piece of toast just as Flash finishes the second plait, securing it neatly with a band. Flash stuffs the last bit of toast into his mouth and rushes out, pulling Rach away from the mirror. "For fuck's sake, Rach! Come on!"

22 YOU MIGHT WANT TO THINK ABOUT QUITTING, JAMIE

Flash and Boom are back in class. Flash yawning, his mouth wide open, with Boom slumped next to him and out for the count as Britton sits perched on his desk, facing the class, listening to a dark-haired boy at the front reading the closing lines of Shakespeare's Romeo and Juliet.

> *"Go hence to have more talk of these sad things;*
> *Some shall be--*
> *Pardon -- pardon'ed."*

The boy stops.

"Why's it got that funny mark there, Sir?" he asks Britton.

"Well done for asking, Tunde," Britton replies, explaining, "It's still the same word but it's split so that it rhymes better. So you say, pardon-ed and punish-ed," nodding at him to continue.

Tunde repeats the line again.

> *"Some shall be pardon'ed and some punish'ed"*

Boom, who's been fast asleep, jolts awake with a hacking cough, and interrupts Tunde full flow. He waits for Boom to stop coughing before finishing.

*"For never was there a story of more woe;
than this of Juliet and her Romeo"*

Tunde finishes, exaggerating the 'o' to emphasize the point, making the class laugh.

"Yes, very funny. Thank you, Tunde," Britton replies, with a smile on his face, as Jemima, a redhead in the front row, gives Britton big moon eyes before announcing to the whole class, "That was so romantic, Sir."

One of the boys in the back row turns to his mate and mimes shoving his fingers down his throat. Britton is just about to pick him up on it when he spots Flash mid yawn.

"Late night was it last night, Mr Pritchard?"

Boom starts to cough next to Flash, but this time he can't stop. Hacking himself awake again, he pulls a tissue from his pocket, and coughs into it, speckling it with red and green paint from last night's graffiti. Flash spots the dotted paint and throws Boom a concerned look.

"You might wanna think about quitting, Jamie," Britton says, fishing a pack of cough sweets from his trouser pocket and heading for Boom's desk.

Realising he needs to distract Britton before he spots the tissue, Flash knocks a pile of books onto the floor in front of Britton, who doesn't even flinch.

"Books, Mr Pritchard."

The class burst out laughing as the bell goes, marking the end of the school day.

Mr Britton sighs. A weary, been teaching-far-too-long kind of sigh.

"Go home, year 11s. Get some sleep. I want you back, bright-eyed and bushy-tailed in the morning."

Jemima, the red-haired girl from earlier, pulls a face as she stands up from her desk. "We're not animals, Sir." Ending it with a flirty smile.

"Debatable Jemima, debatable," Britton replies, getting a flirty giggle from her in response. He looks down quickly, pretending to busy himself with something on his desk.

Boom shoves the last of his books into his bag, coughing into his tissue as he and Flash walk out, passing feet from Britton's desk. Flash leans closer to Boom and whispers in his ear, "Need to wear a mask, bro. It's not good for you." They look up, and spot Britton watching them. They immediately pull away, making themselves look instantly guilty. Britton catches it and raises his eyebrows at them.

"Early night tonight, Jamie," Britton says as Boom heads out the door. "You too, Mr Pritchard."

"Sir," they answer together, before hot-footing it out of the classroom.

Behind them, in the now near but empty classroom, Jemima lingers by her desk. Giving a quick glance over at Britton to make sure he's not looking, she quickly folds the waist of her skirt over a couple of times to shorten it. Turning away from him slightly, she undoes one more button on her shirt so the top of her bra shows. She turns back round to face him - making a show of bending down low over her bag to reorganise it several times before finally shoving her books inside. Britton, acutely aware of what's going on, keeps his eyes

93

trained firmly on his computer, ignoring her completely.

Giving up, Jemima throws her bag over her shoulder and walks out past his desk - but not without one last attempt to wind him up.

Brushing past his desk, she reaches the door, glancing back over her shoulder to deliver her final words as seductively as she can. "Hope you get to watch Netflix later and chill, Sir."

Britton turns red, only too aware of the phrase's double meaning. Keeping his head down to hide his blushing face, he tells her, "Have a good evening, Jemima."

Jemima steps out into the corridor, tipping her head back in a silent laugh, pleased with herself. One nil to her in her very own game of Tease The Teacher.

23 DEFINITELY NOTHING TO DO WITH ROMEO AND JULIET

Sitting in the now empty classroom, Mr Britton tips his head back and lets out a loud sigh. He scrubs at his forehead with the base of his hand as if scrubbing hard enough might actually rub out all of the stress and frown lines embedded there after years of teaching in one of the city's most challenging secondaries.

Pulling himself upright, Britton stares at the pile of books in front of him. It's a daunting task, like facing an opponent at the start of a fight. He lifts the top one from the pile, opens it, looks at it and sighs. Whoever's book it is has written a single sentence in scruffy handwriting with multiple blots of ink in just one line. Next to the sentence is some kind of unidentifiable brown stain, which Britton has a scratch at, and sniffs, before pulling a face as if to say to himself, 'why did I just do that?!'

Pinching his forehead between his finger and thumb, Britton reads the sentence silently in his head. With a despondent look, he picks up a pen and circles several of the words within the sentence in bright red ink, correcting each spelling mistake before adding: "A single sentence does not constitute homework, Damien. Please come and see me after class."

Britton slaps the book down next to him but instead of reaching for the next one at the top of the pile, he sorts through them until he gets to Boom's book halfway down. Boom's real name, Jamie Johnson, is written on the front in a fluid, creative font. Not quite graffiti, but the letters definitely have an artistic flair to them.

Opening the book at Boom's last piece of homework, he flicks through the pages to see how much he's written. There's several pages of work, six or seven - a novel, almost, in comparison to the last student's work. Boom's handwriting is surprisingly clear and neat; his arguments well thought out - and - running alongside several of his main arguments are little sketches in the margin to help illustrate each point. Where he's written, 'many refer to Romeo and Juliet as star-crossed lovers', Boom has sketched the silhouette of two lovers next to the phrase, intertwined in a kiss. Above them, two hearts, divided by a lightning strike.

Britton's face lights up as he reads Boom's answer. Thank god for one good student, he thinks to himself. One good student might just make all the hard work worthwhile, especially if Boom does something with it. Carrying on reading, Britton reaches one particular paragraph and stops to write alongside Boom's words - 'a really well thought out point, Jamie. Well done.'

Turning the page, he stops to look at an unexplained sketch at the top of the margin. Glancing at the text - then back at the drawing - Britton frowns, muttering to himself under his breath.

"Definitely nothing to do with Romeo and Juliet. Not unless Shakespeare had them abducted by aliens."

It's Boom's first graffiti sketch with Feisty in it, with the two aliens standing at the top of the spaceship, welcoming Red the Angry Bird, with tits, and next to it, the phrase: "Welcome, Feisty Bird."

Britton gives up trying to work out what the sketch is about and finishes Boom's final paragraph instead. He gives Boom an A+, circling the mark in red pen to give it more emphasis. Returning to Boom's sketch, Britton lets his pen hover over it for several seconds before writing two question marks in the margin next to it. Britton shakes his head before closing Boom's book. He then stands, ready to leave.

24 LIKE I SAID. STAY AWAY FROM HER

Britton steps out of his classroom wearing a large bag over his shoulder and carrying a huge pile of books in both hands. An elderly male cleaner, in his 70s, mops the corridor in slow, methodical strokes whilst listening to something on his headphones. Britton nods at him as he closes the classroom door behind him, somehow managing to lock it before heading down the corridor towards the exit. Passing the library on his right, his attention is drawn to a blue light, emanating out of the room from one of the computers. Frowning, he stops to peer into the room through a small glass window.

He spots Boom sat in front of one of the computers lined up against the wall in a long row. The lights are off, so the room is in darkness, apart from the eerie glow from the computer. Completely engrossed by what he's reading, Boom doesn't even notice Britton peering through the window. He pulls away and heads back towards the exit, and out into the school car park.

It's dark outside and Britton's car is one of only two left. The car park is lit by lamp posts, several of which have a CCTV camera attached to them, trained onto the parking spaces below.

Britton leans on his car door, balancing the large stack of books against the glass as he reaches for his car key stuffed inside his trouser pocket. There's a quick darting movement from behind, making him jump, and he drops the pile of books in a messy heap at his feet. He turns round to find Flash grinning at him, leant against the car next door.

"For God's sake, don't any of you have homes to go to?!" Britton says, forgetting himself for a second as he regains his composure.

Flash grins.

"Sorry, Sir, didn't mean to make you jump. I'm just waitin' for Boo--" he stops to correct himself, "Jamie."

Britton throws him a look. "Students shouldn't be here beyond a certain time, Mr Pritchard."

"Don't worry, we're leaving soon, Sir," Flash replies, with a grin.

Britton opens his mouth to speak but it hangs there as his attention is drawn to a girl, racing towards them in the dark. Flitting in and out of sight as she darts between the cars and shadows, it's only as she reaches them that they see who it is. It's Feisty. And she isn't happy.

Racing up to Flash, she shoves him hard in the chest, pushing him backwards into the car with a thud. Gripping a screwed-up piece of paper in her hand, she shoves it in his face, shouting, "Where is he?!"

He takes a guess. "Boom?" - forgetting they're not supposed to mention their tags in front of the teachers. Without thinking, he adds, "He's in the library. What's your problem any--?"

Britton shakes his head at Flash in disbelief as Feisty sprints off towards the school, leaving Flash mid-sentence. Sensing trouble, they race after her, crashing through the school doors and into the corridor, just as Mr Ellington, the school head, storms into the library where loud shouts can be heard. The elderly cleaner stands in the corridor, headphones out, mouth wide open - broom mid-air - as his eyes follow first Mr Ellington, then Britton and Flash as they burst their way into the library.

Britton and Flash arrive just in time to see Feisty slam Boom hard against a bookshelf, sending a row of books crashing to the floor. Shoving his letter to her mum in his face, she yells at him, "How was THIS supposed to help?! Poking your nose into my fucking business!"

Mr Ellington grabs Feisty by her arm, and pulls her away from Boom, who's stood in silence, shaken by the confrontation.

"Stop it now, Mercedes!" he says, pulling her back further.

Feisty pulls away from his grip, like a dog straining at its leash, before breaking free and taking another run at Boom. Inches from his face, her features contort with anger. She slams the letter into his chest, shouting,

"You think you know the answer to everyone else's problems. But how is *any* of this supposed to help?"

Right at the end though, her voice cracks, giving away her emotions. It's only for a second though, but it's long enough for everyone to see what's there. The devastation of being abandoned and a mum that's absent.

Regaining her momentum, she waves the letter in Boom's face again, screaming at him as Ellington drags her away.

"What's the fucking point of telling her *'it's not*

personal?' My dad left her for a woman, half her age, after twenty years of marriage, Jamie. *Twenty years*. Of course it's fucking personal. What he's telling her - *us* - is twenty years of love, kids. None of it's good enough. It was all a bunch of shit. We're shit!"

And with that her voice breaks, and she starts to sob. Mr Ellington escorts her out of the room, leaving Britton behind with Flash and Boom. For a moment they're all too shell-shocked to speak. After what feels like minutes, but is actually only seconds, Britton tips his head towards the door, leading Flash and Boom outside into the fresh air.

Standing by the school gates, Britton looks them both in the eyes. His gaze darts from one to the other, and back again, before addressing them both with a serious face.

"Like I said. Stay away from her. I know she's got a lot going on in her life right now, and ultimately she's not a bad person. But Mercedes is in a lot of trouble right now and if you're not careful she'll drag you both down with her."

25 THE TAG LUNAR SOUND FAMILIAR TO YOU?

Boom stands outside a tatty-looking pub, in the heart of a rundown residential estate, just one of many local council estates, made up of grotty tower blocks and concrete playgrounds. He's in school uniform still, surrounded by skateboarders dressed casually from head to foot in t-shirts, caps and sweats. Approaching from the pavement in trackie bottoms and a new pair of fancy trainers, is Flash. He reaches Boom and chucks a bag of clothes at him.

"I'm not even gonna say anything!" he tells Boom, obviously narked.

"I'll give 'em back tomorrow," Boom replies, a little too sharply.

"What you antsy with me for, bro?" Flash throws his hands up, but then carries on, comedy style, just to let Boom know he's not really pissed off with him.

"You're the one who fucks my clothes up all the time, G. Gets paint all over them. Should go for a job as a painter decorator when you leave school. Got your wardrobe all sorted already."

Boom laughs. Flash pauses for a minute, then looks at Boom.

"What d'you think Britton meant earlier? 'Bout Feisty?"

Boom shrugs.

"Still gonna take her with you to buy paint tomorrow?" Flash asks him.

Boom shrugs. Almost like a 'sure, why not?'

Flash scuffs his feet, acting like an embarrassed teenager all of a sudden."

"What?" Boom asks him.

"Do me a favour? Ask Feisty about bras for me."

Boom bursts out laughing. It's game on now.

"Like what? Size? Colour?!"

"No, you twat. Rachel needs a bra. And I ain't got a fuckin' clue about how you go 'bout getting one."

Boom starts laughing. Flash scowls, but he's trying not to laugh at the same time.

"You go to the shop, pick one you like and buy it," Boom jokes.

Flash laughs. "No, dickhead. I mean. How do you know what size you are?"

Boom mimes grabbing a pair of boobs in front of him.

"Like this!"

"They don't do that, do they?!" Flash asks, half-serious.

Boom laughs, shaking his head, and Flash takes a swipe at him. Boom ducks his head just in time. Flash is about to give it another go, when he spots a police car approaching slowly from the opposite side of the road. Judging by the speed of it, they're doing a recce.

More worryingly, however, is The Cat... who they spot crossing the road behind the cop car, completely oblivious to its presence as he walks along the road, head down, texting.

"Ah shit," Boom says to Flash under his breath. "Can't get his attention without the cops spotting us. And him."

As the car pulls up outside the pub, all the teenagers scatter. Flash and Boom dive inside the pub while the skateboarders head off, pedalling their feet frantically to escape the cops. Officers Matthews and Wilson - the same cops who arrested Flash the other night - jump out of the car and head towards the pub. But as they reach the entrance, their path is blocked by a young mum struggling to fit her buggy through the door. Her screaming toddler's strapped inside and they have no option but to stop and help her through. Officer Wilson lifts the buggy into the air, manoeuvring it through the door to allow Matthews to go inside.

Just across the street, The Cat draws level with the pub - looking up just in time to spot the cop car parked in the car park with Wilson hovering by the entrance. Cursing to himself under his breath, The Cat stuffs his phone into his pocket and dives between two parked cars.

Matthews wanders back outside, shaking his head. Annoyed, he tells Wilson, "Missed 'em." They jump back into their patrol car and take one last look back towards the pub before driving off.

A minute later, Flash and Boom pile out of the pub, looking for The Cat, but he's nowhere to be seen.

"Shit! Did the cops get him?" Flash asks panicked, looking at Boom.

They hear a cough and walk over to where a line of cars are parked. Walking over to them, they spot The Cat, propped up Spiderman style between two cars - hands and feet pushed either side of him, lifting his whole body weight off the ground like a gymnast - pure muscle strength alone keeping him up. He grins at them before letting out a loud, pained groan as he releases his muscles and drops to the floor. He gives Boom and Flash the bird as they laugh at him, dragging himself back up onto his feet.

He takes a second to compose himself before telling them, "Found out who that guy was the other day by the way. The one from the playground, remember?" There's a beat, before he continues. "The tag Lunar sound familiar to you?"

"Lunar?! No way!" Boom's excited.

"Used to tag all the trains right?" Flash checks. "Aint seen his name in a while."

The Cat leans in conspiratorially. "That's 'cause the BTP got him. He's up in court next week. Two years minimum apparently."

"Two years?!" Boom baulks. "You'd get less for murder." Then off their faces, "Well, maybe not quite."

"Explains why he didn't want to stop and chat though," The Cat says, raising his eyebrows at Boom and giving him a pointed look.

"On that note," Boom says, "time to go. Before the feds come back."

And with that, they turn heel and head off into the estate.

26 CHILL, WILL YA?!

Boom's sat at a bus stop, slouched at the end of a bench; hands stuffed deep in his trackie bottoms and his hood pulled tight over his head, looking every inch the troublemaker. There's a bus due any minute and the pavement's packed, but somehow Boom's got the bench to himself. Any passengers that are standing under cover with him keep their distance, choosing to hover at the edge of the shelter instead.

An old woman, in her 80s, is making her way along the pavement, towards the shelter, but she's struggling to make her way through the crowds of people - partly because of how narrow the pavement is and partly because all the other passengers are either too busy chatting, or too engrossed in their own world, to notice an old lady with her shopping trolley. In the end, she gives up trying to squeeze past politely, and bashes into their ankles with the spikes at the end of her trolley, making them move. Boom's clocked her though and watches as she approaches. As she enters the shelter he gives her a quick nod and smiles at her before shuffling along the bench to give her space to sit down. The old woman takes one look at him and how he's dressed before shuffling her way to a corner of the shelter, where a young mum stands with her two young kids, who are busy poking faces at each other.

Annoyed by the diss, Boom shakes his head and slumps down even lower on the bench, shoving his hands deeper into his pockets.

His attention is grabbed by a blue Ford Fiesta as

it pulls up alongside the shelter. Feisty jumps out of the passenger seat and slams the door behind her, walking away without looking back. The passenger window slides down and Feisty's dad leans across the driver's seat to shout something out the window.

"We haven't finished talking yet, young lady!"

Feisty spins round and in full view of everyone at the bus shelter, raises her arm high into the air and in a ceremonious gesture, with a huge amount of flair, she flips him the bird.

"Fuck you, arsehole!"

Boom can't help himself. He starts to laugh as he catches the shocked faces of the other passengers, including the old lady and the young mum. Intrigued, he watches as Feisty approaches looking a lot more 'made-up' than normal. For the first time ever, she's in a skirt, which she wears with a stylish, fitted denim jacket. Her face is fully made-up instead of its natural state - with eyeliner, mascara as well as some bright, red lipstick. She plonks herself down next to Boom, as everyone around her stares at her. Boom looks at her with an amused smile on his face.

"Take it the talk went well then?"

He's laughing, making Feisty laugh too. Several of the passengers give them a disapproving scowl, which only makes them laugh even harder. Feisty gives Boom a playful slap on the belly, pretending to be annoyed that he's managed to make her laugh when she's trying to be grumpy.

"He only agreed to the meeting 'cause Ellington told him he had to. Wouldn't have done it otherwise," she tells him.

"And?" Boom asks.

Feisty rolls her eyes.

"Well, Ellington was up for suspending me. But then dad managed to talk him out of it. Basically told him everything that's been going on over the past few months.

"Awkward!"

"For him maybe. Not me. Made himself look a right cunt."

The young mum spins her kids round so their backs are facing Feisty, and glares at her. But Feisty hasn't even noticed and carries on talking.

"Promised Ellington he'd try and patch things up. Spend more time with me and Summer if he gave me one more chance--

"That's a good thing, right?" Boom asks her, looking at her sensitively, knowing it's a big thing for Feisty underneath all her pretend 'don't care' attitude.

For once Feisty answers Boom straight, dropping the attitude and fake bravado.

"Yeah," she says, smiling sweetly at Boom. "It's what I've wanted all along if I'm honest. I've missed him."

Boom squeezes her hand, happy for her. Feisty pauses for a few seconds though, before adding, "We'll see though. I'm not holding my breath."

The mum with the kids is still staring at Feisty, following everything she says. This time Feisty's spotted her and starts mouthing off at her.

"What's your fucking problem?! Never seen a girl in a skirt before?!"

The woman bundles her children out of the shelter, while everyone else shuffles awkwardly on the spot, pretending not to listen. Boom shakes his head at Feisty, laughing.

"Chill, will ya?!"

The bus pulls up and everyone surges forward - leaving a space for Boom and Feisty to jump on first. Feisty clocks it and laughs, telling Boom: "I should be rude to people more often!" She taps her card on the ticket machine and heads upstairs to the top deck.

27 THIS WHOLE LOOK. THE SKIRT. MAKE UP. IT SUITS YOU

Boom sits on the front seat next to Feisty, watching the world flash by in a companionable silence. Boom glances at her and smiles. She can't help herself, and grins back - just for a second - giving a true reflection of what she's really like underneath her life-hardened exterior. Sweet, funny even, underneath all the cynicism her dad has left her with.

"What?" she asks, laughing.

Boom circles his face and lips in the air with a finger, referring to her make-up.

"This whole look. The Skirt. Make Up. It Suits You."

Feisty grins. "Thanks."

They sit side by side, not talking, until Feisty breaks the silence. Too embarrassed to look him in the face, she tells him, "Sorry for being such a dick. You didn't deserve it. You were just trying to help."

"Oh. You mean when Ellington had to drag you off me you mean? When you nearly gave me a black eye? That?"

Boom's enjoying making her squirm. But not in a mean way, he's just being playful.

Feisty doesn't answer. But a second later, asks him, "Why won't you do it?"

This time Boom knows exactly what she means. Turning to face her, he tells her: "Just give up will ya? I'm never gonna do it. It's not what it's about for me."

"It could be though," Feisty says.

"Besides. I thought you'd feel differently about it now. You know. Now you've made peace with your dad and all that," Boom adds.

Feisty glances out the window. "I do. It was just a question."

She glances at him, one last time, before giving up. She turns to face the front, watching the street below flash by as the bus heads into the centre of town.

28 THEY JUST GAVE YOU A WELL FILTHY LOOK

The bus stops by the shops in the centre of town and Boom and Feisty jump off. Boom dives straight off the main street and down an alley, followed by Feisty. They reach a grimy looking shop, with bars over the window, that looks a bit like a DIY shop; simple and basic, selling what it sells without trying to sell itself. Boom dives inside, followed by Feisty.

Inside, the lights are dim, giving the shop a dingy feel. It takes a second or two for Feisty's eyes to adjust, but when they do she can't help herself, her eyes are all over the place, taking it all in. Rows and rows of moving metal cages on wheels line the concrete floor, giving the shop a kind of warehouse feel. Inside each of the cages - which are only accessible by unlocking a padlock at the front - are cans of paints. Like the ones used by Boom and Curl for graffiti, but divided according to colour and shade or the specific type of effect they give.

There's a few different brands, but the shop seems to mainly stock Montana. Feisty walks alongside the cages, reading each label. Montana Hologram Glitter. Montana Granite Effect. Montana Chalk. Montana Nightglow and Montana Primers. So many different effects, she wouldn't even know where to begin.

She's so busy taking it all in, and trying to process it, that she hasn't clocked the other couple in the shop, walking from cage to cage browsing. Boom has though, and follows them closely, his eyes flicking impatiently between them and the two shop assistants behind the counter. He makes a show of scratching his head before glancing up at the CCTV cameras positioned at various points around the shop. Boom watches the couple leave, without buying anything, before his eyes drift back to the shop assistants, deep in conversation behind the counter. Feisty has her back to them so can't see their faces.

Boom's eyes are all over the shop, until they stop at some cans of paint lined up on a top shelf next to him. Just three of them, the only ones that aren't locked away in cages. He shuffles closer, glancing over at the two shop assistants who are still deep in conversation. He leans in towards Feisty, his eyes fixed in their direction, and whispers in her ear-

"They just gave you a well filthy look!"

Feisty spins round to look at Boom, who tips his head over to where the two shop assistants are still deep in conversation. Feisty marches over to them and lays into them.

"Don't give me the evils then fucking pretend you didn't by standing there chatting! What's your fucking problem with me?! Thought I was gonna nick somethin' did you?!"

Behind her, Boom reaches up to the top shelf and grabs the cans of paint - making the most of having Feisty as a distraction. He stuffs the cans down the front of his hoodie, walks over to where Feisty is still having a go, and pulls her out of the shop before they call the police.

"Come on!" he says, pretending to be indignant. "We can get paint somewhere else!"

The two shop assistants look at them in shock, not sure what just hit them - or what just happened.

29 EVEN LAWYERS DO IT

Boom bundles out of the shop with Feisty in tow. He pulls a can of paint from under his jumper, gives it a shake and holding it close to his hand, tags the door of the shop on his way out... the door already heavily-adorned with various other tags (a symbol of the business itself).

Feisty looks at Boom, confused. "Where'd that come from?"

"Same place where these came from," he replies, grinning as he pulls the other two cans out from under his jumper. Smiling, he continues-

"Picked them up while you were busy shouting at the shop assistants."

Feisty still doesn't get it. "I thought everything was locked away."

Boom gives one of the cans a shake. It's half-empty.

"Got myself some ex-display ones, didn't I? Enough to keep me going for now though," he replies with a casual shrug.

A smart-looking professional wearing a knee-length camel-coloured cashmere coat approaches from the high street. Feisty takes one look at him and instinctively tugs at Boom to get away.

"Chill," Boom replies. "He's one of us."

Feisty frowns at him. "Really?!!" She doesn't believe him.

"Not all graffiti artists are teenage delinquents

like me and Curl," Boom smiles. "Graffiti artists do it because they love it. It's a form of art to them. But even more, it's a form of expression, communication. A lot of them start young but turn their lives around. Get themselves all the sensible things in life like everyone else - a Job. Mortgage. Family. But they still go out bombing, 'cause it's what they love. They want to keep their voice. And it's a way - if you like - to keep rebelling against 'the combine." Boom can see Feisty's confusion and stops himself to explain. "It's from a book. One Flew Over The Cuckoo's Nest. There's a character in it called the Big Indian and it's his way of describing society and the way it controls us. All of us. Graffiti allows us not to be controlled. To be alive. Move to the beat of our own drum. Plus nothing beats the adrenaline buzz," he adds, grinning.

Feisty gives him a look. She's still not got her head around the constant fear of being caught every time they're out.

The posh-looking man, now only feet away, reaches the shop entrance. Feisty clocks his bag, a fat leather briefcase like the ones lawyers carry their court papers in. Feisty looks him up and down, whispering to Boom.

"Looks more like a boring lawyer to me," she says.

"But that's what I've been trying to tell you," Boom says. "There's loads of graffiti artists who are highly-paid professionals during the day who still sneak out in the middle of the night to do what they love. Maybe not loads, but definitely enough to surprise you. People in their twenties, thirties, forties... And yeah, there's even lawyers doing it. There's this one guy everyone knows about. Puts his paints in his bag along with all his court papers. It's the perfect disguise. Feds take one look at his bag and don't even bother to search him. Never been stopped once. They just assume the reason he's out at three in the morning is some case he's working on."

The man clocks Feisty looking at him and flashes her a cheeky wink as he enters the shop, laughing as he goes. Everything about him screams 'professional' - including an inbuilt arrogance at the fact he can do what he does and still get away with it.

"Fucking hell!" Feisty starts laughing, shaking her head in surprise. "I would *never* have guessed!"

"Maybe I should use him as a distraction next time instead," Boom says, dropping it into conversation and flashing Feisty a cheeky grin.

It takes a second or two for the penny to drop, but then Feisty realises she's been had. "You fucker!" she laughs, landing him a punch straight to the stomach - half mad and half amused at his ingenuity.

"You could've got me arrested!"

"Nah!" Boom replies, laughing. "I wouldn't have let it happen." There's a pause before he adds, "But I knew you'd be a good distraction. You're always good to give someone a mouthful or two."

"Go fuck yourself!" Feisty laughs, taking another slug at his stomach as they head off down the alley and back towards the High Street.

They reach the shops, where the street is teeming with people. Boom stops.

"You alright to get the bus back by yourself?"

"You not coming?" Feisty looks disappointed.

"I need to get Flash some clothes. He'll never speak to me again if not," Boom replies.

Feisty tries to hide her disappointment by giving Boom a casual shrug, before turning to walk away. "I'll see you at school tomorrow. But I won't let on I know you this time," she adds, with a smile.

She heads off quickly, making sure she disappears quick enough for Boom not to notice her face, and for her to give the game away. He stands there watching long enough to make sure she reaches the right bus stop, before heading off. But he's missed her face entirely. It's only when she reaches the bus stop that Feisty lets her act drop, and the bravado drains out of her like a deflating balloon. Gutted to be going home alone, she lets out a loud sigh. Or more to the point, gutted to be going home without Boom.

30 HOW COULD I BE SO FUCKING STUPID?! TO FALL FOR HIS BULLSHIT AGAIN?!

It's another school day, and throngs of kids pile through the school gates. Feisty's head bobs along amongst the masses, swept along like jetsam in a tide. She passes Boom, who's stood on the pavement waiting for Flash. Their eyes drift over at the same time to some fresh graffiti daubed on a pillar at the side of the school gates. Sensing each other's presence, their eyes drift over everyone's heads and they catch each other's eyes for a second. Their gaze flits back quickly to the graffiti, and they give each other a secret smile before passing each other like complete strangers.

The bell goes, and the students speed up, heading for the school entrance, making sure they get to registration in time.

Inside, a couple of the older lads play tag along the corridor, jostling their way past the other students, still sleepy from the night before. Everyone heads for their lockers, unlocking their padlocks and dumping their coats inside. They take out their folders and pencil cases before stuffing their bags inside their lockers and slamming them shut.

Mr Britton is patrolling the corridor before registration and spots Feisty flouncing down the corridor, her skirt hitched up and giving it attitude - but for the first time ever - with a huge smile on her face. Raising his voice loud enough to be heard over the masses, he shouts across at her.

"Lessons start in *two* minutes, Miss Havara."

Waiting for the backlash, Britton does a double take as she flashes him a friendly smile before replying with a polite, "Sir." Britton is so taken aback he stops dead in his tracks, standing in the corridor with his mouth wide open. Watching from a distance and laughing, having watched it all play out in front of them, are Boom and Flash. Slapping each other's arms, laughing, they're in shock themselves.

Feisty's phone rings and Britton's teacher's instincts kick back in. "Put it away till break time please, Miss Havara! Bell's about to go!" But it's too late, Feisty's already answered. There's only a few students left in the corridor now. Most of them are safely inside the classroom, apart from a handful of stragglers including Feisty, with Boom and Flash.

They watch as Feisty listens to whoever's talking for a few seconds before her face darkens and she shouts down the phone, "You're fucking kidding me!" She hangs up and in a storm of anger charges at the lockers. She lays into the row closest to her, kicking them with her foot, leaving several dents and making the Year 7, who's struggling to empty his bag next to her, jump out of his skin. He drops his bag in shock, its contents spilling out across the floor. He watches, eyes wide, as Feisty boots his bag - along with what's left of its contents - down the corridor in a fit of fury.

"What d'you think you're doing, Mercedes?!" Britton shouts. Feisty spins round to face him. "Fuck off!" she shouts, making sure she does it as loudly as she can before flipping him the bird and crashing through some double doors to the outside - the dramatic scene, a full 360 degree turnaround from a minute earlier. Flash can't help himself, and starts to laugh, but is caught out by Britton, who is not amused. "Adam! Jamie! Class! Now!" He stops to check on the Year 7 boy, whose eyes have welled up, and is about to head after Feisty when Boom beats him to it. Flash tries to stop him but for once in his life he's not fast enough, and Boom pulls away and is out the door in seconds. Both Flash and Britton shout after him at the same time.

"Jamie!"

"Boom!"

They look at each other, Flash realising he's just given Boom's name away again but hoping Britton didn't catch it properly. He's about to sprint after Flash but Britton points him in the direction of the classroom. "Not you as well, Mr Pritchard."

As Flash takes a seat at his desk, Britton pokes his head through the classroom door, telling his students, "Class. Start reading where you left off last time and read *in silence* until I get back. Any talking, or misbehaving, and all of you will be in detention after school. Got that?" No-one speaks. Britton shuts the door behind him, heading off down the corridor, towards Mr Ellington's office.

Outside in the empty playground, Boom manages to catch up with Feisty and grabs her by her arm. Wild like a banshee, she spins round to face him, her finger hammering the air in front of her to emphasise every point she makes, letting it all spill out before Boom even gets a chance to speak.

"*How* could I be so fucking stupid?! To fall for his bullshit AGAIN?! He promised Ellington he was going to make a fucking effort with us. But surprise, surprise. Carla and Max get back from being away at her parents and he doesn't want anything to fucking do with us! He's just cancelled AGAIN!"

"I get it," Boom says, speaking in a slow, calm voice in an attempt to diffuse her anger. But it has the opposite effect.

"No you don't! He's a fucking arsehole!" she shouts, tears welling up in her eyes. Her voice starts to crack as she thinks about what she's saying. "I've always blamed Carla. But it's not her, is it? It's him. 'Cause if he really wanted to see me he would. But he doesn't, does he?" It's not a question though. She doesn't need a reply. Her voice cracks completely, and she has to swallow several times to get rid of the lump in her throat before she continues. "He's my dad. And he doesn't give a shit. About me, or Summer."

She starts to cry. Boom steps closer and pulls her head into his chest and holds it there, gently stroking the top of her head to comfort her, like before. Eventually her breathing slows and all the fury and anger releases from her body. She lifts her head up, looking directly into his eyes for a few seconds, and before he has time to do anything about it, Feisty pushes herself up on her tiptoes and kisses him. Boom tries to pull away, conscious he doesn't want to take advantage of her when she's down.

"Trust me, you don't wanna get involved with me," he says, with an ironic laugh. "Not really a good bet as far as relationships are concerned. Got too much of my own shit going on to be any kind of use to anyone else," he says.

Feisty's not giving up though. She just wants him - and will do anything to have him near her again. So she does what most people do when they really like someone and fakes the nonchalance. "I'm not asking you to marry me for fuck's sake! I just wanna kiss you." She gives him a naughty smile and pulls his head closer and starts to kiss him again.

Boom tries to pull away but she's got him this time. She gives his top lip a playful bite, pushing her tongue deep into his mouth and playing with his tongue as she pulls herself into him, pushing her breasts up against his chest so he can feel how much she wants him. And with that he gives up. Allowing himself to be the teenage boy that he is, wanting - no *needing* - that physical release, he shuts his eyes and kisses her back. Feisty opens her eyes for a second, watching his face intently for some kind of reaction, a hint of how he really feels. But there's nothing. At least nothing she can read.

Annoyed, she pulls away from him and without warning, starts to have a go at him. "You wanna lie down like some sad pathetic dog and take all their shit, you go for it. Me? I'm gonna do something about it!" And with that she storms off, leaving him to think about what she's just said.

Boom stares into the distance, deep in thought; and stuck with the reality of his own situation. An abusive stepdad, who he's forced to watch beat the shit out of his mum every night. And being completely powerless to do anything about it.

31 WOMEN. THEY'RE ALL STUPID, RIGHT?

Boom arrives home from school and heads up the stairwell, reaching the top where his front door is. Instinctively, he slows down as he approaches his front door, hanging back to listen. He edges forward slightly so he can peer through the kitchen window to see if his stepdad is in. His mum is stood at the kitchen counter so he lets himself in but walks in to find the kitchen in chaos. There's a huge pile of sandwiches stacked in front of her, grated cheese and other ingredients spread out across the counter. He's about to say hello when he spots the blood pouring from a cut at the side of her eye, and he stops in his tracks.

He spots movement from the corner of his eye and jumps. It's Oli, standing in the inner corridor, disconcertingly quiet, not saying anything or looking at anyone as he pulls on his luminous works jacket. It's a scary, powerful silence. A powerful, brooding presence that sucks the life out of everyone in the room, draining Boom of all his energy and filling him with fear.

Boom watches Oli as he shoves his feet into his steel-capped boots and walks back into the kitchen. Boom knows he's seen him but Oli pretends he hasn't, brushing past Boom in the tiny space without a word. Boom's face and his mum's say it all. The silence is terrifying. Boom's mum keeps her head down as she stares at the sandwiches, at a loss as what to do next. She can feel Boom looking at her, but she doesn't look up, and every few seconds wipes the blood that's pouring from her face with her sleeve. She keeps her head down, speaking to Oli in a timid, almost whisper. "I didn't know what filling to do."

Oli looks at her with disdain.

Boom's mum is visibly terrified and as hard as she tries, she can't hide the shake in her hands. Whatever she says she knows will be wrong, but she tries to blag it for Boom's sake, trying to placate Oli with a fake breeziness which belies the terror she feels inside.

"I thought I could do you a bit of everything. That way you can choose what you want. So I've done some cheese, and some egg, ham and…"

She trails off as Oli completely blanks her, slamming things down on the kitchen counter as he makes his way around the kitchen. She trails off, the facade gone; jumping every time he bangs the counter. Her body is stiff and tense; acutely aware of every nuance of Oli's whilst Boom stands there, forced to watch it all. He can see the games Oli is playing but like his mum he's too scared to do anything. When Oli walks over to him to acknowledge him for the first time that evening since walking in, Boom visibly flinches. Oli stops, inches from his face, with a nasty smirk on his face.

"Women. They're all stupid. Right?"

Boom's mum flashes Boom a look that says, 'just do it.' Boom looks at Oli and through gritted teeth replies, "Yeah. They're all stupid."

OIi leans into Boom's mum's face, as close as he can go without actually touching her. Staring directly into her eyes, he tells her: "See. Even your own fucking son thinks you're stupid."

With that, he turns on his heels and heads out, slamming the front door behind him.

Boom's mum lets out a stifled sob and bursts into tears. Boom walks over to her and hugs her. He reaches over to the radiator where Flash's t-shirt - the one with the policeman giving someone the bird - is drying and he pulls it off, gently wiping the blood from his mum's face, taking his time and making sure he is as gentle as he can be.

"I don't think that by the way. You know that, right?" he tells her, his voice choked. "I think you're amazing and brave and beautiful, and I'm… sorry."

"I know," his mum replies, still crying. "You did the right thing. I don't want him to start on you." She blows out hard, trying to catch her breath and calm herself before continuing. "I meant what I said, Jamie. Please. Just humour him. Long enough till you can go."

"But--" Jamie's about to argue with her but she's not letting him have this one.

"For once, Jamie, I'm right. You know I am. You've seen what he can do. You've seen it first hand. You saw what he did in front of that little boy the other day. Please. Just stay out of it. I don't want him to start on you. I'd never, ever forgive myself."

She breaks down again, letting Boom hold her. She wipes the tears from her face and starts to stack the sandwiches into various different lunch boxes.

"Fucking bastard left these here on purpose, I'm sure of it," she says. Boom catches his mum's eye and they start to laugh, letting go of all their stress. They stop laughing, and his mum asks him, "Would you mind dropping them to the depot for me?"

"What, all of them?" Boom asks her.

"I dunno. Yeah, probably. If you don't he'll just say he wants the ones you left here, so just take them all," she adds. She's in her permanent state of confusion and indecisiveness, any confidence she ever had to make simple decisions, well and truly beaten out of her after years of physical and mental abuse from Oli.

Boom picks up the sandwich boxes, shoves them into his bag and heads for the front door; his parting shot to his mum -

"You're right, he is a fucking bastard."

And for a second, the freedom of it makes them both smile.

32 WHO'S YOUR STEPDAD?

Boom reaches the train depot and heads for a mobile in front of him, marked reception. A dark-haired man in his 40s, wearing a high visibility jacket and hard hat, is behind the counter, checking the CCTV cameras in front of him, flicking from one to another, reviewing the footage. Satisfied, he gets to his feet, pulls a clipboard from a hook on the wall in front of him and places it on the counter to run through a schedule of repairs. He's just about to head off when Boom walks in, rucksack on his back. Boom looks at the bloke and gives him a polite nod.

"Can I drop some lunch off to my stepdad? He forgot it."

The man behind the counter is distracted and keeps his head down like he's trying to remember something.

"I'll be with you in a second. I've just gotta make a note of something." He runs through the schedule a line at a time with his pen, and without looking up asks Boom, "Who's your stepdad?"

"Oli Campbell," Boom replies.

The man looks up immediately, a look of pity on his face. He lets his brain process the information for a second or two before trying to cover his reaction.

"He's in the hanger. I'll show you."

He steps out from behind the counter and gently steers Boom back to the entrance with his hand. Boom's already clocked the man's change in attitude. Someone else who knows what a bastard my stepdad is, he thinks to himself. The man points Boom to a hanger, a couple of minutes walk away at the far end of the compound, over some rail tracks and past several metal huts where equipment is stored. There's a couple of trains next to the hanger, either under repair or being cleaned, graffiti daubed all over the sides. Boom smiles to himself.

The man hands Boom a hard hat.

"Strictly speaking, I should walk you over there myself, but I might leave that one for you if you don't mind. Just be careful when you're inside the hanger, that's all. Don't touch anything and come straight back when you've found him. And make sure you check out with me before you leave."

He grins as Boom steps onto the tracks.

"They're not live by the way. Just in case you were wondering." Boom looks down nervously at his feet, "Shit. I didn't even... think."

The man laughs, tipping his head to a repair shed closest to them. "I'll be in there when you're ready to leave."

Boom nods at the guy before making his way down the tracks, crushing the weeds with each step of his feet. His face darkens as he approaches the hanger, clocking the graffiti on the side of a train that's being cleaned. Thick, black unintelligible letters - definitely not the work of a pro, he thinks to himself - as he pulls back the giant bi-folding doors of the hanger just far enough to squeeze through.

Once inside, Boom waits a second, allowing his eyes to adjust to the light. It's still quite dark inside, despite the lights that are on at the back of the hanger, which has a high roof but no skylights. Boom peers down the tracks to the back of the hanger, where a train is pulled up alongside a raised walkway, just like the platform of a station. Music blares out of a speaker on a bench at the back, which has tools laid out all over it. Boom starts walking towards the bench but stops, momentarily freezing as Oli jumps down out of the driver's cab. Oli doesn't see Boom and heads to a dirty sink next to the workbench, outside a single toilet cubicle. Boom watches Oli for a minute as he scrubs his hands with a nail brush, leaving behind an oily residue in the sink; Oli completely oblivious of his presence - any kind of noise within the hanger itself drowned out by the music.

He's about to shout across to Oli when a woman steps out from the back of the train and approaches Oli. Boom watches as the woman - Paula, a work colleague of Oli's - walks over to where Oli is and turns off the music. Boom knows he needs to move, but can't, transfixed instead by what he knows is about to happen. Frozen to the spot, he watches Paula, who in her 30s is about ten years younger than his stepdad, walk over to Oli and push him up against the wall. Placing her hand on his trousers, she starts to massage his crotch making him groan with pleasure. Boom's disgusted. He can feel a rage filling his veins and he wants to explode at the injustice of it. His stepdad treating his mum like shit whilst all along carrying on with another woman at work, but he can't move.

Frozen to the spot, Boom can't seem to pull himself away. Even from several feet away, Boom can hear Oli's voice, loud and echoey in the hanger as Paula uses the base of her hand to rub his balls through his trousers.

"You're gonna make me come," he says, his voice the low familiar - and to Boom - brutal, gravelly voice that belongs to only him.

All of a sudden, Boom's instinct to survive kicks in. He knows Oli will go ballistic if he spots him there, and remembering the man back at reception wonders if he'll come looking for him if he's gone too long. He dives behind the front of the train, resting his head back against the carriage, a look of pure disgust on his face. Paranoid that even his breathing is too loud, or that Oli will spot him at any minute, Boom glances around the hanger looking for a way out - but the only way out is the way he came in and that's too risky 'cause Oli will definitely spot him if he tries leaving now. Stuck, Boom peers slowly out from behind the cab to check where Oli is now.

Oli has flipped positions with Paula, and now it's her who's pinned against the wall, while he slathers her neck with kisses. His large, fat hands struggle to pop open the top button of her shirt as he moves down to her breast. He pulls her bra to one side. Cupping her breast roughly in one hand, Oli bites her nipple. Whatever he's doing is turning her on though, and she leans back against the wall, groaning in pleasure and pushing her crotch towards him. Boom feels like he's going to be sick and he has to hold his hand in front of his mouth to stop himself from gagging. He rests his head back against the train, whispering to himself to stay calm, sick at the thought that anyone could ever find his violent bully of a stepdad attractive. "Just breathe," he tells himself. The noises at the back of the hanger are getting louder, more sexual, and Boom has to cover his ears with both hands to block out the sound. The noises stop for a second, and he hears Paula ask Oli, "Why don't you sleep here for the night? Tell your wife you've got a night shift."

"I can't," Oli replies.

Paula's hand travels back down to Oli's trousers and she undoes his zip, sliding her hand inside his pants to play with his cock.

"What's the matter? Don't you want me?" she teases.

Oli groans. "You know I do, babe. I'd like to force myself inside you right now."

Paula laughs, but Boom's disgusted. How can she find that sexy? She's obviously got no idea of what he's capable of. He gets back up on his feet, desperate to find a way out, but stops to listen as he hears Oli tell Paula, "Besides, I don't like leaving her alone with my boy. Last time I stayed out, I got home and she was passed out cold on the sofa. Paralytic. With the stove on. Could have set fire to the whole bloody flat. With my boy in it too."

"You fucking liar!" Boom says under his breath, furious, but still trying to escape without being spotted. He peers back round the side of the train, desperate to leave.

Oli's stood in front of Paula, her skirt hitched up just above her waist as he shoves his fingers inside her pants, pushing them deep inside her and moving them in and out, as fast as he can; a little rough, as he whispers something dirty in her ear. Paula grabs his arm for a second, "Not so hard, babe." Oli's face is tucked to the side of her, next to her cheek, so she can't see his reaction but he's pissed off. He's not someone who likes being told what to do, but he manages to hide his reaction as he kisses her neck, telling her, "I thought you liked it rough?" Paula giggles, "I do, babe, you were just getting a bit frisky there, that's all." Oli raises his face level with hers and gives her a slow, dirty grin, keeping his eyes trained on hers as he starts to move his finger in and out a bit slower this time. "Better?"

"Hmmm." Paula groans in pleasure, closing her eyes again as he continues to play with her. But Oli's not finished yet, filling her head with lies as he whispers-

"Sometimes, when she is awake, she gets…"

He trails off. Waiting for her to ask him.

Paula looks up. "What?"

"She gets angry and…" Oli trails off, biting his lip as if he's struggling to tell her the truth. "Hits him."

Paula looks shocked. "His mum hits him?" Oli nods.

It's too much for Boom - and he lashes out from where he's hiding, smashing the side of the train with his fist; slamming the metal as hard as he can. "You lying arsehole," he mouths, tears of anger and frustration in his eyes.

The noise startles Oli and Paula and, instinctively, they pull apart quickly. Paula hitches her skirt back down and Oli scans the hanger. He can't see anything but he tips his head towards the entrance. They walk out, side by side, chatting to each other like innocent work colleagues.

As they pass, Boom ducks down low behind a metal trolley in front of him and doesn't move until he hears the door of the hanger slide open and shut, and their voices melt away.

Furious, Boom slams the side of the train again with his fist, this time shouting angrily at the top of his voice. Grabbing his rucksack, he walks over to the sink where he hurls Oli's lunch boxes at the wall. One of the lids pops off and a cheese sandwich falls out. Boom pulls it apart, smearing it around the dirty sink, and sticking it back together again before putting it back inside the container and sealing the lid. He pulls out the rest of the sandwiches and does the same, before putting the lids back on and stacking the boxes in a tidy pile somewhere where Oli will see them.

Just above them on the bench, there's a key rack with an array of keys marked 'spares'. There's a staff notice board next to it, with the words 'w/c 10th September: 3691'. He's not a hundred percent sure, but Boom thinks it's the code to get into the hanger. He picks up a pen and scribbles the numbers on the front of his hand before taking all of the keys from the rack and walking over to Oli's train. He places the bundle of keys on the floor and works his way through them, one by one, until he finds the one that opens the driver's cab. He slides the key off the key ring and stuffs it into a hidden pocket inside his phone before walking back to the key rack and hanging the rest of the keys back up. Picking up his bag, he heads for the hanger entrance, sliding the heavy door shut until it locks. Turning his hand so he can see the numbers he's scribbled down, he keys in 3691 and waits until a green light flashes and the lock clicks open. "Bingo!" he says, before heading back to reception, looking for the man to return his hard hat to.

33 YOU HEAR THAT, ARSEHOLE?
YOUR TIME IS UP

Boom weaves his way through a busy market, packed with stalls. He's nearly home and he's been walking for a bit, so he's calmer now. But there's something different about him; something steely in his expression, a broodiness that wasn't there before. He's no longer dominated by fear. He passes a string of market stalls: an electrical stall selling all types of radios and batteries; a clothes stall; a food stall selling all the basics from biscuits and cereals right through to a fancy dress stall. Boom ducks to avoid a pair of glittery 70s flares hanging from a peg tied to the corner of the plastic tarpaulin sheltering the stall from rain. Boom passes a child's angel outfit, with white muslin wings, and some kind of superhero outfit he doesn't even recognise, and then, right by the stallholder, some kind of Greek outfit, with a long cloak and crown of some sort. The stallholder, an old woman in her 70s, catches Boom looking at the costume, frowning as he tries to work out what it is. "Nemesis. The Greek goddess of divine retribution and revenge," she tells him.

Boom stops in his tracks. He turns to look at her. "What was that?"

"The outfit. I could see you trying to work out what it was. It's Nemesis. The Greek goddess of divine retribution and revenge."

Boom looks over at the green crown attached to a plastic bag, sealed with the costume inside. Going by the picture on the front of the pack, there's wings in there too and some kind of cloak. Boom pulls some notes from his back pocket, "I'll take it."

"Party is it?" she asks him.

"Something like that," he replies, keeping his reply short.

The old woman glances at Boom, taking his face in. Her age means she's learnt to read people well. And somehow she just knows. Or maybe it's the recognition of someone who's been through it herself. But whatever it is, she lifts the costume down on the end of a long pole and hands it to Boom. "Tenner, please," she says, before adding, "Hope you get to enjoy it."

Boom hands her a tenner and stuffs the costume into his rucksack before heading off. He reaches home, pulling open the door of the tower block with a kind of determination that's replaced the fear and trepidation he normally displays. He's always hated Oli, but what he saw today… he's got even more reason to hate him.

Boom opens the front door of his flat and dives inside, darting through the kitchen and into his bedroom, locking the door behind him so no-one can come in.

Stripping off, he throws on fresh joggers and a hoodie, and reaches into his rucksack for the outfit. Spreading it out over his bed Boom takes it all in - a crown, woven entirely from fake leaves; an hourglass filled with sand; a long, white cloak and a pair of wings. Boom picks up the hourglass and frowns. "Bizarre," he mutters to himself, thinking it must be something to do with someone's time running out. He pulls a piece of paper from the plastic bag. It's some kind of information, which he reads out loud.

"Nemesis was the goddess of indignation against, and retribution for, evil deeds and undeserved good fortune. She was a personification of the resentment aroused in men by those who committed crimes with apparent impunity, or who had inordinate good fortune. She directed human affairs in such a way as to maintain equilibrium. Her name means she who distributed or deals out."

Boom flips the hourglass over, studying it for a second or two as the minuscule grains of sand trickle their way through the tiny gap between the two glass vessels.

"Your time is up, fucker," he mutters to himself. Realising the importance of what he's just said, Boom's face takes on a hard look as his eyes refocus on the tiny grains of sand. "You hear that, arsehole? Your time is up."

34 I'LL DO IT

Feisty sits at the kitchen table with Summer, watching a YouTube video on her laptop. It's a group of graffiti artists who've filmed themselves painting trains. Summer sits beside her, scowling. There's a light on above the table, but the other half of the room is in darkness like the rest of the house, giving it a slightly eerie feel.

Summer doesn't look impressed.

"You can't just vandalise whatever you want just 'cause you feel like it."

"It's a train company!" Feisty tells her. "It's not like they can't afford to clean it up."

But Summer's happy to give some attitude back. "Yeah, well, if everyone had that attitude we'd all be screwed 'cause all the money it costs to clean the trains would just push up the cost of the tickets. So not that smart really, is it? And besides, how would you feel if someone did that to something that belonged to you?"

"I don't own anything anyone would want to graffiti, do I?" Feisty replies sarcastically, rolling her eyes.

"You could be suspended any minute because of your behaviour at school and now you've gone and got yourself mixed up in all this shit too!" Summer replies. "If you get locked up 'cause of it, what am I gonna do?!"

She looks upset. All of a sudden, Feisty gets why Summer's being so pissy with her. She's about to put her arm around her when a flurry of tiny stones, like gravel, shower the window, making them both jump. They sit there for a minute - frozen to the spot - waiting to see if anything else happens. With the rest of the room in darkness, their faces are illuminated in the light, making everything look much more intense. Feisty gets to her feet and walks reluctantly towards the window. Summer follows, holding her sister's arm tight, staying behind her until they reach the window just above the sink.

They peer out into the darkness, their eyes adjusting to the light, searching for whatever it was that caused the noise. They can see the reflection of the light in the glass behind them, and then the room behind, lying in darkness. Feisty thinks she spots something. Nervously, she leans forward, peering through the window into the dark. She can see the bushes, but nothing else. But some kind of instinct tells her there's something out there. Her body tenses with fear. As they stare out into the dark, a face appears at the window, making them both scream. Whoever it is hears them and ducks back out of sight, but Feisty has spotted the grey hoodie and shakes Summer's hand off before heading for the front door.

"It's ok, I know who it is."

Feisty walks along the dark corridor to the front door and opens it. Boom is stood there, pacing a tiny area in front of the door, round and round like some caged animal. He's agitated, scrubbing and tearing at his head with both hands, leaving his hair rough and dishevelled; totally oblivious to how he looks. He carries on pacing, deep in thought. There, but not there.

"You ok?" Feisty asks, genuinely concerned.

Boom carries on pacing for a second or two, staring at the ground, before replying, "I'll do it."

He doesn't have to explain. She knows. But whilst she's worried about him she also doesn't want to let the opportunity go.

"What changed your mind?" she asks.

Boom doesn't answer. Feisty steps out onto the path and pulls Boom towards her, holding him close until he calms down. Giving him a chance to have back what he's given her. He stands there rocking in her arms. "I hate him. I hate him. I fucking hate him." Until finally, he's still.

Feisty cradles the back of his head with her hand. Boom looks at her and smiles, and before she knows what she's doing, Feisty leans in for a kiss. It's gentle and tender and for a second Boom responds... needing that touch... before he realises what he's doing and pulls away.

"What? Neither of us are seeing anyone," Feisty replies, trying to play it casual.

Boom stands there, holding his head in his hands, like the troubled soul he is.

"Sorry. I just don't want to give you the wrong impression. You're a really nice girl and all that but like I said before... I don't do relationships. I've got too much shit in my own life to even think about anyone else."

Feisty cuts him dead in his tracks, desperate to hide how mortified she is at getting it so wrong. "It was just a fucking kiss, alright? I don't wanna be your girlfriend. Now, when do we start?" she asks, changing the subject quickly.

"Two thirty. Your dad's garage. Don't be late."

And with that he spins back round, heading off into the dark, troubled and dazed. He stumbles into the hedge, rights himself, and heads off down the path and out of sight.

Shutting the front door behind her, Feisty leans back against the cold glass. She closes her eyes, mortified by his response. "Fuck it!"

35 WHERE IS HE?

The Crew - Flash, Curl, The Watcher and The Cat - stand outside a tumbledown shed in the middle of a field by the side of a carriageway. No-one's speaking but Flash keeps checking the time on his phone obsessively. It's 2.50 a.m.

Glancing around the hut, he takes in his surroundings. The walls are strong but the roof is in tatters, with barely any tiles left, and large, gaping holes looking out into the sky.

"You told him we were out of town, right?" Curl asks him.

Flash nods, flicking back to his Whatsapp messages from earlier. He checks again to see if Boom's sent anything, but there's nothing. He chews on his lip, conscious the others are watching.

The Watcher's looking at him. Flash shakes his head, adding: "He's never been a no show before." He sounds worried.

Curl pulls his phone out and turns on the torch. Stepping outside the hut, he shines it down a field and onto a farm track that runs parallel with the hut and towards the carriageway, some hundred feet away. But there's nothing. No sign of anyone. Conscious of how bright the light is, he flicks it back off and turns to face the others.

"So whatcha wanna do?"

Flash looks at them. "Made all this effort. Might as well get started. If he shows up, we can beast him later."

The Cat smiles at the thought and turns to The Watcher. "Signal?"

The Watcher whistles the first line of WIZ KHALIFA'S 'See You Again'.

"Bro! That's one of my favourite songs," says Flash, as The Watcher heads off in a straight line until he's far enough away to get a clear view of not just the hut but the track and the road as well.

As The Cat and Flash stand back and watch Curl spray his first letter onto the side of the wall, Flash logs back into Whatsapp. There's a message he sent five minutes ago, asking Boom where he is, but there's still no reply from Boom. Worried, Flash sends him another one... "You ok, G?"

He waits a few seconds but he can see Boom's not online. Frowning, he swipes the App off, and turns to look at Curl's work so far - two beautifully, elaborate letters on their way to forming a word.

36 BLURRY HOUR

It's late and Feisty's house lies in complete darkness, every house in the street the same. Buried beneath her duvet, she's curled up fast asleep - the covers pulled over her head. Only the shape of her body gives away the fact she's actually in there, somewhere. Her curtains are drawn, but a sliver of moonlight shines through a tiny gap.

Her alarm goes and she bolts upright, almost like she's been waiting for it, whacking the alarm quickly before she wakes the whole house. She takes a few seconds to come round and rubs her eyes before checking the time. It's 2 a.m. Boom's 'blurry hour' as he calls it - the time of night when most sensible people are asleep. Feisty yawns, a huge mouthful of a yawn, before throwing off her covers. Keeping the light off, she shuffles over to a chair on the opposite side of the room where she's laid out all of her clothes. Feeling her way with her hands, she gets dressed in the dark, picking up a warm, thick cardigan and zipping it up over her pyjama top. She then pulls a pair of jeans over the top of her pyjama bottoms and pulls on a pair of thick, woolly socks before shoving her feet into a pair of trendy trainers and pulling her coat on. Using her hands to feel her way around her room, Feisty makes her way to a chest of drawers at the side of her bed where she's left her phone and house keys. Turning her phone on, she waits for the logo to spiral onto the screen and illuminate her darkened room. Flicking through her messages, she clicks onto Boom's profile before messaging him. 'Leaving now.' She then shoves everything into her coat pocket and creeps out into the hallway, shutting her bedroom door quietly behind her.

Out on the street, in the heart of Boom's estate, a cold frost bites through the air. Boom's tower block looms ominously in the dark, its shady presence stretching high into the sky. Across each storey, a checkerboard of lights dot across the various flats where the night owls are still awake. But it's late and most of the residents are fast asleep.

Slumped on a step at the side of the building, sheltered only partially from the weather by the bins, is Boom, who's drifting in and out of consciousness in a fitful, torturous kind of sleep. His head is pushed against the icy cold of the brick wall and his whole body shivers as he shifts his body around in his sleep in an attempt to stay warm. His hands are stuffed deep inside his pockets as subconsciously he draws his jacket tighter to his body. He's got his headphones on, and now inside his head, we hear the music pumping loudly inside his brain, so loud it's deafening. But Boom's so exhausted he'll sleep through anything right now and his eyes stay firmly shut.

A vibration in his pocket stirs him until he's halfway between catatonic and awake, caught between the need to be awake and the need to stay asleep. Boom's phone continues to vibrate until he's fully awake. Reluctantly, he stretches his limbs out, letting the cold in, until he's forced to stand, jumping up and down on the spot in an attempt to get warm. Removing his phone from his pocket he checks the time. It's 2.30 a.m. Shivering violently with the cold, Boom rubs his legs briskly, jumping around on the spot until he warms up, but it's so cold the air is just fogging up in front of him as he breathes. He checks his messages, opening Feisty's one from earlier. He clicks on it, reads it, and then spots Flash's message, still unread. He pulls it down from the top of his screen, reading it without opening it, and sees the "You ok, G?" He hovers over it for a second but then thinks twice, grabbing his rucksack instead and heading out into the dark.

37 SO HOW D'YOU LIKE YOUR PROFILE, GRAFFITI BOY?

Feisty strides along the pavement, her pace fast, her head down. She's got the walk of an urban teenager - fake bravado with a slight bounce in her step; a signal to those around her that she's not scared. But the bravado falls off in an instant as a man steps out of an alleyway next to her as she passes. She lets out a high-pitched squeal, making the man jump. Muttering an apology under his breath, he scuttles away quickly. Feisty pulls her hood up over her head, and speeds up even faster, staying close to the walls and hedges as she walks, away from people's sight lines.

A car drives past slowly with two men inside. They spot her and wind the windows down as they pass. The two men, both fat, middle-aged and balding, look her up and down, leering at her tits as they pass. Feisty clocks it and spins round on her heels, in disgust, to give them the bird, shouting, "Go fuck yourselves, 'cause your wives won't want to, you fat, ugly bastards!"

But the second she's said it, she regrets it. Terrified, she watches as the car slams to a halt at the end of the road and the driver flings open the car door and jumps out. Clinging to the edge of the door, the man shouts: "Who d'you think you're talking to, you little slag?!" He's rough, and nasty too, with no boundaries as to what he says, to who.

Feisty starts to shake. She looks back over her shoulder, desperate for someone to pass, but for a city street it's unusually quiet, even for that time of night. "Damn it. Come on, someone. Anyone," she mutters to herself under her breath, clocking the man as he stands by his car door, looking like he's about to break away at any second and make a run for her. She lets out a sigh of relief as two men, in their 20s, round the corner and start walking towards her. They're slightly pissed, and having a laugh, totally oblivious of the trouble ahead, until one of them clocks Feisty and the terrified look on her face. He's about to walk over to her to check she's ok when the driver of the car shouts over to him.

"I wouldn't if I were you," he says, in a loud, clear voice.

The guy's built like a brick shithouse; fat, but a real powerhouse of pure, over-exercised bulging testosterone, his neck so thick it makes the rest of his body look slim. The two lads take one look at him and speed up, staring at the floor as they pass, only too conscious they've bottled it but too scared to stop and help Feisty out. Feisty panics, muttering to herself as she tries to find an escape route.

"Fuck! Think Mercedes, think!"

She stands there in the middle of the pavement, fully lit up and exposed, but feeling safer under the light than out of it. Frozen to the spot, she waits for the inevitable as the driver leaves the car and starts striding towards her. Unsure whether to run or face him, she decides to stay, reasoning with herself that at least the road is well lit.

The man strides towards her, like something from a science fiction movie; his muscles so huge he can't even rest his arms by the sides of his body. Stopping just in front of her, the man takes one look at her and smirks, leaning forward just enough to let his mouth brush hers, in a slow, intimidating move. Speaking in a low, gravelly voice, he tells her: "Bet you'd kill for a bit of cock in you right now, wouldn't you?"

Terrified, Feisty starts to shake violently, unable to look the man in the face in case it makes her even worse. The man lets out a deep throaty laugh, not the least bit bothered about what he's doing to her, which only makes Feisty even more scared.

The man takes a step forward until his erection is digging into the side of her leg.

"Please don't," Feisty says, so quiet it's almost a whisper. Clearly terrified about what's going to happen next, she turns her head, flinching as the man picks up a chunk of her hair and brushes it against his neck in a slow, controlled movement.

Terrified, but feeling like whatever's going to happen is going to happen, Feisty decides she may as well go down with a fight. But it takes all her effort to contort her face into something that doesn't resemble pure fear. She bites down hard on her jaws as she tells him:

"Wife had enough of your tiny dick has she?"

The man yanks at her hair until his face presses against hers. Reaching down, in the middle of the street, to pull his cock out of his tracksuits bottom, he tells Feisty, "Like to try would you? See how tiny it really is."

Shaking with fear, Feisty looks away as the man starts to play with himself, pushing against her, gripping her hair so tight she can't move. Feisty starts to cry, until the sounds of a cop car hits the air, just streets away. The man pauses, in two minds whether to ignore it or not. But as the sirens get closer, the second man leans out of the passenger seat, shouting to his mate to get moving. "Let's go!"

The driver yanks Feisty's hair hard before releasing her, telling her: "Next time you won't be so lucky."

As the sirens grow closer, the man races towards his car and jumps in, driving off at speed before the cops spot him.

Feisty drops down in a heap in the middle of the road, hyperventilating with shock. Conscious the sirens are getting closer, she staggers over to a low garden wall at the side of the road, and throws up; squatting behind some bushes until the cops pass.

Hunched in a tight ball in front of the hedge, Feisty starts to sob, wiping the snot and tears from her face as she struggles to bring her breathing back under control. She looks down as her phone beeps. It's a message from Boom.

"Two mins away. Where are you?"

Hands shaking, she types "same", pressing send before walking back onto the main road and turning left towards the busier part of town. She walks under a railway bridge before reaching a car sales yard at the side of the road, with a tall wire fence running around its perimeter. A line of cars are parked in front of the building and at the rear a huge pile of tyres are stacked on top of each other, several feet high. Feisty stops to peer inside the fence, her eyes adjusting in the light until she spots Boom, leant against the mobile waiting for her. How did he get inside?

She pulls a set of keys from her pocket, unlocks a padlock on the front gate and lets herself into the compound. She takes one look at Boom, and shouts across in a loud whisper, "Keep your head down. Camera won't see your face."

Having learnt from The Cat, Feisty takes a running jump towards the CCTV camera and hurls herself up towards it last minute, knocking the lens away from her until it faces the mobile. The camera now points to the wall of the mobile, where a sign above the entrance reads 'EAST END MOTORS.'

Feisty signals to Boom to hide at the back of the building, behind the tyres. Walking up to the entrance of the mobile, Feisty unlocks the door with her keys and disappears inside for a couple of minutes before joining Boom, who's slumped behind the stack of tyres at the back of the building. "Done. Camera, security lights, alarm. Everything," she tells him.

"So we're safe?" Boom asks.

Feisty nods.

It's hard to break a habit though and Boom glances back anyway to check the road. Feisty clocks it and grins, much more secure than normal. She clocks Boom looking at her. "What?!" she asks him, indignantly. Boom smiles. "Well, normally, you're the one pacing up and down. In front of all the street lights where everyone can see you! But tonight you just seem… I dunno. Calm, I guess."

Feisty stares down at her trembling hands, still shaken by her confrontation with the man. "Ha, yeah.

Well. I've got a personal interest in this one," she replies, trying to bluff it out. "You ready?"

Boom nods, pulling the nemesis outfit out of his bag. He pulls the cloak over his head and slips the mask onto his face before carefully balancing the crown on top with both hands, almost like it's real. He stands, adjusting the crown so it doesn't slip. "What d'you think?" he asks her, his voice muffled behind the mask. The only thing left to identify him now are his trainers; strangely out of place with the long cloak. Boom looks down at his feet, raises one foot and wiggles a trainer in the air. "Go well with the outfit don't they?" he laughs, behind his mask.

Feisty ignores the humour, looking super focused as she replies, "Let's go for it." She pulls her phone from her pocket and lines the video up ready to go.

"No feet remember," Boom mumbles from behind the mask. He turns to face the building, then looks back to Feisty before giving her a nod and running full pelt towards the building, gripping a can of paint in one hand, bag of paints in the other.

Feisty hits record. Holding her phone horizontal, she follows Boom, stopping just in front of him to film the movement in his hands, giving life and pace to the video. Choosing her angle, she moves back and forth, from side to side, filming like a proper director before going in close to follow Boom's hand as he holds the can close to the wall. She holds the camera steady as the picture starts to take shape.

Boom's 'piece' shows a man, standing in a

hospital ward in a green gown, with clearly distinguishable features. It's Feisty's dad, standing next to a woman, lying in bed, cradling a newborn baby in her arms. It's his girlfriend, Carla, with their baby Max; both of them happy and smiling.

Boom glances at Feisty, his mask on camera. But not even the colour of his eyes can be seen from behind the mask, it's too dark. He looks away, reaching for a can of paint. He gives it a shake and we hear the unmistakeable rattle of the bearings before Boom sprays a jet of paint onto the wall, forming a thick grey line next to the man.

Through the camera lens, we see the picture take shape. The line becomes a large window, a viewing area onto the ward. And through the glass, we see two girls… desperately banging on the glass to try and get the attention of the man stood the other side. Boom sketches their outlines, revealing just a sliver of a face on the girl closest to the wall. A young sweet face, contorted with anger but at the same time sad; a single tear rolling down her cheek. Boom stops for a minute, watching as Feisty takes it in. She signals for him to continue, and Boom drops the can back in the bag, swapping it for one more. A can of bright red paint.

Popping the lid off the can, Boom directs a jet of paint at the wall, tracing some letters in garish, unforgettable red… SINS OF THE FATHER, just below where Feisty's dad is standing. Boom turns to face the camera and Feisty holds the lens steady for a second before hitting stop.

Feisty stands in front of Boom's piece for a second, taking it all in, before telling him in a calm voice,

"Great job." And then the adrenalin kicks in and she starts to laugh hysterically… unable to stop. A clear act of revenge against her dad for all the hurt he's caused her.

Boom grabs Feisty by the arm, keeping her focused. "You ok to lock up?" She nods, still laughing.

Boom hangs back, leaning against the wall, waiting for Feisty as she runs back into the mobile to reset the lights and security system before locking the door behind her.

As she races towards Boom he breaks into a run alongside her. They race through the compound to a hole in the side of the fence, where someone has cut through the wire with some cutters. Boom slips the cloak off from around his body, along with his mask and crown, and stuffs it back into his rucksack before ducking through the hole in the fence, holding it open for Feisty to follow. She looks at him, still laughing hysterically from all the adrenalin. "Why didn't we just go through the gate? I had keys." Now it's Boom's turn to laugh. "Oh yeah. I forgot."

The two of them race through the streets, Feisty's laughter setting Boom off too. Diving down an alleyway, away from the main drag, Feisty stops to rest, bending over to place her hands on her legs as she tries to control her laughter. She lets out a squeal and throws her head back in delight as she recounts in her head what they've done. "We did it!"

She leans into him and kisses him firmly on the lips. "Thank you," she tells him, taking in every bit of his face. Boom looks at her, and for a moment, no-one moves. Feisty's shaking - maybe from adrenalin, maybe a little bit from what's about to happen. Boom looks at her, and gently brushes her face with his hand. "You ok?"

Feisty nods, before gently taking his hand and guiding it towards her breasts, telling him, "Be gentle." Boom leans in and kisses her gently on the neck. But for Feisty all the longing and wanting of the past few weeks hits her and she spins herself around until she's facing Boom, shoving him up against the wall as she drags her open mouth along his face - brushing her lips along his forehead, cheeks, nose and then slowly down over his lips, before giving him the gentlest of kisses.

This time Boom doesn't try to fight it.

Remembering something, Feisty keeps her eyes trained seductively on Boom as she pulls her phone out and brings up the video of Boom in his nemesis outfit. She's somehow managed to get it uploaded onto a social media account already, under the name 'Graffiti Boy.' Feisty hits play, and Boom watches as the video is introduced with the words, "This is for every son or daughter who has been let down by a parent." Feisty leans in towards Boom as he moves his head closer to hers to watch the video, watching it to the end where he turns to face the camera in his Nemesis outfit, and the video stops.

Feisty looks at him and slowly, seductively, licks his face, asking him, "So how d'you like your profile, Graffiti Boy?"

Boom groans, trying to contain his pleasure enough to answer. "Graffiti Boy? Is that what you're calling me now?!" he replies laughing. "I like it," he adds, "Just make sure there's no way to trace you - or me - via the account."

"Don't worry, I've been careful," Feisty tells him, smiling and grabbing him by his T-shirt and pulling him towards her as she leans back against the wall, throwing her head back and opening her mouth wide in pure animalistic passion as she brings his head down to her chest. Keeping her voice slow and level, she whispers in his ear - "So you gonna fuck me, or what?"

Boom stops for a second, making sure he sets the record straight. Because as much as he wants this, he doesn't want to hurt her either. "I meant what I said earlier. I'm not good at relationships."

"I've got it," Feisty replies, pulling him closer and biting his lip to shut him up. She sticks out her tongue and slowly licks his cheek, dragging it into his ear where she flicks it around before whispering to him, "I just want you to fuck me."

Boom lets out a loud groan and lets go. Unzipping his trousers, he pulls out his cock. Holding it in one hand to keep it firm, he carries on kissing her whilst using his spare hand to undo her trousers. He struggles for a second to work out what's going on, until he realises she's wearing two pairs of trousers. Laughing, Feisty pulls her pyjamas down far enough for Boom to push his cock inside her.

"Oh fuck!" he groans, as he feels the warmth. He starts slowly before getting gradually faster, until he's fucking her up against the wall, putting his hands gently behind her head to stop it from banging against the brick. Feisty holds her head close to his, her expression hidden, as she grimaces in pain as he enters her, struggling to hold it in as she takes a sharp breath in.

"You ok?" he asks her, stopping for a second as he notices how quiet she is.

"Don't stop," she tells him, pulling him back inside her. He lets out a quiet groan and collapses against her as he comes, resting his head against the wall.

They stand there in the dark for a second or two, both cold, until Boom pulls himself out of her. He brushes Feisty's arm gently. "You sure you're ok? Wasn't the most romantic of places, I know," he smiles. Feisty pulls her coat around her and smiles. "I'm fine. Now come on, let's go." As they walk away, Boom pulls her gently towards him, Feisty letting her head rest on his shoulder as they walk away.

38 WE KNOW

Boom checks the time as he climbs the stairs to his flat. It's 4 a.m. He reaches the balcony and stops, exhausted and tired, every last drop of adrenalin drained from his body. He turns towards his front door, jumping as he spots his neighbour peering nervously out of his front door in the direction of his flat. He throws Boom a sympathetic look before retreating to the safety of his own home. Boom stands on the balcony listening to Oli beat the shit out of his mum from inside their flat. Her cries of help not even reaching a pinnacle before he can't bear it any longer. His face contorts as he faces his front door, spitting the words out as if Oli was stood there in front of him. "You piece of shit. I'll get you back for this!" and with that he spins back round and heads down the stairwell.

Back at her house, Feisty stands in front of the bathroom sink, staring at her reflection in the mirror of the bathroom cabinet. She takes herself in, looking for some kind of sign - any kind of sign - that something's changed. But there's nothing. Nothing visible anyway.

She puts the plug in the sink and pours herself some warm water, sliding down her pyjama bottoms to give herself a wash, as her knickers drop to the floor, around her feet. There's blood on them. She reaches for a flannel inside the cabinet and dips it into the warm water, gently washing herself as she soothes away any soreness.

Outside, street lamps light up the darkened pavements; the sky a dark, silky black. Boom's feet pound the pavement, angry and fast, their pace in line with his mood. There's a sense of urgency about him. He crosses a road and looks up. And then we see…

He's stood on the pavement, opposite the train depot where Oli works.

Boom stops in front of the high wire fence surrounding the depot. Walking down the side of the fence, Boom heads for the shadows, reaching into his rucksack to pull out a pair of wire cutters which he uses to cut a tiny hole at the bottom of the fence, just big enough to pull back the wire and climb through. Boom throws his bag through the hole, then follows, bending the wire back again the other side to disguise the hole before sprinting off in the direction of the hanger where Oli's train is kept.

Boom reaches the building and keys in the numbers on the keypad. The alarm beeps briefly then stops, giving Boom the all-clear to slide the door back and enter the building. Sliding the heavy doors shut behind him, he stands in the dark for a while until his eyes adjust to the light and he knows it's safe to use a torch. He turns on his phone, and shines it around the hanger, lighting up Oli's work station at the back of the building… the toilet and the sink, before coming to rest on Oli's train, parked up alongside the platform undergoing maintenance work.

Boom checks out the CCTV camera by the front of the door, high above his head. Picking up a concrete tile from a pile stacked by the door, he hurls it at the camera, smashing the lens and breaking the camera off its arm, sending it crashing to the floor. There's shattered glass everywhere. Boom picks it all up, along with the camera and broken arm, and hides it inside a box underneath a table next to the door.

Using the side of his trainer, Boom kicks any shattered glass that's left into a pile next to the box. He then makes his way to the back of the hanger, to Oli's train.

Boom opens the case of his phone and slides out the key from earlier, using it to unlock the driver's cab. He steps into the cab, putting his rucksack down on the floor allowing him to shine his torch around the inside, studying each wall in turn. He stops at the back wall, behind the driver's seat, the same wall that links the driver's cab to the carriages behind. There's a large expanse of cream wall that's completely bare. Reaching into his rucksack, Boom pulls out a can of black paint, gives it a shake, and sprays it onto the very bottom of the wall behind the driver's seat, testing how well it sets on the surface. He shines his torch onto it and is about to give the paint another quick test when he hears voices approaching from outside. "Fuck it," he mutters to himself panicking.

Flicking his torch off, Boom stands there in the dark... waiting and listening. The voices get louder. There's a male and female, and they're getting closer. The door of the depot slides open and Boom dives down low, swearing to himself. "What the fuck?!"

The man and woman are talking in low whispers. Boom's struggling to hear what they're saying and has no idea how close they are. Sticking his head up above the controls, he tries to make out where they are but it's pitch black outside and he doesn't want to give himself away. Staying low, Boom tugs at the door that divides the driver's cab from the carriage next door. It's stiff, almost like it's stuck. He tugs at it again, but starts to panic as the couple's voices drift back into earshot. The woman laughs as she gets closer. Panicking, Boom peels his bag off his back and puts it down on the floor, giving himself enough traction to tug at the door until it releases.

"I hope you bought the candles!" the woman laughs, right outside the driver's cab. It's Paula!

"Shit!" Boom panics. Squatting down low on the floor, Boom picks up his paints and shuffles into the carriage next door, only just managing to slide into the next door carriage seconds before a man's heavy-footed steps can be heard making their way up the steps into the driver's cab. The man, (Boom's pretty sure it's Oli), pulls a giggling Paula up into the cab and slams the door shut behind them, the sound reverberating around the silent hanger.

Paula stops giggling for a minute and takes a deep breath in. "What's that smell?"

"Must have sprayed the trains today," the man replies. Horrified, Boom realises he's stuck in a very dangerous situation... just feet away from Oli.

Clinging tight to his paints to stop them from clinking, Boom moves his bag across the floor, making his way across the carriage, millimetre by millimetre. His face contorted with fear, he's absolutely terrified. Terrified that at any minute he'll make a noise that will give himself away and terrified as to what Oli will do if he finds him.

Boom freezes as the two of them stop talking; moving only when they start to talk again.

Oli's voice is loud and clear, both him and Paula talking at normal volume in the cab next door. Boom's inches away from the safety of a seat that he can hide behind when the dividing door behind him starts to slide open. He freezes, bracing himself for the inevitable, when he hears Oli tell Paula, "Nah. Let's do it here. Give me something to think about tomorrow when I'm driving the trains." They slide the door back shut again, but leave it partially open so their voices drift through to where Boom is now hiding behind a seat.

Too scared to move back any further, Boom listens to the sounds of their kisses getting noisier and wetter, grimacing as he listens to his stepdad fuck Paula. Oli grunts and Paula lets out a loud moan, "Oh babe, yes!" Boom's disgusted. There's a loud thud against the wall, and Boom freezes, terrified. But the thud becomes rhythmic, louder and faster, in time with Oli's grunts as he fucks Paula up against the wall of the cab. There's something carnal, animalistic about their noises. It's just fucking, pure and simple.

Paula's voice drifts through the door as she tells Oli, "Gently, babe!" Oli laughs, a deep throaty laugh, telling her: "What's wrong, don't you like it hard?" Paula lets out a low, guttural moan of pleasure as her body slams against the wall next to Boom's head, crying out at the same time as Oli lets out a loud grunt as he comes. Boom stays low, squatting behind the seat, shaking violently as he tries to calm himself down; the thudding a reminder of the daily attacks Oli makes on his mum. On the edge of tears, Boom's forced to listen as Oli zips up his trousers. He's close enough to hear the sound of the zip as it carries through into his carriage.

"Time to go," Oli tells Paula, who has her arms wrapped around Oli's neck and is trying to kiss him. He pushes her away, not too roughly, but forcefully enough to make her stop. "Don't wanna get caught. Guards'll be round in an hour or so." Boom inches his head around the side of the seat, just in time to catch Paula's face. He pulls back, waiting until the door of the driver's cab slams shut behind them.

It's only when he hears the huge doors of the depot slide open, and shut, that Boom gets back up, kicking the feeling back into his feet as he slams the side of the carriage wall with his fist. "Bastard!"

Pulling his phone out of his pocket, Boom turns the torch on, positioning it so that it shines directly onto the expanse of wall behind the driver's seat where he started to spray earlier. He grabs some paint from his bag and gives it a shake before writing in stiff, angry movements, the words: "OLI'S FUCK TRUCK" in thick, black capital letters. Stepping back to admire his handiwork, he gives the can another shake before writing just below it: "WE KNOW."

Boom shoves the paint back into his bag, opens the cab door, and jumps out onto the track, stepping back to admire his handiwork before hot footing it out of the hanger.

39 HEARD THE YARD GOT A VISIT

Flash is in school uniform, slumped against a lamp post opposite his block of flats, waiting for Boom. His eyes scan everyone as they enter or leave the building. It's an icy winter morning and with every breath out Flash sends a plume of fog streaming out of his nose. Struggling with the cold, Flash lets his usual chilled air slip a little and he breaks into a mini rant.

"Where the fuck are you, bro? Got better things to do with my time than freeze my tits off waiting for you!"

And with that, he propels himself off the lamppost, heading off in the direction of school.

Seconds later, a bleary-eyed Boom stumbles out of his flat and heads down the stairwell. As he reaches the next level, he pauses. A familiar figure leans against the handrail, facing in his direction... almost like he's been waiting for him.

It's Lunar, the graffiti artist who's up in court for tagging trains; the guy from the park who wouldn't look Boom in the face.

Now it's Boom's turn to act shady. Having been super keen to talk to Lunar before he now wants to avoid it like the plague. Everything about his body language screams 'don't talk to me.' Boom clocks Lunar but looks away quickly pretending not to have seen him. He carries on walking but Lunar stops him in his tracks with a casual, but pointed, "Heard the yard got a visit."

Lunar takes a slow, deep drag on his fag,

watching Boom's face for a reaction.

Boom gives a casual shrug in reply, and Lunar laughs. He knows. Growing up on the street, he can read body language a mile away, and he's got Boom sussed a million times over. Boom's keen to get away but he knows he can't go until Lunar lets him, but Lunar's making the most of watching him squirm under his gaze. Their eyes lock, and for a moment no-one speaks, until Lunar tells him, pointedly, "Whoever it is needs to look out for The Feds. Transport Police have got their own graffiti unit."

Lunar starts telling a story. "This one guy, he's proper special he is. Makes it his job to catch fuckers like me." Adding sardonically - "And he did." Lunar stares at Boom, waiting for some kind of reaction but Boom's playing it cool. Lunar studies Boom's face for a sign of the turmoil inside. Anything. A sideways glance, small twitch of the face. But there's nothing.

Boom, however, can feel the heat rising in his face. He doesn't know if he's managed to hide it or not, but all he wants to do is shout at Lunar - "Fuck off staring at me, will ya?!" But he can't.

Lunar stubs his cigarette out on the floor in front of him before continuing. "Anyway, this cop. All the writers know him. I mean, ALL the writers." Lunar adopts a Yorkshire accent for the next bit, telling Boom, "DC Brightly from Yorkshire. Mean-looking mother fucker he is too." He laughs, "He's got this pinched face. Like a fox. All sly and wily." Lunar pinches his cheeks together and screws up his eyes till he's painted the picture.

Lunar continues in his normal speaking voice,

"Fucking hates us. Each and every one of us. It's like he's got a personal vendetta against the lot of us. But, get this" - he looks up at Boom and the adrenalin starts to flow through him, building up the energy and suspense of his words as he talks - "Once he's on to you, that's it. You may as well give up then and there. 'Cause I'm telling ya, he don't stop. Not till he's got you well and truly locked up. Never to breathe fresh air again." Lunar stops, the enormity of it hitting him, before his storytelling takes a dip to match his mood. "I should know. He managed to track me. Didn't have a fucking clue. Turns out he was tracking me for months. Tracked my workplace, my girlfriend. Followed my mum home from work one day. Even spoke to the fucking bus driver on my route to work for fuck's sake. He's like the fucking terminator. Won't give up 'till he's got you. I didn't have a fucking clue what I was up against. Not a fucking clue."

Boom's visibly nervous now but Lunar's forgotten all about him. Lost in his own fate, he recalls an image of Brightly in his head. "Proper arrogant bastard he is too. Wore a Banksy T-shirt to arrest me, the cock. Like it was some joke to him."

Unable to remain quiet any longer, Boom tries to shrug off Lunar's stories, telling him, "Don't know why you're telling me all this. I wasn't even out last night."

Lunar's head jolts up and he gives Boom a wry grin. "Who said anything about last night? I never even mentioned when it was."

Boom tries desperately to cover his tracks. "I just assumed it was from what you said."

Lunar looks Boom straight in the eye. "Like I said. Whoever it was needs to be careful. Brightly's a…" He pauses to find the right word, "Nasty fucking bastard. That's what he is."

Still trying to keep up the casual act, Boom tells Lunar, "I've gotta go. Can't be late for school." And with that he hurtles down the stairs, bursting out through the entrance to the flats at a hundred miles an hour, flustered and stressed. Bashing his forehead with the base of his hand, over and over, Boom mutters to himself, "You fucking idiot, Boom. You fucking idiot."

40 GRAFFITI BOY. WE MEET AGAIN!

Feisty sits on a kerb that runs around the edge of the school car park. A group of friends huddle round her, engrossed, as they check out Graffiti Boy's profile on her phone. She looks up as Mr Britton pulls into the car park next to them, clocking him through the windscreen.

"Time to go!" she mutters to the group, swiping her Apps shut as Britton climbs out of his car, feet from where they're sitting. But he's been a teacher too long not to clock their shiftiness in an instant - quickly scanning their bodies for signs of anything suspicious.

"Mercedes. Angel," he says, aiming his instructions at the two girls he knows, "Get yourself to class now. Bell's about to go any minute." And with impeccable timing, the bell goes and the group slopes off, with one of the boys muttering, "Sir," in Britton's direction as they leave. "Nice to know at least one of them's got manners," Britton mutters to himself under his breath, frowning as he watches them leave before picking his own bags up and heading towards school.

Crossing the playground at a pace, he slows as he clocks large pockets of kids on their phones, all too engrossed to even notice him. Peering over the backs of one group of lads sat huddled on a bench, Britton clocks a video they're playing on Instagram. It's Boom's SINS OF THE FATHER piece, filmed through Feisty's camera.

"Any particular reason why you're all watching an illegal activity on your phones when you should be in form?" Britton asks, making them jump. Freaked out by the presence of a teacher, the one with the phone shuts the video down instantly. The group gets up quickly and heads towards school, walking with their heads down, glad they got away it... for once.

Tucked behind one of the pillars at the side of the school gates, away from Britton's eyeline, is Flash. Leaning back against the wall, he blows frosty clouds of air from his mouth as he waits for Boom. Staring at the end of the road, he spots him walking towards him, head bent and studying something on his phone. Boom gets closer, totally oblivious to the fact Flash is there. Flash watches him transfixed, smiling cheekily as he passes, thinking about whether to make him jump or not - but in the end waiting to see if he looks up before he speaks. He waits till Boom draws level with him before pushing himself off the wall, asking him, "Where was you last night, bro?" He trails off as Boom spins round and he clocks his face. "Jeez, what happened to you?"

"Didn't get no sleep," Boom replies, flat and drained.

"What? None at all?"

Boom shakes his head in response. Flash peers at Boom's phone to see what's got his friend so distracted. Boom tries to pull his phone away but he's too slow. Flash clocks a photo of someone Boom's pulled up, reading the headline out loud. "British Transport Police and its Very Own Weapon of Mass Destruction - DC Brightly, Enemy Number One to Graffiti Artists everywhere."

"That's some heading," Flash tells him, scanning the story for a second as he tries to work out why

Boom's reading it. He makes a mental note of Brightly's face in his head, pinched and mean-looking just like Lunar described him.

"What you reading 'bout trains for?" he asks Boom. But before Boom replies they hear a shout from across the playground. They look up and spot Britton stood on the steps leading into school. "Mr Johnson. Mr Pritchard. This is starting to get boring. Get yourself into class. Now!"

They pick up the pace, heading into school, past their lockers and straight to class where sluggish students make their way to their seats - teenage style, like they're wading through treacle. They're just about to take their seats at the front of the class when Britton looks up, and directs a girl to their desk instead. "Adam. Jamie. Please take Sienna's desk for today. Sienna, up at the front please." Sienna, a moody-looking girl with piercings up her ears as well as through her nose and cheeks, makes her way to the front of the class, scowling at Britton.

"Any reason for that particular look Sienna, or can I assume it's because you fancy a lunchtime detention as well as a day of intense observation?" he quips. Sienna doesn't answer but slams herself down in protest without even looking at him. Her friend, a tall girl with long brown hair worn loose at the sides with two top knots on the crown of her head like a character from Star Wars, sits down next to her, smirking.

Britton starts the register, calling out the students' names one by one - Ali, the trouble-maker at the back, Sienna at the front, Adam (aka Flash) second row back with Jamie (Boom) next to him, and two more rows of boys next to them - jumping from table to table, and around the room, until everyone's ticked off. He then gets to his feet and turns the projector on behind him, revealing a picture of a wild but handsome, long-haired man in a passionate embrace with a strong, beautiful woman. Something a little 'Gone With The Wind', but wilder.

"So. Class!" Britton injects loudly, in an attempt to jolt the apathy out of them. "Can anyone tell me *why* Wuthering Heights is still so popular 150 years after it was written?"

"It's not," Ali mutters from the back of the class, to a roomful of sniggers.

"Thank you for that, Mr Ali, but I think you'll find that most academics, as well as anyone with any knowledge and love of reading, or interest in human psychology, would completely disagree with you. Anyone else care to answer?"

Britton stares across a sea - ocean even - of apathy, before continuing. Pacing up and down between the rows of tables in an attempt to stir up energy, he continues: "The reason why Wuthering Heights is still so popular is because its author, Emily Bronte, manages to capture some of life's strongest emotions. Emotions that years later, all of us - even you Mr Ali, despite how nonchalant you pretend to be - can identify with. Things like Jealousy. Love. Betrayal."

Britton lingers over the words, emphasizing each one in turn for dramatic effect. He glances across at Boom, who for once in his life (despite his complete lack of sleep) is awake in class, sketching something down the side of his book. "Jamie!" Boom jumps, assuming he's done something wrong. "What other emotions could you write about today that were just as relevant 150 years ago?"

Boom looks down at the sketch he's drawing, the tip of his pencil resting on a clenched fist. Pressing down a little too hard on the nib of his pencil he snaps it, blotting the picture. He clenches his teeth, before replying. "Anger?"

"Anger! Good one, Jamie," Britton replies, his eyes scanning the faces of his class as he directs a question their way. "Anyone here been angry before?" It's a rhetorical question, but still, he'd like *some* kind of engagement from the class. Instead he looks for the sleepy faces - which is pretty much all of the class - and heads their way, firing questions at them until he gets a response.

Britton reaches the desk of a bored male student, slumped on his desk with his head on his hands and totally disengaged. Britton pauses for a second before slamming a hand on the desk, causing the student to shoot upright in his seat, scaring him half silly and making the rest of the class laugh at his expense.

"What about *revenge*, people?!" Britton says with passion, spinning back round and heading straight for Boom, his star pupil, desperate to find someone to share his love of story. Louder and louder, he waves his hands in the air like an actor performing a piece, directing his questions to Boom as he reaches his desk. "After all, what could be more satisfying than taking revenge on someone who's hurt you?" Britton sits on the edge of

Boom's desk and does a quick mental log of the clenched fist in the margin of his notebook, before spinning back round to tell the rest of the class, "It may not be the 'right' thing to do but it sure makes you feel better" - spinning back round to Boom as he adds, "Right, Jamie?" Boom freaks out. He has no idea what's going but he can feel the paranoia pumping through his blood. *'What the fuck does Britton know?'* Flash clocks Boom's look, and silently mouths to his mate, 'what?'

Britton heads back to the front of the class, where he presses a key on his laptop to bring it alive. Linked to the whiteboard at the front of the class, it brings up a critique by a respected journalist writing about Wuthering Heights. Reading it aloud, he continues: "Wuthering Heights is, I quote.."

As Britton continues, his back momentarily turned to face the board, Flash mouths to Boom, "You ok?" Boom replies with an unconvincing nod. Desperate to get Flash's attention away from him, he pretends to focus on what Britton's talking about as he continues, "It is about the vindictive soul of a wronged man… a horror story."

Britton glances back at the class just to check no-one's doing anything they shouldn't be but misses Sienna as she tucks her mobile back onto her lap, scratching her head to district his gaze. Flash and Boom catch the movement though. Sitting one row back, and directly behind her, they wait until Britton is back facing the board before craning their necks to take a sneaky peak at what she's watching. Boom takes one look at it and starts pinching his forehead between his finger and thumb, letting the enormity of what he's done sink in.

It's Feisty's Social Media feed, with endless images from his graffiti video at Feisty's dad's garage last night, entitled "Sins of the Father". Flash, meanwhile, has no idea why Boom looks so stressed. Scribbling the words, Graffiti Boy, on the back of a notebook with a huge question mark next to it, he shoves it under Boom's nose when Britton's not looking. Boom shrugs, but Flash is on to him. Boom looks away, just in time to catch Sienna turn round and give Ali a look. Glancing down at her phone, she gives him a subtle nod before sharing the link with Ali. Boom watches as Ali glances down at his lap to check Sienna's message as it comes through on his phone.

"Mr Ali!"

Britton raises his voice, making Ali jump. Annoyed at getting caught out, Ali sighs loudly as Britton strides over, holding his hand out for his phone.

"You 'aint allowed to take my phone," Ali tells him, with attitude.

Britton gives him a wry look, before calmly replying.

"Oh, I think you'll find I am Mr Ali. If you'd like to check the school's mobile phone policy, I think you'll find you have agreed not to use your phone in class unless directed by the teacher."

Ali slumps in his chair.

"Your phone please," Britton tells him.

Ali hands it over, reluctantly, giving Britton the chance to check out what it is. It's Boom's video again, frozen on screen.

"Graffiti Boy. We meet again!" Britton

comments out loud. Boom's freaking out in his seat as Britton tells Ali, "Maybe you can talk Mr Ellington through the video when you see him over your lunchtime detention, Mr Ali."

"You're fucking kidding me," Ali mutters, loud enough for Britton to hear.

"And for that you get two detentions Mr Ali. Must be your lucky day. Now off you go," Britton tells him.

"What?!" Ali replies, all attitude. "I ain't done nothing wrong."

"Any more arguing and we'll make it a week," Britton tells him, waiting for Ali to move. "Mr Ellington's office, **now**, Mr Ali."

Ali gets up, kicking his seat back and sending it crashing against the wall making the whole class jump.

"I'll make sure you get your phone back at lunch so you can spend your detention talking Mr Ellington through the video you thought you'd watch in class, instead of listening to my lesson," Britton tells him, enjoying himself now.

As Ali skulks his way to the classroom door, the bell goes, but Britton halts the rush as the class jump up out of their seats. "Wait!!" The class watch, eagle-eyed, as Ali disappears through the door. A second later, Britton gives them the nod, and they pile out after him and are gone in seconds, leaving just Flash and Boom behind.

Boom, who's a little freaked out by his video going viral with his classmates, is just about to head out with Flash, when Britton calls him back. Flash, as loyal as ever, hangs back with Boom but Britton quips, "He doesn't need you to hold his hand, Mr Johnson."

Alone with Britton, Boom stands at the side of his desk - waiting for some kind of retribution. He keeps his head down, waiting for the shit to hit the fan. Britton studies his star pupil for a second, pausing to emphasise whatever he's about to say, before telling Boom, "I've been going over some of your pieces, Jamie. They're really good. One of them in particular..."

All Boom hears is "piece". Convinced he's about to cop it, he stands there shifting his weight from one foot to the other, head down, pulse racing. But when it doesn't come, he looks up, watching Britton as he flicks through the pages of his notebook, passing sketch after sketch until stopping at one of a man in a hospital gown (from the Sins of the Father sketch).

Britton turns the page, stopping at Boom's next piece of writing, entitled 'Modern Poets.' Boom frowns for a minute, confused.

"Take your essay on modern poets for example," Britton continues, causing Boom to let out an audible sigh of relief. "The quotes you use. Your arguments. They're brilliant. It's 'A' level standard and beyond," he adds, flashing Boom a look that's a mix of pride and encouragement. He looks Boom straight in the face as he adds: "I know it's still a way off yet Jamie, but have you ever thought about University?"

Boom laughs. It's not just relief at escaping capture, it's also the ridiculousness of Britton's suggestion. Britton responds with a frustrated, "Why is that such a crazy idea to you, Jamie?"

He looks at Boom, who's staring at the floor,

before continuing.

"You're bright, Jamie. *Really* bright. You're getting straight As even though you pretty much sleep through every lesson - which by the way I let you get away with because you obviously work really hard outside of class to make up for it. And because I think there's a little more to your story than meets the eye."

He watches Boom squirm under his scrutiny but decides not to push it.

"Just because no-one from this school has gone to Uni before, doesn't mean you can't Jamie. The open days are coming up next month. I'd like you to visit some of the universities with me, Jamie."

"Thanks Sir, but it's not really my thing," Boom replies.

"Why?" Britton asks him, challenging him for an answer.

Boom shrugs. "I like it here."

"Jamie. You're a teenager. Teenagers normally can't wait to leave home. Please don't tell me you're any different because I just don't believe you."

"Well, I am," Boom replies, refusing to look Britton in the face.

Britton doesn't get it, so tries again.

"Just because you like living here, Jamie, doesn't mean you can't go away to study and move back later."

But Boom's not convinced. All he can think about is leaving his mum on her own with Oli - something he's adamant he won't do. Britton has one final attempt at changing his mind.

"Would you at least think about it, Jamie? It would make a real difference to you. To your life, your future."

Boom gives him a non-committal shrug, before throwing his rucksack over his back and replying, "Can I go now?"

Britton replies with a disappointed nod. Boom's halfway across the classroom when the head, Mr Ellington, knocks on the door. He leans in and nods at Boom before launching straight into conversation with Britton, so Boom has no other option but to hear what's being said.

"Interesting video," Mr Ellington tells Britton, making it clear he's now seen Ali. "Some kind of revenge graffiti by the looks of it. At a mechanics garage in Brooker Street. So could be someone local maybe. It makes some kind of reference to being let down by a parent. Not really the kind of thing we want our students to be watching though," he adds, moving to one side to let Boom pass.

Boom squeezes through the door, just as Britton asks Ellington, "What about the police. Are they involved?"

"I've just spoken to them now," Mr Ellington replies. "And they're looking into it. In the meantime, I think we need to get the tutors talking to the students about it in form time."

Boom stands the other side of the classroom door, shocked at the momentum his video has picked up. Unsure of just what the hell Feisty has got him into.

41 EVERYTHING STINKS TILL IT'S FINISHED. WHAT'S THAT ABOUT?

Flash pounces on Boom as he bursts through a door and into the playground.

"What did Britton want?"

Boom shrugs. "Wants me to go to some poncey Uni somewhere to study. Didn't say what, just thought that I should."

Flash's mouth drops open and stays there, hanging. Boom looks at him and laughs.

"What's the matter with you?!"

But Flash doesn't respond how Boom thinks he will.

"University? Bro, that is sick!"

Now it's Boom's turn to look at Flash like he's crazy, but Flash jumps in quickly before Boom has a chance to diss him.

"What?! You always say you wanna leave this shithole. Well now you can. Maybe this is how you do it. Go to some posh uni somewhere, get yourself a job, nice flat overlooking the river - then I can move in." He flashes Boom a cheeky smile, adding, "I want my own bedroom though. And kitchen..." and after a little more thought adds, "and living room, so I can entertain the laaadies without being disturbed."

Boom laughs, giving his mate a playful punch in the stomach. He's just about to say something when they're disturbed by a whistle from the other side of the playground. It's Curl, with two of his mates. They walk over to them only to find Boom's Graffiti Boy profile open on Curl's phone.

Curl's friend leans over his shoulder and reads the profile out loud.

"Just 'cause we're teenagers doesn't mean we have to sit back and take whatever it is the adults decide to do to us. We all deserve to have a voice. Have people respect our opinions, whatever age we are."

Boom looks surprised. He didn't write that but he knows who did.

Curl's mate continues reading.

"So if you're scared, angry or hurt, get in touch. I'll write any message you want, post it on your profile, as well as mine. Whatever it takes to get your voice heard. Because REVENGE, as they say, is sweet."

Boom shakes his head, furious that Feisty's made it so confrontational. And all about her.

There's a couple of quotes below Boom's profile, which Curl's mate reads out loud to the rest of the group.

"You may write me down in history with your bitter, twisted lines. You may trod me in the very dirt, but still, like dust, I'll rise." The boy screws his face up as he adds, 'Mary Angelou. Angelow. Don't even know how to pronounce that." He looks at the rest of the group, "Who is she, anyway?"

Curl reads the final quote below that, one by Dr Seuss. "Everything stinks till it's finished.' Sounds ominous." He catches his mates by surprise by adding, "My dad used to read his books to me. He's a children's author innit?"

Boom steps out of the circle as his mates carry on

chatting. Pulling his phone out of his pocket, he brings up an image of Brightly from earlier. Using his fingers to enlarge Brightly's photo, he stares intently at the detective's face. A sense of foreboding written all over his face.

42 D'YOU KNOW ANYONE WHO MIGHT'VE GOT IT IN FOR YOU?

Oli's at the depot, making his way across the train tracks towards his manager's office; the Portakabin at the front of the compound surrounded by fencing, the one Boom visited. Oli's in his work clothes, looking even more threatening than usual with his pumped up demeanour and wearing his hard hat, steel-capped boots and fluorescent jacket.

He reaches the Portakabin just as a pinched-faced detective exits his boss's office. It's Brightly, the famed graffiti detective Lunar told Boom about - 'enemy number one' to graffiti artists everywhere.

Oli eyes him suspiciously on the way past but unlike most people who come face to face with Oli, Brightly holds his own - completely unphased by the anger simmering just below the surface. Oli, who's not used to someone standing their ground against him, spins round to watch Brightly leave, brushing past him on the way into his boss's office - a little too brusquely for it to be an accident. Brightly clocks it, locking eyes with Oli until he's passed him and leaves the cabin.

Oli's boss, Dave Field, is sat at his desk, waiting for him. A stocky, bald-headed guy in his 40s, he gives Oli a forced - slightly nervous - smile as he walks in. Oli sits down, deadpan, and waits for his boss to speak. Not even bothering with pleasantries.

"Have you any idea why someone would have said...?" Dave trails off, aware straight away it wasn't the best question to ask Oli, especially straight off the mark. Oli gives him a hard stare. Despite his size and weight, his boss looks flustered, stumbling over his words as he continues. "Not that I, err... I'm not saying I think it's... you know, true or anything. It was just pretty specific... " Adding quietly, "that's all." He trails off, only too aware that Oli is staring him out. He clears his throat and starts again. "D'you know anyone who might've got it in for you?" he asks, blurting it out.

"Wouldn't be sitting here if I did, would I?" Oli replies, in a rough, sarcastic voice.

Dave continues. "The man you saw a minute ago. The one you passed in the doorway. He's a detective from the British Transport Police. DC Brightly." There's a pause, before he adds: "He might want to have a chat with you at some point."

"What'd I wanna talk to the cops for?" Oli replies sarcastically.

"I just thought you might want to find out who did it, that's all," Dave tells Oli, annoyed at himself for letting Oli scare him like this, but feeling his face flush as Oli stares him out.

"Whoever it is I'll kill 'em when I find out who they fucking are," Oli replies.

"Might not be a good idea." Dave attempts a joke, but trails off as Oli sits stoney-faced opposite him.

Oli gets to his feet before his boss can say anything else. "We done here?" he asks rudely.

Dave nods, shuffling through a pile of papers on his desk in front of him until Oli leaves, shutting the door behind him.

"Fuck," Dave mutters to himself, relieved to see

the back of Oli.

Outside the depot, Oli heads back towards the hanger where Paula is waiting for him. Gripping a spanner in his hand as he walks, the tightly-pulled tendons in his hand are the real indication of the pent up anger and aggression he hides from the rest of the world. Everyone apart from Boom and his mum that is. Oli passes two track engineers on the way. He catches their eye and they look away quickly.

Oli reaches the train hanger, where Paula is stood outside, waiting for him and nervously smoking a fag. Staring at the floor, she scratches the dirt with her foot before looking up at him. "I think we need to take a break."

Oli's grip on the spanner tightens. Luckily for Paula, she's totally oblivious to just how dark his mood is. "Just for a bit. Just till things die down, that's all." Oli shrugs. Taking it as a sign of compliance, Paula leans in to give him a kiss on the cheek before walking away.

Oli clenches his jaws shut tight and waits until Paula's out of sight before hurling his spanner against the wall of the hanger. The sheer force of it dents the hanger and sends the spanner landing with a clatter onto the track in front of him.

The two track engineers glance up from their work, catch Oli glaring at them and look away again quickly.

43 INTERESTING!

Brightly's slumped against his car at the side of the road, facing the depot. It's not the usual police car, however. It's a beaten-up Citroen AX, over 20 years old with rusty hubcaps and inside the driver's cab, a choke, that fills the entire car with a strong smell of petrol whenever the engine starts. The best undercover cop car if ever there was one. Not fast, not flash, but enough to get him from A to B without giving the game away.

Brightly stands there, waiting and watching, his eyes trained on the entrance and his hands stuffed deep inside his pockets. Call it copper's instinct but something's telling him to wait. He watches Paula and Oli through the metal fence. Watches as Paula says something to Oli before walking away and Oli throw his spanner against the side of the hanger in a fit of anger.

Brightly raises an eyebrow and carries on watching. He watches Paula head out of the depot, onto the street, where she heads straight for a red Fiesta parked at the side of the road. She climbs into the passenger side and leans over to give the driver a kiss on the cheek.

A wry smile crosses Brightly's face. "Interesting," he mutters to himself.

He pulls a small notepad and pencil from his pocket and makes a note of the car's plate as it pulls away.

44 HAVE YOU RUN THAT CHECK FOR ME YET?

Oli's blue Toyota pulls up outside his tower block. He jumps out, heads for the flats and throws open the entrance door, into the lobby. Rage personified.

Up on the balcony - across the stairwell from Oli's flat and hidden from view - Brightly stands smoking, his back to the stairwell. He leans over the edge to catch any movement in and out the front of the building and keeps his gaze on the street below as Oli makes his way up to the top of the stairwell and reaches his floor. Brightly sneaks a sideways glance as Oli pulls his key out and lets himself into his flat.

Brightly spins round to face Boom's flat. Keeping his eyes trained on the bright red door, and the rusty door number swinging from its nail, Brightly pulls his mobile out of his pocket and calls work.

Speaking in his distinctive Yorkshire accent he tells the person the other end, "I'm here now." There's a pause before he asks, "Have you run that check for me yet?" There's another pause as he waits for the person on the other end to speak before continuing, "He got in about an hour ago but the stepdad's just got home now."

He falls silent for a minute as he listens, before adding, "Oli. Oli HANSON. Hotel, Alpha, November, Sierra, Oscar, November. And his stepson is Jamie. Jamie Johnson. Same surname as the mum."

45 PLEASE DON'T DO IT. PLEASE DON'T DO IT

Oli storms inside, blissfully unaware of Brightly hanging around outside. His huge bulk of a body makes his presence felt. Walking straight into the kitchen, he runs his dripping nose along the length of his arm and glares at Boom and his mum who are sat at the table in silence, waiting for the onslaught. They're both on high alert, waiting for trouble. Boom's mum wears a battered, shapeless cardigan but Boom's in a new grey 'DC' hip hop cardigan - looking every bit the cool street kid. But despite 'the look', Boom's only just managing to keep it together. Him and his mum sit rigidly in their seats, every muscle in their bodies clenched, each drop of adrenalin pumping at a fierce ferocity around their bodies. Their eye movements track every single movement Oli makes, no matter how small, as they wait for the explosion they know is coming.

Behind them, the oven fan whirrs quietly in the background, but neither of them move. Instead they sit like mutes, able only to watch as Oli slings his dirty work jacket over the back of his chair before making his way into the inner hallway to kick off his boots, sending them crashing into the wall and leaving a grubby mark on the paintwork. He bends down to pick them up and, unnervingly, places them neatly side by side on the shoe rack; his careful precision a scary reminder of the calculated control he likes to have over the people in his life.

Boom's mum watches from the kitchen but looks

away quickly as Oli walks back into the room, careful not to let him see her watching him. He slams himself down on the seat next to her, the sheer bulk of his body filling the gap next to her tiny, slender frame, emphasising her vulnerability.

She gets up out of her seat and, without speaking, picks up a stack of plates she left on the side earlier and places them onto the table, one by one, nervously stretching in front of Oli as she places Boom's plate in front of him, and then Oli's. She's trying desperately to keep it together for the sake of Boom, but her hands give her away. As she turns back round to pull off the oven gloves that are hanging on a rail at the front of the cooker, her hands shake uncontrollably. Pulling a tray of fish fingers and chips out of the oven, she struggles to keep the tray steady and places it on top of the cooker for a minute to calm herself.

"Hurry up. I'm hungry. What's the matter with you, you stupid bitch?" Oli grunts from the table.

Hiding her face from Boom, and trying hard to keep herself composed, she picks up the tray again and walks over to the table, where Boom is watching her nervously as she struggles to stop her hands from shaking and dropping the tray. Boom watches his mum shovel the food onto her plate first, using a metal spatula, spilling some onto the table next to her. As she stretches over him to pick them up and place them back on the plate, she accidentally knocks Oli's arm with the edge of the oven tray. Oli leaps up out of his seat and knocks the tray out of her hands, catching the edge of the table and sending food and plates crashing to the floor.

"You burnt me, you clumsy bitch!" he yells. Oli looks across the table at Boom, whose face is a mix of pure anger as well as fear. He leans over the table, bringing his face down level with Boom's until it's just inches from his, and asks him in a slow, threatening voice. "Got a problem with me, have you?"

Boom clenches his jaws, the movement visible under his skin. Oli notices it and gives Boom a half smile, half sneer. Boom shakes his head in response, and looks away, staring at the wall in front of him. Ashamed of not being able to help his mum, Boom sits there shaking his head to himself, unaware he's even doing it, but his head filled with shame and guilt. Shame at sitting there every day watching his stepdad destroy his mum. Guilt at not having the strength to do anything about it.

Oli turns to Boom's mum who is still stood beside him shaking and shouts, "Why's the food all over the fucking floor still?" Boom's mum stands there, frozen to the spot, until Oli yells at her to move. "PICK IT UP!" he shouts, kick-starting her into motion with a heavy dose of fear.

Boom watches helplessly as his mum gets down on all fours, scrabbling round the floor picking up food. The fish fingers have broken in half and have turned soggy, the breadcrumb coating sticking to the floor. Boom's mum tries to scoop them off the floor using her hands but gives up and ends up shovelling them up with a spatula. She tips them back onto the oven tray, conscious that Oli is watching her every move as she digs the last fish finger out from below the cooker. One of Oli's thick, curly hairs has stuck to it and it's covered in dust. She tips it off the spatula, shaking it extra hard to get it to come off and then sits back down at the table, her head down.

"Well?" Oli asks her calmly.

She looks at him in confusion, but the look of horror on Boom's face says it all. He knows exactly what Oli is about to do. He turns his head to face the wall, the words turning over silently in his head, over and over, *"Please don't do it. Please don't do it."*

Oli flies up out of his seat. Grabbing Boom by the scruff of his collar, he yanks Boom towards him, screaming in his face - "Want me to start on you too, do you?! Cause I will. You fucking know I will, you fucking piece of shit! I see what you're doing. Disrespecting me for that fucking bitch of a mother of yours!"

Oli drops Boom as abruptly as he yanked him up. Picking up his wife's plate he tips her untouched food onto his own plate, before shoving it into his mouth, eating with his mouth open. Boom thinks Oli's confrontation with him has managed to divert Oli's attention from his mum, but Oli's head is spinning, thinking about Paula. All that keeps playing over and over in his head is how she told him she didn't think it was a good idea to see him any more. Every time it comes into his head he slams his fist down hard on the table, making Boom and his mum jump. Aware they're staring at him, Oli lets his mouth fall open, revealing a mouthful of half-chewed food. Getting some kind of perverse pleasure out of his grossness, he keeps his mouth wide open, watching their faces for a reaction.

He takes one look at the tray of crushed food on the tray in the middle of the table, covered in dust and hair, and tells Oli's mum, "Eat up then."

Boom's mum takes one look at the food and freezes. Oli smiles at her, a perverse kind of smile, before tipping the contents of the tray onto his wife's plate. Holding her gaze, he pulls her plate towards him, clearing his throat until he brings up a mouthful of phlegm. Still smiling, he opens his mouth and lets a thick string of phlegm drip slowly onto her food before pushing the plate back towards her. He lets her push the food around her plate for a few seconds before bursting into a rage.

"Fucking eat it!"

Boom watches in horror as his mum shovels up a forkful of food. She places it in her mouth, retching as she attempts to swallow. Oli slams his fist as hard as he can on the table, sending cutlery flying as he jumps up out of his seat, making her choke on her food. Retching, she pulls a thick black curly hair (one of his) from her mouth before swallowing, retching some more after she's swallowed.

"Fucking bitch!" he yells, lashing out at her plate and sending it crashing to the floor before grabbing his coat from the back of his chair. Pulling it over his arm he heads for the door, slamming it shut behind him as he leaves, leaving Boom and his mum sitting side by side in a stunned silence.

46 MALE OR FEMALE?

All the Crew - everyone, except Boom - are sat on a high wall, lined up like soldiers; kicking their legs to pass their time as they rip the shit out of each other.

"You alright up here, Watch?" Curl asks the Watcher loudly, playing to his audience.

The Watcher, who's been keeping an eye on everything going on around them, looks at Curl like he's mad. "Yeah. Why?"

"Just you're looking a bit wobbly, that's all," Curl says, staring at his hands to downplay it a little.

The Watcher screws his face up at him, shaking his head. He looks away, watching the car park opposite, and misses the wink from Curl to Flash. Quick as a dart, Curl reaches behind Flash and gives The Watcher a shove from behind, knocking him off the wall and onto the ground below.

The Watcher topples off to a loud cheer from the rest of the Crew, managing to land on both feet before looking up at Curl and flipping him the bird, as the Crew sit lined up, laughing from the top of the wall.

A second later, Flash jumps down and heads off in the direction of the estate. His back to the Crew, he raises his hand high above his head in a farewell gesture as he walks away.

Curl shouts down from the top of the wall. "Where you going, G?"

"Find Boom," Flash shouts back, without turning round. "Laters."

As he approaches home, and the familiar entrance to his and Boom's block, Flash is oblivious to the fact he's being watched. Over on the opposite side of the road, Brightly's propped up against his car, leaning on the bonnet to watch the entrance to Boom's block of flats. He's on his mobile, mid conversation, but with his eyes honed on the entrance. He spots Flash and his eyes narrow, making him look even more pinched-faced.

Brightly leans forward, straining to make out Flash's face as he passes. But like all the teenagers round here, Flash's face is hidden by his hood, pulled tight round his face to cover his features. Brightly's still trying to make out his face when Boom steps out of the flats, onto the pavement, making Brightly sit even further forward in an attempt to make his face out, but Boom's is hidden too. Despite Brightly not being able to make either of their faces out, his eyes are on lock down, a hunter with his eyes on the prize.

"Could be him," Brightly mutters to the person on the other end of the phone. "Same jumper," he adds as he takes in Boom's cardigan, the same grey 'DC' hip hop one he was wearing in his mum's flat earlier. "Just can't make out his face."

As Flash and Boom head off together, Brightly jumps in his car and follows, trailing them at a distance from the opposite side of the road. He stops at the end of the street as Flash and Boom dive into some basketball courts in the centre of the estate; courts with a high, metal cage surrounding the outside and shrouded by tower blocks.

"Where'd you get to earlier?" Flash asks Boom.

Boom gives Flash a non-committal shrug. Flash studies his friend's face for a second or two before deciding to let it go. He sits down next to Boom, placing his arse on the ground as Boom pulls a sketch pad out of his jacket and starts to draw. Flash watches in awe for what seems like a long time before he remembers his phone, and pulls it from his pocket, along with his headphones. Shoving the buds into his ears, Flash flicks through the tunes, stopping on a particular song to hit play. They sit side by side in companionable silence as Boom draws and Flash listens to his music, both in their own personal heaven, until all of a sudden, Flash sits up, excited, and hands Boom his buds.

"Check this out."

Boom shoves Flash's buds into his ears, leaning back against the metal fence and shutting his eyes to listen. All of a sudden he's somewhere else, the music transporting him from the soul-destroying tower blocks of East London to the glitzy world of David Arnold's 'Diamonds are Forever', featuring David McAlmont, singing loudly in Boom's ear…

"Diamonds are forever; They are all I need to please me."

Flash pulls the buds from Boom's ears. He looks at his mate with unquenchable excitement. "Well?"

"Well, what?" Boom asks, perplexed.

"The singer," Flash replies, bouncing about like an excitable puppy. "Male or female?"

Boom screws his face up at Flash like he's crazy. It's a given surely. "Female."

"Wrong!"

"No way!!" Boom's shocked.

Flash flips his hand in the air, like a winner. Pulling the earplugs out of his phone so they can listen together, Flash pulls the video up on YouTube.

Boom leans closer to Flash to watch the video and they sit there, shoulder to shoulder, watching as the masculine figure of David McAlmont walks into shot and he starts to sing.

"No fucking way!" Boom laughs, totally shocked.

"Sick, right?" Flash is laughing too.

They watch as McAlmont parts a glittering curtain of beads and is transformed, re-entering the room as his glamorous counterpart from a Bond movie. A man still - but this time in a tight, white bodysuit, with painted cherry lips, feather boa and diamond choker.

Boom sits there with his mouth open, gobsmacked but mesmerized as McAlmont sashays over to a clean, white bed with fluffy cats on it, their fur pumped up and teased within an inch of their lives.

McAlmont's cherry-toned voice pulls them in. Boom watches in amusement, with a smirk on his face, as the singer bends over the cats, stroking and moving as seductively as possible.

"Check out those pussies!" Boom grins, naughtily, setting Flash off. They sit there, snorting with laughter, like naughty schoolboys.

McAlmont delivers a stinging blow to the pianist's face as he sings the next line.

"Woah!!" Flash and Boom react in unison.

"How sick is that, right?" Flash asks his friend...

leaving it a second before giving Boom a naughty smile, winding him in with, "Is it wrong to say I quite like it?"

Boom takes the bait, telling Flash, "You know you can tell me anything, right G?"

Flash laughs, joke over. Or so he thinks.

But Boom's not letting up. "Rach would always help, I'm sure." He leaves it a second, before telling a puzzled Flash, "You know. If you ever wanted to experiment. With lippie and heels and all that" - and then, with a really naughty look on his face and barely managing to contain his laughter, "Pussies on the bed maybe."

They crumple up with laughter, keeling over onto the floor and holding their sides, laughing hysterically. Flash just about manages to calm down enough to tell Boom, "Just 'cause I like this song, don't mean I'm a batty boy, bro."

"Wouldn't matter if you were, darling," Boom replies camply, licking his finger and circling it over the top of his t-shirt exactly where his nipple is.

Flash laughs. "That is just wrong, bro."

They're still laughing when Boom's phone rings. The initials FG flash up. Flash takes one look, and all of a sudden the atmosphere takes a heavy dive. Boom answers, with Flash slicing his hands in front of his throat, trying to get Boom to 'kill the call.' Boom mouths to Flash to leave him alone, listening to what Feisty's got to say before telling her, "See you in twenty."

He hangs up, to a look from Flash.

"What does *she* want?" Flash asks as Boom gets to his feet. He doesn't even need to say it. His tone alone is enough to tell Boom he's not impressed. Flash may have been forced to hang out with her, but anything outside of the Crew, he doesn't want to know. All he knows is Feisty made Boom do all the revenge graffiti and filmed him doing it, so to him she's nothing but trouble.

"Wants to do another piece," Boom replies. Flash's face darkens and he sits there shaking his head.

"It's ok," Boom tells him. "This one's an important one. A one-off. Never to be repeated. Then I'm done. Forever. Finito."

"So you say," Flash replies, unconvinced.

Flash watches silently as Boom gathers up his stuff and heads off in the direction of the main road. Flash kicks the metal fence in frustration, muttering to himself under his breath, "What you playing at bro?"

He looks up, catches the back of Boom's disappearing figure and shouts, "Make sure she knows you're done!"

Boom throws his hand up in recognition, but doesn't turn round. Choosing to carry on walking instead.

47 THIS BOY I WAS SEEING…

Boom's in Feisty's neck of the woods now, metres from her house. As he reaches the end of her drive, she jumps out from behind some bushes high on adrenalin. He jumps. Laughing in delight, she punches his arm in jest. "How sick was today? The whole school was talking about it. We're famous, innit!"

Boom isn't impressed, and he makes sure she knows it. "Is that all this is to you? Some kind of ego boost?"

"What the fuck's your problem?" Feisty asks him, straight on the defensive.

"I'm not even sure I want to be on Social Media. The only reason I agreed in the first place was 'cause of your dad. 'Cause I felt sorry for you," Boom replies.

Feisty flies at him. "Sorry for me?! I'm some pity case, am I?! It's me who feels sorry for you, not the other way round. You can't even--"

"Fuck this," Boom says, shaking his head and walking away.

Feisty's blown it. But she knows she can't do it on her own, so she races after him, tugging at his sleeve to get him to stop. "Sorry, I'm a twat. I didn't mean it. Don't go. Not until you've seen this at least."

"I'm not interested," Boom replies, shaking her off.

She tries again, tugs a little harder this time.

This time Boom loses it and pushes her away. "Whatever shit you've got planned just keep me out of it!"

Feisty pulls her phone out and hits play on a video, holding it up in front of his face as she trots alongside him forcing him to watch it before he has time to push her away again.

A girl's face appears on the screen. Blonde, sweet... fourteen, fifteen at the most. Her face swollen and pink from crying.

Boom stops in his track and looks at Feisty. "That's Louisa. From my block. She's on the same floor as me. Her dad died last year."

"I know," Feisty nods. She looks Boom in the eyes. "You need to see the rest of it."

She presses play again and the video continues with Louisa talking to camera.

"This boy I was seeing," she says. "He's eighteen. Broke up with him, last week. But now he won't leave me alone. Says he's going to tell my mum we slept together unless I get back with him." There's a pause before she continues. "She'll kill me. I can't tell her. She's always warning me not to do anything 'cause I'm underage. But he keeps following me, threatening me, telling me he won't give up till I go back to him. I'm scared."

As if to illustrate the point, Louisa's ex, a tall, white guy, (18), approaches her from behind. "Oh shit." It's Feisty's voice as she clocks him approaching. The guy walks towards the camera and gives Feisty a hard shove, knocking her phone to the ground. There's a scuffle of feet and in the background, Louisa shouting and sobbing, "Leave her alone!"

"I 'aint leaving her alone. Or you. Not till you

come back to me. You've got me for the rest of your life, babes!" It's Louisa's ex in the background, threatening both of them, before Feisty's face appears in full view of the camera as she bends down to press stop on the video.

Boom stands there, his face dark. Feisty looks at him for a minute without speaking, trying to figure out exactly what's going on in his head but she hasn't got a clue. But to Boom, it's not just the violence, but the threats too - the sheer panic it invokes in him - hurtling towards him and gripping his throat in fear, just like every time Oli walks into a room. A stark reminder of just how helpless violence makes its victims feel. He takes one look at Feisty and tells her, "I'm in."

48 I DIDN'T KNOW YOU TWO KNEW EACH OTHER. ARE YOU TWO MATES?

Brightly's sat in the driver's seat of his beaten-up Citroen, opposite the entrance to Boom's flat. Yawning, he's holding a huge cup of takeaway coffee in one hand, resting with his elbows on the wheel to prop up his head, his eyes on the flats. He spots movement and turns his head to spot Boom approaching with Feisty, their faces hidden.

Brightly sits up, spots Boom's DC cardigan again - and the girl. He shoves his coffee cup into his lap, pinching it between both legs to hold it steady, swearing to himself as he struggles to wind down his window before Feisty and Boom disappear. "Jesus fucking Christ, I need a new car," he mutters to himself. In his rush to get his phone out in time, Brightly knocks his coffee cup over, spilling hot coffee on his lap and all over the seat. "Damn it!" he curses, wiping the coffee off his trousers with one hand whilst pointing his phone in the direction of Boom and Feisty with his other. He takes photo after photo as he tries to capture some of their features. Watching as they enter the flats, Brightly grabs some tissue from the side door and wipes his lap and seat, before scanning the photos. He zooms in closer, unsure if he's got anything or not. Calling work, Brightly launches straight into conversation as soon as someone picks up. "Might have got a visual, not sure. Could be the same kid as earlier. Same jumper. Same walk. And there's a girl too. Can you run a check for me? Soon as poss." He hangs up, sending the photos straight to his work contact.

Inside the tower block, Boom climbs the stairwell with Feisty. She turns to look at him as they walk, "She'll probably ask why you're there. Just tell her I asked you 'cause you could show me where she lives. Otherwise she might guess who you are." Boom nods and carries on climbing the stairs to his floor. But instead of turning left to his front door, he makes a right, walking along the balcony several doors down until he reaches Louisa's flat. "It's this one," he tells Feisty, stepping back to lean against the wall, letting Feisty take the lead.

Feisty leans forward and rings the doorbell. There's the sound of someone shuffling down the corridor inside, and the door opens to reveal Louisa, the young, sweet girl from the video. She looks at Feisty. "Thanks for coming…" She trails off, spotting Boom leant against the wall.

She flashes a big smile his way. "Jamie. What are you doing here?" Her eyes flit between Feisty and him, and back again. "I didn't know you two knew each other." And then, to their muted response, "You're not *him* are you?"

Boom plays dumb. "Who?"

Feisty looks at Louisa, making a big deal of shaking her head. "Nah. Jamie knew where you lived."

Louisa glances at Boom for confirmation but Feisty jumps in quickly to distract her. "He said he'd do it."

Louisa looks happy, but worried at the same time. "Really?"

"Yeah," Feisty replies, noticing Louisa eyeing up Boom, who's keeping his gaze directed at the floor.

There's a spark of attraction, definitely from Louisa's end at least, and a jealous Feisty has just caught wind of it. Annoyed, she tells Louisa, "That's all I came to say, anyway."

She glances back at Boom, who's looked up, and is now smiling at Louisa. Feisty grabs him by the arm. "Come on. Time to go. Gotta find our man."

Louisa smiles sweetly at Boom as they leave. "Bye Jamie."

Feisty pulls Boom away but it's not until they're round the corner and he hears Louisa's front door shut that Boom shakes Feisty off, telling her in an annoyed voice. "Don't keep pulling me, alright?"

49 YOU FUCKING ARSEHOLE!

Feisty and Boom make their way along a busy urban street, in the dark. They pass a corner shop, with a fruit and veg display lined up on the pavement outside. A teenager, a bit younger than Boom, no more than thirteen at the most, is standing on the pavement blocking their way. The boy hands some money to his older brother, who heads into the shop for him, in some kind of shady deal. The boy moves to one side to let Feisty and Boom pass. Boom gives the teenager the briefest of nods as he passes but his attention is distracted by a group of rowdy revellers outside the pub opposite, The Golden Lamb. He's about to move on when something captures his attention.

"You fucking arsehole!"

The teenage boy looks at Boom, ready to square up, but quickly realises Boom's not talking to him. He follows Boom's gaze to a couple across the road, on the edge of the pavement, making out in full view of everyone. It's pretty intense, with some heavy petting going on as the guy gropes the woman's breasts as he slips his tongue inside her mouth, moving his hand down to grab her crotch, not giving a shit who's watching.

The teenager looks away in disgust. "For fuck's sake."

Even the revellers have had enough by the look of things, and one of them shouts something across to the man, who flashes him a look back, sending the drunk back to the group without another word.

The only people left watching are Boom, and a man leant against the entrance of the pub, his face hidden by a cap pulled down low over his eyeline. The couple are locked together still, the man's body bent towards her, his crotch thrust hard into her leg as he cups her arse cheeks with both hands. The couple are kissing like they're seconds from fucking - right there and then in the middle of the street. The man pulls away for a second and whispers something in the woman's ear and she looks up, laughing.

It's Paula. And the man - his face in full view now, his hands still cupping her arse - is Boom's stepdad, Oli.

Boom loses it. Without thinking, he boots an empty coke can laying on the pavement in front of him. It whistles into the air, missing the teenager and his mates by inches. Disgusted and furious and a million other things all at the same time, Boom storms after Feisty; passing the group of teenagers, who instead of saying something about the can, move to one side to let him pass.

Outside the pub, the man with the cap lifts his head up slightly. Pint in one hand, his gaze follows Boom. Making sure Oli's not watching him, the man takes his cap off to give the top of his head a rub. It's Brightly. He watches Boom with intense interest as he storms off down the street, towards a girl (Feisty) who's stood waiting on a street corner ahead of him. She waves at Boom, signalling to him to follow her down an alley on the left, before diving out of sight.

Close up, Brightly raises an eyebrow. "Bingo!"

He places his half empty pint on the step of the pub entrance and walks away... job done.

50 I JUST DON'T GET YOU SOMETIMES. YOU WERE FINE EARLIER

Boom follows Feisty down the alley. Seconds later they're off the main drag and back on a residential estate, surrounded by tower blocks. Everything about Boom screams anger, his body language, his air... Feisty turns back a couple of times to glance at his face, but her instincts tell her not to say anything.

They keep walking until they reach a shabby-looking tower block, destined to be demolished at some point in the near future. Feisty checks out the number on the entrance before telling Boom, "This is it." She looks at him, still brooding with ill content.

"You alright?"

"Yeah." Boom replies in a shitty, monotone voice.

Feisty's staring at him, trying to work out what's happened between here and home. Boom clocks her looking at him. "What?!"

For once Feisty doesn't answer back. She shrugs, letting him vent whatever he needs to vent. Boom pulls his rucksack off his back and throws it on the ground in front of him.

Feisty checks out her watch. "It's still quite early." Boom rummages through his paints, answering her with a, "Don't care. It's dark." But as soon as he says it, they hear someone approaching from the end of the street and Feisty panics. "Fuck!"

Boom grabs his bag and pulls Feisty into a bin cupboard by the entrance of the flats, knocking Feisty's phone from her hand as he pulls her inside. In the rush to hide, neither of them notice, and Feisty's phone remains exposed on the pavement.

Hiding in the dark, there's barely space for either of them to move. Feisty's shoved up against Boom, her head level with his chest. She looks up at him, the intensity of it getting to her, and for a second they stand there, staring into each other's eyes, waiting for whoever it is to pass. Phased by the physical proximity to Boom, Feisty shuts her eyes, unable to look at him any longer, worried that if she keeps looking at him she'll give her feelings away.

They stand there, their bodies pressed together, until the footsteps fade and Boom reaches forward to push open the door. He steps out onto the pavement, leaving Feisty standing there for a second or two, giving herself just enough time to compose herself before heading out onto the pavement after him.

She spots her phone on the pavement and bends down to pick it up. "Shit! I didn't even notice I'd dropped it! That could have been bad."

"For fuck's sake. Have you got all the videos on your phone?" Boom snaps.

"I'm not that stupid." Feisty replies testily, annoyed at Boom for breaking the spell.

"Really?" Boom's proper shitty now. Not his normal self at all, but Feisty's had enough and loses it with him.

"Why are you being such a dick today?!"

Boom ignores her, reaching back into his bag for a can of paint. "Just play the video will ya?"

Despite her barbed demeanour, Feisty has to look away quickly. Boom implying she's stupid has got to her more than she let on and her eyes are watery with tears. Feisty brushes her hand over her hair like she's trying to sort it out, but surreptitiously brushes the tears away instead with the base of her hand. More subdued than normal, she tells Boom, "I just don't get you sometimes. You were fine earlier."

"Yeah well," he replies, non-committedly.

"Yeah well, what?" Feisty pushes him on it.

"Just play the video will ya?" Boom snaps.

Feisty sighs. She pulls up the video of Louisa, converting it to full screen on her phone and letting it play out in full for Boom to listen to while he works. Boom shakes a can of paint in his hand as Louisa starts to talk, spraying an outline on the wall of the tower block in front of him.

As Louisa's voice kicks in, Feisty hits pause, remembering something. "Shit. I need your phone otherwise I can't film you."

Boom pulls his phone from his pocket and hands it to Feisty. Reaching into his bag, he pulls out his nemesis outfit and places his mask over his head to keep his face hidden. When he's done he nods at Feisty to start the video again, and Louisa's voice kicks back in. Gentle, sweet… and scared. Her fear spurs him on, desperate to help at least one female in his life who's suffering at the hands of an abusive bully.

Boom's whole body language changes as he listens. He works in silence alongside the video, making sure he hears everything Louisa says, her words spurring him on to do a good job. Giving one of his cans a good shake, he speaks briefly to Feisty, "Turn it up a bit, will ya?" As he listens to Louisa talk about her ex - following her home, his threats to never let her go - his body gets more and more uptight, like a tightly sprung coil; his sharp, angry movements a reflection of the torment inside his head.

Feisty watches him, perplexed. "Did something happen en route? You were fine at the flats."

Boom ignores the question and in the waiting silence we hear Louisa speak.

"He just keeps showing up, threatening me. Threatening to tell my mum we've slept together. He's got some dodgy photos of me too. I can't believe I was that stupid to send him them. I dunno what he's going to do with them. I'm *really* scared."

Boom chucks his can of paint back in his bag, making Feisty jump. Shaking a fresh can, he sprays a thick black outline of a figure onto the wall, before grabbing a coloured can and adding some flesh coloured pink to the face.

Feisty stands behind him, filming him in widescreen to fit it all in. It's starting to take shape now. Boom's a talented artist, he's only done a few lines of paint but already the expression is there. The man has a cold, expressionless face. He's kitted out in full military uniform. It's Korean dictator, Kim Jong Un.

As Louisa carries on talking, Boom draws a second man, in a suit and tie, with thin eyebrows and a thin moustache... a slightly geeky, comical face. It's Syria's dictator, Bashar al-Assad. And after him, a dark, black sweaty skinned man with glasses - Zimbabwean

President Robert Mugabe.

Boom has painted them standing in a semi-circle in the background, with a modern-day teenager stood in front of them. Tall, white, 18. As Boom completes the final touches, we see it's the face of Louisa's attacker, her ex. Standing back to get a clear view of his work before he signs it off, Boom steps forward, picks up a can of black paint and adds: *"Some dictators don't need a country to control people."*

Underneath it he writes, *"If anything happens to her, we'll know it was you"*, initialising his work with GB (for Graffiti Boy).

Boom spins round to face the camera and stands there for a second or two as footsteps approach. Feisty cuts the video dead, helping Boom gather his stuff as they make a run for it.

Boom peels off his Nemesis mask and wings, stuffing them into his bag before breaking off from Feisty, crossing the road diagonally at a pace. It's a safety move, going separate ways so they're less likely to get caught and if they do get caught it's just one of them, not both.

Feisty stuffs her hands into her pocket and crosses where the cars turn into the road, acting like she's on her own and nothing to do with Boom. It's not till she's further up the street and completely out of sight from the tower block that she looks up, watching Boom as he storms ahead of her.

He cuts back onto the High Street where he stops suddenly to stare at The Golden Lamb on the opposite side of the road. The pub where he saw Oli kissing Paula earlier.

Feisty races onto the High Street behind him, clocking his dark mood the second she spots him. She slows down to wait with him, arriving flustered and out of breath. She watches his face for a second or two. Without looking at her he asks, "You ok to get home from here?"

Feisty shrugs. "Sure."

A look of jealousy crosses her face as it dawns on her where Boom might be going.

"You off to see Louisa?"

Boom looks at her, confused. "No, why?"

"Just thought you might be that's all. I said I'd let her know in the morning how it went," Feisty adds.

Boom's not really taken it in though - lost in thought as he stares at the pub opposite. His mind replaying the images of Oli and Paula over and over in his head.

Feisty runs her hand along Boom's arm, trying to get him to look at her. "I thought maybe we could head back to mine. Stay the night if you wanted," she adds, with a flirty smile.

She's pretty much spelling it out for him. She wants him. In her bed.

But Boom doesn't even look at her.

"There's something I need to do. I'll see you in the morning," he replies, slinging his bag over his back.

Feisty takes a step back to let Boom pass as he heads off down the high street in the opposite direction. She watches him for a second before letting out a loud sigh, kicking the ground in frustration. Spinning on her heels she heads home, pissed off with how the night ended. Gutted that Boom doesn't fancy - or want her enough - to stay the night.

Up ahead, Boom rounds a corner, walking to the end of the street before taking a right, down an alley, and into a familiar, more industrial area. Keeping his head bowed, he crosses the road, stopping outside the train depot. Oli's workplace.

Circling the perimeter of the fence, Boom pulls his hood tight round his face to hide his features as he looks around, checking the lampposts to see where the hidden cameras are.

Moving down the side of the fence, he squats down low, keeping his hood pinched tight to his face. He tries the fence with his hand until he finds the ready-made hole he cut in the wire on his last visit. Checking the cameras one more time, he climbs through the hole. He throws his bag through first, then follows. Pushing the fence back into place from the other side, before heading off in the direction of the train hanger.

51 FOR FUCK'S SAKE OLI, LET HIM GO. HE'S JUST A KID

It's morning, and Oli makes his way to the train hanger; his huge mouth opening in a wide yawn, before heading inside. He walks to the workshop at the end of the hanger, where his train is, ignoring the other workers as he slings his bag on the floor beside the train.

The two track workers from the other day stare nervously at him, with a bucket of liquid, and a long brush, by their feet. Next to them, a young apprentice, 16, glances nervously at the cab of the train, waiting for Oli to spot the huge picture on the side of it.

Then finally, sensing everyone around him staring at him, Oli looks up; aware that no-one's said a word to him, or to each other, since he got in. He frowns, before following their gaze to the cab.

Someone (Boom) has painted him and Paula on the side of the train, kissing outside The Golden Lamb Pub, late at night, surrounded by drunken revellers. In the picture, Oli's hand is groping Paula, rubbing at her knickers through her jeans, whilst his mouth feeds on her lips. Boom's managed to make the picture look pretty disgusting, showing the relationship for what it is. Pure, emotionless lust.

Oli takes it in for a second before exploding.

Lunging for the apprentice, Oli lifts him up off the floor by his collar, screaming obscenities in his face. The apprentice is clearly terrified, and begs Oli to let him go.

"Please. Let me go. It wasn't me. Please."

"Well who was it then?" Oli screams in his face, "Cause it weren't me, that's for fucking sure. So it's got to be one of you CUNTS, cause we're the only ones with the code." Furious rounds of spit fire in the apprentice's face as Oli continues his tirade. "And it's gotta be YOU, cause this all started last week when YOU started."

The apprentice whimpers, trying hard not to cry. "It's not, I swear. Please. Let me go. It wasn't me, I swear."

One of the track workers steps forward. He's clearly scared, but at the same time he's had enough of watching Oli bully the boy.

"For fuck's sake, Oli, let him go. He's just a kid."

Oli glares at the man, but puts the apprentice down. The young boy is visibly shaken, and close to tears.

Still furious, Oli picks up a spanner from the track in front of him and hurls it at the train. The spanner bounces off the side of the train, missing the apprentice's face by inches. The apprentice screams, before bursting into tears. There's a stunned silence in the hanger. But Oli doesn't give a shit and glares at the apprentice in disgust.

"I'm gonna FUCKING KILL whoever did this!"

The apprentice covers his face and sobs quietly into his hands, as the two track workers watch in silence as Oli lays into the train, kicking the sides with his steel-capped boots, over and over in a furious assault until he runs out of energy and is forced to stop.

52 LOOKS LIKE THE BLOODHOUND'S ONTO SOMETHING

Back in his office, manager Dave Field gets up out of his seat to show DC Brightly out. It's still only 8 a.m.

"Are you sure you don't want to talk to Oli while you're here?" Field asks him.

Shaking his head, Brightly is adamant. "Probably best he doesn't know I was here either. Just for now anyway."

Field raises an eyebrow, curious to know what's behind all the secrecy. Wondering if there's more to Oli's story than he knows.

Later, at the offices of the British Transport Police, two young trainee officers, no more than eighteen or nineteen, walk out the office on the way to a job, dressed in the bright yellow waistcoats and logo'd hats of the BTP. They glance back into the open plan office, through a huge expanse of glass running 360 degrees all the way around the room, to where Brightly is sat studying something on his computer.

"Look's like the bloodhound's onto something," the first one comments.

"How can you tell?," the second one asks.

The first officer adopts a thick Yorkshire accent, mimicking Brightly to a tee. "'Cause every time he gets a hunch about something he starts stroking his pretend goatie. Watch."

The other one watches as Brightly pinches his

chin between his finger and thumb, running his finger over his chin like he's stroking a beard, except there's nothing there. "Oh yeah! Never noticed that before."

A senior officer walks into the corridor behind them, and the two trainees immediately bolt upright, making themselves look instantly suspicious. The officer raises an eyebrow as he passes, not having to utter a word for them to suddenly remember where they should be and scuttle off in the direction of the car park.

Back in the office, Brightly's still stroking his chin as he studies some CCTV footage filmed from the road outside the train depot where Oli works. He watched it play out for real, but sits watching it again as recorded video footage. The camera shows Paula leaving the depot, walking along the pavement to a waiting red Ford Fiesta, where she climbs into the passenger seat, leaning over to kiss the cheek of the driver, whose face is hidden.

Brightly clicks on a second file, this time outside Boom's flat. Using his mouse to slow the footage down, Brightly watches as a teen (Boom, hidden by the hood of his sweater) walks up to the block of flats in a grey cardigan, with the letters 'DC' on the left breast. Brightly zooms in closer, but Boom's face remains hidden by his hood.

Seconds later, Oli's Toyota pulls up and Oli jumps out, entering the block of flat after Boom. Brightly skims through the footage, watching closely until he spots Oli coming back out of the building, climbing back into his car and driving off again.

There's nothing for a few more minutes until Flash (his face hidden) walks up to the entrance and is met by Boom (his face also hidden) outside the entrance. They bump fists in a greeting and walk off together. Brightly narrows his eyes, studying the way they walk, looking for something to distinguish one from the other. He then fast forwards an hour to where the teenager (Boom) returns with a girl (Feisty, again her face hidden). He pauses the footage for a second to make a note of the time. 10.30 p.m.

The two of them enter the flats, returning back onto the street some 20 minutes later (which would have been their visit to see Louisa).

"That's a lot of movement for a week night," he mutters to himself.

Deep in thought, he pauses the CCTV footage, trying to piece it all together in his head. The times. The people. The possible reasons.

As he's sits at his desk, stroking his chin, his boss, Detective Sergeant Meadows, walks over to check on his progress.

"Anything?"

Brightly shakes his head in response, still stroking his chin.

Meadows hands him a piece of paper. "Maybe this'll help. Burrows was gonna call it in last night but then his wife went into labour."

The piece of paper has three names on it. Oli Hanson and Lorraine and Jamie Johnson (Boom and his mum).

"The names of everyone who lives at 201 Falcon Towers, on the Burnley Estate. Which you've already got. But - turns out it's a regular call out for the feds. Six times in the last three weeks. Domestic violence. Including a nasty attack on a neighbour, who was too scared to make an official complaint."

Brightly sits up in his seat. He might be onto something now. He pulls up some fresh CCTV footage, from last night, titled: GOLDEN LION PUB (April 14). Filmed high up from the top of a lamppost, the footage shows the group of teenagers outside the shop with the fruit and veg. Brightly lets it play out until Boom shows up in his grey DC cardigan, his face hidden, watching something across the road (Brightly knows it's Oli and Paula) before kicking a can high in the air in frustration, missing the group of teenagers by inches. He pauses the tape to make a note of the time. 10.40 p.m. He spots the girl (Feisty) with him. "Interesting."

Brightly then cuts to the next piece of footage outside the pub, rolling it back to just before 10.40 p.m before letting it play out in real time as the cameras pick out Oli making out with Paula on the pavement outside the pub, surrounded by drunken revellers. Even though they're drunk you can still tell how uncomfortable it's making them feel and all of them take several steps back to get away from the heavy petting.

Sergeant Meadows stands behind Brightly, frowning; trying to follow what's going on. But Brightly hasn't finished yet. Keeping the other files open, he pulls up another file entitled TRAIN DEPOT, also dated April 14.

This time the camera captures a youth skirting the fence around the depot, scanning the area for cameras before finding a corner of the fence where he squats down low. He throws his bag through a hole in the fence before climbing through after it. The youth races across the tracks to the giant hanger at the back of the depot where Oli's train is kept.

Brightly rewinds the footage to where the youth is circling the fence. He zooms in close but still can't make out the boy's face. He then zooms in closer to the letters on the boy's cardigan. The letters DC marked clearly on the left breast. Brightly then clicks back to the footage outside the pub, and then back to the footage outside the flats, checking out the cardigan the mystery youth is wearing each time. In every shot, the letters, DC, are clearly marked on the left hand side of the cardigan. Brightly flicks back to the last bit of footage opposite the Golden Lion pub then back to the footage outside the train depot, making a note of the time on both videos. He sits there quietly, stroking his imaginary goatee.

Sergeant Meadows raises his eyebrow from behind Brightly.

"You onto something?" he asks Brightly, who's still stroking his chin.

"Not sure, Sarge," he replies.

"Well, keep me posted," Meadows tells him, walking off with his hands in his pockets.

Still stroking his chin, Brightly picks up his phone to dial a contact. He waits for them to pick up before telling them, "I need you to enhance some images for me."

53 IT'S OK. YOU CAN SIT DOWN NOW, JAMIE

Flash and Boom are sat in class. Britton is stood at the front facing his students, making sure he can see everyone.

Flash is reading to the class from his copy of Wuthering Heights with Boom asleep on the desk next to him, his head on his hands. Britton, however, is choosing to ignore this fact as usual and lets him sleep.

Sitting at his desk reading, Flash is unable to contain his endless energy. Surging through his body, his legs jig up and down under the table, making him want to just get up and run. As he reads, Flash's leg bangs the table, causing a steady, rhythmic tapping. Britton nods at him to stop. Flash makes a conscientious effort to shift his legs away from the top of the table, before continuing to read.

"I pulled its wrist on to the broken pane and rubbed it to and fro till the blood ran down and soaked the bedclothes."

Unable to sit still for long, however, he tips his chair back onto two legs. Britton watches, mesmerized, knowing it doesn't matter how many times he tells Flash, he'll still keep doing it. He carries on watching, waiting for the inevitable.

"Still it wailed," Flash continues, "Let me in!' and maintained its tenacious grip, almost maddening me with fear."

At that point, Flash tips back just that little bit too far, landing on the floor with a loud crash. Boom jumps up out of his seat, startled, knocking their desk to the floor with an even louder crash, making the girls scream. Some of the boys at the back of the class start cheering.

"Calm down everyone. It's just Mr Pritchard up to his usual."

The class start to laugh as the shock subsides. But as they relax, Boom stands there frozen to the spot; startled to the point of terror, something heavy playing out in his mind as he stands there poised and ready to run.

"It's ok. You can sit down now, Jamie," Britton tells him.

But Boom doesn't move. Flash picks the desk up off its side, placing it back on all four legs before sitting back down on his chair, tugging at his friend's sleeve.

"Try four legs next time, Mr Pritchard. They're a great new invention that work well apparently," Britton quips, making the class laugh but Flash blush with embarrassment.

Boom's still standing there though, completely out of place within the seated class. Flash looks at him concerned and nudges him from the side. "Bro."

Boom stands there tugging at his hair in the same distressed way he did the night he turned up at Feisty's. Britton looks at him concerned.

"Jamie!" Britton manages to capture Boom's attention. "Are you ok?"

Boom 'comes to'. Realising what he's doing, he lowers his hands and grips them tightly together.

"I'm fine, Sir," Boom replies, before sitting back

down.

Britton frowns, concerned, before turning back round to face the whiteboard to write a phrase down for the class to copy.

Back at Boom's desk, he feels a message vibrate on his phone. Making sure no-one, except Flash, is looking, he checks his messages. It's from Feisty telling him to check Graffiti Boy's Insta account.

Logging on to his account, Boom pulls up the latest video he did getting back at Louisa's ex. There's a huge thread of comments below it. Everything from 'not cool, intimidating a young girl younger than you', followed by the hashtag #standuptobullies to 'Well done for standing up to this bully. Hope he learns from it.' But as the thread goes on, the messages get more and more dark, with the final one reading, 'If her ex doesn't kill himself, I will.'

The bell goes, marking the start of break-time. Boom's the last to leave, staring at his phone in his lap, still in shock at the reaction his post is getting. He gets up, walks to the front of the class, and hands Britton his dog-eared copy of Wuthering Heights before leaving.

Britton looks up briefly, clocking the sketch Boom has drawn on the inside cover of the book. An angry fist, punching through a wall.

Britton looks at it and frowns.

54 GLAD SOMEONE'S GOT THE SENSE TO STAY OUT OF IT!

It's break time, and a repeat of the other day - with groups of teenagers huddled over their phones. Nothing unusual as such, except instead of the self-inflicted solitary confinement of each teenager bent over their own phone, this activity's a bit more social, with something capturing their attention all at once.

Flash is walking around the playground with Boom, who's studying something on his phone.

It's his Graffiti Boy profile, including the latest video he filmed for Louisa, referencing his outfit he filmed in as "Nemesis, the Greek goddess of divine retribution and revenge", making it perfectly clear what all his videos are about - Revenge.

There's a string of comments under the video and Flash only has to look at the first one to know Boom should be worried.

"You're in deep shit now bro. What d'you do it for?"

Boom doesn't look up but keeps skimming through the comments as they walk - clearly worried about what he's done, but in too deep to admit it. Too engrossed to notice anyone else around them, they pass Curl, sitting with The Watcher. Curl whistles over to Boom, to capture his attention.

"Yo, Boom. You coming tonight?"

The Watcher grins, jiggling his chest about like a pair of boobs.

"Depends on a certain little lady, right bro?" he laughs, adding in a high-pitched piss-take voice, "Feisty, Feisty, I love you Feisty."

Boom ignores him, too busy trawling through the messages on his page to really notice. The Watcher is about to take the piss again when he spots a tall white boy, about 18 and definitely not a school kid, storming through the school gates and into the playground (it's Louisa's ex).

"Aye, aye," he says, his instincts kicking in. Even from here, he can see this person's trouble.

Mr Britton steps out onto the playground just at that second. He clocks the groups of teenagers hovering over their phones and is about to approach one group when he spots Louisa's ex storming through the playground, heading towards a much smaller white boy, twelve-year-old Hayden, who's telling some kind of joke to his friend next to him. Hayden doesn't spot Louise's ex until it's too late however - looking up just in time to get a blow to the nose, which sends blood spurting out in front of him in a fierce red jet.

Within seconds, all the students circle around the two boys as Louisa's angry ex reins blow after blow on Hayden, screaming abuse at him as a sobbing Hayden tries to defend himself by shielding his head with his arms.

"Thought it was funny to bad mouth me, did you, you little shit? Spread my face all over where I live? Thought that was funny, did you? Did you?!"

Standing several feet away - and the only person in the whole of the playground stood as far away from the fight as possible - is Boom. The only one backing away from trouble instead of circling it with the usual morbid fascination of a teenager.

Realising Louisa's ex thinks his graffiti is Hayden's work, he stands there trying to figure out if there is anything he can do to stop the fight whilst at the same time not wanting to get involved... but it's obvious the fight is sending his stress levels through the roof. While everyone else is preoccupied with the fight, no-one even notices Boom, stood by himself on the edge of the tarmac, tugging at his hair in clumps and cranking up the music on his headphones in an attempt to drown out the fight.

Boom watches through a haze in his head as Britton rushes into the fight, struggling to hold onto Louisa's ex, who tries desperately to wriggle free from his grip, kicking at his legs to try and bring him down. The boy catches Britton's leg, lashing out again to kick his knee out from under him, sending Britton flying to the ground. Britton lets go of his grip and the boy escapes, racing across the playground and out through the school gates, onto the streets beyond.

"Bugger!" Britton swears to himself before realising in an instant that all the kids have heard him swear. Wobbling back onto his feet, he tells them, "What's everyone staring at? Go!"

As the crowds disperse, Britton bends down to help Hayden back onto his feet. The young boy's in shock and his body is shaking uncontrollably. Britton looks over to one of the boy's friends and barks instructions at him.

"Take him to reception, make sure he's seen by

a first aider. And keep his nose covered!"

He jumps back as a spurt of blood jettisons out of Hayden's nose, missing him by inches.

Britton stands there in the playground watching the students disperse back into school. He catches Boom standing by himself on the edge of the playground and waits until everyone is safely inside before wandering over to him.

"Glad someone's got the sense to stay out of it!"

He walks back into school, leaving Boom by himself in an empty playground; music blaring in his head as he tries to wipe the fight - and the guilt - from his mind.

55 YOU'D BETTER WATCH YOUR BACK, GRAFFITI BOY, 'CAUSE I'M COMING FOR YOU!

Flash is stood at the lockers, surrounded by the usual end of break bustle, except this one is even more chaotic than usual as the students buzz with adrenalin, picking apart the fight and trying to figure out who the boy was that hit Hayden. Literally every student is talking about it as they pull their books out of their locker and transfer them into their bags in time for class. Flash isn't in his locker though. Instead, he's stood in front of it, locked on his phone. Reading the final comment posted on Graffiti Boy's profile - "You better watch your back, Graffiti Boy, 'cause I'm coming for you!"

Worried, Flash bites his lip, trying to think it through for a second until the sound of Mr Ellington's voice bellows through the corridor, kick starting him - and everyone else - into action.

"Everyone grab their bags and head into the hall now please! We have an emergency assembly!"

Flash swaps a confused look with the other students. Shoving his phone into his pocket, he pulls some books from his locker, shoves them into his bag and heads for the hall.

56 HAYDEN THINKS IT'S GOT SOMETHING TO DO WITH LOUISA CHAPMAN IN YEAR 10

Mr Ellington paces back and forth at the front, waiting for the last of the students to file into the hall and sit down. The students chatter noisily to each other as they wait to find out why the emergency assembly has been called, until Mr Ellington throws a look their way, silencing them in seconds.

Flash is one of the last to slope into the hall. As he sits down by the entrance, he catches Boom's eye the other side of the room. No sooner has he sat down, than Mr Ellington addresses the room in a loud, clear voice filled with authority.

"The fight you just witnessed I've been told has something to do with some revenge graffiti posted on a particular Social Media account last night," Ellington starts. "Now some of you may have seen the video. Some of you may not. But, what I need to tell you is that ANY form of vendetta against anyone, be it in writing, in person, or in this case over Social Media, IS ILLEGAL and anything that is recorded - as in the case of Social Media - is classed as defamation and could get you into SERIOUS TROUBLE with the police. I repeat, SERIOUS TROUBLE. So let me make myself clear. If any one of you has anything to do with this video then you need to watch your back from now on, because you have committed a serious crime which the police are now looking into. And if any of you are thinking of any copycat behaviour, please don't."

Flash looks up, worried, catching Boom's eye the other side of the hall. Boom looks away quickly.

"You should also know," Mr Ellington continues, "that the school DOES NOT tolerate this kind of behaviour and if I find ANY of my students committing this type of revenge crime, you will be suspended immediately whilst the matter is looked into by both the school and the police. Do I make myself clear?" he asks, emphasising the question and waiting for all the students to respond before he lets them go.

"Yes, Mr Ellington," they reply in unison.

The head tips his head towards the door, signalling for the student in the front row, closest to the door, to file out first. Row after row of students follow, filing out one by one, passing Mr Ellington and Britton as they talk in hushed voices at the front of the hall.

Boom keeps his head down as he passes, but hears just enough to know he's in trouble.

"Any idea who was behind it?" Britton asks.

"Not the graffiti," Mr Ellington replies, "but Hayden thinks it's got something to do with Louisa Chapman in Year 10. They hang out together, and it's her voice in the video. She just broke up with her boyfriend, who's turned nasty apparently. Police are ID'ing the teenager who hit Hayden as we speak and are going to call me back as soon as they know anything."

Boom slows his walk down in an attempt to hear more. "Do you think it was one of our students?" Britton asks, adding, "I'm not sure any of them would even know who the dictators were." Just as he says this though, Boom looks up and they catch each other's eye for a second. A light bulb switching on in Britton's head as Boom passes.

57 ALL I WANTED TO SAY WAS JUST STAY AWAY FROM THE TRACKS, BRO. IT 'AINT WORTH IT

Flash and Boom walk through the council estate, on their way home from school. As they reach the entrance to their tower block a car slows down next to them, and Lunar jumps out in a suit and tie. He catches Boom's eye, and tips his head, signalling to meet him inside, under cover of the block.

Flash walks loyally with Boom, but Boom stops at the bottom of the stairwell next to Lunar, telling him, "Sorry bro, d'you mind?"

Flash shakes his head, pissed off that he's been given the brush off, but Boom tells him, "Just best you don't know too much, that's all. No point dragging you down with me as well."

Boom watches as Flash heads up the stairwell, taking the steps two at a time. He waits 'till Flash reaches the top and turns the corner before speaking to Lunar. "What?"

Lunar looks shaky, scared and vulnerable all at once.

"Got my sentencing tomorrow," he tells Boom, before adding in a scared voice, "And I'm going down." He waits a second before looking Boom straight in the eye. "All I wanted to say was just stay away from the tracks, bro. It 'aint worth it."

58 LIKE I STAND A CHANCE WITH HER WITH YOU LOT AROUND!

Flash and The Crew - all except Boom - are hanging about outside the Lord Protector Pub. There for the night, perched high on a 12-foot wall, swinging their legs and just messing about like typical teenagers. Flash in the middle, with The Cat and The Watcher either side and Curl at the end, and plenty of banter.

A familiar looking girl walks towards them. She spots them up ahead and screws her face up, bracing herself for the onslaught. She keeps her head down and pretends she hasn't seen them, but she can feel their eyes on her as she gets closer.

The Watcher spots her and taps Curl on the shoulder and winks. He nudges Flash, tipping his head in the direction of the girl. It's Nicole Folsey, the girl who caught Flash with his trousers round his ankles outside the school. Apart from the fact she's stunning, you can tell she's a cool girl, someone both the boys and the girls get on with. Someone that Flash, quite obviously, has a massive crush on. He takes one look at The Watcher's face and spots the wind up before it even hits, telling him, "Just don't do it, bro. You know it 'aint cool."

But The Watcher knows he's got his audience, and before Nicole is close enough to hear, he leans in towards Flash and gives him a full-on pout, puckering his lips up for a kiss.

"Fuck off, will ya?!" Flash replies, shaking his head at his mate, trying not to smile at the same time.

As Nicole gets closer, the line falls silent as they watch her pass. She may have her head down, and be walking as quickly as she can to get past, but her squirm is palpable. It's not just Flash waiting for the wind up, but her too…

Flash shifts nervously from one leg to leg to the other, wobbling slightly and glaring at his mates to keep their mouths shut as she passes. He can see the wind-up building in The Watcher's eyes, and even the others are looking at him, begging for more. Flash slaps him hard on the belly to keep quiet. But the move catches him off balance and he starts to wobble, tipping backwards off the wall before The Cat and The Watcher only just grab him in time before he falls. Barely managing to smother their laughter they help straighten him back up, but then make a thing of brushing down his t-shirt for Nicole to see.

The Cat winks at The Watcher, and leans in for a stage whisper, making it loud in Flash's ear.

"Say something then, lover boy."

Nicole pretends not to have heard, but she obviously has because she picks the pace up, keeping her eyes even more focussed on the pavement than before. Flash glares at The Cat and goes to elbow him in the stomach. The Cat darts backwards, but wobbles, grabs Flash, and nearly takes him with him over the back of the wall. Curl and The Watcher piss themselves laughing, grabbing the both of them to save them. It's like an episode of Laurel and Hardy on loop.

Flash catches Nicole's eye as she passes directly below, spots her awkwardness and panics, deciding to say something - anything - just so she doesn't feel awkward like they're talking about her, which they are, but he doesn't want her to think they are.

"Alright, Nicole," he says, flashing her one of his megawatt smiles.

The Crew let out a snigger. Nicole looks over and scowls at Flash. Flash throws his hands up in the air to defend himself, but before he realises what's happening, he's lost his balance and topples backwards off the wall.

Nicole looks on in shock as Flash tips backwards, throwing his long legs up in the air... the last part of him to disappear behind the wall. There's a flash of gold trainer and then he's gone. There's a stunned silence, followed by a THUD as Flash hits the ground. No-one moves for a second, and then Flash lets out a groan.

"Why'd I have to make such a dick of myself in front of her, *EVERY FUCKING TIME*?" he groans to himself, forgetting he's in earshot of everyone else.

Now the shock's subsided, the crew start to laugh. And properly laugh. Doubling over on top of the wall, pissing themselves laughing at Flash's expense; the image of his long, skinny stork legs disappearing over the back of the wall forever burnt in their memories. Even Nicole has to bite down hard on her lip to stop herself from laughing.

Curl steadies The Cat and The Watcher as they dangle over the back of the wall to rescue Flash. Still pissing themselves laughing, they yank him back up, helping to steady him as he reaches the top.

Nicole looks over at Flash, genuinely concerned. "You ok?"

Mortified, Flash replies with a brief nod of his head.

She smiles and carries on walking.

Curl grins. "She cares about you, bro." The Crew start laughing again, as Curl adds, "Must mean she likes you."

"Yeah right," Flash replies, "Like I stand a chance with her with you lot around!"

And that's it. Piss take time. Curl does a perfect impression of Flash, his arms flailing like a broken windmill as he mutters the words he wanted to impress her with before falling backwards of the wall. "Alright, Nico--oooole!"

"Fuck you, mother fucker!" Laughing, Flash shoves Curl off the wall and watches him fall, before jumping off and walking away.

Curl looks up. "Where you going?"

"G. You know we was only messing right?" The Watcher asks, genuinely concerned they might have upset him.

Flash screws his face up, like he's mad. "Don't be stupid! Used to you lot by now. Just checking on Boom."

"Yeah, where is he?" asks Curl.

Flash shrugs, walking off as he replies, "I'll let you know when I find him."

59 CONSIDER IT DONE

Boom is sat in his bedroom in the pitch black. His computer screen glows blue in front of him and he's slumped in front of it, leaning on both elbows, head down and broken; listening to Oli screaming abuse at his mum from the lounge. As he listens he pinches and pulls at his hair, wanting to feel the pain as a way to try and block out what's happening at home.

"Some prick vandalised my train, made me look a right cunt and got me in trouble with the boss 'cause the fucking new kid put in a complaint about me. And you ask if I had a good day! NO-- I-- FUCKING-- DIDN'T-- HAVE-- A-- GOOD-- DAY!" Oli screams at her.

Boom hears the hard slap, as Oli lashes out at his mum. Then silence, just for a second, before a loud thud, as Oli hurls her body at the wall.

Boom can't stand it any longer. He pulls his headphones on and cranks the music up until it hurts his ears, loud enough to drown out the sound of Oli beating up his mum.

Now all he hears is music.

No more slaps. No more thuds. No more screams or shouts. Just music. Pumping loudly in his ears, taking away the pain.

Boom sits in front of his computer, eyes shut, jaws clenched; pushing his headphones as tight to his ears as he can. Focusing only on the beat of the music. The lyrics and the melody. Just long enough to start feeling himself breathe again.

There's a flash of blue, and a message pops up on Messenger, from someone called SkaterDude. Boom opens his eyes.

"Been with my Crew since I was 11. Me and my bestie set it up."

It's a message on Boom's Graffiti Boy account. And whoever it is, is getting straight to the point, with a flurry of messages.

"Known him 15 years. Never had an argument. Not once. But this new guy starts, and all we've done is fight."

"Told my m8 I'd stolen the lyrics to one of the songs he penned, but I wouldn't do that. He's just causing shit."

"Ended up fighting with my m8 over it. Proper punches, the lot. And now he won't speak to me."

The blue glare from the computer lights Boom's face up as he types his reply one-handed. Keeping his other hand free to keep his headphones pinched as tight to his head as he can.

Making slow progress he types, "Where are you?"

"Cromwell Towers," the reply comes back. "Tower block opposite the Lord Protector. You know it?"

"Shit!" Boom swears out loud to himself, remembering that's where he should be right now.

A second or two passes before SkaterDude sends another message.

"You still there?"

"Yeah, sorry," Boom replies, adding, "What's

your m8's name?"

"Hovis."

"??" Boom types, with a thinking emoji next to it.

"'Cause he's brown," then…

"They call me snowie." with a laughing face next to it.

Boom replies with a "LMAO" before continuing, "And poison boy?"

He waits a few seconds for SkaterDude to type his reply.

"Lyrics. Fancies himself as a bit of a rapper."

Boom pauses for a minute, and another message flashes up from SkaterDude.

"U still there?"

Boom leans back, stares at the screen for a minute before typing, "CID" (consider it done).

He's about to turn his screen off, but logs back into Messenger. His final reply to SkaterDude.

"It'll be there in the morning."

Boom turns his screen off, grabs his bag, and heads out into the corridor. As usual, it's pitch black. And silent now. Just the glow from a light spooling out from underneath a gap in the bottom of the lounge door at the end of the corridor.

Boom heads for the toilet, pushing the door shut behind him. Keeping the lights off, it's the same routine as before. He climbs onto the toilet seat, opens the window, and shoves his bag out onto the balcony, and follows.

60 NO IT'S NOT OK. SHE'S A FUCKING EMBARRASSMENT

Boom tumbles through the toilet window onto the balcony below and lands awkwardly on his elbow. He gets up and gives it a rub as he heads for the stairwell. But just as he reaches the top, he hears someone calling his name. It's Louisa, her head poking out from behind her front door.

She looks at Boom, concerned.

"You ok?"

She's obviously heard the noise coming from his flat, and now he doesn't know what to say.

"I'm fine," he says, in an attempt to shut down the conversation.

Now it's Louisa's turn to look awkward.

"Sorry, I didn't mean to... I just wanted to check you were ok, that's all."

Boom nods, and heads off down the stairwell, into the night.

Now outside, Boom heads for the main road, music pumping loudly in his ears. There's a brief pause as a text pops up from Flash.

"Change of plan. C U at mine."

Boom spins back round and heads back into the flats, heading up the stairwell, past his flat, and up several more floors until he reaches Flash's place. He taps gently on the front door, a rhythmic beat they obviously use just for each other.

Flash opens the door but instead of letting Boom

in he asks "Where was you earlier?"

Boom's visibly stressed still, and replies with a simple, "You gonna let me in or what?"

Flash steps aside to let Boom in, studying his face on the way past and clocking his mate's sombre mood. He puts his hand on Boom's arm, stopping him from going into the living room.

"What's going on?" he asks.

Boom just shakes his head, so Flash continues. "What you talking to Lunar for? Are you and Feisty working the trains, is that it?"

"No!" Boom's quick to shut him down. "We did her dad's garage. And the piece for Louisa. But that's it."

Flash isn't convinced, but he lets Boom off the hook for now and follows him into the living room.

As soon as they walk in, they're assaulted by the noise of the telly, cranked up to full volume. The lights are off and Flash's mum is slumped on the sofa, watching TV. Her eyes are red and her head rests heavily on a cushion.

Flash's sister, Rachel, sits on the sofa opposite. She looks up as Boom enters the room and flashes him an awkward, embarrassed kind of smile. Flash's mum suddenly becomes aware of Boom's presence, and raises her head off the cushion to greet him. Rachel rolls her eyes, waiting for it. Her mum's eyes are puffy and her speech slurred as she greets Boom with a friendly welcome.

"Look who it is! My favourite friend. I mean my favourite friend of Adam's."

Rachel scowls, sighing heavily from her seat opposite.

Flash gives Boom an apologetic look, like they've done this all before. But Boom looks at him as if to say, 'don't worry about it.'

"Mrs Pritchard," Boom replies, smiling at Flash's mum.

Flash's mum waves her hand exaggeratedly over her head.

"I keep telling you. Just call me Rosa."

She tries to sit up but rolls off the sofa instead, landing in a drunken heap on the floor.

"For fuck's sake!" Rachel says out loud.

"It's ok, Rach, we've got this," Flash tells her.

"No, it's *not* ok," Rachel replies. "She's a fucking embarrassment!"

Mrs Pritchard tries to roll herself back up onto all fours to bring herself to standing, but she's too pissed. When that doesn't work she tries pulling herself up by gripping tight to the edge of the sofa, but even then she just falls straight back over.

Boom taps Flash on the arm, and together they gently lift Flash's mum by the underarms and bring her up to standing. She's just about to thank the boys when she starts retching and stumbles out of the room.

Flash's sigh is weary, like it's just something he lives with now. But just because he's used to it, doesn't mean he likes it. He turns to Boom.

"You ok to help Rach with her homework? She's stuck on some history you'll probably know the answer to."

"How come you're not doing any tonight?" Rachel asks Flash.

"Because unlike you two smart arses, I is dumb. Whereas you two on the other hand need to make the most of you God-given smartness and use it to get out of this shithole and make something of your lives," he tells his sister, with a smile.

Boom throws his arm around his mate. "Clever 'aint just about grades, my friend. Clever is about being street smart. Like you. Getting on with everyone. Like you. Making everyone's life the richer just by being in it. Like you. 'Cause it don't matter how much money you've got in this world, or how big you house is. If you 'aint got your mates, then you 'aint got anything. And you, my friend, are loved by each and every one of your mates, a thousand times over."

Flash is visibly moved by what Boom's said, and for once he's speechless. An embarrassed silence follows, before Rachel interjects with a, "Enough of the love in, already," before miming sticking both her fingers down her throat to make herself sick.

Flash gives her a good-natured punch on the arm as Boom sits down next to her. But before Flash can join them, his phone beeps with a message from the Crew. He scans it, then tells Boom, "Rendezvous, one hour."

"Better get on with it then," Boom tells Rach with a smile.

61 JEEZ. WOULDN'T WANT TO GET ON THE WRONG SIDE OF HIM

A pair of feet in red trainers, with luminous green piping around the edges, hurtle down the stairs, followed by another pair of trainers just behind them. It's Flash, in yet another pair of brand new trainers, followed closely by Boom. As they race down the stairs they laugh noisily, giving each other playful shoves as they go.

Flash hits the next level first. It's Boom's floor. He lands with a thudding skid, just as Oli and Boom's mum round the corner. Boom reaches the balcony just behind them, clocks who it is and drops the laughter, instantly.

Boom's mum turns towards them, clocks Boom and flashes him the tiniest of smiles, before looking away quickly before Oli spots her. Oli gives Boom a hard stare and nods at Boom's mum to get inside. She scurries inside the flat, shutting the front door quickly behind her.

"Jeez. Wouldn't want to get on the wrong side of him," Flash comments.

He has no idea it was Boom's mum and stepdad, and Boom doesn't let on otherwise.

Boom frowns for a minute, before telling Flash, "I'll catch you up. Think I left my sketches on your living room table."

They fist bump and Boom barrels back up the stairs, rounding the corner and stopping to lean over the rails to check Flash has gone before walking back down the stairs and stopping in front of his front door. He rests his head against the door, listening to Oli as he beats the shit out of his mum, wincing with every punch.

62 SORRY, CAN'T MAKE IT. I'LL EXPLAIN IN THE MORNING

The Crew are stood by a deserted railway bridge in an expanse of open grassland, in the early hours of the morning.

The Watcher and The Cat are stood on the brow of the hill, keeping watch. Or at least, The Watcher is. The Cat, meanwhile, is performing his usual backflips and handstands next to him.

"Just watch the path, will ya?!" The Watcher tells him, annoyed.

The Cat flips himself back upright, freezing on the spot like a statue. "Better?" he asks.

The Watcher frowns at him, unimpressed. "Ha, ha."

Back at the bridge, Curl and Flash are checking out Curl's old graffiti piece, 'Shit happens'. A thick, black line has been scored through the middle of it.

"Who'd you piss off?" Flash asks him.

"No one," Curl replies. "I don't think."

Flash checks the time on his phone again, glancing to the top of the hill to see if Boom is coming. He pulls up his messages, clicking on Boom's name.

Back at his block of flats, Boom bursts out the entrance, highly agitated and tugging at clumps of hair, really distressed by what he's just heard. His headphones are on and music blasts his head, stopping momentarily as his phone beeps, and a message from Flash pops up.

"You left yet?"

Hands shaking badly, Boom drops his phone. He takes a deep breath and picks it up, replying,

"Sorry, can't make it. I'll explain in the morning."

He then crosses to the opposite side of the road and heads for the Lord Protector pub, where he looks for the Cromwell Towers tower block. Spotting the name on the front of the block, Boom walks across the road to the entrance before checking out the expanse of bare brick on the side of the building.

"Perfect," he mutters, before dropping his paint bag on the floor in front of him, checking out the street lights as well as all the shops, buildings and walls for hidden CCTV.

It's 1 a.m so he's fairly safe, but it's a huge risk he's taking. Normally there's always someone covering his back, but it's like a switch has flicked in Boom, he just doesn't care any more. His life's already shit so he's got nothing left to lose by making it any shitter. He may as well get caught if that's what it takes for him to feel something. Something other than the huge sense of despair he normally feels.

Boom paints a curled-up snake, wrapped up in a giant spiral. Running along the length of its scales are the lyrics to Eminem's song **Lose Yourself** scrawled in thick, black letters. The scales themselves are a beautiful light green, with a pink sheen to them.

"If you had one shot, or one opportunity..."

Rubbing his hands together, Boom realises he's

forgotten to wear gloves this time, and his hands are covered in a pink and green glaze. "Damn it!"

Boom shakes his can of paint, thinking of a message for Lyrics. When he's done, he crosses the road and starts walking back towards his piece, filming it on his phone to post.

63 I WASN'T GOING TO SAY ANYTHING, IT'S JUST... MY MUM'S LAST BOYFRIEND. HE WAS THE SAME

Boom walks slowly through the night to his flat, where only the more hardcore of the teenagers are still hanging about in groups in the car park in front of the block. He's wearing his rucksack on his back, but if anyone really wanted to find out what he's been up to, all they'd need to do is take a closer look at his hands, which are covered in the pink and green paint glaze from earlier.

He passes Louisa, huddled on a wall, sandwiched between her friends. She looks up as Boom passes and leans in to say something to her friends before jumping off the wall and running after him.

"Jamie! Wait up."

Boom turns round to face her, and she continues quietly so no-one can hear. "I just wanted to say I hope you're ok. I could hear it from mine."

She knows. Boom looks mortified. Louisa places a hand gently on his arm.

"I'm not meaning to make you feel uncomfortable. I wasn't going to say anything it's just... My mum's last boyfriend. He was the same. I just thought you might want someone to talk to about it. Someone who knows what it's like."

Boom's never had anyone talk to him about it before. Not even his neighbour. It's normally the thing that no-one mentions, so it's weird to be spoken to about it so openly.

Louisa is persistent though. Her face caring.

"Maybe you do, maybe you don't. But what I'm trying to say is, I know what it's like, not being able to talk to anyone about it. And I know what it's like to have to sit there and listen to it, and feel so helpless. Worthless even. 'Cause you feel like you should be doing something about it, 'cause it's your mum, but you can't 'cause you're just too... petrified."

She's hit a nerve and she knows it. "Why don't you come up? Please. Mum's out. We can just talk."

Boom looks at her. "I'd like that."

Back in the car park, Feisty is leant against one of the cars, scanning through the message notifications on Graffiti Boy's profile. She spots one from SkaterDude, obviously sent before his messages on Messenger.

"Graffiti Boy. Can we talk?"

Feisty frowns. She looks Flash up on her phone, and calls him, waiting for him to pick up before asking, "You don't know where Boom is, do you? I've been trying to get hold of him all night."

She waits a second to hear his reply, before asking, "What time was he supposed to meet you? Hmm. Ok, thanks."

She hangs up, frowning again. She gets up off the car and stretches. She's about to start walking home when she spots Boom by the entrance of his flat, chatting to Louisa, who has her hand on his am. Her face drops and she tears up instantly, hurt written all over her face.

Too shocked to move, she watches as they head inside together. She bashes her head with her hand,

251

furious with herself.

"You've done it again, you fucking idiot. Believed some bloke who doesn't give a fuck about you."

Some teenagers are staring at her, looking at her like she's crazy. She glares back at them before storming off into the block of flats to find out what Boom's up to.

She reaches Louisa's flat, but there's no sign of Boom or Louisa.

Feisty hovers outside the flat for a second, staring at the front door. She lifts her hand to knock, but then stops herself, looking around for somewhere to wait instead. But there's only the balcony, in full view of Louisa's flat, so if Boom comes out he'll just spot her straight away. So instead, she heads up one flight of stairs, stopping halfway where the stairs turn the corner; sitting down to rest her back against the block of concrete below the handrail where she can hide from Boom, but still have a good view of Louisa's flat. She leans her head back and waits.

64 I'D RATHER BE BEATEN MYSELF THAN EVER HEAR THOSE SCREAMS AGAIN

Louisa and Boom are stood in her kitchen. No-one talks while the kettle boils and Louisa makes them both a tea. Boom watches her silently, his head immersed in his own thoughts.

"Sugar?" Louisa turns to ask him.

Boom shakes his head. "No, thanks."

"Do you wanna go through to the living room?" Louisa asks.

Boom nods, and follows her through to the other room, where they sit down side by side on her sofa. Louisa waits until Boom takes a sip of his tea, before starting to talk.

"Has it been going on long?"

"'Bout six years. Ever since he moved in," Boom replies. He laughs, an ironic kind of laugh, not a happy laugh, before adding, "Made sure he waited a few months though. Just enough to get settled in and make my mum think he loved her before he started beating the shit out of her."

Louisa looks at him sympathetically. "That's how people like that work." She waits a second before asking, "How old were you when your dad died?"

"Eight."

Louisa rests a hand on Boom's arm. Boom looks at her before opening up.

"That was the thing about Oli. It was a year after

my dad died, so I guess, I dunno, I don't know what's normal. But when I look back at how my mum met him, it's like all the signs were there from the start. 'Cause he seemed ok. But he just seemed to appear from nowhere. Like he'd spotted her from afar. How vulnerable she was, and then came to find her. Met in the pub one night. Told her a sob story about how he'd lost his wife, and how he knew how she felt--"

"What, and he hadn't?" Louisa interrupts.

"Nah. Made it all up. Just to get under her skin. Started doing things to 'help' her. Mend her car. Help with stuff around the house."

"What did you think of him?"

"Well, at first Mum was really careful not to let him in when I was there," Boom replies. "Not 'cause there was anything dodgy going on. I think she just realised it would have been too soon for me to have another man in the house so soon after dad died. 'Cause all I wanted was my dad back. So I guess I only had what she told me. That he was this nice guy who was just being a friend to her. But now I can see how manipulative he was. Making sure he was always there to help whenever she needed it. Making out he was a friend. Giving her someone to rely on when she was vulnerable. Telling her this whole sob story until one day I think she thought she'd help him out by letting him move in." Boom stops for a minute, before adding. "He told her he'd been thrown out of his flat without any notice 'cause his flatmate had told some lie about him. Now I know it was just a lie to get my mum to let him move in with us."

"Nice guy," Louisa quips.

Boom laughs, appreciating the dark humour from someone who understands.

"What about you?" he asks, giving her a gentle smile.

"Remember the electrician?" Louisa asks him. Boom nods. "Well it was him. Asked mum to marry him, moved in, and bam! Same as you."

She takes another sip of her tea, before adding, "It was only a few months. So not as long as you. But I don't think I'll ever forget the sound. It's like the sound of their screams are burnt in your memory forever..." She trails off, going quiet.

"You ok?" Boom asks.

Louisa starts to cry. "I'm sorry. I was supposed to be listening to you, not the other way round."

"It's alright. Come here," Boom tells her, pulling her towards him and wrapping his arms around her in a gentle hug.

Something about the hug just makes her let go and she sobs loudly, remembering what her mum went through. Struggling to talk because she's crying so much, she tells Boom,

"The thing I hate the most is, I hate..." Composing herself enough to speak, she pulls back from Boom to look him in the face as she tells him, "I hate myself for letting it happen. I just used to sit there and listen to him beat the shit out of my mum and I didn't do anything. I just let it happen," she breaks down, sobbing uncontrollably.

Boom's close to tears himself now.

"He's the guilty one, not you."

There's a pause before he adds, "I'm exactly the same. Every time, I think I'm going to do it. Grab the bastard by the neck and sling him against the wall. Beat the shit out of him like he does my mum. Get him out of our flat. And I'm bigger than you too. But when it comes to it, I can't. It's the fear. I keep telling myself he's only a man. And I'm a man. But the fear just paralyses me. Freezes you to the spot. Sometimes I'm so scared, I feel like I can't even breathe and it takes me hours to feel normal again."

"Have you told anyone?" Louisa asks him.

"No way!" Boom replies. "He'd kill her, kill me. I'm sure of it." Recalling what happened to his neighbour a few weeks back he tells her, "Remember a few weeks ago? My neighbour?"

"Shit! Was that your stepdad?" Louisa asks him, shocked.

Boom nods.

"We'd tried to escape. He was supposed to be staying out all night. He never stays out all night, ever. But he told my mum he was. So I persuaded mum to run away. Never come back. Get away, once and for all. But as we were leaving, mum spotted his car pulling into the car park, so we knocked on the neighbour's door and asked him to take us in…" he trails off, guilty at the memory. "Ended up beating the shit out of him." Boom winces, as he recalls what Oli did. "Kept kicking him in the ribs with his boots on. The steel-capped boots he wears to work. Thought he was going to kill him. Anyway, when we got home he beat my mum up too. Burnt the only picture she had left of my dad. The one of them on their wedding day. And then he told her he'd kill her if she ever tried to leave again. So that was that."

Louisa takes Boom's hands in hers. "Look at me."

Boom looks up, eyes level with hers, as she tells him,

"She *will* get out. Both of you will. You have to believe that. I don't know when, or how. But you will. You just have to wait for the right moment."

But Boom doesn't share her belief. He's had too many years of Oli to ever think he'll escape. "I dunno."

"You will Jamie. I promise. And if I can help you do it, I will. I promise. Because I don't think I'll ever forget how awful it was for the rest of my life. I don't think you can. And if I can help someone else get out of it, I want to."

Louisa gets up and wanders out of the room for a second before returning with a magazine article in her hand. She passes it to Boom.

"Do you remember the guy who won X Factor a few years ago? Looks a bit like one of the Jackson Five, don't know why... had this amazing voice. Could hit all the high notes," Louisa says, pointing to a picture on the front of the article. It's X Factor winner, Jahmene Douglas.

"Yeah. I remember him," Boom says.

"His dad was violent. You can tell he went through it just by all the things he says. About being so scared, he couldn't move."

She starts to read from the article, the bits that mean something to her.

"Domestic violence is in my DNA, it's in who I

257

am. I'd rather be beaten myself than ever hear those screams again." She looks at Boom. "That's exactly how I feel."

Boom nods.

Louisa continues, talking with passion.

"It's a really good article. He talks about how the fear was still there, even after his dad had gone. But how he started to change all that. Finding something to focus on, setting yourself a dream and working towards it. Like painting a picture of what you want your life to be, rather than what it actually is. Turning a negative into a positive."

Louisa folds the page shut, telling Boom, "It's a really good article. You can borrow it if you like. I thought it might help."

Boom mulls it over as Louisa hands the magazine to him. "Painting your negative into a positive. I like it."

He looks at Louisa. "It's kind of a relief. To be able to talk to someone about it. Someone who understands. *Thank you*."

Boom smiles at her, adding, "I should go. It's getting late. Even for me," he laughs, looking at the 3.30 a.m time on the clock. "How did that even happen?!"

Louisa laughs. "Amazing how time flies when you're talking about fun things," she laughs ironically, making Boom laugh too.

He gets to his feet and picks up his mug to take into the kitchen with him.

"I mean it. Thank you."

Louisa opens the front door to see him out.

Outside the flat, Feisty is slumped on the

stairwell, half asleep. She hears Louisa's front door go and jolts awake. She gets up, peering over the handrail, so she can see Louisa and Boom from the stairwell.

Boom holds his arms wide, inviting Louisa in for a hug. They hold each other close for what seems like an eternity before Boom gives her a gentle kiss on the cheek, telling her, "You're amazing. Thank you."

Feisty's face flares with jealousy as she watches them break away with a warm smile. Louisa stands there watching Boom walk back across the walkway to his flat before shutting his front door behind him.

Louisa shuts her front door.

In a fit of anger, Feisty punches the brick wall with her hand, hurting herself in the process. She yelps in pain as she grips her injured hand with her other hand, tears rolling down her face as she kicks the wall with her foot.

"Fuck you, Jamie Johnson! Fuck! You!"

65 WE'LL SEE ABOUT THAT, YOU MOTHER FUCKER!

Boom's still smiling as he enters the flat but stops as soon as he sees his mum at the table. She's got her head down and she's rocking back and forth in large, swinging movements.

"Mum!"

His mum looks up. Her whole face is black and blue. Oli must have beaten her badly for all the bruising to come out so quickly. She's about to say something, when her phone rings. It's Oli. She listens for a second before replying,

"I'll send him down now." She hangs up, turning to Boom to ask him, "Could you drop his work bag down to him? He's waiting in the car."

"What's he doing getting his work bag now? It's 3.30 in the morning?" he asks his mum, but when she doesn't answer, "Mum?!"

"I don't know. I don't care. Jamie. Please. Can you just do it?"

Boom nods, not wanting to upset his mum. He grabs Oli's bag and heads down the stairs and out into the car park, highly agitated and pulling at his hair, full of hate and loathing for his stepdad, but dreading the confrontation too.

As he leaves his flat, Boom doesn't notice Feisty stepping out onto the stairwell behind him where she's been waiting for him. She's limping slightly and still holding her hand. She pauses for a second, before deciding to follow him. As Boom heads out through the main door, in a highly anxious state, Feisty rushes him from behind, giving him a hard shove. Boom looks stunned and stands there motionless as she screams abuse at him.

"Fucking twats, the lot of you."

"What you talking about?!" Boom asks her, annoyed at the ambush.

"I saw you. With Louisa," she yells at him.

"So?"

"What d'you mean, *so*?! You slept with *me*!" Feisty shouts.

"What, so now I can't speak to another girl ever. Is that it?!" Boom replies, incredulous.

"That isn't what this is about and you know it," Feisty shouts at him. She shoves him hard, sending him flying backwards, and he hits the ground awkwardly, banging his elbow.

Feisty starts to cry, but they're angry tears too. Sad because she's hurting, angry because she's annoyed at herself for letting someone hurt her again.

"You were my first," she tells him, watching Boom's face as the information sinks in.

He tries to stand but Feisty shoves him back again, sending him flying backwards onto his behind. This time though, Boom's had enough.

Losing it 'cause he knows he's still got Oli to face, he shouts, "You think I've got time for this shit in my life?! Just fuck off!"

Boom gets to his feet but Feisty's not finished with him yet. She's about to give him another shove when Boom takes a step back, telling her, "You know what? I've done nothing but stick up for you. From the start. But they're all fucking right about you. You are just a crazy nutter. A fucking angry, bitter, *shitty* person!"

Completely destroyed by his words, Feisty stands with her head in her hands, sobbing, as Boom storms off to the car park, where Oli's waiting for him in his blue Toyota.

Boom strides up to the car and taps on the driver side window. Oli lowers the window, and clocks his work bag in Boom's hand.

"Stupid bitch forgot to give it to me."

"What did you just say?" It's the first time Boom has ever challenged Oli.

Oli finds it funny though and looks at Boom with a smirk on his face, repeating it again more loudly and more clearly, "I said, stupid bitch forgot to give it to me."

Boom looks at him in disgust and drops Oli's bag onto the pavement with a thud. There's a pause, just for a second, whilst Oli decides whether to jump out of the car and beat the crap out of Boom or not. But instead, he remains icily calm, telling Boom with a smirk,

"You never did have the balls to stand up to me, you gutless little shit."

Oli opens the driver door, picks up his bag and throws it onto the passenger seat before driving off at speed. Boom watches him leave, telling the back of Oli's disappearing car,

"We'll see about that, you Mother Fucker!"

Boom reaches behind his back for his rucksack and jangles the paint cans, checking they're all there.

And then he heads off in the direction of the Industrial Estate, followed at a distance by Feisty.

Back in the car park, the teenagers have all left. The only movement is from inside a car parked in the furthest point of the car park. The driver winds their window down by hand, a stiff, clumsy movement, and peers out after Boom and Feisty.

It's DC Brightly.

His eyes narrow and he starts to stroke his chin between his finger and thumb. A sure sign he's onto something. Following his hunch, he pulls the choke out and starts the engine.

Knowing exactly where he's heading.

66 TWO TIMING DIRTY CHEAT AND LIAR

A trainer'd foot (an adult one) grinds a cigarette butt into the ground. Dressed in jeans and t-shirt, it's DC Brightly in his undercover guise. He's parked off the junction opposite the train depot where Oli works.

Leaning back against his car, he waits and watches; stroking his chin. Brought here on a hunch.

His hunch pays off though when sure enough, Boom appears a minute later. Brightly watches as Boom crosses the road, looking back over his shoulder every few seconds to make sure no-one's around. Reaching the perimeter fence, Boom goes back to the same spot as the other day. He pushes the hole in the fence and climbs through, sprinting off in the direction of the giant train hanger.

Brightly hangs back, waiting for the second figure - the mysterious female he saw arguing with Boom earlier. Several seconds later, the girl (Feisty) comes sprinting across the road in a dark blue jacket, diving into the shadows as quickly as she can to keep herself hidden. She squats down in front of the stretch of fence that Boom climbed through, pushing at the wire until it loosens. She wriggles through but she's not quite gauged it right and her coat gets stuck on a sharp piece of wire. Panicking, she yanks at her coat to get herself free but manages to rip her jacket in the process, leaving behind a small piece of dark blue material.

Clearing the fence the other side, Feisty checks her hood is still over her face before sprinting off towards the train hanger, in the same direction as Boom.

Brightly crosses the road behind them and follows them through the gap in the fence.

Feisty slows down as she reaches the hanger. Convinced Boom's going to be inside, she panics, freezing to the spot when she sees him outside the hanger, standing in front of the entrance and painting something straight onto the giant sliding doors that lead into the hanger.

Terrified he's going to spot her, she dives behind a skip to the side of the hanger, piled high with planks of old track wood, sheets of plywood and old seats torn from the carriages. She pulls her phone from her pocket and checks it's on silent. She stands there for a minute or two, regulating her breathing before she relaxes, peering out from behind the skip to see what Boom is up to. He looks back over his shoulder, nervously. Aware he's taking a huge risk doing this on his own.

Feisty ducks back behind the skip and waits a second or two, before peering back out, looking to see what Boom's drawn on the hanger doors. Making sure its size does it justice, Boom has filled one of the hanger doors with Oli's face. It's still the outline of it for now, but the large, ugly, oversized features... they're all his. Feisty pulls out her phone and tries to film Boom, but she's too exposed.

Ducking back behind the rubbish, Feisty looks at the top of the skip, trying to work out how high it is and if she could pull herself up over the top of it to climb inside and use the rubbish to stand on and hide behind. Stuffing her phone into her pocket and zipping it up to make sure it doesn't fall out, Feisty picks up an old seat that's fallen from the top of the skip and uses it to stand on - giving herself the height she needs to climb safely into the skip. Pulling herself up onto the outer edge of the skip, she rests there for a second as she works out how to climb inside the skip without making any noise. Resting uncomfortably with her stomach pushed against the rim of the skip, Feisty slides along her stomach and reaches across diagonally to the outer rim the other side, grabbing the edges to hold herself steady before allowing her feet to drop silently into the skip.

As she drops down though, she accidentally knocks a piece of plywood, sending it falling to the bottom of the skip with a loud clanking noise. Boom looks up nervously. Feisty doesn't move, praying that Boom will just think it's an animal of some sort, making its way across the compound late at night. Keeping her eyes shut, she breathes a sigh of relief as she hears the shake of a can, and Boom spraying a new line, a new colour onto the door of the hanger.

Testing the rubbish with one foot to make sure it won't move, Feisty climbs onto one of the old seats, and grabs the outer rim of the skip to pull herself up onto the edge, to give herself something to rest on as she films Boom. Angling her phone until it's horizontal, she presses record, her eyes hard and icy. Whatever reason she's filming Boom for, it doesn't bode well.

Peering through the lens, Feisty watches as Boom fills Oli's ugly, giant face with colour. She carries on filming as Boom puts his can of paint down in front of him and studies Oli's face. Satisfied that he's made it large enough and ugly enough for all to see, Boom puts the can back in his bag and pulls out a can of black paint.

Giving it a long shake, he starts on the adjacent door, forming a word in giant black letters. He starts with a T, then a W and O. Feisty watches through the camera lens as a sentence takes shape.

TWO TIMING DIRTY CHEAT AND LIAR.

Boom steps back to admire his work. Feisty leans forward, trying to capture Boom's face but slips. She grabs the edge of the skip as one of the planks of wood she's standing on slips, dropping her down into a large hole by the side of the wood. She takes a minute to rebalance herself, making sure her feet are secure on a new plank of wood before letting go of her grip on the skip.

The wood is balanced at an angle though, so it's like resting on a precarious slide but she shifts from one foot to the other until she feels balanced again. Holding her phone horizontal in both hands, she opens Boom's Instagram page and brings up his Graffiti Boy profile.

"You think you can fuck with my feelings, well fuck you Jamie Johnson, I'm gonna fuck with you back!" she mutters to herself.

She clicks on the button to add a video, bringing up the one she's just filmed of Boom painting Oli on the side of the hanger. But Feisty hasn't noticed Boom leave the spot where he was standing to finish a cigarette. Taking his final drag, he walks towards her with the butt in one hand, clearing his throat as he chucks it - still lit - into the skip.

The butt hits Feisty on the side of her cheek,

making her jump. She drops her phone, which disappears down the large hole at the side of the wood, making a noise. Boom jumps. Now super nervy, he decides to get going, peering back over his shoulder constantly as he sprints back towards the hanger. He grabs his bag, stuffs the cans of paints inside, and legs it back to the front of the building where the hole in the fence is.

Feisty waits a couple of minutes until she's sure he's gone, then shifts her feet, leaning forward to grab the edge of the skip again to give herself something to hold on to so that she can grab one of the planks of wood and use it to fish about at the bottom of the skip to try and find her phone. She moves it around from side to side, but it's impossible in the dark.

"Damn it," she mutters to herself in the dark.

But she can't go home without her phone. It's her only form of communication, but more than that, it's got incriminating evidence on that could be tracked back to her.

Holding tight to the edge of the skip, she tries to lower herself further down into the hole to get some kind of gauge on how deep it is. But she lowers herself too far, and doesn't have the strength to pull herself back up again.

She manages to pull herself up far enough just to rest her head on the side of a plank, but then her hand slips and she falls backwards hitting her head on the side of the skip, knocking herself unconscious. Her body goes limp and she slumps to the bottom of the skip.

Brightly - who has been watching all along, hidden from sight - steps out of the dark and into the light of one of the security lights. Realising something is seriously wrong, he sprints towards the skip.

Minutes later, and Brightly is stood next to a waiting ambulance parked outside the depot entrance, empty but with its doors open and a light on in the back. The main gates to the depot are open now, giving a clear exit for the ambulance crew to get through on their return. He listens as a radio kicks in at the back of the ambulance, and the crew radio through details of Feisty's injuries to control.

"Caucasian girl, 14/15 years of age, unconscious with a blow to the head. No other obvious signs of trauma. We're on our way back to the ambulance now."

Seconds later and the ambulance crew - one male, one female - make their way through the gates to the waiting ambulance, with Feisty lying unconscious on a stretcher. Walking behind them is Oli's boss, depot manager Dave Field. The ambulance staff slide the stretcher onto the ambulance and secure the doors. The female crew member walks around to the front of the ambulance and starts the engine, waiting for her colleague to join her. But first he makes his way over to Brightly, handing him a badly smashed up phone. It's Feisty's, damaged in the fall.

"Not sure if you can do anything with this or not. Found it at the bottom of the skip where she was," he tells Brightly, tipping his head in the direction of Feisty.

Brightly nods. "Thanks."

Dave looks at Brightly. "You think it could be evidence?"

"Depends what's on there," Brightly replies.

The ambulance man pulls a piece of paper from his pocket, scribbles his number on it and hands it to Brightly.

"That's my number if you need it. We should know more when we get to hospital."

Brightly and Field stand side by side, watching as the ambulance drives off. Then, without a word to Field, Brightly starts to skirt the fence looking for the point of entry - the hole in the fence where Boom and Feisty climbed through earlier. Bending down, he pushes the fence, loosening the wire where the hole's been cut and pushed back into place. Putting on a pair of latex gloves, he runs his finger around the edge of the hole until he finds what he is looking for. A tiny piece of dark blue material stuck to the fence, torn from Feisty's coat when she got stuck. Lifting it off the fence, Brightly reaches into his pocket for an evidence bag, places the material inside and seals it.

67 GOOD LUCK WITH THAT!

Back at the police depot, a technician is working late in the workshop. He stands in front of the kettle, yawning, as he waits for it to boil. Behind him, the remnants of a laptop are spread out over the counter top where he's been working. There's pieces everywhere, but each of them laid out in a methodical manner.

He looks up as Brightly walks in.

"You're working late," he comments.

"Could say the same about you," Brightly replies. "Any luck with the footage?"

The technician shakes his head. "Fraid not. Couldn't see their face."

"Damn it," Brightly says, before pulling Feisty's badly smashed up phone from an evidence bag in his coat pocket. He hands it to the technician.

"I need to find out who this belongs to and if there's anything salvageable on it. Photos, videos, anything on social media, text messages. That kind of thing. As soon as you can."

The technician takes one look at the phone before replying, "Good luck with that!"

Brightly shrugs, still hopeful. "This one's priority."

"Add it to the pile," the technician says, yawning wearily.

Brightly drops the nice approach. "Anyone got a problem with it, speak to the boss."

The technician is too tired to argue and turns his

back on Brightly, walking over to the kettle to make himself a coffee.

68 HAVE YOU ANY IDEA WHAT YOUR DAUGHTER WAS DOING AT THE TRAIN DEPOT, MR HAVARA?

Brightly walks into a dark, open plan office. He switches his computer on, and is about to turn the lights on, when his mobile goes. He picks up, listening for a second before replying, "Tell him to wait. I'll be there as soon as I can."

He hangs up, turns his computer off, and heads outside to the car park. It's late and it's cold, and his knackered old car doesn't have any heating, other than a couple of fans that just about manage to blow out warm air after a long run of at least half an hour or so. Grumpy and cold, Brightly jumps in his car, shivering, and hunches his body up over the wheel in an attempt to generate some heat, before heading off through town and up the main hill towards the hospital.

Brightly pulls into the hospital and parks in one of the drop off bays, throwing some police ID onto the ledge in front of the main windscreen, just in case. Walking through the main entrance, he takes the lift to the second floor, where he heads for Jenner ward. He arrives, flashing his badge at the two female staff behind the desk who are entering data onto the computer. Expecting him, they nod, and point him in the direction of a side room at the end of the corridor.

"Room 113, at the end," the sister tells him.

"Thanks," Brightly replies, in a habitual manner without much warmth.

Too tired to be bothered to be friendly to someone who can't be friendly with her, the sister carries on working, not bothering to look up as she tells Brightly, "Her dad's in there with her now."

Brightly's about to repeat another thank you but with the sister already typing away at her computer he carries on walking. The sister, and nursing staff next to her, wait until he's halfway down the corridor before they look at each other and roll their eyes.

Brightly walks into a side room, where Feisty is asleep on the bed. She has a drip in her arm, and she's connected to a machine monitoring her heartbeat. Her dad's sat on a chair next to her, head down, busy on his phone so it takes a second for him to notice Brightly.

"DC Brightly, British Transport Police. How's she doing, Mr Havara?"

Feisty's dad looks up, taking Brightly in as he flashes his badge. "She's heavily sedated at the moment so she's sleeping a lot. She's in quite a lot of pain."

Brightly hasn't got time to waste though and with the pleasantries out of the way, he gets straight to the point.

"Have you any idea what your daughter was doing at the train depot, Mr Havara?"

"No. I don't see that much of her at the moment. Me and her mum split up a few months ago, and I've got a… (he looks awkward)... young baby. It's all a bit tricky at the moment."

Brightly doesn't comment, but continues with the questions.

"So was she staying with you last night, or your wife?"

"My wife."

"Any chance I could speak to your youngest daughter? Summer, isn't it?"

Feisty's dad's guard goes up, registering the fact the detective has already done some homework on his family already.

"Probably best if you leave it to the morning detective. It's still the early hours and I'd rather let her rest for a bit. She was a bit shaken when she saw her sister earlier. I'll call you when she wakes up."

Brightly nods. He's about to leave the room when he spots Feisty's coat hanging on a chair at the back of the room. The same dark blue coat she was wearing when she broke into the depot. His police-trained eyes spot the rip on the arm, but his face doesn't give anything away.

"Would you mind if I borrowed your daughter's coat, Mr Havara?"

Now Feisty's dad really does look suspicious.

"What d'you want her coat for?" he asks, his defences well and truly up now. "I mean, I know she's been in trouble at school," he adds, "but it's never for anything serious." There's a pause, before he adds, "What is this *really* about, detective Brightly?"

"We just need to rule her out of our investigations, that's all Mr Havara."

"Investigations for what?" Feisty's dad asks.

"I'm afraid I'm not at liberty to say," Brightly replies, with a curt smile.

Feisty's dad reaches for Feisty's coat and hands it to Brightly. Worried, he watches the detective leave.

69 DOES YOUR SISTER LIKE GRAFFITI, SUMMER?

It's 7.00 a.m. and the streets are quiet. Brightly pulls up outside Feisty's house in his beaten-up Citroen. He gets out, his face frozen in his usual expression. He's had hardly any sleep, so he's already tired and not in the best of moods.

He walks up to the front door and knocks, waiting for it to open before flashing his badge at a shocked Summer.

"Summer Havara?"

Summer gives Brightly a suspicious look. She nods silently. There's no way she's going to volunteer anything to a cop unless he prises it out of her.

"DC Brightly, British Transport Police," he says, as Summer lets him in. "Did your dad tell you I was coming?"

"No. He's coming over in a bit."

"Hmm," Brightly replies. "Is your mum in?"

Summer nods, leading him down the corridor and into the kitchen where her mum is sat at the table in her dressing gown and slippers.

She looks up, her face blank and her mood low. She seems absent, like her head's anywhere but in the room. Quite clearly depressed.

Summer's aware of it, making sure her mum knows who Brightly is. "Mum. This is Constable Brightly. He wants to ask some questions about Mercedes."

"*Detective* Constable, Mrs Havara," Brightly

says, leaning forward to shake her hand and making the point he's a detective.

Summer's mum shakes his hand vacantly before sitting back again, staring at a spot on the wall in front of her.

"Mum!" Summer tries again, louder this time.

She looks up. "Sorry detective," she says. "What is it you want to know?"

Brightly knows he could play on her vacant demeanour if he wanted to but to do this properly, he has to do it by the book. "Mrs Havara. Are you ok if I ask your daughter some questions?"

Summer's mum doesn't respond straight away, so Brightly repeats his question, a little louder this time. "Mrs Havara. I need to ask your daughter some questions. Are you ok with that?"

She gives him a vacant, empty stare but nods her head slowly. Summer, who's stood behind her mum, gives the detective a fake smile as he turns to face her. He pulls his notebook out of his pocket and just to unnerve her, starts to make notes before beginning his questions. He stops scribbling after a few seconds or so and looks up at Summer.

"Would you say you and your sister are close, Summer?" Brightly asks.

Summer nods. But Brightly's not letting her get away with it. Not now he's got the mum's permission.

"Sorry? You'll need to respond I'm afraid, not just nod. So that I can make a note of your responses," he tells her.

Summer glares at him, a little bit of Feisty

coming through in her attitude. "Yes, Constable, I would."

Brightly looks at her and forces a smile, knowing exactly what she just did there, omitting the word 'detective' again. But he knows how to knock any smugness out of her and goes straight for the kill. "What about graffiti, Summer. Does your sister like graffiti?"

Summer drops her bravado in an instant and she feels her face flush a deep red. She tries to shrug off his question, but when she sees he's still looking at her, waiting for her reply, she tells him, "She likes art, detective."

"Some people don't think of it as art, Summer," Brightly replies coolly. "Some people think of graffiti as an act of vandalism." Continuing, "It's important you tell me everything you know Summer. Otherwise, Mercedes could get herself into all kinds of unnecessary trouble for something that doesn't even have anything to do with her."

He trails off, waiting for Summer to speak, but she remains silent. He waits for what feels like an uncomfortable amount of time before slipping his hand into his pocket and pulling out a card with his number on. "Here's my number if you think of anything."

Brightly turns towards the door. "I'll let myself out," he says, before nodding at Summer's mum, "Mrs Havara." He doesn't wait for a response and heads out of the kitchen towards the front door.

Summer stares after him, her gut telling her it won't be long before she sees him again.

70 MR ELUSIVE HIMSELF

Flash is sat on a low wall just in front of the car park facing his tower block. He's in school uniform, waiting for Boom. He's tired and he's pissy, and he's got a bone to pick with his best mate.

Boom stumbles out of the entrance, emotionally drained - and just tired of his life. But before he can even take a step forward, Flash has hijacked him. Stepping into his personal space to piss him off.

"Where was you last night, then?" he asks Boom, in a pissy voice.

Boom tries to shrug him off.

"Blow us out for Feisty again, did ya?"

"I wasn't with Feisty," Boom replies.

"Then where was you?!" Flash asks.

Boom doesn't answer. Giving up, but clearly pissed off with his mate, Flash walks off ahead. Boom follows behind, in silence, his face troubled. Lost in thought, his fingers tug at his hair as he walks.

Back at school, Britton keeps his eye on the playground from the confines of his classroom, hugging a hot mug of coffee in both hands and taking the occasional sip as he peers through the window, his eyes flitting from one student to the next.

He spots The Watcher and The Cat standing on top of a length of wall.

The two friends are standing in a companionable silence, waiting for Flash and Boom to appear. Without a word, The Cat flips straight up into a handstand and without falling off, walks the entire length of wall, feet in the air, like a gymnast.

"Get down will ya?!" The Watcher tells him urgently.

"What's your problem?" The Cat counteracts back, but The Watcher just shakes his head.

"You're drawing attention to us. That's my problem," he replies, tipping his head towards the classroom where Britton's stood at the window watching them. The Cat flips back onto his feet just as Flash and Boom walk through the school gates.

"Mr Elusive himself," The Cat comments to Boom, clearly pissed off with him for something. He's just about to walk over to him, when Curl cuts in from nowhere, shoving his phone under Boom's nose, forcing him to take a look at something. The Cat and The Watcher stride over, keen to hear what Curl has to say to Boom.

"You're still alive then," Curl says, super arsey to Boom. "Well, just in case you was wondering, cops nearly got us last night. No thanks to you though, we got away. But I'm sure Flash has told you all about it already. Just in case you give a shit."

Flash shakes his head, super quiet for once.

"Why's that my fault?!" Boom asks Curl defensively.

"Because in case you'd forgotten, it was supposed to be us two doing the piece last night. Took too long, just me. Broke the first rule of writers. Overstayed our welcome..."

"Something came up. I couldn't make it," Boom

replies, keeping it vague.

"What? This you mean?!" Curl asks, hitting play on the video that's lined up on his phone, which he's still got shoved up under Boom's face.

The Crew watch as Boom's revenge piece from last night flashes up on Graffiti Boy's Insta page. Flash takes one look at the 250,000 views and can barely contain his shock.

"250,000! No way! Fuck!"

"Yeah, turns out wonder boy here's got quite a following," Curl replies sarcastically. "Guess that's why he don't want to hang with his mates no more!"

"That's not it. And you can fuck off calling me wonder boy too," Boom tells him as the video continues to play.

Filmed by the Lord Protector pub, it's the green and pink snake he painted, with the words to Eminem's Lose Yourself written along its scales and below it, the words, 'Never let Lyrics come between old mates.'

"Kind of ironic, don't you think? Wonder Boy," Curl asks, piling on the sarcasm. "Cause I always thought your mates were important to you. But obviously, Feisty's more important to you now!"

"I thought you said you weren't with Feisty last night!" Flash jumps in, annoyed.

"I wasn't!" Boom replies, getting more and more agitated.

But Curl's angry and still hasn't forgiven Boom for their near miss with the cops last night. "So let me get this straight. Are you saying you wasn't with her before or after The Protector, or you wasn't with her before or after the train depot?"

"What?!" Boom looks shocked.

"I said, are you saying--?" Curls starts again, but Boom interrupts him.

"You said the train depot."

Curl shakes his head, not believing Boom doesn't know what he's talking about.

"You know she's in hospital, right?" he asks. But one look at Boom's face is enough to tell him he really doesn't know what he's talking about.

"Fell into a skip apparently," Curl continues, "knocked herself unconscious. Ambulance crew took her in. Still there now."

"Shit!" Boom's face has gone pale.

Flash looks at him. "You didn't know?"

Boom shakes his head. "I didn't know she'd gone to the depot. She must have followed me there," adding, "Fuck. What was she doing?"

Flash looks concerned for his mate now, all traces of anger gone.

"Filming you?"

"Fuck, I hope not," Boom replies. "I've checked the page. There's nothing on there," he tells the group.

"What were you doing there anyway?" The Watcher asks him. "And why the fuck didn't you get one of us to come with you. We could've been a look out for you."

Boom shrugs. "I didn't want to drag you into my shit."

The Watcher's just about to push him for more, when Flash remembers something.

"Shit. Bro. I meant to tell you. Someone called

the ambulance crew. I thought it was you."

"Shit." Boom looks anxious. Aware that someone could be on to him - but who? Brightly? He starts to tug at strands of his hair. The Crew watch him in shock for a second or two before Boom slopes off in the direction of the school.

71 WHAT THE FUCK HAVE YOU DONE JAMIE?!

Standing in front of the cubicles in the boy's toilet, in front of a long length of mirror, Boom stares at his reflection. His face serious.

Pulling his mobile from his pocket, he clicks on his Insta page, and pulls up the Lyrics video from last night. The total number of views has already gone up, in just a few minutes, in the time it took for Boom to walk into school, go to the toilet and step out to wash his hands.

Boom looks at the number, now totalling 286,000.

He looks up, staring at his face in the mirror, as he asks himself,

"What the fuck have you done, Jamie?! What the fuck have you done?!"

72 SO ARE YOU GOING TO TELL ME WHAT'S GOING ON, JAMIE?

Flash, Boom and the rest of the class are sat at their desks, diving to catch their homework books as Britton frisbees them back to each student in turn.

He throws one to a girl in the front row, then Flash, who has to dive forward over his desk to stop his book missing the table.

"Again Adam," Britton tells Flash, who rolls his eyes and sighs.

"Don't sigh, Mr Pritchard," Britton tells him. "If you did it properly the first time then I wouldn't have to ask you to do it again." Britton is clearly frustrated, but years of being a teacher has taught him not to take things too personally. He chucks the next book at Ali.

"As for you, Mr Ali," Britton quips in a weary voice, "You've been at school long enough to know that one sentence does not count for homework. I want five pages from you by the morning!"

"Oh what?!" Ali replies with attitude.

"That's *six* pages by the morning please Mr Ali!" Britton tells him, before asking him, "Anything else you want to add to that?"

Ali shakes his head, scowling at him.

The bells goes and the class bundles out. There's one more book left on Britton's desk… Boom's. Open halfway through, on a page where he has sketched some graffiti letters, SOTF (sins of the father, Boom's piece he did for Feisty to get back at her dad).

Boom clocks it as he approaches Britton's desk, and he stops in his tracks as Britton asks, "So are you going to tell me what's going on, Jamie?!"

Boom thinks the game is up. He stays silent as Britton flicks through his book, waiting for Britton to stop on another page where he's sketched some other graffiti. But Britton skims past them. Boom tries to hide his frown, puzzled. Britton flicks back a few more pages, then stops, checking the date before telling Boom,

"Six weeks ago. A+," Britton carries on flicking through his book. "A week later, another A+. Week after that, an A-. Still good." Britton flicks through to the last few weeks of work. "Two weeks ago, a C. Last week, D. This week, not even a pass. What's going on, Jamie?"

Boom shrugs.

"Is everything ok at home?" Britton asks him.

Boom looks worried. "Yeah, why?!" he replies, defensively.

"Because usually when an exceptional student starts dropping grades all of a sudden it's a sign there's something else going on in their lives," Britton tells him. "And it's normally something to do with home."

He looks at Boom, waiting for an answer, but Boom stands staring at his feet. Britton waits a few more seconds for Boom to reply, before telling him, "I can't be seen to be making exceptions for you, Jamie."

"Then don't," Boom replies.

Britton sighs. Giving up, he hands Boom his book back, telling him, "I want the last piece of homework back on my desk first thing tomorrow."

Now it's Boom's turn to sigh. He stuffs his book back into his rucksack and heads outside.

73 WHO THE FUCK IS BRIGHTLY, AND WHAT DID YOU DO TO MY SISTER?!

Flash and Boom are walking the usual route home after school, in silence for once as Boom walks with his head down, deep in thought.

He looks up suddenly, telling Flash, "I need to go and see Summer."

"Who's Summer?"

"Feisty's sister."

"I'll come with," Flash tells him.

"It's ok. I don't want you caught up in all my shit. The less you know the better."

Flash ignores him. "I don't know what you were doing and I don't care. I won't ask. I'm just coming for moral support, ok?"

Boom shrugs, leading the way to Feisty's house.

Reaching Feisty's house, Boom gives a quick glance over his shoulder to check the coast is clear before heading up the path to Feisty's front door. Flash takes a step back, watching as Boom gives the door a gentle tap, using the same rhythmic pattern they always use.

"Bro, I thought that was special to us," Flash quips, breaking the ice and making Boom laugh with a bit of banter.

They stand there for a second or two before they hear footsteps and Summer opens the door. She's in her pyjamas.

She takes a second to process who it is before lunging at Boom, shouting,

"Who the fuck is Brightly, and what did you do to my sister?!"

Boom throws his hands up in defence.

"Nothing! I didn't even know she was there!" He tries to calm things down as he introduces Flash. "This is my mate Flash. Feisty knows him. He's part of the crew."

Summer glares at them and is about to shut the door on them both when Boom gets in first, and sticks his foot in the doorway to block her.

"How is she?"

"Conscious," Summer tells him, sarcastically.

"I swear. I didn't know she was there," Boom tells her.

Summer stares at Boom, trying to work out if he's telling the truth or not. There's a beat, before she asks, "She films you, doesn't she?"

"Was she filming me then?" Boom asks her.

Summer shrugs. "Dunno."

"Have you asked her?" Boom asks.

"I haven't been able to talk to her. She's been out of it on medication," Summer tells him.

"Have the cops been round?" Boom asks. The big million-dollar question.

Summer nods, and Boom bites his lip, worried.

"Who was it? Did they give you a name?"

Summer nods. "Yeah. Brightly. DC Brightly. Right sarcastic twat."

Boom starts picking at his hair with his hand.

"What d'you tell him?"

"Nothing! I'm not that stupid!"

Boom starts to pace the path in front of her,

getting more and more anxious.

"I'm not saying you are," Boom tells her, "I just need to know what they know."

Boom's eyes are wide, like a startled animal. Bringing himself out of his thoughts, he tells Summer, "I've gotta go. But do me a favour. Let me know if he comes back. And tell Mercedes I hope she's ok."

And with that he turns on his heels and heads back down the path at a pace, followed by Flash, leaving Summer wondering how much Boom knows.

74 I JUST WANTED TO CATCH YOU. SEE IF YOU'D HEARD ABOUT LUNAR

Drained from all the worry, Boom reaches the top of the stairs by his flat, Flash by his side. He's about to head inside when he hears a 'psst!' from behind.

It's Louisa, with her head poking out of her front door, waiting for him. He walks over with Flash in tow. She smiles at Flash, takes one look at Boom's face and gives him a big hug.

"You look like shit. You ok?"

Boom laughs. "No. But I will be. I hope."

"I just wanted to catch you. See if you'd heard about Lunar," she says.

Boom shakes his head, not sure if he wants to know.

"Got three years. Conspiracy to cause criminal damage."

"Three years?! Fuck!"

There's a noise from the living room and Louisa looks back quickly to see what it was.

"I better go. Text me later."

Louisa shuts the door behind her.

Flash takes one look at his mate, and says,

"Leave the trains, bro. Whatever you're doing it for. It's not worth it."

Boom gives his mate a friendly slap on the arm, thanking him for the warning.

"It's ok. I'd already decided that. Pretty much straight after I found out about Feisty falling into the skip."

They bump fists and Flash hurtles up the stairs, looking back over his shoulder to shout, "Laters" to his mate.

75 HE'S NOT HERE

Boom lets himself into his flat, tensing as he enters. His mum is sat at the table, staring at the charred thumbnail-sized photo of her husband, the one Oli nearly destroyed after the fight with his neighbour. Weirdly though, she's not trying to hide the photo. Instead she holds it gently in one hand, stroking it with a finger and smiling.

Boom's eyes dart round the kitchen and along the corridor, looking for signs of Oli.

His mum smiles at him, unusually relaxed and calm. Happy almost.

"He's not here," she tells him, shaking her head to herself, a relaxed smile on her face.

Boom looks at her, confused, trying to work out what's going on. She's still holding the photo in her hand, which is starting to stress him out.

"What you doing? He'll go nuts if he sees it."

His mum looks at him, tears welling up in her eyes as she smiles. "He's not coming back."

"What d'you mean he's not coming back? Mum, what have you done?" and for a horrible minute, Boom thinks his mum might have done something to Oli.

She laughs.

"Believe me, I'd have done that years ago if I was going to. He's gone. Left me for someone at work, apparently," and starts laughing. She starts to lose it completely, struggling to get the words out because she's laughing so much, "Anyone else would be gutted if their husband left them for someone at work, but I couldn't be happier!"

And then Boom starts laughing too, and rushes over to hug his mum, wriggling free for a second to ask,

"Are you sure? You're absolutely sure?"

"Absolutely," she laughs. "Told me I was a fat bitch who'd let herself go and that he was leaving me for this woman at work who was much prettier, much slimmer than me. And you know what? I don't fucking care! I've never been so happy in all my life!"

"Mum!" Boom laughs, shocked at hearing his mum swear for the first time in a long time.

She looks at him laughing, swearing even more now that she can. Making Boom laugh. Ecstatically happy, she shouts,

"I don't give a flying fuck! He can think I'm a fat, ugly cow for all I care. I'm free!"

The pair of them stand there hugging in the middle of the kitchen, swaying from side to side, laughing and hanging on to each other as tight as they can, as Boom's mum shouts over and over, "We're free! We're free! *We're free!*"

76 WHAT YOU SO HAPPY ABOUT? HAS IT GOT SOMETHING TO DO WITH THAT LOUISA CHICK?

Boom heads out for the night to meet the rest of the crew, passing his mum in the kitchen, who's stood by the front door, smiling, as a locksmith changes the locks. The guy drills the last screw into a new double-bolted lock and checks it's on properly before handing Boom and his mum a new set of keys each, telling them,

"The gold one does the main bolt and the long silver one does the chubb lock at the bottom."

"Thank you," Boom's mum tells him. "You have no idea how much this means to us."

The guy smiles at her, placing his bill on the kitchen counter. "It's got the payment details on there, as well as my contact details. Any problems, just call me."

He heads out, leaving Boom alone with his mum. Holding his keys in his hands, Boom checks in with his mum.

"Are you sure you're ok me going out? I can stay in if you want."

His mum smiles. She leans forward and gives him a kiss on the forehead.

"I'm fine. I'm actually looking forward to having some time on my own for the first time in years."

Boom smiles at her. "I love you."

"I love you too," she replies.

As he shuts the front door behind him, Boom's mum sits down at the table on her own and starts to cry, a mixture of regret and relief.

The Crew are at the basketball courts where Boom and Flash meet, huddled under a broken street lamp, waiting for Boom. The court is only half lit, surrounded by tower blocks looming into the night sky all around it.

The Watcher stands over them, keeping watch, as Curl shows the others his sketch, using the light on his phone. The only other person stood up is The Cat - as active as ever, bouncing a ball back and forth between his legs before slamming it into a basketball net. He races back to the start and does it all again, loop after loop. The Cat slam dunks the ball into the net and saunters over to the Crew, grinning.

"Haven't you dumbarses come up with anything yet?" he asks, laughing.

Flash knocks the ball from his hand and hurls it at him. The Cat makes a sound like a whizzing bullet before catapulting backwards into a flip - like a scene from The Matrix - making sure he dodges the ball as it spins towards him. The ball misses him by inches and The Cat lands back on his feet laughing, giving Flash a very smug-looking bird in the process.

"Too slow, mother fucker!"

The rest of the Crew - including The Watcher - are too busy laughing to notice someone step out of the shadows and grab The Watcher from behind, making him shout out in shock.

"Woahh! What the fuck?!"

He spins round to find Boom standing there in

front of him, laughing. He looks in high spirits.

"Losing your touch bro!" he laughs, ribbing The Watcher.

"Where'd the fuck you come from?" The Watcher asks him. "You literally came from nowhere!"

Boom nods at a hole in the corner of the fence and laughs. He's literally buzzing with fun and energy. Flash looks at him like he can't quite work out what's going on, studying Boom's face in detail as he tries to work out why he's so happy. It's been a long time since he's seen him like this.

"What you so happy about?" he asks him. "Has it got something to do with that Louisa chick?"

"Who's Louisa?! How'd I miss that?" The Watcher asks.

"We're just mates!" Boom laughs, but grins at Flash, before adding, "Unlike lover boy here, who still hasn't worked out how to get his end away with Nic-ooooole!", waving his arms in the air and reliving the moment when Flash fell off the wall.

Flash laughs, giving Boom a slug in the belly.

There's a beat, and Boom pulls a piece of paper from his jeans and throws it into Curl's lap. Curl catches it and unfolds it so the rest of the Crew can see it. Boom has sketched a saying which Curl reads out loud for all to hear.

"Just when the caterpillar thought the world was over, it became a butterfly," giving Boom a cheeky grin as he adds, "Bit deep for you, 'aint it?!"

"Bit gay you mean!" The Watcher quips, making Flash laugh, and earning them both a slap in the gut. Boom gives a casual shrug.

"Sums up how I feel right now."

"What, gay?" The Watcher jumps in, quick as a flash.

The rest of the Crew laugh, enjoying the moment, as Flash studies Boom's face from the side, thrown by the new 'happy' Boom.

77 IT'S NOT CONCLUSIVE, BUT I'D SAY JUDGING BY THEIR BUILD AND HEIGHT, AND THE WAY THAT THEY MOVE, IT'S THE SAME PERSON

Brightly's sat with the technician, who's got some CCTV images frozen on a computer screen in front of them. They're the same clips Brightly looked at before, but this time the technician's managed to zoom in closer. The images are of Boom outside his flat, the train depot and the pub where he saw Oli kissing Paula. You still can't make out his face but the technician has put some kind of measurement on the screen next to the pictures and is studying the person's movement.

"It's not conclusive, but I'd say judging by their build and height, and the way that they move, it's the same person," he tells Brightly.

He gets up off his seat, and in a much more upbeat voice tells Brightly, "But what I *do* have is a match for the coat."

He walks over to the counter top and picks up Feisty's coat, along with the piece of material still sealed inside the evidence bag.

He hands it back to Brightly, with a print-out showing the exact same pattern on both pieces of cloth.

"Which means," the technician tells Brightly, "whoever is the owner of this coat was the person filming at the train depot the other night. Which must also mean, they probably know the identity of Graffiti Boy here."

Brightly punches his fist in the air, in triumph.

"Thanks," he tells the technician, getting up out of his seat and putting his coat on, as he heads out the door - his prey in sight.

78 WHAT WAS THAT LOOK? THE OTHER DAY, WHEN I ASKED YOU IF FEISTY LIKED GRAFFITI?

Summer is sat at the kitchen table next to her mum, eating her dinner in silence. There's a knock at the door, and Summer looks up.

"Go away!" she mutters to herself, but sighs as whoever it is knocks again.

Annoyed, she gets up out of her seat and walks down the hallway to the front door in her pyjamas. She opens the door only to find Brightly stood in front of her, flashing his badge and a smug-looking smile.

"Can I come in?"

"Sure," she replies, barely able to hide her feelings about him this time.

Summer leads Brightly down the hallway and back into the kitchen, where her mum is sat at the table spooning a tiny amount of food into her mouth in an attempt to eat.

Brightly nods at her, "Mrs Havara", before tipping his head towards an empty chair at the table and asking, "D'you mind?" But before she gets a chance to answer, he sits down next to them, sandwiched awkwardly between them both but looking like he doesn't give a fuck.

This time, he gets straight to the point. He puts Feisty's coat on the table directly in front of Summer, pointing out the tear in the arm. "See that? It was torn climbing through a fence."

"And?" Summer replies, trying to play it down,

but it's obvious from her face that she's panicking.

Brightly's in his element. Reeling her in - knowing full well he has his kill in sight.

"It's Mercedes's coat, isn't it?"

Summer looks down at her lap as Brightly continues, watching her face closely for a reaction.

"The tear in the arm matches a piece of material we found stuck to the fence at the train depot. It's now being used as evidence."

Summer doesn't speak.

Brightly pauses for a few seconds, enjoying the awkwardness of the moment. He leans in towards Summer, continuing,

"That and the coat form two pieces of evidence linking your sister directly to a crime scene, Summer. So if you don't want her to go down for this, you better start talking."

For all her bravado, Summer's still quite young and as tough as she's trying to make out she is, she's not able to handle the pressure. She bursts into tears.

Brightly looks at her, pushing forward without an ounce of sympathy. "What was that look? The other day, when I asked you if Mercedes liked graffiti?"

Summer cracks. "It's not her. She doesn't do it. It's someone else."

"Who then?" Brightly asks.

"I've only met him once. He goes by the name of Boomshakalaka," Summer tells him. "Boom for short."

"Boom?"

Summer nods, watching as Brightly scribbles it in his notepad.

"Think you'd recognise him if you met him again?" Brightly asks.

Summer screws up her face, then nods, slowly. Reluctant to get involved, but knowing it's now inevitable.

Minutes later, Brightly walks back down Feisty's drive carrying her coat. He climbs into the front seat of his car, calling Meadows on his mobile,

"We're onto something Sarge. Can you ask the lads to talk to the feds and see if they've noticed any local graffiti with *Boom* in the signature? Local council might be able to help too." There's a pause before Brightly adds, "She's met him. Doesn't know his real name though but we should be able to get a photo ID by tomorrow."

He waits a second while Meadows says something before telling him, "Boom. As in explosion. Short for Boomshakalaka. Yes Sarge, I'm heading back now. See you shortly."

And with that he starts the engine and pulls out into the road, heading straight back to the police station where his boss is waiting for him.

79 IT'S RISKY. HE'S GOT A BIT OF A TEMPER, BUT IF YOU THINK IT'LL WORK, YEAH, WHY NOT? JUST BE CAREFUL

Brightly's sat at his desk, next to Meadows, watching the CCTV footage of Boom kicking the can in anger after spotting Oli kissing Paula.

Unbeknown to him, the two ginger-haired cops are stood behind him, taking the piss, stroking their chins between their fingers and thumbs, mimicking Brightly as he stares at the screen, thinking.

Brightly pauses the footage just after Boom kicks the can.

"Are you one hundred percent sure about this?" Meadows asks him.

Brightly nods. "It'll get exactly the reaction we're after."

"Hmm," Meadows replies, pausing for a second before continuing. "It's risky. He's got a bit of a temper, but if you think it'll work, yeah, why not? Just be careful."

"He doesn't scare me," Brightly replies with an arrogant, confident tone.

80 HOW WELL D'YOU THINK YOU KNOW YOUR NEW BOYFRIEND, MRS…?

Brightly walks up a front path leading to a terraced house. He knocks, and Paula opens the door. Brightly flashes his badge at her, setting her off in a panic.

"Has something happened--?" she asks, but Brightly's pre-empted her question already.

"Don't worry, everyone's fine, Mrs… " he trails off, waiting for her to fill in the gap with her married name (even though he knows it). But Paula replies, "So, why are you here?"

"DC Brightly, British Transport Police," Brightly says, introducing himself. "I'm here about the graffiti that was done about your new boyfriend," he tells her, pausing to emphasise the word 'boyfriend'.

Brightly's looking for a reaction, goading her by referring to Oli as her 'new boyfriend'.

"Do you know who did it?" she asks, but Brightly doesn't answer, replying instead with a question.

"How well d'you think you know your new boyfriend, Mrs…?"

He's doing it again. Rubbing salt in the wound, looking for a reaction.

"I know there's some stuff going on at home to do with his wife and son…" she trails off, not wanting to use the words 'domestic violence'.

"I don't think it's his wife, Mrs..." Brightly trails off, looking at Paula. "Your new boyfriend's got quite a nasty temper on him as it goes. Neighbours call the cops out on a regular basis. Beat the shit out of one of them, a couple of weeks ago. Broke some ribs, kicked him in the head with his work boots. The neighbour was too scared to report it though, so he got away with it." Watching her face closely, he adds, "Again."

Brightly turns on his heels, shouting back over his shoulder, "Like I said. How well d'you actually know your new boyfriend?"

Paula stands on the doorstep shocked, watching as Brightly climbs into his car and drives off.

81 I NEED YOUR HELP. I'VE DONE SOMETHING REALLY STUPID

Paula is sat on reception at the train depot, with the phone pressed between her neck and ear, taking a message. She scribbles it down on a post-it note and waits for the caller to finish what they're saying before telling them,

"Yep, yep, I will. Thanks for calling."

She walks into her boss's office with the message. Dave is on the phone and signals for her to take a seat for a second. He finishes the call, hanging up as she sticks the post-it note under his nose.

"That's the number for the quote. I said you'd call them back this morning."

Dave smiles at her. "Thanks. Can you do me a favour? I need to speak to Oli about something. Can you walk over there for me and let him know?"

Paula looks nervous. "Sure."

Making her way across the train tracks towards the hanger, Paula spots an argument outside the huge sliding entrance. Oli's got the young apprentice pinned up against the wall by his neck, while the other two track workers stand there, too shocked to move.

Her instinct is to run towards the hanger but like the others, she's frozen to the spot with fear. Oli is terrifying. He shouts abuse in the young apprentice's face - not caring how young the lad is or how scared he is.

"I'm gonna fucking kill you, you little prick! What the fuck did you think you were playing at with your latest little stunt?!"

Oli slams his fist into the young boy's stomach, making him retch.

It's enough to kick start the two track workers out of their stunned silence and they race forward at the same time and pull Oli off the young lad. But it takes both their strength to yank Oli off, as he launches blow after furious blow into the lad's stomach.

Paula looks terrified, holding her hand over her mouth to stop herself from making a noise. She shuts her eyes, unable to watch any more, but still forced to listen as one of the track workers shouts at Oli to try and calm him down,

"Just leave him alone for fuck's sake. I keep telling you, it's not him."

Somehow they manage to pull Oli off of the apprentice, the older of the two track workers yelling at him.

"Get out of here. Now. And don't come back until you've calmed down."

Paula opens her eyes, catching Oli's eye as he walks past. She stands there, stunned, as the apprentice leans forward, his hands on his knees, retching. He retches a couple more times before throwing up, fear and adrenalin pumping out of his body in a huge, projectile vomit.

Paula can't watch any more. Feeling faint, she leans against a shed. She pulls out her mobile and dials. Someone picks up, and she tells them,

"I need your help. I've done something really stupid."

82 I'D LIKE YOU TO LEAVE NOW

Paula is stood in the living room, her curtains drawn despite the searing daylight outside. She's with her brother - a bulked-up man with a 'no messing' kind of look on his face. Someone who isn't going to let someone like Oli intimidate him or his sister. His presence still isn't enough to calm Paula down though. She paces the carpet next to him, absolutely petrified at the thought of having to face Oli when he gets back. Every few seconds she pulls the curtains back the tiniest of amounts to stay hidden while she looks out for him.

"It doesn't matter how many times you look. He's still not there," her brother says.

"You didn't see it. It was really scary, Col," she tells him. "He didn't give a shit we were all there, he just laid into him. Thought he was going to kill him. Probably would have done if we hadn't have been there. I had no idea." There's a pause, before she adds, "What the fuck have I done?"

Paula's brother puts his hand on her shoulder in an attempt to calm her down, but it's not working. She pulls the curtain back again and spots Oli, heading up the path, one step closer to entering her house. Her brother takes one look at the state she's in and heads for the front door, telling her,

"I've got this."

He walks through to the hallway, approaching the front door just as Oli puts his key in the lock. But the security lock's on and he can't turn his key.

Paula's brother waits for Oli to take his key out

of the lock. He puts the chain on and calmly opens the door to confront Oli. Oli takes one look at him and asks,

"Who the fuck are you?!"

Oli tries to step inside the house but Paula's brother blocks him with his foot, keeping the chain on. Staying calm, he replies,

"I'm Paula's brother. And I'd like you to leave now."

Oli is about to say something but takes one look at the size of Paula's brother's arms before turning on his heels and heading back down the path, with a face of thunder.

Paula's brother waits until Oli reaches the end of the path before shouting after him. "I want you to leave her alone from now on. Here. Work. Everywhere. You got that?", before adding, "Your stuff's by the gate."

As he reaches the gate, Oli bends down, and without looking back, picks up a rubbish sack stuffed full of clothes. He throws the bag into the back of his car before driving off, screeching loudly as he pulls away.

Paula's brother walks back into the living room. Now it's his turn to be worried.

"Get your stuff. You're coming home with me."

Paula nods. She grabs her coat and heads straight for the front door.

83 I WAS THINKING. MAYBE WE COULD GO AND SEE MY SISTER

Oli's blue Toyota pulls up outside the tower block where he lives (or used to) with Boom and his mum. He climbs out and leans back against his car to stare up at his old home.

Inside the flat, Boom and his mum are busy in the kitchen. Boom's mum is frying some eggs in a pan while Boom gets everything ready, fetching the cutlery and plates. Both happy to be doing simple things in each other's company, without Oli sucking the life out of them.

"I was thinking. Maybe we could go and see my sister."

"Auntie Em?" Boom replies. It's like a blast from the past. "Haven't seen her in years."

"Yeah well," Boom's mum replies sadly. "That's another thing he wouldn't let me do."

Boom stops to give his mum a proper bear hug.

"Yeah, well now you can do whatever the fuck you like."

"Jamie!!" she says, but with a smile on her face.

"It'd be nice," Boom smiles. "I remember Auntie Em. She always used to make me laugh."

There's a noise at the door as someone tries to turn a key in the lock. Boom and his mum flip instantly into high alert, their bodies seizing up as Oli's bulky silhouette reflects through the frosted glass of the front door.

"Go away!" Boom shouts. "This isn't your home any more."

Oli ignores him, continuing to try and turn his key in the lock and cursing loudly when nothing happens.

"We've changed the locks!" Boom shouts through the glass. He instinctively pulls his phone out of his pocket, just in case.

Oli kicks the door in frustration. It goes quiet for a minute before Oli tries another tactic. He puts on a pleading voice, telling Boom's mum,

"I made a mistake. I'm sorry, Lorraine. I love you. Let me back in love, so we can talk about it?"

"Don't listen to him," Boom tells his mum. A minute passes in silence and then Oli flips out, laying into the door and kicking at it in his steel-capped boots, trying to force his way back in.

Boom's mum instinctively cowers down low in a corner of the kitchen. Gently, Boom pulls his mum to her feet and guides her through the kitchen and out into the hallway, where he pulls the door shut behind them so they no longer have to listen up close to Oli's shouting and swearing. But even with the door shut, Oli's hate is palpable - a relentless monster that just won't leave them alone.

Boom's about to dial 999 when suddenly all the shouting, the pounding... stops. Boom and his mum look at each other for a minute, without moving, before Boom gets up, telling his mum,

"Wait there. I'll go and see what's happening."

Boom places his hand on his mum's shoulder to

calm her down. "I'm not going to do anything stupid ok." He hands her his phone. "If he starts up again, call the police."

Boom walks back into the kitchen and approaches the front door, his movements slow and controlled. His senses are on red alert, waiting for a sign that Oli's still there - a noise, a cough, his bulky silhouette... but there's nothing. Boom stands there in the silence... listening, waiting. As he relaxes he takes a deep breath in - the silence broken by a loud knock at the door. Boom jumps, letting out a terrified scream. His mum screams, shouting at him from the hallway. "Don't open the door!"

A voice shouts through the glass, "Police. DC Brightly. Can you let me in, Mrs Johnson?"

84 MUST BE HARD, BEING THE ONLY KID. HAVING TO WATCH HIM DO THAT TO YOUR MUM

Boom leans over the kitchen sink and peers through the window just to make sure it's not one of Oli's traps. He spots Brightly and lets out an audible gasp.

"What?!" Boom's mum asks, panicked.

"It's ok. It's not him," Boom shouts back to her, as he takes in Brightly, stood in front of the window, flashing his police badge at him. Boom pales, taking in the significance of Brightly being there. Knowing Brightly's onto him now, even if he doesn't know it's him yet.

"Everything alright?" Brightly asks through the window, not letting on if he saw Oli a minute ago or not.

"Hmm," Boom replies, too shell-shocked to reply properly.

Brightly catches movement from the hallway, and spots Boom's mum picking herself up off the floor. He's clocked it, but he doesn't react. Instead, he waits for her to walk into the kitchen and make her way to the front door. Her guard's up, even though he probably saved her skin.

"Sorry, who are you?" she asks.

Brightly flashes his badge. "Detective Constable Brightly Mrs Johnson, from the British Transport police," he tells her.

"British Transport Police?" She looks confused.

"That's right. I'm investigating some graffiti vandalism at the train depot where your husband works."

"Oh," she replies, distracted; her brain still playing through what just happened with Oli. "Sorry," she tells him. "I'm a little distracted. Come in. Would you like a drink?"

"Tea please," he replies.

Boom's mum nods at the kitchen table, inviting him to sit down. Boom sits down next to him, protecting his mum (and to check out how much he knows). He keeps his head down though so he doesn't have to look at Brightly as he watches him.

Boom's mum places a hot drink in front of Brightly and sits down.

"I'm sorry, why did you say the Transport Police were involved again?"

"I head up a specialist division, Mrs Johnson. Tracking down graffiti artists."

Boom can feel his face burning. If he could stop his mum from talking, just by willing it to happen, he would. But she carries on with her questions.

"I know there was some down at the depot recently. Have you found out who did it? Is that why you're here?" she asks.

Brightly's had his eyes on Boom the whole time, watching him closely for any kind of reaction.

"Where's your husband now, Mrs Johnson?" Brightly asks.

Boom looks up and exchanges a look with his mum.

"He left me. A few days ago. I changed the

locks," she tells him.

"Why's that, Mrs Johnson?" Brightly asks.

"As if you don't know," Boom thinks to himself, aware that Brightly knows more than he's letting on.

"He's not a nice person, detective..." she tells him, trailing off.

Now highly stressed - both at the thought of Oli as well as worrying about why Brightly is sitting there in his kitchen - Boom refuses to look up. Terrified he'll give something away.

Boom's mum won't stop asking questions though. Boom's finding it hard not to squirm in his seat, wondering why she won't stop. *"It must be nerves,"* he thinks, as his mum asks Brightly, "What's the link to my husband? With the graffiti I mean."

"Well, it seems he was very good at pissing people off, Mrs Johnson," he adds wrily.

"What d'you mean by that?" she asks.

Boom is becoming more and more uncomfortable. His discomfort with the conversation emanating out of him like invisible soundwaves.

Brightly keeps his eyes on Boom as he delivers the next punch. "What I'm saying is, whoever did the graffiti didn't just choose the depot by mistake. It was a deliberate attempt to get back at your husband for something, Mrs Johnson."

Boom can't take the pressure any more. He gets up out of his seat muttering to Brightly,

"Excuse me a minute. I need the loo."

Walking into the hallway, Boom enters the toilet, shutting the door behind him. He wiggles the handle a couple of times to make sure it's locked. He turns on the tap, running cold water over his wrists for a few seconds before splashing his face in an attempt to calm himself down. Then, without using the toilet, Boom flushes, before heading back out into the corridor, slipping quietly into his bedroom and shutting the door behind him, scanning the room for traces of anything graffiti related.

Spotting his rucksack with his paints in, Boom picks it up off the floor making sure to be extra careful not to clink the cans of paint inside. He opens his bedroom window and ties the bag to a nail at the end of the window ledge so that it dangles below the window sill, out of sight. He closes the window, scouting the room a second time, looking for anything else that might give the game away to Brightly.

Boom spots Flash's old t-shirt scrunched up on the radiator to dry, the one he got the paint on. He picks it up and gives it a good shake. It's the t-shirt with the policeman on, giving someone the bird... covered with droplets of grey and luminous green paint from the spaceship graffiti.

He hears movement in the corridor outside. Quickly, he stuffs the t-shirt under his mattress at the end of the bed and sits down at his computer and turns it on. Just in time - as Brightly knocks at the door, entering before Boom even has a chance to tell him to come in.

Brightly attempts a smile, his eyes lingering over a poster that Boom's drawn and stuck to the bedroom wall above his bed.

"Like art do you?" he asks.

Luckily for Boom it's not a graffiti piece, so it's not going to give the game away. Not immediately anyway.

Boom nods.

"You've got a real talent for it," Brightly adds.

"Thanks." Boom replies, squirming under the scrutiny of the sharp-eyed detective, but knowing it would be weird not to respond at all.

Keeping his eyes trained on Boom, Brightly adds,

"Must be hard, being the only kid. Having to watch him do that to your mum. You must feel quite helpless. Like there's nothing you can do to stop him."

Boom doesn't reply. He doesn't want to give his emotions away, not with this cop (only too aware he's being led into some kind of trap).

Brightly stands there, brazenly scanning the room for evidence, as Boom's mum walks in behind him. His eyes scan the floor under Boom's bed, but there's nothing. But then he catches it. A tiny piece of grey material, sticking out from underneath the mattress at the end of Boom's bed. Right at the very moment Boom catches it too.

Boom shuts his eyes, cursing to himself inside his head. Aware it's too late to do anything about it now.

Brightly walks over to Boom's bed and tugs at the material, pulling Flash's t-shirt out from under the mattress. Before he even has a chance to stop her, Boom's mum pipes up,

"I thought you'd got all the paint out of Adam's T-shirt."

317

"Damn it!" Boom thinks, shaking his head.

Brightly shakes the crumples out of the t-shirt and holds it up in front of him, making a real show of laughing at the picture.

"Your mate's t-shirt, is it? Mind if I borrow it? It's right up my boss's street. Might try and track a new one down for him."

Brightly hands Boom his business card. "Just tell your mate. Adam was it? Tell him to call me if he wants his t-shirt back."

Brightly leaves with Boom's mum. They shut the door behind them, leaving Boom to take in what just happened.

"Fuck it! **Fuck it!**" Boom swears to himself, gripping his head with his hands.

Back in the kitchen, Boom's mum sees Brightly out, closing the door shut behind him. She sits down at the table and sighs. There's a knock at the door, and she opens it again, expecting to see Brightly. But it's Oli. He shoves his foot into the doorway to stop her from shutting the door and gives her a wide smile before punching her in the face, sending her flying to the ground.

Hearing the noise from his bedroom, Boom comes rushing out of his room. But it's too late. Oli barges his way back into the flat, slamming the door behind him. Picking Boom up by his shirt collar, Oli hurls him back into the hallway, locking the door behind him. Leaving himself alone in the kitchen with Boom's mum, to do anything he wants to her.

Picking up his phone and earplugs from where he left them on his desk, Boom slides himself into his wardrobe and sits down. Hearing a loud crash from inside the kitchen, he slides the door shut and cranks his music up as loud as it will go. He sits there in the dark, rocking quietly, bashing his forehead with the palm of his hand. Over and over, until his phone pings, offering a brief distraction as a message pops up from someone called LolGirl.

"Can you help me, Graffiti Boy? My boyfriend raped me and I want everyone to know what he did so he'll never do it again, to anyone."

Something about her situation and what's going on in the kitchen between his mum and Oli makes something flip inside of him. Determined to at least try and help someone in a vulnerable situation for once, Boom climbs out of his wardrobe, walks over to the window where he pulls up his bag of paints before climbing out onto the ledge, and onto a flat roof just below. Throwing his rucksack onto his back, Boom stands at the very edge of the roof, gauging the height, before jumping to the ground below.

Landing on his feet, he heads out into the night. With absolutely no fear this time.

85 YOU LOLGIRL?

The air's got a bite to it.

Anyone else would be cold, but not Boom. Not tonight. Tonight he's on a mission, fuelled by anger and revenge and a determination that no-one, or nothing, will stop him from doing what he's about to do.

Sitting waiting for him, on the wall surrounding the car park in front of his block of flats, is 14-year-old LolGirl. A streetwise looking girl, with bleached blonde hair, far older looking than her actual years. She's sat on the wall, pretending to read a magazine with her head down. But even with her head down you can feel trouble oozing out of her.

Boom walks over to her.

"You Lolgirl?"

She nods.

"Have you got it?" Boom asks.

The girl nods, handing Boom the magazine she's been reading. "Inside front cover. In thick, black letters." She looks at Boom, before adding, "Make sure you get him for me, will you?", before walking off.

Boom opens the magazine, and a passport-sized photo falls out. It's the girl, sitting next to her boyfriend, the one she says raped her. And inside the front cover of the magazine, a name. Written in thick, black letters.

Jake.

Next to it, LolGirl's written the name of a nearby tower block where the boy lives, along with the number of his flat. Boom absorbs the information for a second or two before pulling his lighter out of his pocket and setting fire to the magazine. Waiting for it to burn out before chucking it into the bin and walking away.

86 GO FUCK YOURSELF OLD MAN!

Boom reaches a grey, pebbledash tower block, one he's not been to before. Angry rap music pounds in his ears as he enters the building, willing him onwards and upwards. Boom strides up the staircase, taking the steps two at a time. This time not giving a damn who sees him. He reaches the tenth floor, walking out onto the balcony that winds itself around the whole of the building, a full 360 degrees, with a staircase at both ends.

He takes a left, checking out the door numbers as he walks. He stops in front of a brown door and slings his bag down, pulling out one of his cans of paint.

For once, Boom's not even trying to hide his face, he's too angry. He works with his hood down, out in the open and in full view of anyone who passes. No nemesis outfit. No hoodie. Just him.

And he doesn't give a fuck.

Rap music pounding in his ears, Boom starts to draw the outline of a person on the door, someone lying on their back.

An elderly man in his 80s walks past, leaving heavily on a stick down one side of his body. Born in a generation of people who stood up for their beliefs, the old man takes one look at Boom and waves his stick at him, shouting, "Oy! What d'you think you're playing at?! I'll call the police!"

"Go fuck yourself old man!" Boom replies, glaring at him.

It's not him. Boom wouldn't usually swear at anyone, much less a vulnerable, older person - but Oli's fucked with his head, and right now it's the only way Boom can release all his pent-up anger and frustration at the way Oli has messed with his life, as well as his mum's.

The old man knows trouble when he sees it, and shuffles past, heading into the safety of his own flat and shutting the door.

In a separate part of the City, Flash and the Crew are hanging out at one of their usual haunts, the Lord Protector Pub. The Cat is performing his usual stunts, hanging upside down from the top of a wall by his feet.

Curl's sat on the pavement below him, sketching his latest piece onto a notepad that rests on his lap. Flash is sat next to him, head bent, scrolling through pictures on his phone, looking for inspiration. Every now and then Flash looks up at The Cat, hung upside down by just his feet, before asking him,

"Seriously bro, how d'you do that?"

Curl hangs there without slipping, replying with a dramatic flourish,

"Because I am not human. I am a cat!" Before adding sheepishly, "Think I need to get down. I feel a bit dizzy."

The rest of the Crew let out a laugh, before The Watcher walks over, whistling an alert.

"Someone's doing graffiti at a tower block two streets over. No hood, no mask. Completely naked. No visuals but sounds like it could be Boom."

"What the fuck's he playing at?" Flash asks, racing off to help his mate, followed by the rest of the

323

Crew.

Back at the flats, Boom's still spraying the walls, hood down still and fully exposed - or "naked" as The Watcher calls it. Angry rap music pounds in his ears as he mutters to himself under his breath,

"Why d'you have to come back for, you nasty *fucker*?"

His words are laced with anger and hate. Not only is he taking a huge risk by painting while fully exposed in the open, he's also attracting attention by making himself look like an angry, crazed person, standing there muttering to himself.

The anger fuels his creativity though and his work is taking shape already. Looming large over the front of the door is a close up of a teenage boy, about 15 or 16 years of age, lying on top of a young - and very frightened looking girl… LolGirl. The boy has her pinned to the floor, his face twisted with hate. His hands reaching for the zipper on his jeans, the scene a clear depiction of what he's been told.

Rape.

Approaching Boom from the nearside stairwell is a dark-haired boy with a closely-shaven head. As he gets closer, his face sharpens into view. It's the boy in Boom's picture.

He spots Boom, takes one look at the graffiti on his door, and completely flips out.

"What the fuck?!" he says, racing over to where Boom is continuing to paint, refusing to stop even though the boy's just arrived back.

He grabs Boom by the neck and pins him to the

wall, laying into him with punches. Boom tries to fight back but the way he's been pinned gives him no room for manoeuvre. The boy swings his arm back, ready for another punch, when someone grabs him from behind and yanks him off of Boom.

It's Flash. Coming to Boom's rescue.

Two police vans pull up on the street below, screeching to a stop at the side of the pavement. A string of riot cops pile out, with a police dog in tow, barking loudly as they head inside the tower block.

Boom and the accused boy are too busy fighting to even notice the police, but Flash is on it.

Down below, the rest of The Crew have arrived now too, panting and out of breath. Stopping at the end of the street to catch their breath, they catch sight of the police vans pulled up outside the tower block where Boom could be in trouble - and freeze. Standing there for a second or two, they try and work out what to do next.

The Watcher grabs them by the arm, pulling them towards the car park at the front of the flats, where they duck down behind some cars to watch what the cops are doing. The Watcher pulls out his phone and calls Flash on his mobile.

Back up on the tenth floor, Flash picks up, telling The Watcher, "I'm on it!" He hangs up, before telling Boom and his assailant, "Feds are on their way up!"

The boy isn't having a bar of it though, and ignoring Flash, he starts laying into Boom again. He's pissed off and angry and talking with his fists. "What the fuck have you drawn that on my door for, you cunt?!"

"Cause people need to know what you are Jake!" Boom replies.

There's a shout from the top of the stairs, and the boy's dad, a balding man in his 40s, spots the fight and drops his bag on the floor, racing towards them. Except the boy's not called Jake.

"Tom!"

Grabbing Boom by an arm, he yanks him off his son, shouting, "What the fuck are you doing?!"

Boom takes one look at the boy, hears the name Tom and realises he's been had.

"Tom?! Shit!"

Every other time Boom's done his research first. But this time he was so screwed up over Oli, and his desire to get back at him, he didn't bother. And now he's fucked up, majorly. Realising what's happened, Tom takes one look at Boom and shakes his head, looking at him like he's pathetic.

"What? You didn't think to check it out first?! Well, maybe you should have. 'Cause if you had, you'd have realised she's a fucking nutter who's been stalking me ever since I finished with her five months ago. If you don't believe me, speak to the police!"

Boom stands on the balcony, running his hands through his hair. "Sorry man. I'm so, sorry. Sorry." Pissed off at himself for being so stupid and worried about the trouble he's got himself into.

Down on the street below, one of the police vans gives a short, sharp burst of a siren, reminding everyone they're there, and breaking through the angry bubble they've been stuck in for the last half hour.

Grabbing his paints, Boom shoves them into his bag - this time not giving a shit about the noise, 'cause after all he's just been stupid enough to stand there spraying the door in full view of everyone passing and getting it completely wrong.

As the cops get closer, the shouts get louder - and even the dog seems to be getting more crazed with its barking.

Flash leans over the balcony and spots the cops five floors down. There's about six of them.

"Shit! We've got to go!" he tells the others. He spots the dog, with Brightly up front, and motions for Boom to take the staircase opposite.

"You go that way. I'll head 'em off!"

Tom and his dad dive inside their flat, eager to hide from the cops even though they've done nothing wrong, because like everyone else in the vicinity they have a healthy distrust of the police.

Boom, meanwhile, races to the end of the balcony, reaching the stairs opposite.

Flash is still stood outside the door with the graffiti on, however, quickly scanning the area for any clues that may have been left behind. He spots a can of paint that Boom has somehow missed and shoves it into his trackie bottoms. He's about to go when he takes one last look back at Boom's graffiti.

"Damn it Boom!" he mutters to himself, pulling the can out of his pocket to use it to spray over the so called 'rapist's' face. A small ball of paper falls from his pocket, but Flash doesn't notice. Realising the cops are now really close and gaining on him, Flash legs it off down the stairwell (the opposite one to Boom) before he is caught.

As he disappears from sight, the Police Dog reaches the tenth floor, racing up the other set of stairs and down the balcony towards where Boom and Flash were stood a minute or two ago, followed by two of the younger, fitter cops.

Just behind them, an eagle-eyed Brightly has spotted the balled-up piece of paper that Flash dropped. Call it copper's instinct, but Brightly knows it's something important. He opens it up to find a receipt for a pair of trainers from Sports Direct - giving the date and time of sale. It's pretty much the only time Flash has ever bought a pair of trainers in his life.

"Bingo!" Brightly says to himself. Knowing tracking the purchase should be pretty easy.

Down on the staircase below, the Police Dog is giving chase to Flash. With the dog gaining on him, Flash reaches a part of the balcony that juts out over the pavement below. Doing a quick mental calculation in his head Flash works out he's two floors up, a good twelve feet or so, and takes one last look back at the dog as it gains more ground. Not stopping to give it a second thought, Flash climbs up onto the balcony - and jumps to the ground below.

Seconds later, the Police Dog reaches the balcony and stops. It's going crazy, pawing at the wall and barking, circling the spot where Flash has just been stood. The two young cops catch up, panting heavily as they lean over the wall and watch as Flash disappears through some waist-high grass at the back of the flats.

Back at Tom's front door, Brightly pulls an evidence bag out of his pocket and places Flash's shop receipt inside of it, bagging it as evidence.

Elsewhere on the Estate, Boom's still on the run - unsure how much of a head start Flash has given him, but too frightened to stop. Hurtling through an unfamiliar car park, Boom ducks behind a car, peering back over his shoulder to check if it's safe to stop. Having escaped the cops, Boom leans back against the car, panting heavily.

87 WHAT T-SHIRT? AND WHO THE FUCK'S BRIGHTLY?

Flash is pacing his hallway. Back and forth, back and forth, while everyone else sleeps. A shadow passes the glass on his front door and a figure appears. There's a tap, that's barely audible. Flash opens the door to find Boom stood in front of him, his face a picture of blind panic. Flash steps aside to let him in, and they walk down the hallway together without a word, passing the first room (Rachel's) and then the second, where Boom mouths to Flash,

"Where's your mum?"

"Asleep," Flash signs, pointing at the bedroom door.

Creeping into the lounge, they shut the door behind them. They turn on the lights, dimming them straight away to keep the light low.

"You got it?" Flash asks.

Boom nods, reaching into his bag to pull out his laptop. He sits on the floor in front of a low table where he opens it up and logs straight into his social media accounts for Graffiti Boy.

Flash reaches over him and starts to type something into the Google search bar...*How long does it take to delete a Facebook account?* Twitching with urgency, Boom leans over him, following the thread with his finger as he reads out loud,

"It may take up to-- no way! Shit that's months!"

"Wait, it's ok," Flash tells him, reading: *"While we are deleting this information, it is inaccessible to other people using facebook.'* It's ok. You're in the clear."

Boom is super twitchy though... more like how Flash is normally with all his excess energy. But he can't relax until he's deleted all of the accounts associated with his pseudonym, Graffiti Boy. The two of them sit in intense silence as they delete the accounts, one by one. Facebook (set up for the oldies); Insta; Snapchat; YouTube and Twitter. Hitting the last DELETE button, Boom sits back and lets out a huge sigh. Flash looks at him,

"That everything?"

Boom nods, his body visibly relaxing. He shuts his laptop and is about to crack some banter, when he remembers something.

"What?!" Flash asks, catching the alarm on Boom's face and bracing himself for the next bit of bad news.

"Brightly's got your t-shirt."

"What t-shirt? And who the fuck's Brightly?"

"The cop from the British Transport Police. The one in the newspaper article. He heads up their graffiti unit."

"Wait. What?" Flash asks, taking a second or two to catch up. And then it hits him. "The guy you were looking at. On your phone. Him?" Boom nods. "Shit Boom! What the fuck?! Shit!"

Boom stares at the ground.

"How'd the fuck he get my t-shirt?" Flash asks.

"He came round. To speak to mum about the graffiti at Oli's work. Saw your t-shirt poking out from under my mattress and took it back to the station with

331

him."

"Shit! This is serious Boom!" Flash says, spinning round in a blind panic. "It's got paint on from your spaceship piece. He'll be able to match the paint with the paint on the t-shirt, won't he?"

"That was at the Industrial Estate. He won't even know about that. And even if he's seen it, he won't link the two together. Brightly's just after me for the stuff on the trains."

"What makes you so sure?" Flash asks. "Fuck Boom. My DNA's gonna be all over it..."

"I told you," Boom replies. "He's not interested in the other stuff. He probably doesn't even know it's out there. He just cares about the trains."

"Exactly *how* busy have you been on the trains?" Flash asks him. When Boom doesn't speak, he pushes for an answer. "Go on!"

"I've done a few."

"How many's a few?!"

Boom shrugs. "I don't want to tell you too much, G," he tells Flash. "It 'aint I don't trust you. You know that, right? I just don't wanna drag you into all my shit."

"Bit late for that, bro. I'm now fully feet-first, all the way, never-to-come-unstuck immersed, up to my neck in all your shit right now," Flash replies, super unhappy.

"But the fact it's your t-shirt is a *good* thing, bro," Boom tells him. 'Cause if he traces it back to you, all you gotta do is try and draw something and he'll know straight away it 'aint you. 'Cause you could't draw a fucking stick man if your life depended on it." Boom's trying to make light of the situation but Flash isn't laughing.

Boom tries again. "Plus I'm hardly gonna let you take the rap for something I've done, am I?"

Flash is pissed off now. "Why'd you let her drag you into all this shit anyways?"

"Who?" Boom asks him.

"Who d'you fucking think?! Feisty of course! That's who. I told you she was trouble."

"She's not my favourite person right now either," Boom replies. "But to be fair to her, she didn't know I was doing the trains until she followed me. I did that shit on my own. To get back at Oli when I found out he was shagging some woman from work."

"What?!" Flash asks.

"Yep," Boom replies. He checks the time on his phone. "Bro. It's 3.a.m. Can we talk about this in the morning? I'm shattered."

Flash sighs. He disappears out the room for a second, returning with a spare duvet and pillow for Boom. "You might as well stay. Sofa's all yours."

"Thanks," Boom replies.

"Hmmm," Flash replies, shaking his head at all the shit Boom's dragged him into before disappearing back to his bedroom where he climbs into his bed and falls straight to sleep, forgetting to set the alarm on his bedside cabinet.

88 CAN I HELP?

Brightly's stood outside the front of a Sports Direct shop. It's still early and other than the odd person cutting through the town centre on their way to work, there's no-one else about. The metal blinds are still down on all the shopfronts, but the lights are on in Sports Direct and you can see movement inside the shop as the staff get ready to open up.

Someone walks up to the metal rollerblind from inside the shop and hits the button on the mechanised device that rolls it up. The young, female shop assistant jumps as she spots Brightly, stood on the street directly outside.

"Sorry, didn't mean to make you jump. Is the manager there?" he asks.

The young girl nods, throwing him a funny look, like he's a whinging saddo for showing up this early. He flashes his badge at her, enjoying the instant change in attitude as she takes in his police status.

"DC Brightly, from the British Transport Police."

He follows her to the front counter and pulls up a photo of the receipt that Flash dropped from the night of the chase on his phone.

"I need to see if you can track someone down for me using a receipt."

The girl walks over to the storeroom door at the back of the store, leans through and bellows, "Rob!"

89 NO WAY WE GONNA MAKE THAT

It's the morning, and Flash and Boom sprint along the pavement, reaching the school gates exhausted and out of breath. The playground's deserted and the gates locked. They give them a rattle to see if there's a way in, but they're padlocked.

"Shit!" Flash says. "That's all I need. Another call home."

Boom checks his phone. "We're still only three minutes late. We might just make it," he says, adding a little less hopefully, "If we can find a way in."

"We're gonna have to ring the intercom," Flash replies.

Boom's eyes run the length of the wall that skims the boundary.

"No we're not. Come on."

They race down an alleyway that runs down the side of the school and stop halfway along. Flash takes one look at the wall, which is 12-foot high, and tells Boom, "No way we gonna make that!"

Boom ignores his pessimism. "Chuck your bag over."

"You sure about this?"

Boom nods, "Just do it."

Flash takes one look at the wall and decides to do it Olympic-style, spinning round several times like a javelin thrower before letting go. Him and Boom watch as the bag goes flying. But it doesn't quite make it, landing instead on top of a tall bush next to the wall.

Now it's stuck about ten-foot up, which means a leg up at the very least.

"You big girl!" Boom adds, having a good-natured laugh at Flash's expense.

Flash laughs. "Fuck you. I'd like to see you do any better."

Boom gives Flash a winning look, before picking up his own bag and attempting a different approach. This time he forgets the spins, standing steady as he bends down in a low squat before propelling himself, and the bag, upwards as high as he can go. They watch as the bag clears the wall, a smug smile creeping over Boom's face as he turns to Flash.

"What was that you were saying?"

Flash gives him the bird. "Now we just need to work out how to get my bag down." He walks over to the bush and tries to push his way through all the foliage to find a foothold somewhere within the branches. Flash is battling with the bush as the branches keep springing back in his face, making Boom laugh.

"Bro, this is like watching a comedy act."

"Fuck off and help me, will ya?" Flash asks, getting annoyed as the branches keep springing back in his face, making Boom laugh even more. "We're running outta time."

Boom walks over and gives Flash a leg up, wobbling precariously as Flash pushes himself up off of Boom's hands, which he's got clasped together in a kind of ready-made platform.

"Steady as she goes!" Flash says, mimicking the voice of a posh sailor from an old black and white movie as Boom wobbles all over the pavement with him.

Boom starts to laugh at the ridiculousness of it, along with Flash's dodgy impersonation of a posh person, and before they know it, they're both struggling to contain their laughter - Boom laughing so much he can't even put Flash down. Flash grabs his mates ears to hold on, making them laugh even more. Soon they're crying with laughter.

"Stop wobbling, you twat!" Flash tells him, making Boom laugh even more.

"Oh for fuck's sake!" Flash says, waiting for the inevitable, as Boom can't hold it together any longer. He drops Flash headfirst into the bush, making Boom laugh even louder.

Flash has landed in just the right position though, and with an excited punch in the air, he grabs his bag and chucks it back down to Boom, who's laughing so much he can't even catch it. Flash jumps down after it, covered in leaves, making Boom laugh so much his sides ache. They sit there on the pavement for a few seconds, just laughing, before they manage to calm themselves down.

"We better go, bro," Flash tells Boom, with a bit of branch still sticking out the top of his head. Laughing, Boom pulls it out of his hair, before walking over to the wall and forming a platform with his hands again, for Flash to climb up onto. He hoiks Flash up and onto the wall, where Flash locks his feet together for a second until he gets his balance, before throwing himself off the other side. Boom takes one look at the bush, scrabbles up its branches and onto the top of the wall, where he jumps up and off, disappearing after Flash.

Grabbing their bags the other side, they race towards school looking for a way in. Flash spots a fire door that's been propped open and dives through, followed by Boom, making sure they're off the playground before anyone spots them.

90 BUT THERE YOU ARE, STAYING UP TO THE EARLY HOURS, JUST PISSING IT ALL AWAY. AND FOR WHAT?!

Britton is taking the register on his computer as his form group sits there reading - or at least pretending to read. He's just about to mark Boom and Flash absent when they burst through the door, sending it crashing against the wall, making everyone jump. They stand there, in the entrance, panting and trying to catch their breath, Flash with leaves in his hair and stuck to his blazer.

The class laugh at the sight of them, but Britton cuts them dead, his manner curt. "Nice of you to join us, Mr Pritchard. Mr Johnson."

His tone catches them off guard. Flash and Boom exchange a puzzled look. Normally, Britton would be annoyed, but this time he looks genuinely angry and they can't work out why.

"Sorry Sir, we forgot to set the alarm," Boom tells him.

Britton marks them present on his register, refusing to look at them as he replies,

"Good job we don't all do that, isn't it? Sit down."

They sit down in silence. Even Ali, at the back of the class in his usual spot, knows not to make one of his usual wisecracks.

The class read in silence until the bell goes at the end of form time, and the class empties. They pile out, passing Britton's desk, several at a time. Britton waits for Boom to pass, and stops him in his tracks. "A word, Jamie."

His tone says no messing. Flash lingers next to Boom, but Britton ushers him away. "Mr Pritchard, whose name did you hear? Yours or Jamie's?"

Flash throws Boom a look that says, 'hope you're ok' before walking out, leaving a bemused Boom to face the wrath of Britton. Boom stands there, perplexed, trying to work out what's going on because in all the time he's had Britton as his teacher, he's never - *ever* - seen him this angry before. Not even when he's slept through one of his classes - which is quite often as it goes. So... *this* - he doesn't get...

"Why were you late?" Britton asks him, getting straight to the point.

"I stayed at Fla..," Boom corrects himself. "Adam's house last night. We just forgot to set the alarm. Sorry, Sir."

"What time did you go to bed?" Britton asks.

Boom looks shocked by the level of questioning. "I dunno... late."

"How late?" Britton asks him, staring at Boom until he gets an honest response.

Boom pauses for a second, before replying truthfully. "3 a.m, Sir."

It's enough to light Britton's fuse. "Really Jamie?! Well it's nice to see you're taking your studies seriously."

He's not shouting but it's the first time Britton has ever raised his voice that much to him. It's just not something he does, not even with students like Ali, 'cause he knows if he does, he's lost the argument. But this time, he just can't help himself. He takes a deep breath, visibly trying to calm himself down.

"So what were you doing that was so important you couldn't get to bed till 3 a.m?" he asks Boom.

Boom stands there like a surly teenage and shrugs, the apparent complacency of it, setting Britton off again.

"Is that the best you've got for me? A shrug?!" Britton asks, still really angry. Shaking his head, he levels his gaze with Boom. "Do you wanna know why I'm so angry, Jamie?"

But now it's Boom's turn to be riled. "How come you're having a go at me and not Adam?" he asks, frustrated at the injustice of it.

"I'll tell you why, shall I?!" Britton rants, pointing his finger at Boom. "Because unlike you, Adam doesn't waste his talents away. Unlike you, who up until recently was managing to get straight As despite the fact you sleep through pretty much all of my lessons. But I know you care, Jamie - and that you *have* tried - because I've seen you in the library after school when everyone else has gone home. So what's gone wrong? Tell me!"

Britton pauses for a second, waiting for an answer, but nothing comes. "All I see is this wasted talent, Jamie. And it is *so* frustrating. *So*, frustrating, when year after year I see a sea of bored faces, and then I have you. This bright, talented, creative student who could pretty much do anything in the world they set their mind to. Take themselves places they've never dreamt of. But there you are, staying up to the early hours, just pissing it all away. And for what?!"

Britton stops. Aware he's sworn when he shouldn't have, but aware he's close to doing it again if it'll make Boom take him seriously.

Boom laughs.

But he doesn't mean it in a disrespectful way. He's just laughing at the fact another adult (apart from his mum) has got his back for once. That someone has actually noticed the extra hours and all the work he's put in and the fact Britton *does* actually care what happens to him. But Boom just doesn't have any control over his life right now.

But all Britton hears is the laugh and he's not impressed.

"Why's that so funny?! I mean for Christ's sake, Jamie. There's students who would kill to have half your brains. Get outta here and make something of their life. But you're happy just to sit back and let all your talent go to waste. If you want to do well in life, Jamie, you've got to be determined. Take the knocks and then get back up and start again. But there's no point me telling you any of this if you can't see it for yourself, is there? You need to start taking some responsibility for what happens to you in your life, Jamie!"

But now it's Jamie's turn to lose it.

"Oh, really? It is, is it?" Boom asks, his voice laced with sarcasm. "So if I - 'take responsibility' - as you call it for what happens in my life, everything's going to be ok, is it? Everything will turn out all rosy? Is that what you're telling me?"

He's thinking about Oli now and how controlling he is, and how much he's fucked up his life as well as his mum's.

"You wanna be sarcastic with me, Jamie, fire away," Britton replies. "I could be sarcastic with you too if I wanted. But what I want is for you to start listening. Before it's too late. Nothing makes me more frustrated than seeing a bright pupil like you throw it all away just because you can't be bothered. Look at me." Britton pauses to make sure he's got Boom's attention. "Yes, life is hard. But you can always do something about it, Jamie. Turn stuff around. Please don't throw it all away by being stupid."

Jamie can't contain his anger any more. "With all due respect, Sir. You know fuck all about me or my life!"

And with that, he storms out of the classroom, slamming the door behind him.

91 TALK OF THE DEVIL

DC Brightly is sat at his desk, staring at his computer, with his boss and the two ginger-haired cops next to him. Brightly's explaining the significance of Flash's t-shirt to them all.

"Jamie - that's Mr Hanson's stepson - had it in his room, hidden under his mattress. So he quite clearly knew it would be of interest to me."

Sgt Meadows interrupts him, "Who does it belong to again?"

"His mate Adam. According to Jamie's mum."

"Surname?" Meadows asks him.

"I've put a call into the school so once I hear back, we can ID them."

"We need to do that without them knowing we're on to them," Meadows says.

Brightly looks slightly annoyed at being told the obvious. "It's ok, I've got it covered, Sir."

"Hang on a minute though," the first ginger-haired cop interjects. "If there's no evidence linking either of them to the graffiti at the depot then why are they even suspects?"

"Because all the stuff against Mr Hanson is about revenge. So ask yourself. Who would hate him enough to do it? A workmate maybe, there's been a couple of incidents at work where he's roughed up one of the apprentices. But why would an apprentice care who Mr Hanson was shagging? He wouldn't."

Brightly pauses for a minute to let it sink in with everyone, before continuing,

"Turns out our Mr Hanson is pretty nifty with his fists. Likes to beat the shit out of Jamie's mum every night, according to the neighbours. The feds get called out pretty much most nights. Never by Jamie though. So maybe the revenge is a way for him to feel like he has some kind of control over it. And maybe, just maybe, he gets Adam to do his dirty work for him."

"Makes sense," Sgt Meadows comments.

"Both lots of graffiti were pretty specific," Brightly says, showing them photos of Boom's handiwork at the depot... 'Oli's Fuck Truck' with the words, 'We know' - and the second piece on the giant sliding doors leading into the hanger, identifying Oli and Paula as lovers, with the words 'Two timing dirty cheat and liar' written under Oli's face.

"What about his bit on the side?" the second ginger-haired cop asks, keen to impress Meadows.

"What about her?" Brightly asks.

"Has she met Jamie? Who does *she* think might have done it?"

"Don't think she'd have a fucking clue. She was all over Jamie's stepdad 'til I told her what he was *actually* like. And even then, I don't think she really believed it until she saw him beating the shit out of someone at work the day after my visit."

"What about the paint, on the t-shirt? Does it match any of the colours at the depot?" Meadows asks.

"No," Brightly replies. "But when I went to see Mercedes' sister - that's the girl who injured herself falling into a skip and whose jacket matched the piece of material left on the fence - she told me her sister had been hanging out with someone called Boom. But neither of these pieces have been signed off. They're both anonymous," he says, pointing back at the photos from the train depot.

"What? So you think there could be a link between Boom and the train guy? Or could they be two different people?" Meadows asks.

"Dunno but it's worth investigating," Brightly replies. "If it's the same guy, and we find his work somewhere else, we might be able to get a match on the paint. Forensics can match the paint particles on the t-shirt to the paint particles in the graffiti, and bingo! We have our man."

"So what are we looking for here?" Meadows asks.

Brightly clicks on a photo of Flash's paint-stained t-shirt, which the forensics team has taken. "Whatever the picture's of, it's a mix of at least these two colours, dark grey and luminous green. It's pretty unusual, so should be easy to spot when you find it. And whatever it is, it's probably been signed off with the tag 'Boom'."

"What about the girl's phone?" Meadows asks. "Anything on that yet?"

"Not yet, Sir," Brightly replies. "It's taking a bit of time 'cause of the condition it was found in. Pretty much smashed up. But you never know, we might get something out of it. The only other thing we're waiting on is the receipt from the night of the chase."

"What you think that might be linked to the same guy?" Meadows asks him.

"Right now, I'm not ruling anything out,"

Brightly tells him.

Meadows looks impressed. "Good work."

Brightly's phone pings with a notification.

"Talk of the devil. The receipt belongs to… Bingo! Adam Pritchard. Goes to Jamie's school. Got to be the same guy," he says, getting up out of his seat excited, as he adds, "Only one way to find out."

His phone pings with a second notification.

"Interesting," Brightly says, reading it. "Pritchard's got a caution for shoplifting. Two years ago. Pair of trainers. Hardly worth the effort. Seems like one of our guys has a bit of a fetish for trainers."

"Where are you off to now?" Meadows asks him.

"School, Sir. Gonna get Mr Trainer Boy ID'd."

"Stay in the shadows for now," Meadows tells him. "Don't wanna let them know you're onto them and blow all your hard work."

92 YOU SURE? IT DEFINITELY WASN'T THE OTHER WAY ROUND?

Brightly's sat in the driver's seat of his beaten-up Citroen, parked at the side of the road, several hundred feet from where all the students are piling out of Boom's school. Next to him, in the passenger seat, is Tom, the boy from the tower block LolGirl accused of rape (the one she told Boom was called Jake). Sitting behind them in the back is Tom's dad, the one who pulled Boom off of his son.

They watch as the students leave school - their eyes focused and concentrating too hard to speak. It's Tom's dad who breaks the silence.

"Is this the only exit?" he asks.

"Yeah," Brightly replies. "They've got an electronic signing in system so students have to clock in and out every day, and the only way out is via reception and these gates."

But Tom's dad is not listening, sitting forward in his seat the same time as Tom, as they spot a familiar face… or two. Brightly clocks it straight away and his eyes follow their gaze to two students, piling out of the school gates chatting. It's Flash and Boom.

Brightly knows the look on Tom and his dad's face - so without even asking them if they've got a match, he lifts a camera up to his face that's he's been holding in his lap. He zooms in close and takes several photos in quick succession.

Flash and Boom are blissfully unaware they're being watched as they walk along, Flash telling Boom,

"Just take it as a sign you weren't meant to get caught this time," he says. "Just don't get complacent."

"Don't worry. I'm leaving the depot well alone from now on. And everywhere else for that matter too for a while," Boom replies.

Back in the car though, Brightly's got all the confirmation he needs, as Tom tells him, "The one on the left. He's the one who did the graffiti. The one chatting to him came to help him."

"You sure?" Brightly asks him. "It definitely wasn't the other way round?"

"One hundred per cent," Tom replies.

Brightly looks at Tom's dad for confirmation, even though he already knows the answer.

Tom's dad looks at Brightly and nods.

93 I'D SAY YOU'VE GOT YOURSELF A MATCH

Brightly's back at the office, with Meadows and the two trainees. Pinned to one of the computer screens in front of him are a couple of photos he took of Boom and Flash as they left school - one's a close up of their faces, the other's a wide shot, showing a bit more of their general gait.

Brightly's pulled up some CCTV footage on the computer next to them - which he's frozen, ready to play. It's the same footage he looked at before but now he's got more to go on. He looks at the others.

"Ready?"

They nod.

Brightly clicks play and the footage of Flash and Boom outside their flats kicks in. The video stops and he clicks a second file, the one showing Boom (in disguise) skirting the perimeter fence at the depot before diving through the hole and racing across the tracks before disappearing out of sight.

Brightly pauses the footage.

"So? What d'you think?"

Meadows nods. "You can't see their faces. But yeah, looking at the way they walk, their whole stance and body shape. I'd say you've got yourself a match."

The other two cops nod as well.

Meadows looks at Brightly. "So what you gonna do?"

Brightly smiles - a happy, smug kind of smile. "Start closing the net."

94 ALL I KNOW IS SHE STARTED HANGING OUT WITH HIM A COUPLE OF WEEKS AGO

Summer's eating dinner at the kitchen table with her mum. The light's dim, casting eerie shadows across the table and no-one speaks. Summer watches her mum with a worried expression, her gaze following her fork as it chases the food around her plate, never actually going anywhere near her mouth. She looks depressed. And thin.

There's a loud knock at the door. Summer jumps, but her mum doesn't react and carries on chasing her food around her plate. Summer frowns, wondering who's stupid enough to knock on their house at dinner time.

She gets up to answer the door. She opens it, takes one look at Brightly and her face drops.

"Mind if I come in?" he asks, looking every bit like the cat that got the cream.

Summer doesn't smile or speak. Instead she leaves the door open for him, turns on her heels and walks back to the kitchen without a word. He follows her down the corridor in the dark, entering the kitchen where he sits down next to Summer, directly across from where her mum is sitting. Brightly takes in the darkened room, the eerie shadows and the vacant expression on Summer's mum's face. He looks at her, trying to engage with her directly.

"Are you happy for me to question your

daughter, Mrs Havara?" he asks.

Mrs Havara doesn't respond, so he tries again.

"Mrs Havara?"

This time she nods, distractedly.

Brightly pulls his trump card from his pocket, and slides it across the table to Summer. It's the picture he took of Boom and Flash walking out of school together. Brightly watches Summer's face closely. Waiting for a reaction... and he's got it. The tiniest flicker of recognition, then shock as she realises he's on to them, and then gone, almost before it appeared. But just enough for him to know he's onto something.

He points at Flash and Boom in the photo.

"Do you know these boys, Summer?"

Summer looks at him, nervously.

"Is that a yes or a no?" he asks, pushing her.

Summer still doesn't answer, so Brightly ramps it up a gear.

"You do know that Mercedes could get convicted for this if she's linked to the graffiti, don't you?"

Summer looks terrified, fear making the words pour from her mouth before she can stop herself.

"That one there," she says, pointing to Boom. "He's called Boom" - and then, off the back of Brightly's questioning face, "It's his tag. What graffiti artists use as their signature."

"I know what a tag is," he tells her. "Don't forget I jail graffiti artists for a living." Clocking Summer flinch at the mention of jail, Brightly continues, "So what else can you tell me about him?"

"Nothing. All I know is Mercedes met him a

couple of weeks ago."

"Do you know his real name?"

Summer shakes her head.

"How did they meet?"

Summer shrugs. "I don't know. Sorry."

Acutely aware of his intense interest in her replies, Summer's scared her vague answers are just going to piss Brightly off even more, which she already knows won't end well. But she actually *doesn't* know anything about Boom, other than he's good at maths, he's into graffiti, and he's been hanging out with her sister for a couple of weeks.

"What about this one?" Brightly asks, pointing at Flash.

"I've never met him."

"Ya man," Brightly says, pointing back to Boom. "Does he draw?"

Summer's not even sure how to answer. She's not even sure if Boom can draw. Just that he's part of a crew. But she wants to give Brightly something, *anything*, just to get him off her sister's back. But she can't lie.

"I'm not sure. Sorry."

Brightly gets up out of his chair, pulls his card out, and slides it across the table towards Summer.

"If you think of anything, call me. Anything that might link this 'Boom' guy - or his mate - to the graffiti. At the depot, or anywhere else."

Brightly gives Summer's mum a brief nod, "Mrs Havara", before heading out, back down the corridor in the dark and letting himself out the front door.

95 THINK WE MIGHT HAVE GOT AWAY WITH THAT ONE

It's late evening, about 10 p.m, and Flash is waiting at the lamppost outside his and Boom's block of flats. He's dressed in trackie bottoms and a hoodie and faces the entrance, waiting for Boom. Except this time, Boom comes pounding up the pavement behind him. He's got his paints on him, but he's still in school uniform. Flash gives him a funny look.

"G! Why you still in uniform?"

"Had to go do some stuff for mum. Didn't have time to change," Boom replies.

Flash rattles Boom's rucksack which is tied tight to Boom's back, just to check he's got his paints.

"You got your paints though," Flash says, confused.

"Just grabbed them quickly in case I didn't have time to go home and get changed. Which as it turns out, I didn't."

Flash shrugs, dismissing the questions in his head, until he happens to glance back at Boom and catch something in his look. Boom's gone quiet and is walking with his head down, deep in thought.

"You ok, bro?"

Boom looks up. "Yeah, I'm fine."

Flash knows not to push Boom on it, so he pulls a ready-rolled spliff from his rucksack instead and hands it to Boom. But just as he hands it over, a police car turns into the road, the two cops' inside looking in their direction.

"Fuck it!" Boom says, his hands instinctively reaching behind his back to touch his paints.

"Back to me!" Flash tells him, spinning round with his back to the cops.

"It's ok. I've got it," Boom tells him.

"G! Back to me!" Flash says with a sense of urgency. "If they see you with that they're gonna search you and find your paints."

"I owe you," Boom tells him gratefully, spinning round quickly so the cops can't see him hand the spliff back to Flash.

Flash takes it off him, tucking it into a zipped pocket behind his waistband.

"Think we might have got away with that one," Flash says, but as he logs the cop car picking up pace, adds, "But - just in case - eyes left for the great escape." Flash subtly tips his head towards a pathway to their left that runs between two sets of houses. Sensing Boom dithering, Flash tells him, "G, go!"

"But I don't want to leave you on your--" Boom replies, interrupted by Flash.

"Seriously G, you seen the state of them? Right fat bastards," he jokes. "I'll outrun 'em in seconds. If they find your paints, who knows what'll happen? Might be enough for Brightly."

It's enough to spook Boom. "You're right. Laters."

Boom ducks down the alley, too fast for the cops to pull over and follow. Ducking out of sight, he peers back round the end of the alley, watching as the cops pull up alongside Flash and jump out. He can see them talking to Flash, who empties his pockets out before taking his bag off his back and emptying the contents on the pavement. Boom lets out a sigh of relief, but then stops as one of the cops walks back to the cop car and opens the boot. A police dog jumps out onto the pavement and runs over to Flash, barking like crazy.

"Ah shit," he mutters under his breath.

He watches as the cops say something to Flash, who reaches into the hidden pocket of his waistband and pulls out the spliff and a big bag of weed. One of the cops walks back over to the car and opens a door, waiting for Flash to climb in. Once he's in, the cops pull off, heading for the station.

"Fuck it!" Boom says, punching his fist into his hand in frustration, guilty that his friend just took the rap for him. Pulling out his phone, he messages Flash's sister, Rachel, typing the words, "Flash said eat without him. He's gonna be back late."

He then heads off, guilty as shit that Flash got caught.

96 YOU COMING OR WHAT?!

Boom heads home, through the estate, passing tower block after tower block. He passes a tall wall, in front of an entrance... some writing catching his attention as he passes. Scrawled in the middle of the wall, halfway up, in line with most people's eyeline, are the words - "Five reasons why it's great to be alive". And then nothing. Like whoever wrote it couldn't think of five reasons. Or, Boom thinks, maybe it's supposed to be interactive. And whoever passes needs to add a reason.

Looking around him to make sure the coast is clear, Boom squats down low, shielding his bag from view as he pulls out a can of paint. He gives it a good shake, and underneath the words, paints the number one. Then right next to it, writes:

1. Friends. Amazing, BEAUTIFUL, loyal friends (underlining loyal, as he thinks of Flash).

He writes the number two underneath, leaving it blank for the next person to fill it out. He chucks the can back into his bag and heads off. But before he rounds the corner, he stops, double backing until he's back in front of the wall. Pulling the same can back out of his bag, he draws a number three, four and five below the number one and two, talking to himself as he writes 'friends' next to each number. Drawing a lightning strike next to each one to represent Flash, he tells himself, "You are the luckiest G around, Jamie Johnson. You have your mum, you have Flash and you have the rest of the crew. You is lucky, lucky, lucky."

Finishing his five reasons, Boom heads back to his block of flats. Still high on the euphoria he feels when he thinks about friends, Boom forgets for a second what he might be coming back to. Just as he turns his key in the lock, he hears angry shouting coming from the living room. He enters the kitchen, which is in the dark, and stares down the corridor to the closed door of the living room, where all the screams are coming from.

And then it starts.

The heavy punches, his mums sobs.

And Boom can't bear it.

Walking into his bedroom, he walks straight over to the wardrobe, slides the door open and climbs inside, pushing his headphones tight to his ears.

As he buries himself into his shoes, and tries to hide, his phone pings with a message from Flash.

"Any chance your mate could pick me up from the police station?"

But even with his music cranked up as loud as it can go, Boom can still hear Oli beating the shit out of his mum, who's no longer sobbing but screaming instead. And it's just like Louisa said. The kind of scream that's burnt into your memory, a scream you'll never forget.

Boom rocks back and forth, trying to create some kind of inner calm, but all he feels is traumatised.

His phone pings with another message from Flash.

"Bro. You coming or what?! I'm soaked. It's properly pissing it down."

But Boom can't move, obsessed instead with the

sounds of his mum's screams and the rhythmic rocking, back and forth, back and forth.

As he rocks, his phone rings and Flash's name comes up. Boom answers, but as he picks up the music cuts dead - meaning all he can hear is Oli beating his mum up. He's desperate to get Flash off the phone. Flash can't hear it his end though and is clearly annoyed with Boom - the sound of heavy rain forcing Flash to shout to be heard.

"Bro. Where are you? Thought your mate was good for a lift."

But Boom's too distracted by what's going on to answer him properly.

"I can't hear you," he tells Flash.

But Flash isn't impressed and shouts even louder. "Then turn your fucking music off bro!"

Close to tears, Boom tells him, "I've got to go."

"What d'you mean you've gotta--?" Flash asks, angrily, but is cut dead as Boom ends the call.

Boom turns his music up as loud as it will go, making him wince as the sound throbs in his ears. As he sits there rocking, a message pops up from Flash.

"I took the rap for you, G. And you can't even be bothered to talk to me! So much for friendship! FUCK YOU!!"

But Boom's too distressed to reply, waiting until Oli's exhausted himself and finally stops beating his mum. With no more screams or shouts, Boom sinks down into the bottom of the wardrobe and instead of moving, shuts his eyes, drifting off into a fitful sleep.

97 I'VE TAKEN A LOT OF SHIT FOR YOU. BUT LAST NIGHT REALLY TOOK THE FUCKING PISS

Boom steps out of his flat onto the balcony, dressed in school uniform, with a piece of toast hanging from his mouth. He shuts the door behind him and walks along the balcony to the stairwell. He looks exhausted, depressed almost - all the usual spark gone from his eyes. He's like a soldier stepping straight out of a battlefield back into normal life. Everything normal on the face of it, but in reality, just... flat and low, everything out of sync.

As he steps out onto the street, he glances over to where Flash normally meets him by the lamppost, but Flash isn't there. He sits down on the pavement to wait for him, his head bent, completely and utterly broken. Minutes pass and he realises he's been lost in all his thoughts. He checks the time on his phone. He's now late. His legs feel like lead but he forces himself to run, heading for school.

Boom slows as he reaches the school gates, giving himself time to catch his breath before the bell goes. He's completely drained, not an ounce of emotion left to give. He spots Flash and some of the Crew up ahead, sitting on the wall at the side of the playground. Flash sees him and turns his back, causing the others to look at him in surprise. Boom's in half a mind whether to approach Flash or not, too exhausted and drained to be able to handle any more drama after last night. But he walks over anyway, walking straight into an awkward silence. No-one speaks for a second. Boom looks over at Flash and says, "Sorry about last night."

It doesn't even sound like him. His voice is flat and drained of any life.

Flash doesn't reply. He doesn't even look at Boom. Boom tries again, the situation so awkward that even the Crew are squirming with embarrassment.

"I couldn't get out the hou--"

Flash flips round, furious. Up till now he's been holding it in, but now it's out he lays into Boom with a tirade of words.

"I took the rap for you last night you fucking dick! The least you could have done is show up with a lift home! Instead, I had a four mile walk home in the pissing rain, 'cause my 'mate' - *who I took the fucking rap for* - couldn't give a shit! You couldn't even be bothered to take your fucking headphones off to hear me talk! Far too fucking busy listening to your fucking tunes instead!"

The rest of the Crew look shocked. Never, ever, would they think Flash and Boom would fall out like this. Instinctively, they take a step back, giving them space to work it out between them.

Boom's close to tears, but Flash is too angry to notice. Boom tries to explain, grabbing his mate by the arm in an attempt to explain himself.

"It wasn't like that. I had stuff going on. I--"

"Do you know what?! I've taken a lot of shit for you! But last night really took the fucking piss!"

Boom tries to grab him again, but Flash has had enough.

"Just fuck off! I'm not interested in whatever bullshit you've got to say!"

He gives Boom an angry shove. Boom topples backwards, knocking his head on the wall behind him.

And that's it.

He crumples and starts to sob, freaking out the rest of the Crew who've never seen him cry before.

But Boom doesn't give a shit. Not any more. He's had enough. All the years of shit… the fear. Never being able to talk to anyone about it. How hard it is. How it kills you inside. And now his best mate hates him. So as far as Boom's concerned, he's got nothing to lose by just letting it all come out.

"You wanna know the real reason I couldn't make it last night?" he asks Flash.

Flash's face is drained of colour, shocked to see his mate in the state he's in. One look at Boom and he knows this isn't going to be good.

Boom doesn't wait for an answer. "My stepdad, Oli, gets great satisfaction from beating the shit out of my mum every night. And I mean *beat*. Once a night if she's lucky. More if she's not. Most nights I'm lucky to even get out the door. But then I'm guess I'm lucky I can get out. 'Cause my mum sure as hell can't."

He doesn't care that the rest of the Crew are now staring at him in stunned silence. As 'streetwise' as they like to think they are, they all look devastated. Empathy - and shock - written all over their faces. But Boom doesn't care. He just carries on. Telling them - for the first time ever - no holds barred, just how shit his life really is.

"Most nights I have to climb out the bathroom

window just to get out, so he can't stop me. But it makes me feel like crap. Because while I'm free, she's not. My mum's the one who has to stay there and cop all his anger and hatred. My mum's the one who does it to protect me. I swear the fucking psycho is gonna kill her one day."

He pauses a second before continuing,

"In fact, last night..." Boom trails off, having to compose himself before he can continues. "Last night, I thought he had. It's the worst I've ever heard it. He pretty much turned over the whole flat, before beating her unconscious. So yeah. That's why I didn't make it out last night."

Flash is looking at him with tears in his eyes. Visibly moved by what Boom's just told him.

Ignoring everyone around him, Boom gets up and walks out through the school gates and into the street, ignoring the bell as it goes.

The Crew watch him leave, too shocked to speak or follow.

98 IT'S LIKE IT WAS THERE ALL ALONG, JUST STARING ME IN THE FACE

Flash jogs along a narrow, grassy pathway by the edge of a canal, shouting for Boom.

"Jamie!"

He's in his school uniform, having left just after Boom. He spots a trail that's been beaten through the undergrowth, leading up over the bank, and decides to follows it. Stepping out onto an overgrown track at the top, he looks for Boom and spots him several hundred feet away, slumped against a wall with his headphones on. Flash walks over and sits down next to him, reaching for his phone so he can turn the music off.

"I'm sorry I pushed you. And for being a dick. I didn't know. I was just angry."

Boom laughs. "Bit of a common theme in my life right now." Quick to add off the back of Flash's face. "That wasn't a dig by the way."

Flash looks at Boom. "Why didn't you tell me?"

Boom shrugs.

"You know what's weird?" Flash tells him. "I didn't have a fucking clue. Really. But now I do, it's like... it's like it was there all along, just staring me in the face. One minute you're having a right laugh with all of us. The next you're on your own, listening to music and not wanting to be with anyone."

"Music's the only way I can drown it out," Boom says, trying to explain it to his mate. "Cause it's always there. <u>Always.</u> Spinning round my head. If I shut my eyes, I can literally hear it, even when I'm not there. The punches. The kicks. My mum, screaming."

Flash is looking at him, like he's going to cry, but Boom carries on.

"The worst bit's the silence though. 'Cause then you're just thinking 'he's done it. He's finally killed her'."

Flash takes his mate's hand and gives it a tight squeeze as Boom continues,

"Remember that couple we bumped into on the stairs last month? 'Mean-looking mother fucker' is what you called him, if I remember right. Well that was him."

Flash shakes his head. Now he's seen Oli, it all makes sense.

Boom carries on with his story,

"He left for a bit. Last week. Fucked off with some woman from work." Suddenly some light comes back into his eyes, and his sense of humour's back, even if it is a little dark. "Anyone else would have been devastated but my mum couldn't wipe the smile off her face. It was fucking amazing. I got my old mum back, just for a while. Like when my dad was alive."

That Flash gets, having lost his own dad a few years back. He throws Boom a look of understanding, as he continues,

"We were just… happy. But then he came back, forced his way back in, and he's been worse than ever. Like he's gunning for her. Like he blames my mum for everything bad that's ever happened to him, for things not working out with him and Paula."

"Paula? You know her?" Flash asks, shocked.

"Saw them snogging outside the pub a couple of

weeks ago. Brazen as anything. Fucking arsehole."

"I don't get it. If he doesn't love you mum any more, why doesn't he just leave her?" Flash asks.

"Cause then he wouldn't be able to control us any more, would he?"

Flash shakes his head in disbelief. "How fucked up is that?" and then something clicks. "So, those pieces on the trains, the ones attacking Oli. That was you."

Boom doesn't reply. Flash looks at him, worried, telling him,

"Do me a favour, will ya? Stay away from the tracks. The only person you're gonna hurt is you. The best way to stick it to Oli is to get yourself outta here. Like Britton said. Do your thing. Do it well. Take your mum with you and just stick it to the fucker in the best way you can - by being successful and proving to him he doesn't have any power over you any more. I mean it, bro."

Boom smiles, "Lots of people wanna do stuff with their life but they never get the chance, do they? What makes you think I'm gonna be any different?"

"Cause you're an annoyingly talented fucker that's why," Flash laughs. "You were destined to do well."

Boom laughs, slapping his mate on the arm in a friendly gesture.

Flash looks at him, unsure about whether to say something to Boom or not, but then he goes for it anyway.

"There's something I want you to listen to. I think it would be good for you. But it could wait. If you didn't want to listen to it. I mean, you don't have to listen to it now."

"Now. Later. It's all the same to me." Boom shrugs.

Flash reaches into his pocket and pulls out his phone, bringing up an image of Katy Perry on Spotify, her semi-naked body sprawled across some pink, fluffy clouds. It's from The Teenage Dream album. Boom can't help it - he laughs, letting out all the pent up trauma from the last 24 hours.

"I was not expecting that! First some dude in a sparkly dress. Now Katy Perry. Are you sure there's nothing you wanna tell me, G?"

"Like what?"

"Like my best mate is a battie boy after all?" Boom teases.

"I 'aint no Battie boy," Flash replies, laughing, but taking the bants anyway.

"To be fair, I wouldn't give a shit if you were. You know that right? I'd love you whatever."

Flash grins, giving it large back. "Now who's a battie boy?"

Boom laughs. Flash stands, checking the time on his phone.

"Better get back. You coming?"

"I'm gonna stay here a bit," Boom tells him. "I won't be far behind though."

"Ok. Check this out then," Flash tells him, sharing the Katy Perry album with him. "Track four. Firework. Rach loves it. Says it makes her feel like she could do anything she set her mind to. Rule the world if she wanted to!" Flash grins, "It's like it's been written just for you, bro. There's even this one line in it" - and he starts to sing -

"Boom, Boom, Boom, even brighter than the moon, moon, moon."

He's good - but there's something funny about this cool, street kid singing Katy Perry and now Boom can't help but laugh. A proper belly laugh that says everything's ok between them now.

"Seriously, bro. Fuck off back to school before you kill that song."

Flash grins, flipping Boom the bird as he turns on his heels and makes his way back up the track.

Boom leans back against the wall and hits play, listening to the lyrics. But it's not just the chorus with his name in, it's everything. It's just like Flash said - the lyrics could have been written especially for him.

Boom's lost in the words - his eyes welling up as he listens to the lyrics and what they mean. The words that Flash chose specially for him.

He sits there listening to the end of the song, before wiping his eyes with his hand. He gets up, tucks his phone back in his pocket and walks back down the track towards the embankment, and back to school.

99 WHAT'S THAT FOR?

Flash walks in from school and dumps his bag. He heads for the kitchen, passing his mum who's out cold on the sofa. But instead of being upset or annoyed like he would be normally, he stops in front of her, gently lifting an arm that's dangling over the side and placing it back on the sofa. He then heads for the kitchen, where Rachel is fixing herself a snack. She smiles at Flash as he walks in.

"Good day?"

Flash frowns. "Not sure I'd go that far," he replies.

Rachel catches a look in his eye. A real warmth.

"What?" she asks him.

Flash walks over to her and pulls her close for a big bear hug and doesn't let go. Rachel doesn't let go either, smiling into his chest as she asks him,

"What's this for?"

"We're just lucky that's all."

"Really?!"

She doesn't look convinced. But Flash hugs her even tighter, telling her,

"Yeah, we are. We've got each other, Rach."

100 WHAT'S WITH THE WINGS?

Brightly walks out of the police station at the end of a shift and heads for his car. He looks knackered but when his phone rings he picks up, the word LAB flashing up. It's work. He listens for a second before replying, "Just leaving now. Why?"

But whatever the person's said the other end, it's done something 'cause he perks up immediately, alive with some kind of feverish excitement.

"I'm on my way," he says, heading straight back inside the station and through the corridors to the back of the building where the lab is housed. He lets himself in through the security scanner on the door, nodding at the male technician sat in front of one of the computers in semi-darkness, watching a video. The technician hits pause as soon as he sees Brightly, telling him,

"Took a bit of time, but think we've got all of it now."

Brightly sits down next to him as the technician hits play again. It's a video of Boom, pulling on his nemesis wings and mask, running towards Feisty's dad's garage. It's Feisty's early footage - which the lab must have pulled off of her phone after it was handed in. Brightly frowns, watching as the footage reaches the end, panning over the tagline, 'SINS OF THE FATHER'. He leans across the technician and hits pause.

"What's with the wings?"

"Nemesis," the technician tells him. "The goddess of divine retribution and revenge."

"How d'you know that?" Brightly asks him,

impressed.

"Did my research, you know how it is. He wants you to know he's getting back at someone. Listen," the technician tells him, as he hits play again.

Boom's heavily-disguised voice kicks in, telling anyone who's listening,

"This one's for parents everywhere. To remind them that kids are for life, not just for Christmas."

Brightly hits pause again, stroking his chin as he thinks.

"So it's someone's dad he's getting back at?"

The technician nods, rewinding the footage back to where the camera lingers over the two girls banging on the glass, trying to reach their dad. It's Feisty and Summer, their faces hidden, just their long hair poking out from inside their hoodies.

"I don't think it's his though," Brightly says, thinking it through out loud. "His real dad's dead and his stepdad he gets back at through the yard. It's got to be something to do with the two girls, whoever they are."

Brightly's stroking his chin with his fingers, desperately trying to make sense of it all.

"Is there anything else?"

The technician nods, hitting play on the next piece of footage. It's Louisa's revenge graffiti, with her ex stood in front of the dictators. Brightly hits pause for a second, asking,

"It's definitely the same style. We're looking at the same person, right?"

The technician nods, and hits play again.

Watching as whoever's holding the camera crosses the road and walks over to the dingy, worn-out tower block opposite.

"Can you zoom in on that sign?"

The technician zooms in closer, revealing the name of the tower. Brightly makes a note of it in his notebook and watches as the video continues, going through the dictators that Boom has spray painted onto the wall, one by one. There's a large flag behind one of them, with red and blue stripes, and a red star in the centre of it.

"Where's that flag from?" Brightly asks the technician.

"North Korea. And the gentleman in front of it, none other than the country's dictator, Kim Jong Un."

"Of course," Brightly comments, watching as the camera zooms in on the other figures standing in the group, facing outwards so their faces can be clearly seen. He watches as the camera pans around the group, naming each one in turn.

"The Syrian guy. I can't remember his name. And Mugabe. That's Robert Mugabe isn't it?"

The camera pans over the words Boom wrote...
"Some dictators don't need their own country to control people."

The technician hits pause, turning to look at Brightly who comments,

"Not your average graffiti artist then. Someone who's got an interest in world politics too."

"And righting the wrongs," the technician adds. "Or at least, what he sees as the wrongs. There's more," he tells Brightly, as he brings up the Lyrics video, the one Boom filmed, with the Eminem song lyrics that wind themselves along the body of a snake, getting back at the teenager who's trying to divide two friends.

The video (which Feisty must have downloaded from Graffiti Boy's stream) starts at the Lord Protector pub. Boom, who's filming, crosses the road to the tower block opposite where he painted the snake.

"I know that pub," Brightly says, making a note of its name in his notepad again, as well as the name of the tower block.

The video finishes, but there's more to come. The technician turns to Brightly and tells him,

"You'll be interested in this next one."

It's the footage at the train depot. The final film on Feisty's phone, before she fell into the skip and smashed it up. Brightly watches as Boom - who's shown from behind, his face obscured - spray paints the front of the hanger. The footage is a bit shaky as Feisty dives out of sight behind the skip, every now and then, before steadying herself again. Feisty carries on filming Boom as he finishes his piece, seconds before she falls into the skip, smashing her phone and knocking herself unconscious. The final clip finishes and Brightly sits there stroking his chin, over and over. Thinking.

"So we know they're all about revenge. But what's the connection? The depot I get, but why the others?" There's a beat, before Brightly adds, "Can you make out his face in any of the clips?"

The technician shakes his head.

"And there's nothing in there with any luminous green paint?"

The technician shakes his head again.

"Damn it!" Brightly says, slamming his hand on the desk in frustration.

101 GLAD YOU FIND IT FUNNY!

It's a boiling hot day and Flash stands waiting at the school gates. He peers down the street in the direction of where he and Boom normally come from, with a worried look on his face. He spots Boom weaving towards him, walking uncharacteristically slowly. Boom reaches Flash and stumbles, taking a nosedive towards the pavement before Flash catches him and pulls him back upright.

"Shit, Boom! You is hammered!"

Boom can barely focus, he's off his face on alcohol. Glancing back over to the gates to make sure none of the teachers have spotted them, Flash walks Boom over to the nearest house and perches him on top of a low wall that borders the front garden.

Flash balances him there as he reaches inside his bag for his water bottle. Boom sways violently - toppling backwards onto the person's grass and landing flat on his back in their garden. Flash jumps over the wall, peering nervously at the house as he tries to pull Boom back upright, but he's heavy and drunk and it's not a great combo.

"Come on Boom. Get up will ya?!" Flash says, trying to pull his mate back up to sitting.

He manages to drag him back as far as the wall and lean him against it. He then places one of Boom's arms around his neck, in an attempt to pull him back up to standing. But Boom's not having any of it, swaying violently and slurring his words as he tries to apologise.

"I'm drunk. I'm very drunk. I'm sorry."

Flash, who's normally the calm one in the Crew, is stressing out as he struggles to get Boom out of the garden in time before whoever owns the house comes out and spots them there. He looks up, desperate for help, just as Curl walks past with a mate. Curl takes one look at Boom and taps his mate on the shoulder, telling him,

"Catch you later."

He hops over the wall, and runs over to where Flash is still attempting to move Boom. Flash looks like he wants to hug him.

"I'm trying to move him but it's fucking impossible. He's absolutely shitfaced."

"Should be able to manage it between us," Curl tells him, watching the door of the house in front of them.

There's a shout from one of the open windows upstairs.

"See you about seven!"

The thought of someone about to step out of the house sends them into a blind panic, and now they just need to get Boom out of there, quick. Grabbing an arm each, they manage to yank Boom back up onto his feet, but he's swaying really badly and can barely keep his eyes open. His eyes roll back into his head as he starts to tell them something.

"I'm gonna be--"

Boom stops-- throwing up all over Curl. Curl recoils in disgust and drops Boom, who slumps back onto the grass, barely able to keep himself upright. Just then, a thick-set man walks out of his front door and stares at them in disbelief.

"What the bloody hell…?" he says, staring at Boom, and the pile of sick on his grass.

Flash and Curl drag Boom back over the wall, bumping and grazing his legs as they drag him over the top, shouting back to the man as they leave… "Sorry!"

They reach the gates where Boom seems to have sobered up a bit now he's been sick, but the heat's making the sick on Curl's top stink. Flash takes one look at Curl's shirt and starts to laugh.

"Glad *you* find it funny!" he says, giving Flash a pissed off look.

"I don't," Flash tells him, struggling not to snigger, "It's just… funny in a bad kind of way. Here have my jumper."

Flash peels of his jumper and chucks it at Curl.

"I'm not wearing that. It's boiling!"

"Don't think you've got a choice, G," Flash tells him, starting to laugh again.

Curl undoes his school shirt, carefully peeling it off himself so as not to get any sick on himself and stands there holding it in front of him as far away from his body as he can.

"Gross! What am I gonna do with this now?!"

"Stick it in the hedge. You can collect it later," Flash tells him.

Shaking his head, Curl screws his shirt into a tight ball and stuffs it into the hedge. He slaps Flash on the arm and races ahead of him, into school.

Boom is now walking, with Flash, towards the school gate. They pass a Citroen by the side of the road.

It's Brightly, who's sat as bold as brass in the front seat, watching them approach in his rear-view mirror. He winds down his window and shouts out to them as they pass.

"Everything alright there, lads?"

Brightly nods, tipping his head at Flash.

"Adam."

"Yes, thanks officer," Flash replies.

They keep walking towards the school until they're safely inside. But the second they're in, and away from Brightly, the pair of them start freaking out.

"That's the cop you were talking about, isn't it? The one with my t-shirt?"

Boom nods.

"How the fuck does he know my name?" Flash asks, worried.

Boom shrugs it off. "He knows it's your t-shirt."

"Yeah but how did he know *I'm* Adam?"

"He's just messing with our heads that's all. He 'aint got anything on us," Boom tells him. But Flash isn't convinced, staring out the window to the front of the school to check if Brightly's still there or not.

102 WHAT'S THE EMERGENCY?

It's the end of the school day and the students are piling outside, desperate to get home. Boom, however, hovers by his locker, waiting for everyone to leave. He waits for the corridor to empty before looking back over his shoulder and opening the top of his rucksack just enough to grab his books. Using his bag to shield the books, he opens his yellow workbook from the classroom and flicks through all the pages, checking out how many graffiti sketches he's scribbled down the side of his book… Sins of The Father; the Alien one with Feisty's angry bird… There might be more, but the two that he's seen are enough to incriminate him alone. Glancing down the corridor in both directions, Boom slides his workbook out of his bag. Checking the direction of the cameras, Boom puts his bag down next to the lockers, making it look like he's just resting it there, before subtly sliding the book as far as he can behind the lockers. Somewhere where it will never be found.

His phone beeps and Flash rounds the corner in front of him, followed by Curl, and then several feet behind them, The Cat, and then finally… The Watcher. They're walking in front of each other, no-one talking - acting, for all intents and purposes, like they don't know each other. Boom darts up the stairs to the second floor, followed by the rest of the crew. He walks past another set of lockers down a dark hallway to the end, where a storage cupboard blocks the camera pointing in its direction. Boom waits till they catch up before telling them,

"Should be safe here. No CCTV down this end of the hallway."

The Cat can't wait though and asks,

"What's the emergency?"

"BTP are sniffing about," Flash tells them. "They've got eyes on Boom. And me."

"What the fuck?! You idiot Boom!" The Watcher tells him, asking, "Cause of the stuff at the depot?"

Boom nods.

"Why d'you do it anyway?" The Watcher asks him.

"To get back at Oli," Boom tells him.

Any other time, they'd have had a go at him, but after hearing what's been going on at home they get it. No-one says a thing.

"Shit!" The Cat says, recognising the severity of the situation. "They 'aint gonna just give up their investigation, G."

"I know. That's why I'm here," Boom says.

Curl looks worried. "What about Feisty. Is she involved?"

"Nah," Boom shakes his head.

"Thank fuck," Curl replies. "No telling what she'd do if you pissed her off enough. So how d'you know they're on to you?"

"The graffiti cop came round the other night. And he was outside school this morning. Probably been to the depot too. Only person he hasn't spoken to yet is Oli," Boom says.

"Let's hope he don't either, G. Otherwise I'll be

moving you and your mum into mine to live," Flash replies, worried.

"Has he got anything on you?" The Watcher asks.

"Nah. Well. Maybe. Not much," Boom replies.

"What the fuck does that mean?!" The Watcher asks.

"They've got Flash's T-shirt. The one with the cop on. The one I got paint on. And they know it's his," Boom says, eyeing his mate apologetically.

"Fuck Boom! How comes we're only finding this out now?" The Cat asks.

"I just didn't want to get you involved, sorry. The less you know the better," Boom replies.

"Have they got enough to pin something on you?" Curl asks.

"Nah. Not unless they find our Angry Bird piece. But there's nothing to link that piece to any of the others."

"Yeah but if they're investigating all the others, they'll find it, won't they?" The Watcher asks, worried.

"He 'aint gonna go searching round the whole of London looking for one piece," Boom replies, shaking his head.

"Wouldn't put it past him," Flash says. "He's here, 'aint he?"

The Crew look worried.

"So what's he look like, this cop?" The Watcher asks.

Boom pulls up a photo of Brightly on his phone. They hand it round till they've all seen it, studied it and logged it to memory, before Boom sticks his phone back in his pocket. He glances down the corridor, checking for teachers - aware they've been there a while.

"We've gotta go back and cover it up," The Watcher says.

"No way!" Flash says. "He was right outside the fucking school. You telling me he's not got us followed? He even used my fucking name, bro. I'm telling you, he's onto us. We go back and he catches us, we're fucked."

"Yeah but if we don't do it, and he finds the piece, he's got all the evidence he needs to bang one - or all of us - up," The Watcher replies, trying to convince the others he's right. "All he has to do is match the DNA of the paint to the paint on Flash's t-shirt and bang. That's you gone, bro."

"The only reason Brightly would find all the pieces is 'cause dumbarse here - or should I say dumbarse's friend - posted the fucking evidence all over social media," Flash says, looking at Boom.

Boom shoots Flash a look, but Flash jumps in quickly. "Sorry mate, you're the smartest guy I know, but getting involved with Feisty was the dumbest thing you've ever done."

"Just shut up you two," The Watcher says. "We need to work out what to do." Taking control, he tells The Crew, "No more paints from now on. No more sketches. Nothing. If this guy is following us, we shouldn't be carrying anything that could incriminate us, got that?" he looks at Boom pointedly, before continuing, "I think--

He stops, as somewhere on the floor above them,

a door slams. A teacher makes their way down the stairs. He reaches the bottom step, and sensing The Crew there, he turns to stare directly at them.

"You lot. What are you still doing in school?"

They shrug, looking guilty without even trying.

"Home. Now!" the teacher tells them.

The Watcher spins round quickly, with his back to the teacher, whispering to the others under his breath, "Lord Protector in ten."

Suspicious, the teacher walks over to them, making sure they leave. He waits for the last member of the crew to trail down the stairs, before following them outside.

Outside the school, the Crew instinctively separate without anyone having to suggest it. The Cat's first through the school gates, turning left to throw any cops off the scent, just in case they're being followed. Then, Curl, who's with Flash for a change, takes a right, walking in completely the opposite direction to The Cat. Followed by Boom, on his own. And then The Watcher, following up the rear.

As Curl and Flash pass the bush from earlier, Flash tips his head to where Curl stuffed his shirt in the hedge. Grinning, he asks him,

"You picking your shirt up, G?"

"Think I'll wait for a rainy day," Curl counteracts, with a good-natured grin.

Flash starts to giggle, setting Curl off too as they head down the road laughing.

103 WOULDN'T BE SUCH A COCK IF I BLUE LIT YOU, WOULD YOU?

Brightly's in his Citroen, trawling the estates, looking for the missing graffiti piece - the Angry Bird one, with the luminous paint. The one that - if he finds it - could see Boom prosecuted. He's driving at 15 m.p.h, much to the annoyance of a teenage boy behind him who's in a souped-up white Fiesta, with a spoiler on the back, and an adjusted exhaust that roars when he puts his foot on the accelerator. Brightly clocks the kid's face in his rearview mirror, as he slows down in front of one of the tower blocks, checking out its name and looking for signs of graffiti. The kid honks his horn at Brightly, but Brightly ignores him, slowing at the next crossroads to check out the name of the next tower block. This time, the kid behind loses patience - and drives his car up the pavement to overtake Brightly, giving him the bird as he passes.

"Wouldn't be such a cock if I blue lit you, would you?" Brightly mutters to himself as the kid passes.

As Brightly gets going again, he spots the Lord Protector up ahead, opposite the tower block he's come to look at. There's a group of teenagers perched high on a wall outside the pub, their faces not quite distinct enough to make out from where he's at. But it's The Crew, with Boom and Flash in the midst of them.

The Watcher, who's on the end nearest to Brightly, has spotted his beaten-up banger of a Citroen already. While the rest of the Crew are busy having a bit of banter, his eyes are locked on Brightly, watching as the car slows to a stop, before pulling off again - clearly looking for something. Curl's spotted him now, commenting to the others as he jumps down off the wall.

"Looks like the old fella needs a hand finding somewhere."

"What makes you think he's old?" Flash asks.

"Gotta be, driving a shit heap like that. I'm gonna see if he needs directions."

The Watcher jumps off the wall and grabs him by the arm to stop him. "Wait."

Having caught the attention of the others, they look over - watching in interest to see whatever this guy is up to. Boom and Flash clock the car at the same time.

"Shit!!"

They jump down off the wall, hiding behind it as Brightly gets closer, whispering to the others loud enough for them to hear,

"Just act normal."

The rest of the Crew are freaking out, wondering who this is. They keep their eyes on the car as it draws close, watching as it stops next to the Cromwell Towers sign on the tower block opposite, where Boom painted his Lyrics piece. Brightly pulls over to the side of the road, and gets out - camera in hand.

"Fuck!" The Watcher mutters under his breath, clocking Brightly straight away, as the guy Boom showed them earlier.

Aware he's being watched, Brightly walks over to study Boom's graffiti - the one with the snake and the lyrics winding their way along the length of its body. He clocks the tag at the bottom - GB - and mutters quietly to himself under his breath, 'Bingo!' He takes a photo before walking back to his car, looking up to speak to The Watcher before climbing back in.

"Cool graffiti."

"Yeah," The Watcher replies, trying to keep his cool.

He watches as Brightly pulls away slowly, watching as he rounds the corner and is gone. Flash and Boom pop back up from behind the wall, and don't say a word. Only The Watcher has something to say.

"I know we agreed we shouldn't be doing any more graffiti right now, but you saw him. He's actively looking for something. I'm telling you, we need to get rid of that Angry Bird piece as soon as possible. Before he finds it and links it to Boom." The Watcher paces on the spot, before adding,

"I don't like this. Don't like this at all."

104 A YOUNG SLIP OF A THING LIKE YOU?

Brightly's still driving around the Estate in his car, going from tower block to tower block, looking for the missing piece of the puzzle... Boom's Angry Bird graffiti. His phone's on the dashboard in front of him, fixed in a holder to the left of the steering wheel. The phone rings, but the car's not high-tech enough to have bluetooth, so Brightly pulls over to the side of the road to take the call. He listens for a second before replying,

"So have the doctors given the go ahead for me to speak to her this afternoon?"

He goes quiet again, before replying, "Tell the boss I'll be there in ten."

And with that he hangs up, pulling off quicker this time, heading straight to the hospital.

Reaching the front of the building, Brightly pulls over into a drop off bay and slides an official police permit onto the dashboard so as not to get booked. He jumps out of the car and heads inside, walking along the corridor until he reaches one of the wards. He walks straight past the desk, flashing his badge at the nurses as he passes, and heading straight to the end of the corridor where he knows Feisty is, with her dad.

Brightly walks into the side ward. All the beds are empty bar Feisty's, the bed nearest the door. Feisty's propped up in bed, a load of pillows plumped and piled high behind her. Her face is pale and washed out. Her dad's sat on a chair next to her and looks up as Brightly walks in, giving him a curt nod. No pleasantries here.

Feisty's dad catches the look, and even though he's been shit with Feisty ever since he left, he flicks straight to defence mode.

Brightly flashes his badge at them, before getting straight to the point.

"DC Brightly. I'm investigating the graffiti at the train depot in Cranville Road," he says. Then he looks straight at Feisty, addressing her directly. "How are you doing, Mercedes?"

Mr Havara gets in first, cutting Feisty off before she can reply. "She's pretty shaken actually, detective."

"Dad!" Feisty responds, annoyed.

"What?! You're not up to being questioned."

He's protecting her, and Brightly knows it, responding calmly with,

"Really? My colleague spoke to the doctors earlier and they gave me the go ahead to speak to your daughter directly Mr Havara," adding off the back of Mr Havara's unimpressed face, "Besides it's just a chat. Nothing more."

Brightly looks at Feisty.

"Have the doctors said when you'll be back at school?"

Mr Havara jumps in a second time.

"The doctors said she could go back in a couple of days when the headaches have gone. But for now she's still on a lot of medication for her pain."

Brightly looks unimpressed.

"Mr Havara. I appreciate you're looking after your daughter but it's important you let her speak."

Feisty's dad looks at Brightly but doesn't

respond.

"I won't stay long," Brightly tells Feisty, "I just want to ask you a couple of questions." He catches the dread on Mercedes' face, adding: "You don't mind, do you?", knowing only too well that she does.

Feisty shrugs as if to say no though.

"What were you doing at the train depot, Mercedes?" Brightly asks her.

Feisty goes red, having to think on her feet real quick.

"I like graffiti. I heard there was a piece someone had done at the hanger and I wanted to take a photo."

"Were you on your own?" Brightly asks her.

Feisty nods, not quite able to hold his gaze.

"Do you normally wander about late at night on your own?"

"I'm not scared, if that's what you mean," Feisty responds, trying to play it down.

"That's not what I asked."

Feisty looks worried now. Like she knows Brightly's on to her, but isn't quite sure how to throw him off the scent.

"No. No, I don't," she responds. Adding, "But I'm not scared, if that's what you mean."

"A young slip of a thing like you? You should be," he tells her. "There's all kinds of dodgy characters hanging about late at night. You need to take more care of yourself."

Brightly holds his gaze, keeping eye contact with Mercedes as he repeats the question.

"So you weren't with anyone that night then,

Mercedes?"

Feisty starts to panic, struggling to catch her breath - her anxiety getting the better of her. Brightly keeps forging ahead, asking her, "You haven't seen another graffiti piece anywhere have you?" he asks her, "same style, with luminous green paint in it somewhere? I dunno, it might turn out to be impossible to find, but luminous green. I can't imagine many writers using it, can you?"

Feisty's really struggling to catch her breath now, too young and naive to know how to handle Brightly. Only too conscious she could get into a fuck of a lot of trouble for what she's done.

Mr Havara takes one look at Feisty and pulls the red emergency cord by her bed.

"I think that's enough, DC Brightly," he tells him.

Brightly shrugs. He gives them a forced smile, looks at Feisty and tells her,

"Look after yourself. Make sure you get enough rest."

He nods, turning to leave just as one of the nurses turns up to help. She smiles at Feisty, eyeing Brightly as he leaves, asking her, "You alright lovey?"

She turns round to give Brightly another look, but he's gone.

105 HOW ARE YOU?

Boom's back at school, with the rest of The Crew. It's the usual story... making sure they're not standing anywhere near each other so that no-one clocks them together and realises they're a Crew.

Boom's stood with Flash by the gates when The Watcher walks past. Keeping his head down, so no-one notices him talking to them, he tells them, "Tonight. Usual time. We're getting rid of it."

The Watcher heads over to Curl and The Cat and speaks to them in a low voice, obviously telling them the same thing.

The bell goes, and Boom taps Flash on the arm before sprinting off.

"I'll catch you in class. Just need to do something first."

Heading inside the school, Boom hovers by the ladies' toilet, hiding under the stairs as he waits for Feisty to appear. She shows up, usual time; back at school and there to do a last-minute touch up of her make-up before class. Boom waits a few seconds before following her into the toilets, ducking behind the door before he's spotted.

Feisty's inside one of the cubicles, so Boom waits, leaning against the sink facing her so the second she comes out she spots him. Feisty opens the cubicle door and spots Boom standing there and jumps, cornered and unable to escape. Her face drops as she realises he's after answers. Guilty for trying to stitch him up, she remains silent.

"How are you?" Boom asks her.

"Alright," she replies, keeping it short. Not sure what he knows and what he doesn't.

"Are you being funny with me?" he asks, confused by her reaction.

"No," she replies, super defensive.

"Why were you at the train depot?" he asks.

This time Feisty decides to tell the truth.

"I followed you."

Boom doesn't get it. "Why?"

Feisty starts kicking the front of the sink, refusing to look at him. She's got something to say but she can't say it.

"Go on!" Boom tells her, baiting her.

"I wanted to get back at you," she tells him eventually.

"For what?!"

"For dumping me for Louisa," Feisty says, glaring at him.

"I'm not even seeing Louisa, for fucks sake! She's a nice girl and all that but I've already told you. I've got enough shit in my life to worry about right now, without having to think about a girlfriend."

But Feisty doesn't believe him. She thinks he's spinning her a line, her anger bursting to the surface.

"Don't know what you see in her anyway! She's just some stupid kid who got caught up with an eighteen-year-old 'cause she thought it would be 'exciting' then couldn't cope when he wanted what any normal eighteen year old would want."

Boom knows Louisa was bullied, so hearing

Feisty defend Louisa's ex like this makes him flip out.

"What, so you think it's ok for him to follow her home and threaten her, just 'cause she was trusting enough to believe he might be a decent bloke?!"

He looks at her, shaking his head in disappointment. Tired of all Feisty's bullshit and her anger, he turns to leave, telling her, "I'm going."

"That's right. Do the bloke thing. Fuck off when things get awkward, why don't you?" Feisty tells him, sarcastically.

Boom ignores her. He's halfway out the door, when she tells him,

"You're lucky my phone broke."

Boom spins back round.

"What d'you mean by that?"

"I saw you. Doing the hanger doors."

Boom stops for a minute, letting it all sink in.

"Were you spying on me?"

Feisty refuses to answer but Boom still doesn't want to think the worst.

"What were you gonna do with it?"

And suddenly he knows.

"You were gonna post it, weren't you?! Fucking hell, Feisty. I could get done for that!"

Feisty knows she's in the wrong, but she layers on the sarcasm just for him. Talking to him like she hates him, when really she's just hurt.

"Like I said, it's lucky my phone broke."

Boom's really angry now. He manages to keep his distance, but you can hear the anger in his voice.

"Lucky for you it did."

Feisty laughs at him, like he's pathetic.

"Are you threatening me?! Bit pathetic, isn't it?"

Which just makes Boom all the madder. He takes a step closer to her.

"You'd love that, wouldn't you?" he says. "Gives you the chance to play the victim a bit more. Poor old Feisty. Her dad doesn't care about her so she thinks she can get away with anything. Well for the record, no. I'm not threatening you. I just thought you were a mate that's all. But mates don't try and destroy their friends' lives like you have. Good mates, like Flash--"

Feisty laughs, mocking Boom as she interrupts him mid flow.

"Here we go again. The bro love in."

"Fuck off with your sarcasm," Boom tells her. "Flash is everything you're not. Loyal. Funny. Kind. Whilst you? You're just a sad, lonely little individual. So fucked up, you can't even see that what you're doing is sad. They warned me to stay away from you but I stupidly ignored them. Gave you the benefit of the doubt. But why, I don't know. Cause you're just this fucked up, spiteful little kid who doesn't give a shit about anyone, much less their friends. I don't know why I got involved with you in the first place!"

Boom storms out of the toilet, leaving Feisty in tears. Hurt, and hellbent on revenge, she pulls her phone out of her bag, along with Brightly's business card. She dials his number and waits for him to pick up.

"Hi. DC Brightly? It's Mercedes. Mercedes Havara. You know that piece of graffiti you wanted to find? Well, I think I know where it is."

106 THANK YOU MERCEDES

Brightly's on the Estate where Boom did his first piece of graffiti with Feisty, where he drew her as Angry Bird meeting the rest of the Crew. A man in a suit leads Brightly round the back of one of the units, the same unit where Boom did the piece. Brightly reaches the back of the compound and looks up... looking at it in all its technicolor glory.

Boom's spaceship graffiti welcoming Angry Bird to the Crew.

The spaceship itself is made up of two colours. A dull grey for the spaceship, silhouetted by a luminous green glow.

A huge grin spreads over Brightly's face.

He walks over to the wall and scratches the paint with his finger nail, comparing it to the paint on Flash's t-shirt, in a photo on his phone.

He can't tell for sure (at least not until he gets the paint back to the LAB for a match test), but from where he's standing it looks like a 100% match.

"Thank you, Mercedes," he says in his thick, Yorkshire accent, grinning to himself as the final piece of the puzzle falls into place.

107 DO THEY KNOW WHO IT IS YET?

Britton is sat in the head's office, as Ellington fills him in on the latest from Brightly.

"Do they know who it is yet?" Brightly asks him.

"If they do, they're not telling me," Ellington replies.

Britton listens as Ellington continues, "But apparently there's a definite link between the local stuff and the stuff at the depot. It's not your average graffiti artist either. I mean, the work with all the dictators in. There's not many secondary school kids who are clever enough - or even interested enough - to know who they all are, much less use them in such a clever way as to make a statement."

Britton picks up the photos of Boom's graffiti from Ellington's desk, shuffling through them until he gets to the one with all the dictators in, the one attacking Louisa's ex for being a bully.

Something about the style, and what Ellington has said though, has hit home with him.

"I'll be back in a minute," he tells Ellington, getting up out of his seat and heading back into his own classroom, where he sits at his desk, rifling through the students' yellow workbooks.

Britton flicks through the pile several times, looking for something but becoming more and more agitated when he can't find it.

"Come on! Where are you?!" he mutters.

Giving up, he walks over to the store cupboard instead and pulls out the copies of Wuthering Heights he's been working on with the class. Leafing through them one by one, he flicks through the pages in turn until he finds the one he's looking for.

He goes straight for the inside cover where Boom's drawn a picture of a fist, punching its way through a wall - sheer anger emanating from the picture. The artwork done in exactly the same style as Boom's other graffiti.

"Damn it, Jamie!"

The bell goes at the end of break. Britton reaches for a black marker - hurriedly scribbling down some instructions on the white board for his class to follow before he heads outside.

27th February. Wuthering Heights. Read Chapters 22 and 23 in full - and IN SILENCE - until I return. If you finish, work through the questions at the back of the book.

And then he heads outside, clutching Boom's book in his hand.

He spots Boom coming back inside with Flash.

"A word, Mr Johnson," Britton tells him, his voice deadly serious.

Flash looks on as Britton leads Boom away from the school building, heading instead across the school playing field to the far side, where they sit down together on the grass side by side.

108 I MEAN, FOR CHRIST'S SAKE, JAMIE! DID IT EVEN CROSS YOUR MIND TO CHECK THE STORIES OUT FIRST?!

Britton and Boom are sat at the furthest end of the playing field, as far away from the school building as they can be. Britton's still clutching Boom's copy of Wuthering Heights as he talks.

"You know how I knew it was you?" he asks Boom.

Boom tries to pretend he doesn't know what Britton's talking about. He shrugs at Britton; not admitting anything - but not denying it either.

"It was something the cops said," Britton tells him. "And Ellington. About it not being your average student. How it had to be someone really smart. And they were right. There aren't many secondary school students who'd know the names of every big dictator from around the globe," Britton tells him, "but you would."

Boom doesn't answer, bringing Britton's frustration bubbling to the surface.

"I mean, for Christ's sake, Jamie! Did it even cross your mind to check the stories out first?! Rape is a really serious allegation!"

Boom sits with his head bowed.

"Who else is mixed up in all this?" Britton asks him.

"Just me."

Boom's finally admitted it to someone.

"Who filmed you?" Britton asks.

"Feisty. I mean Mercedes," Boom replies.

Britton lets out a long breath. "For fuck's sake, Jamie. I told you she was trouble. I suppose it was her idea to film it in the first place?"

Boom nods. "Feisty filmed pretty much most of my stuff. Apart from the snake one. I filmed that one myself. And the ones at the depot, they were mine too. The last one, I didn't even know she was there. Told me afterwards she'd followed me to the depot. She filmed it all, said she was going to post it all over social media to get back at me. But then she fell in the skip and that was that."

"Why did she want to get back at you?" Britton asks.

"We had a bit of a thing for a while. Nothing serious. But she got it into her head it was more than what it was and then when she saw me with Louisa she got really angry with me and started accusing me of seeing her. Which isn't true. I just know her 'cause she lives up the corridor from me."

Britton sits in silence for a minute, letting it all sink in before opening up the front cover of Boom's book to where he's drawn the fist punching through a wall.

"Has this got something to do with what's been going on?" he asks Boom.

"What do you mean?" Boom asks, uncomfortably.

"Come on, Jamie. Don't play dumb with me. You know exactly what I mean."

Boom curls in on himself, hunching into his

knees and holding himself tight - refusing to even look at Britton. Britton carries on though, pushing Boom for a reaction until it comes.

"You know what I think, Jamie? I think you go home every single night as scared as hell, wondering what you're going to find. Or more to the point, who you're going to find and what's going to have happened to them."

Boom's bottom lip starts to quiver. He's close to tears.

"But the biggest killer of all. The *biggest* killer of all," Britton repeats, "is the sense of helplessness. Isn't that right? There's absolutely fuck all you can do to stop it, even if you wanted to. Which you do. But you're so shit scared, you can't. You can't even move. So instead you sit back and watch someone you love get the crap beaten out of them every single night. You hate them for doing that to someone you love. But you hate yourself even more for letting it happen."

There's something about the way he's so fired up that makes Boom look up.

Tears are pouring down his face. Every word of Britton's forcing him to face up to what he has to deal with on a daily basis. In fact, what he's had to deal with for years.

Boom looks Britton in the eye and something about the way he looks... he just knows. Britton rolls up a sleeve, revealing some harsh red, cigarette burns running all the way up his arms.

"Arseholes exist in every sector of society, Jamie. Not just yours," Britton tells him, before asking, "So who is it then?"

Boom lets out a slow breath of air, weirdly relieved at finally being able to talk so openly about this, and to an adult too. One that understands.

"My stepdad, Oli. He beats the shit outta my mum every night," he tells Britton. Adding, "And I mean, *beats*. You can literally hear the hate in every punch he lands on her. I'm sure he'd kill her if he thought he could get away with it. I hate him. Hate what he's done to her. Hate what he's done to us. Hate fucking everything about him."

Boom trails off, unable to hold his emotions in any longer. A huge sob racks his body. Britton places an arm around Boom, until his breathing regulates itself again and he stops crying.

"Is that why you got into graffiti in the first place?" Britton asks him, "To get out the house?"

Boom nods. "I can't bear being there, night after night. Listening to what he's doing to my mum. She was so happy with my dad. She was a completely different person back then. It's like he's broken her. Like he's deliberately tried to break her."

He continues.

"Every night I shut my eyes and try to sleep. But I can't. That's why I'm always asleep in class. It's the only place I feel safe enough to sleep. I haven't slept properly in years."

Britton rests a comforting hand on Boom's arm, telling him,

"My dad used to beat all of us. Me, my sister. My mum. Didn't seem to have a preference which one it was. We'd all be at the end of his fist at some point or another. Started when I was five years old. Can you believe that? I mean, for fuck's sake. Who beats a five year old?!"

Now it's Britton's turn to catch his breath, waiting until he has composed himself enough to continue.

"Guess I'm one of the lucky ones though. I got out. One of my teachers at school. Saw the signs and got us out. Helped us find a hostel and that was that. One day we just left. Thing is though, doesn't matter how old you are. If you grow up being told you're a piece of shit, you start to believe it after a while. And you never forget how little that made you feel. No matter how old and experienced you become."

He pauses for a second, wanting to emphasise something to Boom.

"But you know what, Jamie? And I'm living proof of this. Just because you've had a shit start in life, doesn't mean it has to be that way forever. People can have awful things - *really awful things* - happen to them when they are younger and still go on and do well. I guess what I'm trying to say, Jamie, is don't give up. Don't let your shit define you."

Boom laughs. A dry, ironic laugh.

"It's funny," he says. "Even now, when I feel like shit. I still can't help thinking about graffiti. What you just said then would make a really cool tagline. *Don't let your shit define you.*"

Britton laughs.

"It would, wouldn't it? Do I get a commission for that?"

"Nah. You should know better than to

encourage a student to do something illegal like graffiti," Boom adds, with a grin.

Britton laughs. A proper belly laugh this time.

"That's what I like about you, Jamie. You're bright."

Boom looks at Britton, suddenly serious again.

"Can I ask you something?"

"Sure."

"How come you don't get frightened in class? When kids throw stuff at you. Like Ali. That time he picked his desk up and chucked it at you."

Britton laughs.

"That?! That was nothing. I had a student lift up a cupboard once and throw it at me. Didn't do a very good job of it mind but he still threw it." Britton carries on, trying to explain to Boom why it doesn't scare him. "I mean, yeah it's serious. But that kind of thing doesn't bother me, 'cause I know it's not personal. They're just kids acting out. Hitting back at all the shit they've got going on in their lives. But what my dad did. That was personal. As long as I live, I'll never understand why he did what he did. To his own wife and kids." He pauses, before adding, "I'm 45 and I still have nightmares about it now."

Britton stops talking and they sit next to each other, side by side, until Britton breaks the silence to ask, "What's your tag?"

"I've got two," Boom replies. "Graffiti Boy, for the stuff I did with Feisty. I mean, Mercedes. And the other stuff. DC, short for Da Crew. Or if it's just me, it's Boomshakalaka. Boom for short. It means happiness.

Something I'd like to be one day. Happy."

"You will be," Britton tells him, before asking, "So why d'you do it?"

"I guess… every other situation in my life, I have no choice but to just sit back and take whatever shit life throws at me. But with graffiti… it's like, for the first time ever I've got a voice. All of a sudden I'm *allowed* an opinion. And sometimes people even listen to me too. Or maybe people just like my art," he jokes.

"Was it Mercedes' idea to graffiti her dad's garage?" Britton asks him.

"Yeah," Boom replies, "but I didn't have to do it. I could have said no. But I felt sorry for her. I got it. And then after that I got a bit of a taste for it, I suppose. There's something really satisfying at getting back at all the nasty fuckers in the world who just do what they want and get away with it. Nasty fuckers like Oli. And it made me feel like I was fighting back for once, instead of sitting back and letting it all play out in front of me."

Britton nods. "And now?"

"Now I just want my stepdad to get what's coming to him," Boom replies.

"You know the best way to do that?" Britton asks him.

"You're about to tell me it's by doing well aren't you?" Boom says, shaking his head.

"You might think it's cliche or stupid, Jamie, but it's right. People like my dad. People like Oli. They don't change, Jamie. Even if they're caught and prosecuted, they'll just move on and do it all over again to someone new. Destroy someone else's life. But fuck him, Jamie! Fuck him and all his anger and hatred. Focus on what *you* want to do instead. The best way to get to him is to show him that you've moved on. That he's still stuck in his angry, bitter little world but you've moved on and you're happy now. And he no longer has any control over you."

Britton makes sure Boom's looking at him for the next bit. "You can do that Jamie, cause you're smart. Go to Uni. Get away from him. Take your mum with you. Do whatever you need to do to be a success. And stay away if you want to, or don't stay away if you don't want to. But if you come back make sure you come back when you're strong enough to handle him. And show him, he's no longer in control of your life."

He looks at Boom, making sure he's taken it all in. Then he gets to his feet and holds his hand out, pulling Boom back up on his feet.

"Come on. I've got a class to teach."

As they walk back towards school, Britton stops and turns to Boom.

"You know I'm going to have to tell Mr Ellington all of this, don't you? And he'll have to speak to the police. But I'll make sure they hear your side of things first so that it counts towards you."

Boom nods.

"I'm sorry," Britton tells him. "You get it don't you? I can't *not* say anything."

"Yeah, it's ok. I get it," Boom tells him, as they head back towards school.

109 YOU STITCHED ME UP!

Britton and Boom walk back into school, relaxed in each other's company. For Boom, it's like a huge weight has been lifted off him and for the first time in years his face looks relaxed, with all the greyness and the stress gone.

But as they round the corner, they find Brightly stood outside the classroom door waiting for them, with the head.

Brightly's wearing a smug look on his face. Worse still though is his t-shirt. The exact same one that Boom borrowed from Flash, with the policeman flipping the bird at someone in defiance. It's like he's getting off on some sick, twisted joke - but this time it's on Boom.

Boom takes one look at Brightly, with Ellington stood next to him - and wrongly, assumes Britton was in on the sting.

"You stitched me up!"

Boom can't believe it. He opened up all his deepest, darkest secrets, and for what? A con?

Britton opens his mouth to deny it, but before he gets a chance to speak he's interrupted by one of the ginger-haired cops, accompanying Curl down the corridor.

Curl's not under arrest but he's clearly there under duress, telling the cop,

"I've already told you. I don't know what you're talking about!"

Trailing behind them is the second cop, who's got his eye firmly on Flash, The Watcher and The Cat as they head towards the others.

Boom's face drops... gutted that he's dragged all his friends into this.

Brightly, though, couldn't be happier and flashes Boom a smug smile.

Ellington, however, is completely in the dark, and isn't happy about it. Turning to Brightly he asks him, "Are you going to tell me what's going on, officer, or do I need to ring your superior?"

The use of 'superior' doesn't go down well with Brightly, but before he gets a chance to answer, Feisty walks into school with her dad. She catches Brightly's eye and looks away again quickly as she heads over to the group, refusing to look anyone in the eye.

Brightly, though, has got everyone he needs right there. Before anyone has even had a chance to speak, he launches into full flow.

"Jamie Johnson, you are being charged with three separate counts of conspiracy to cause criminal damage to the property of Greater London Trains on the 9th, 10th and 14th of May this year, together with five counts of conspiracy to cause criminal damage to various properties in and around London. You don't have to say anything but--

Boom stares at Feisty. He knows it's her who's landed him in it - and he's furious she still doesn't have the balls to look him in the eye. He shakes his head as she keeps her head bowed, in a bid to absolve herself of any blame. For Boom, though, it's like a red rag to a bull. Ignoring everything Brightly is saying, he explodes at Feisty, angrily telling her,

"You could at least have the balls to look me in the face after pinning everything on me," he tells her. "Standing there like you're completely innocent," he goes on, willing her to look up and face the music. He turns to her dad instead, telling him, "By the way. The graffiti at the garage. It was Mercedes' idea, along with the video and the idea to post it all over Social Media. It was meant as revenge. But I don't suppose she told you that, did she?"

Feisty's dad turns to her, shocked. Mercedes tries to deny it, though.

"Jamie said if--"

Now it's Flash's turn to lose it with Feisty because for someone so loyal he can't stand disloyalty in any shape or form. And he lets her know it.

"Jamie?! Jamie?! You know what, Mercedes?! He's done nothing but defend you, right from the start. Despite everything we said about you. But the first sign of any trouble and you're more than happy to sell your friends to the devil, aren't you? You're just pathetic, you know that?"

"That's enough, Adam!" Ellington tells him.

Brightly, though, is lapping it up. Leaving it to play out in front of him, in the hope that if he leaves them to it they'll just end up stitching each other up and making his job easier for him.

He turns to the probationary cops.

"Read them their rights will you? We can call their parents once we're back at the station."

Before Boom is led away, he turns back to Feisty, furious at her for all the shit she's caused.

"Did you *really* just do all of this 'cause of some

crazy batshit idea I'd had a fling with Louisa?!"

Feisty looks up. Strong all of a sudden, she walks over to Boom, stopping inches from his face. Gritting her teeth to compose herself, she tells him,

"I'll tell you why I did it, shall I? Because you used me. Got what you wanted out of me and then casually walked away when you were done."

Boom tries to protest his innocence but Feisty is too angry to let him get a word in. Furious, she goes in for the kill. "I did it because you were just this sad, pathetic, broken little mess. Desperate for someone to listen to you. It was easy."

It hurts, and without even realising what he's doing, Boom's got her pinned against the wall by her shoulders.

"Jamie!"

Boom turns to find his mum standing there, watching him. It's obvious she's been called by the school - but she's arrived at the exact same moment her son is being taken away. But instead of her support, all Boom clocks is the disappointment on her face - his anger a reminder to her of her life at home with Oli. The comparison isn't fair - but nevertheless, it's there.

And he can see it in her face.

Boom drops Feisty in an instant. Wanting to hurt him even more, Feisty takes one look at Boom, and then at his mum, and back to Boom again before telling him,

"Like father, like son."

Boom explodes, screaming in her face. "That nasty fucker is NOTHING like me. And he's *NOT* my father!"

As Boom is led away, he tries desperately to get his mum to look at him, but she refuses.

"I'm sorry. Mum. Please! Look at me! Mum!"

But she carries on staring at the ground - refusing to look at him as he's led away.

110 WAIT! YOU CAN'T. MY MUM'S THERE!

Boom's at the station being interviewed by Brightly, who's sat with his boss to the left of him. Boom's solicitor, Mr Barry, is next to him, listening closely to all the charges against him.

"Where were you in the early hours of May 9th, Mr Johnson?" Brightly asks him.

"I dunno. That date doesn't mean anything to me," Boom replies, a little too cocky for Brightly's liking.

His solicitor peers over the top of his glasses at him, raising his eyebrows to remind him not to talk. Brightly tries again.

"What about May the 10th and 14th? Ring any bells to you?"

Brightly looks at his solicitor before replying, "No comment."

Brightly scowls at the solicitor for shutting Boom down. He leans forward, making sure Boom knows what he's got on him.

"You're aware we have CCTV footage of you entering the train depot in Cranville Road on the 19th aren't you, Mr Johnson? Along with mobile phone footage of you vandalising one of the walls? We also have confirmation from Mercedes Havara that you were there."

"I bet you do," Boom replies sarcastically.

Mr Barry throws Boom another warning look, reminding him to stay quiet.

"We've also got a match on the paint," Brightly tells Boom.

Boom doesn't say anything. But Brightly's got an ace up his sleeve. He sits back in his seat, cool as a cucumber, before telling Boom,

"Think it's time we told your stepdad who's behind all the attacks, don't you?"

Boom goes into a blind panic, his levels of anxiety soaring through the roof as he starts tugging at his hair, imagining exactly what Oli's going to do to his mum when he finds out.

"Wait! You can't. My mum's there!" he tells Brightly. "He'll go mad! Please! You need to send someone round to get her out first."

Brightly doesn't have any empathy for Boom, but tells him,

"There's an officer on their way round there now to speak to your mum."

Brightly stops the interview temporarily before heading out of the interview room to give Boom time to stew it over with his solicitor.

Boom sits there, tugging at his hair. Unable to speak to his solicitor until he finds out what's happened to his mum. His leg taps against the table until Brightly heads back into the room.

Brightly leans across the table to restart the recording machine, speaking into the tape.

"Interview with Jamie Johnson resumed at 14.20."

He then looks at Boom, telling him, "The officer's going to try again in a bit."

"What do you mean try again in a bit?" Boom

asks, his senses on high alert.

"Your mum wasn't there. Does she normally leave the flat?" Brightly asks him.

"She *never* leaves the flat. Only for food. Is the officer there now? Can he try again?" Boom asks, worried.

"I've given my officer instructions not to speak to Oli until they've moved your mum to a safe place."

Just then, there's a knock on the door and a female officer pokes her head round the door. Looking apologetic, she addresses Brightly's boss. Whatever it is, obviously can't wait.

"Sir, can I have a word?"

Brightly terminates the interview a second time, and his boss walks over to the gap in the door where the female officer is waiting for him.

He listens as the female officer whispers something to him. His face turns white with shock.

"Radio the officer NOW. Tell him not to speak to her until he's heard from us," he says, before turning straight to Brightly. "We need back up."

Boom knows something is up. "What's wrong? Is it to do with my mum? Why'd you need back up?" he asks Brightly, with a sense of urgency. Brightly ignores the question. Boom takes one look at his solicitor, telling him, "I need to call my mum."

Back at the train depot, Oli's manager, Dave Field, is sat at his desk, watching the door nervously. A young police officer is stood behind him, positioned in the corner of the room, his hat in his hands. There's a knock at the door, and Field answers.

"Come in!"

Oli walks in. He eyes the cop suspiciously before taking a seat.

"You wanted to see me."

Field's hands are shaking. He clenches them into tight balls under the desk so Oli doesn't spot them, before telling him, "Err. They've charged someone. For the, err… graffiti. Three counts of conspiracy to commit criminal damage."

"Who?" Oli asks him.

Field takes a second to answer. Bracing himself, before telling Oli.

"Your stepson, Jamie."

"My stepson?!"

Oli takes a second to process the information before flipping out. Jumping up out of his seat, he picks up his boss's desk. Field - and the young copper - only just move out of the way in time before Oli manages to flip it over and hurl it across the room, sending the computer smashing to the floor along with his boss's framed photo of his son.

"I'm gonna fucking kill him, the little bastard!" Oli shouts, tearing out of Field's office, slamming the door so hard, it leaves a hole in the wall where the handle smashes into the plaster.

"Shit!" Field says, picking the phone up off the floor. He's just about to tell the young policeman to radio through to control, when his radio kicks into life.

"0274, I repeat. 0274. Are you registering?"

The young policeman holds his radio, his hand shaking violently. He holds the button and opens his mouth to speak.

Down at the police station, Boom's still in the interview room, waiting for the officers to report back about his mum before the interview resumes.

No-one's speaking.

Brightly's boss taps the table with his fingers whilst Boom sits hunched over the table, chewing at the inside of his gum, and tugging at his hair while he waits.

"Have they told Oli?" he asks Brightly, "And my mum. Where's my mum? Have they found her yet? Are they with her now?"

"They're on their way round there now."

"How far away are they?" Boom asks Brightly.

"Twenty minutes."

"Twenty minutes?! That's too long! You need to get them there now. Please!" Boom says, the stress making his voice crack.

But it's all too much for him. He gets up, kicking his chair against the wall in frustration, which prompts a high alert reaction from the cops in the room.

"You need to be there now! You know what he's capable of! He'll kill her if he finds her!"

"Sit down!" Brightly tells him firmly.

But Boom's not listening. Choosing instead to walk himself into a blind panic as he paces back and forth around the interview room. Boom grabs his solicitor by his arm, begging him,

"You've got to get me out of here. Please! I need to know she's ok. Please!"

Mr Barry flashes him a look that says it's

impossible. Boom tries again. "What about Flash? Can I call him? He's in my block. He could go round there now."

Mr Barry looks at Brightly, who gives him the nod. Mr Barry pulls out his phone and waits for the number.

Boom recites Flash's number to him, rapid fire. "Come on, Flash! Pick up!" Boom says, tearing at his hair while he waits.

After what feels like an eternity, but is in fact just seconds, Flash picks up. But not recognising the number, he remains silent - waiting for whoever it is to speak first.

"Is this Flash?" Mr Barry asks in a calm, steady voice.

His voice is posh and clipped. Enough to completely throw Flash. But before he has a chance to ask who it is, Boom shouts over the top of him, making sure he's loud enough for the whole room to hear.

"G! It's me! Can you go to mine, get my mum out. It's an emergency! You need to get her out before Oli finds her. He's on his way over there now. He'll kill her if he finds her. But G! <u>Don't</u> go in there alone. Wait for the police to arrive."

But it's too late. Flash has already hung up.

Mr Barry looks at Boom. "Just try and stay calm."

111 THERE'S NO-ONE HERE

Flash hurtles down the stairwell, reaching Boom's flat on the second floor. Approaching it with caution, he knocks at the door, cautiously at first, but then a little louder when there's no answer.

He pulls his mobile out of his pocket and dials the last incoming number - Mr Barry's phone. He waits for him to pick up, telling him, "There's no-one here."

He can hear Boom shouting something in the background, and shouts back,

"It's ok, bro. She's not here." There's more shouting, some kind of instructions from Boom, and Flash peers in through the kitchen window and bangs on the glass.

"Mrs Johnson! Are you there?"

There's no answer. The flat's empty.

Flash tells Barry, "Tell Boom, she's not here. For definite."

Flash hangs up, a look of relief on his face. Keen to get away, he hotfoots it towards the stairs, his phone still in his hand. But something makes him stop - and without even thinking about it he takes one more look over the balcony for Oli's car.

It's there.

"Shit!"

He's about to sprint up the stairs when Oli comes pounding up the stairs and onto the balcony. He takes one look at Flash, stood outside his front door, and lunges for him. He grabs his phone and hurls it over the balcony into the car park below.

Grabbing Flash by the scruff of his neck, Oli opens his front door and drags Flash inside, kicking the door shut behind them with a steel-capped boot.

Oli pulls out a cigarette and lights it on the stove. Flash stands by the door, ready to escape at any minute - not quite sure why he hasn't already.

But he can't seem to move.

Oli nods at Flash to take a seat at the table. Still in shock, Flash sits down.

Oli remains by the stove, facing outwards so he can keep an eye on Flash. Flash is becoming more and more unnerved by the silence, and the way Oli is eyeballing him. Until suddenly, it hits him.

"Now I remember where I've seen you," he tells Flash. "You're Jamie's mate, aren't you? I saw you on the stairs together the other day." There's a beat, before he asks, "Good mates, are you?"

It's a loaded question but Flash is too loyal to deny the truth.

"Best mates," he replies.

Oli gives it a second to sink in, before asking,

"So you knew what he was up to then?"

Flash's face drops, but he's still trying to blag it so he can get away.

"What d'you mean?"

Oli smiles... not a nice smile.

"Just found out it was Jamie - my own stepson - who was doing all the graffiti at the depot. Bad mouthing me in front of all my work colleagues. Making me look bad."

Flash looks scared now.

"Who said that? They probably got it wro--"

"You expect me to believe that do you?" Oli asks him, taking a drag on his cigarette and blowing the smoke in his direction. "So, did you know then?"

Flash doesn't know how to answer, but replies truthfully, "Jamie never told me anything about the depot."

Oli gives Flash, a long, cold stare, freaking Flash out.

"Go get me his paints. They're in his bedroom."

Flash has never stuttered in his life before, but Oli is shitting him up so much now he's terrified and he starts stumbling over his words.

"What d'you want his paints for?"

Oli screams at him at the top of his voice.

"I said, go get me his FUCKING paints!"

Shaking with fear, Flash walks into the hallway and down the corridor, not even sure where he's going. "I don't know which--"

"Right!" Oli bellows at him, as Flash draws level with Boom's room.

Flash pushes the door to Boom's bedroom and he walks in, talking it all in. Boom's desk, his computer. The wardrobe door still half open. His eyes dart around the room looking for the paints. And then he spots it. Boom's rucksack, filled with all his paints, half hidden under the duvet at the end of his bed.

He pulls it out and stands there, helplessly, as Oli barges in and grabs it off him, emptying the cans onto Boom's bed. He picks up the can of red paint and walks towards Flash with it. Flash starts backing towards the window, trying to get as far away from Oli as possible. Something about the way he's looking at him is really scaring him.

"What are you doing?" he asks, terrified.

Oli pops open the lid and sprays it right in Flash's face. Grabbing Flash by the neck, he sprays it all over his face, his cheeks, up his nose, into his ears, until Flash drops to the floor retching and gagging, barely able to breath.

"What the fuck?!" Flash chokes.

Oli walks out of Boom's bedroom, like nothing happened, leaving Flash writhing on the floor and trying not to throw up over the carpet.

Back in the kitchen, Oli's stood by the sink. Pouring himself a glass of water, he takes a swig as behind him Flash, wheezing heavily, slides open a drawer and pulls out a sharp knife. The one with the biggest blade.

Standing there covered in paint, and wheezing, Flash holds the blade up in front of him.

"Get the fuck out of here!" he shouts, terrified, his voice shaking but jabbing the blade towards Oli to try and get him to leave.

Oli laughs.

"Come on then!" he tells Flash, baiting him. "Do it for your bestie. 'Cause he never had the balls to do it himself!"

Terrified, but in an attempt to protect himself and get rid of Oli, Flash takes a stab at him, desperate for him to leave. Oli steps back and Flash tries again, but Oli grabs the knife off of him and plunges it into Flash's stomach, sending him crumpling to the floor.

Outside the flat, police sirens filter onto the estate. Oli takes one look at Flash, who is lying crumpled on the floor, and races outside.

112 DO NOT LET HIM PAST. I REPEAT, DO NOT LET HIM PAST

A rookie cop, fresh on the beat, stands guard outside Boom's front door, blocking the entrance which has been sealed off with police tape. PC Noble - spotty and with only a couple of years on Boom and his mates - is doing his best to hold it together but he's starting to freak out. Inside the flat, an ambulance man squats on the floor, leaning over Flash as he checks his pulse. Behind him, an older cop in his 40s - PC Adams - moves from room to room, searching the flat.

PC Adams walks back into the kitchen and pulls his radio out of his belt, radio'ing through to control to tell them,

"No sign of him anywhere, Sir."

He glances over at the ambulance man, and Flash; his still warm body, sprawled out over the floor, red paint and blood pooling into a point by his head. The ambulance man takes one look at him and shakes his head, brushing his hands over Flash's eyes to close his eyelids.

"Shit," PC Adams says, as he takes in Flash's baby face and yet another senseless death.

Down on the street below, a cop car pulls up, lights on and sirens sounding. It screeches to a stop outside the entrance, and Brightly, Boom and one of the ginger-haired cops pile out onto the pavement. Before they have a chance to stop him, Boom's broken free and is racing up the stairs ahead of them.

"Fuck it!" Brightly says, knowing whatever Boom finds won't be good.

He grabs the radio from the other cop and radios through to PC Adams and Noble.

"Oli's stepson is on his way up. Stop him at the top of the stairs and do NOT let him past. I repeat, do NOT let him past."

But Boom's already there, barrelling past Noble and knocking him to the ground as he bursts through the tape - only to find what he's known all along he'll find.

Except that it's not.

He thought he'd find his mum. But instead it's Flash. Covered from head to toe by a blood-stained blanket, his body laid out on a stretcher and about to be carried off by ambulance staff.

Boom drops to his knees, wailing.

"Fuck! Not Flash! Fuck, no! Flash!"

Peter Drummond, a major incident investigator who has not long arrived on the scene, approaches Boom from the other side of the kitchen. Covered in an all-in-one paper overall - his shoes, mouth and hands covered too - he pulls Boom to his feet, steering him gently outside. He sits Boom down on the balcony and leans him back against the wall to steady him, talking to him in a calm, steady voice.

"Mr Johnson. Look at me. I want you to take a deep breath. That's it. Keep focussing on me. Take a deep breath in, and out. That's it. In. And out. And again. In and out."

Boom is having some kind of panic attack,

sobbing uncontrollably and struggling to breath. Drummond stays with him until he starts to breathe normally again, watching the crime scene behind him as Brightly seals the door back up with tape whilst giving PC Noble a right royal bollocking for letting Boom through.

"This is a bloody crime scene for fuck's sake, Noble. *No-one* should be in there other than forensics and CID! Do you understand?!"

Drummond ignores the shouting going on behind him and focuses on Boom whose breathing is nearly back to normal. His eyes look vacant though, and he's retreating into himself, sinking into a state of shock.

Drummond pulls Boom over to one side as the ambulance staff make their way through the door with Flash's lifeless body on a stretcher. Making sure Boom doesn't turn round and spot him, Drummond keeps talking to Boom, resting his hand on his shoulder as he tells him,

"If you have any questions, just ask. As long as they're factual and don't compromise the case, I can answer them for you." When Boom doesn't react, he tries again. "Is there anything you want to ask me?"

Boom stares back at him. His eyes wide in a state of shock, he can't even talk. Concerned about Boom - but very aware he's got an urgent job to do - Drummond gets to his feet and signals to PC Noble to get Boom seen to. He watches as Boom is led off before pulling on a fresh pair of gloves. He stands there calmly studying the blood stains on the floor and wall, looking at the pattern and spacing of them before picking up a camera and starting to photograph them.

Boom is sat on some steps by himself at the back of the station. One of the cops is stood several feet away, watching him from a distance.

Dazed and expressionless, Boom leans back against the wall, feeling the cold seep through his clothes to his back and the rest of his body. In fact, it's the only thing he feels. There's no emotion, no feeling. Just...

Nothing.

Staring straight ahead of him, he slips his buds into his ears, pulls out his phone, and pulls up Katy Perry's Firework song - his last reminder of Flash.

The song cuts in halfway through. Boom - who's physically and emotionally drained - stares vacantly ahead of him as he listens to the lyrics.

The lyrics drop back into Boom's head as he recalls his last conversation with Flash. It's the one at the bridge, after Flash came to find him. Flash looking at him really intently as he tells him,

"The best way to stick it to Oli is to get yourself out of here. Like Britton said. Do your thing. Do well. You could take your mum with you and stick it to the fucker in the best way you can - by being successful and proving to him he doesn't have any power over you. I mean it, bro."

And then a flashback of his response. Him telling Flash, "Lots of people wanna do stuff with their life but they never get the chance. What makes you think

425

I'm gonna be any different?

"Cause you're an annoyingly talented fucker that's why. You were destined to do well."

And suddenly Boom can feel again...

A huge knot just below his ribs. It's like a physical pain almost, like heartache, but not, and all he can think about is Flash. How loyal he was; how caring he was towards his mum; how he looked after - and loved - Rachel. What an amazing friend he was to him, and the rest of the crew. How he took the rap for him. How he wanted everyone around him to be happy, always. Pushing him to do well, even if it meant losing his mate for a while. Although he'd never have lost Flash, he knew that. He'd have taken him with him.

But now he can't.

And then an image of Flash pops into his head, as clear as if he was sitting there right in front of him. His huge smile, his bright eyes, alive and teasing, singing the lyrics with his name in, the cool street kid singing Katy Perry -

'Boom, Boom, Boom, even brighter than the moon, moon, moon.'

And Boom can't stop himself. The tears start to flow and they don't stop. The knot beneath his ribs tightening as the song comes to an end.

There's a crackle of fireworks and Boom shuts his eyes, and all he sees is black.

114 ARE YOU OK, SIR?

Mr Britton is sat at the front of his class, lost in thought. The students are reading quietly to themselves, the whole class unusually subdued. One of the girls at the front looks over at him. Catching the expression on his face, she asks,

"Are you ok, Sir?"

Ali looks up and whispers something to his friend. Britton looks over at him and BELLOWS at Ali, unusually fierce for him.

"Anything else from you Ali and you'll be in detention for the rest of the year, DO YOU UNDERSTAND?!"

For once, Ali doesn't give Britton any backchat. His face turns a deep red and he looks down quickly, pretending to read. Two of the girls in the back row give each other a look as if to say, 'harsh!'

The bell goes, and the room empties in seconds - but unlike normal, the students file out in complete silence. No jostling, or pushing, or racing ahead, just a subdued exit. The only sound, the sound of chairs as they scrape against the floor as the students pull them out from under the desk.

The door shuts behind them, and Britton sinks his head into his hands, no longer able to keep up the pretence of any kind of normality. All he can think of - all he *has* been thinking of all day - is Flash, and Boom, and wondering if there was anything he could have done to stop it all from happening.

There's a knock at the door. He sighs, shouting back, "Come in." The door opens, and standing there in the doorway is The Watcher with The Cat and Curl.

"Can you help us rent some suits please, Sir?"

He knows instantly why. For Flash's funeral.

And something about the sincerity behind their question brings tears to his eyes. He can't even speak. He just looks at them and nods.

115 HOW LONG WILL I LOVE YOU?

It's the morning of Flash's funeral and most people have made their way into church and found a seat. Everyone except the last few stragglers who rush quickly inside as the hearse pulls up outside.

Standing in the churchyard outside are Boom, Curl, The Watcher and The Cat; huddled together as they try and work out how to do their ties. The Watcher spots the hearse and gives the others the heads up.

"Hearse is here."

Boom's fidgety and on edge, like the rest of them. Rushing to try and fix his tie, he gets more and more agitated as he struggles with it.

"For fuck's sake. I can't fucking do it."

The Watcher rests his hand on Boom's arm.

"Stay calm, bro. I'll see if the vicar can help. But first I'm gonna ask them to hang back while we sort it out," he says, nodding at the hearse.

Boom stays behind, getting more and more frustrated as he struggles with his tie. But that's not what this is about, not really. It's about Flash. His best mate. The fact he's no longer here. The fact he'll never be here again. And just the harsh finality of that makes Boom want to throw himself on the floor and scream at the injustice of it all. But he's too afraid to let himself go, afraid how he'll be if he says it out loud...that Flash is dead.

The vicar steps outside, into the churchyard, and walks towards them. He looks at them, taking them all in, in that split second. Their stress, their anger; their sense of loss and the sadness that comes with all of it. He's used to it in his job, but there's something special about this group he thinks sadly. These young men - loyal friends, so upset at the loss of their friend.

"Are you ready?" he asks them gently.

But Boom's still fighting with his tie, and loses it in front of the vicar.

"Jesus Christ! I can't do this tie!" he says, before looking at the vicar and apologising. "Sorry."

The vicar flashes him a dry smile. "Jesus Christ might not be able to help you with your tie, but I can."

Boom blushes with embarrassment. The Watcher walks over just as the Vicar is about to sort Boom's tie out.

Behind him, by seconds, is Mr Britton, rushing into the churchyard from the road. He's seen the hearse and is trying to get into church as quickly as possible. He looks up and spots Boom and his mates; a huddled mess of stressed-out teenagers. He catches their suits, and their crisp white shirts, all the effort they've made and their sense of loss, and he can't help it. He feels a lump in his throat just looking at them. He has to brace himself before he can walk over to them. He takes a deep breath to calm himself before walking over, thinking to himself how misunderstood teenagers really are. How underneath all their bravado and know it all, they're just like the rest of us. Insecure, emotional and never as confident as they seem.

He clocks their ties, loose and untied, and walking over to Boom tells him, "Stand still."

He pulls Boom's collar up, reaches for his tie,

and knots it, securing the knot so that it's as tight and as neat as possible. Unable to find the right words to say to Boom, he doesn't say anything. He just gives Boom a quick nod before making his way along the line of friends, fixing their ties one by one until they're done.

Behind them, the pall-bearers are making their way up the path, ready for Boom and his mates to carry the coffin. Britton catches Boom's face as he turns to face the coffin, the reality of it hitting him like a slap in the face. Flash dead, his body right there in the coffin, and somehow having to get himself through the next hour.

Curl looks at Boom... sensing he can't do this next bit. So he holds his hand out and waits for Boom to pass it to him. Boom pulls something from the inside pocket of his suit and hands it to Curl; something special they had made for Flash, just for today. It's a folded-up white cloth, with splashes of colour all over it. Curl takes it from Boom and walks over to the funeral director. He leans in towards him, whispering something in his ear as he hands him the piece of cloth. The man nods, and watches as Curl unfolds the carefully-ironed sheet and drapes it over the coffin.

It's a special tribute to Flash.

Running along the length of the cloth, in large blue letters is the name, 'Flash', on both sides. On the cloth itself, there's embroidered pictures of trainers, lots of them, and some graffiti lettering, and in the corner each side, just one word... family.

The Crew are struggling to keep it together, but they're doing their best.

Just then, Flash's mum and Rachel step out into

431

the sunshine and walk slowly towards the group, ready to take their place at the front of the procession. Rachel is barely managing to hold it together. She takes one look at the coffin cover and her bottom lip wobbles, ready to go at any minute. She walks over to the group and they circle each other, hugging each other tight; Boom clenching his jaws so tight it feels like he might actually crack his teeth. Boom grips Rachel's hand and gives it a tight squeeze before letting it go so she and her mum can take their place in front of the coffin.

The Watcher pushes out a long deep breath, bracing himself for what's coming next. He takes one look at all his mates, and back to Boom, before telling them all,

"Right. Let's do this."

They nod, walking slowly over to the coffin to take their places at each corner before hoisting their friend up onto their shoulders, ready to carry him into church. Boom at the front with The Watcher, two pall bearers in the middle, with Curl and The Cat at the back. Rachel takes her mum's hand and holding it tight, takes her place at the front of the procession.

From inside the church, the organ player plays the first few chords of Ellie Goulding's song, 'How long will I love you'. As the song filters out into the churchyard, the tiny group of friends and family make their way up the path and into church, keeping their eyes focussed ahead of them, unable to bring themselves to look at any of the faces in the congregation. As they enter the church, the cool air hits them, and suddenly the weight of their emotion seems to sink into the coffin itself, the weight of it bearing down hard upon their shoulders causing them to wobble, momentarily, as they struggle not to drop the coffin.

And then they see them.

Hundreds of people, packing the church out and spilling out of the pews and into the gangways. Students and staff, neighbours and friends... members of the local community. Boom's never been anywhere this packed in his life before. Somewhere in his consciousness, he's aware of the music - beautiful and lilting - and the sound of Rachel sobbing at the front, as they make their way up the aisle to a blur of faces and the haunting lyrics of the song.

Boom waivers as he spots his mum, sat by herself and looking like all she wants to do is hold him. He wobbles, causing the coffin to veer to the side for a second. The two pall bearers in the middle steady it until Boom and his mates regain their balance. The Watcher looks over at Boom and mouths, "You ok?"

Boom's eyes are wide, like a startled animal. Clenching his jaws tight, he holds his breath - making sure he doesn't breathe, frightened if he does he'll start to cry. Boom tips his head just enough to let The Watcher know he's ok, and The Watcher turns to give those at the back a nod to let them know to start walking again. The procession makes its way up the aisle to the angelic tones of Ellie Goulding. Boom's head is in a fog, and he's not aware of anyone, until he gets near the front of the church where Mr Britton's face jumps out at him from the front row; sat next to where Rachel and her mum are going to sit for the service. Britton is staring at them, willing them the strength they need to get through this.

The Crew reach the front of the church and as the music stops they slowly lower the coffin onto a platform in front of where the Vicar is standing.

They walk back to the pews, taking their seats in the row behind Rachel and her mum. Mr Britton shuffles along the wooden bench to make way for them, brushing Flash's mum's hand as she sits down next to him. She throws him a grateful look before taking Rachel's hand; holding each other, united in strength.

The Vicar takes a breath, before he starts.

"Today, we celebrate the life of Adam, Acqwon, Isiah Pritchard."

The Watcher can't help it. He looks at Boom, as if to say, "What the fuck?!" as the Vicar continues, "Taken from this world at just 16 years old. Both his mum, and his sister, Rachel, have asked that instead of today being about mourning, it be about celebrating the life of a wonderful son, brother - and friend."

The pause before friend is deliberate. Something Rachel has asked the Vicar to stress. The importance Flash placed on all his friendships, how much he loved them all.

Boom can feel his bottom lip starting to wobble. He looks across as The Watcher reaches out a hand, gripping his hand hard to let him know he's there.

"I'd like to invite Adam's sister, Rachel, to the front now to share some of her special memories of Adam with you," the Vicar says in a loud, clear voice.

The church is silent, and two girls, sitting several rows back, look at each other. They shake their heads in sympathy, glad it's not them having to speak in front of a packed church.

Rachel climbs the pulpit, aware of everyone's eyes on her. She puts her piece of paper down in front of her and swallows several times before starting,

"People always say you don't appreciate what you've got until it's gone," she says, pausing as she glances in the direction of Flash's coffin, but still not quite able to bring herself to look at it. "Well, they're right," she says, continuing, "Adam is - was - an amazing person." She looks at her mum, sitting there in the front row, watching her, and continues, "For my mum, he was a wonderful son. Loving, kind, supportive. Always supportive. And always, always there when she needed him. For me, Adam was…" she breaks off, as tears fill her eyes and she struggles to hold it together.

Several of the girls in the congregation start to cry, the look on Rachel's face enough to set them off.

"Err…" Rachel continues, managing to compose herself. "For me, he was just my amazing big brother. After my dad died, he was always there for me. Pushing me to do well, reminding me how important it was, even though he wasn't really a big fan of school himself."

She realises what she's said, and looks across at Britton, "Sorry."

The congregation laugh softly, as she continues, "When I started to write this, I really wanted to take you back to the start. To all the funny things I remember about Adam from when we were little. But I couldn't.

Because all I really want to do is remember him as he was the last time I saw him. Smiling. Happy. Someone who just wanted everyone around him to be happy too. He was always so good at making people laugh, even if it wasn't on purpose."

Boom looks at The Watcher and smiles, waiting for it…

"He could be really clumsy at times too," Rachel says. "Always tripping up. Falling off his chair in class…"

She glances over at Mr Britton who's smiling into his lap. And then she starts to laugh as she recalls one particular memory.

"He had this thing about trainers. He was obsessed by them. But it didn't matter how hard he tried not to, he always ended up ruining them. I think the longest he ever had a pair without ruining them was two weeks. Until a few weeks ago, when he managed to break his own personal best. One night, that was all."

The Crew smile, knowing what's coming next.

"He'd stood in some dog shit. He'd tried to get it off, of course, but it just made it worse. It went everywhere. Stunk the whole flat out. He had to throw them out in the end."

Rachel spots the vicar looking at her a little strangely. And then she realises what she's just done, and throwing her hands up to her mouth she tells him,

"Sorry vicar."

The Crew look at each other and smile. The congregation start to laugh too, a release from all the pent-up emotion. Rachel takes a deep breath in, determined to finish this. She breaths out slowly, before continuing,

"Adam's friends meant the absolute world to him," she says, turning to look at Boom. "Jamie--"

Boom gives Rachel a nod, before staring down into his lap, silent tears starting to flow. Rachel continues, looking at each of the Crew members in turn as she remembers them for Flash,

"Jamie, Stephen, Leroy, Noah. You were like family to him. Which is just what you've put on the side of his coffin," she says, glancing over to the white sheet that covers it. "He'd have loved that. And I know how much he meant to you too because of the time you took to put his tribute together for today. It's really special, so thank you. And for wearing suits as well," she says smiling. "I know how you all hate looking smart."

And then the smile drops from her face.

"But, before we watch the tribute, there's something I need to say to Adam."

It's so quiet in the church, you could hear a pin drop - every single person in the congregation focussed on Rachel.

"Adam came home from school last week. Walked in and gave me a massive hug and told me how lucky we were. Except I couldn't see it at the time. But he was right. We *were* lucky. Because we had each other. And when you have someone you love, you just need to remember to tell them that. All the time. Whenever you can. And I never did. I never told him I loved--"

Her voice cracks as she loses it, tears streaming down her face as the last few words come out.

"I never told him how much I loved him. But I

do Adam," she says, looking at the coffin, "I really love you. And I'm going to miss you loads."

The Vicar walks over to the pulpit and helps her down, guiding her back to her seat and waiting for her to sit down before nodding at an elderly man sat next to a large screen behind Adam's coffin. The man points a remote control up at the screen, and the Crew's tribute to Flash starts to play on the screen behind the coffin. A montage of photos fill the screen to Wiz Khalifa's song, 'See You Again.' Flash as a smiley, chubby baby. Flash as a child... and later, Flash the spotty teenager with a dodgy Afro and equally dodgy clothes. Charlie Puth's vocals fill the church, a poignant tribute to the loss of a treasured friend.

"It's been a long day without you my friend...

Photos of Flash pop up with all the Crew. Their arms draped around each other, laughing and smiling... capturing that easy, comfortable feeling you get when you've known someone most of your life. All of them lined up on a wall, smiling and posing for the camera; Flash giving Boom a nudge, some kind of banter that's set the rest of them off laughing; followed by several close-ups of trainers - making the Crew and the rest of the congregation laugh.

As the rapping starts the Vicar, who's sat next to the elderly man in front of the screen, leans across to him and whispers,

"I hope they've got the version without all the swearing."

Britton turns round and nods at the Crew,

438

acknowledging the special friendship they shared with Flash.

As the song draws to an end, the congregation sit there in silence for a couple more minutes, taking it all in before getting up out of their seats and filing out really slowly, into the sunshine outside. Not really wanting to leave.

Boom and the rest of the Crew stay seated in the church, staring at the blank screen; linking hands one by one and gripping each other tight as they remember their friend.

116 I'M GLAD I TOLD YOU ABOUT MY PAST, BECAUSE NOW I CAN SAY WHAT I NEED TO SAY WITHOUT YOU THINKING I'M JUST ANOTHER FUCKED UP KNOW-IT-ALL WHO DOESN'T HAVE A CLUE

Boom's stood by Flash's grave, staring at the mound of earth covering the freshly-dug hole. He's the last one left and has been stood there over an hour, unable to bring himself to leave. Because if he leaves, it means it's final.

He looks up, aware of someone walking towards him. It's Britton, who's made his way back to the church and to Flash's grave.

Stopping in front of Boom, he takes his place next to him. Standing side by side, as he tells him,

"I'm glad I told you about my past, because now I can say what I need to say without you thinking I'm just another fucked up know-it-all who doesn't have a clue."

Boom can't help it. He laughs, glancing at Britton's face from the side. Knowing that whatever Britton is about to say is going to mean something.

"Sometimes things just happen in life and no matter how hard you try, you just can't make sense of *why* they happened," Britton tells him, "They just did. But what's important is not to let what happens in life beat you. *Ever*. 'Don't let your shit define you', remember?" Britton smiles, "Because it doesn't define you. When something bad happens, you have a choice. To let it beat you, or to get back up and fight."

Britton pauses for a second before telling Boom,

"Don't let what's happened to you affect you for the rest of your life, Jamie. Yeah, you've had a shit start in life. But not all of it's been shit. You've got a mum who loves you. And the chance to start again. You owe it to yourself to give yourself the life you deserve."

"Think I've fucked up there," Boom laughs.

"No you haven't," Britton tells him. "The court will hear about Oli. What he did to you, and your mum. Plus you've got an exceptional school record. I'll vouch for you. Tell them what an amazing student you are."

"Fucking hell, I've never had so many nice things said about me before. Maybe I should get my best friend killed more often," Boom says, trying to make a joke of how shit things are, but struggling not to cry.

Britton steps closer to Jamie so he has no other choice but to look him in the eye and hear what he has to say.

"You didn't do it, Jamie. It wasn't your fault. None of it was. It was Oli's, and Oli's alone. Adam just happened to be the unlucky one who got caught up in the middle of it."

Boom's trying really hard not to cry.

Britton pauses for a second, studying Boom's face, then tells him,

"Next time I see you, I wanna see the fight in your eyes. It's not good enough just to get by, Jamie. I want to see you *fight* to be here. Not just for you. But for your mum too. But most of all for Flash."

And with that, he walks away, leaving Boom by Flash's graveside, tears streaming down his face.

Mr Britton is taking the register at the front of the class. His whole demeanour tired and weary, just like the rest of the class.

"Ali?" he says, his hand poised over the keyboard.

Ali replies with a "here."

"Considine?" Britton continues.

"Here."

Britton sighs, knowing the answer already.

"Johnson?"

He waits a second, before asking again, "...Johnson?"

He glances over to the desk where Flash and Boom usually sit, taking in the two empty seats. He's about to mark Boom absent when the door opens, and Boom stands there, scared and afraid... but trying.

Boom glances at the desk where he and Flash always sat, and his bottom lip starts to wobble.

The whole of the class look visibly moved to see him there, and Britton has to swallow several times to compose himself before nodding to a seat next to a girl sat by herself at the front of the class.

"Take a seat next to Alice please, Jamie."

Boom looks at him gratefully, before taking a seat at his new desk, right in front of Britton.

Britton looks down at his register and tries again.

"Johnson?"

Britton looks up, catching the look in Boom's eye as he replies in a strong voice,

"I'm here, Sir."

And Britton smiles, knowing exactly what Boom means.

He's here.

Really here.

THE END

GRAFFITI TERMS

Graffiti Writers – Graffiti Artists are not called artists, but writers. This term refers to all graffiti, whether it's words or pictures.

Going 'bombing' – going out doing graffiti

Toy – a bad beginner

Piece – The more detailed work. It's graffiti on a large scale and has taken time to both do and design (you'd always sketch a piece out first on a piece of paper before attempting it on a wall)

Tag – a writer's nickname. Generally quite short, 3-5 letters long, because if you're going out bombing you need to be able to write it quickly and go.

Throw up - Simple outline, simple fill. It's designed to be quick and doesn't change in style. Can be done automatically without thinking – i.e. a tag.

Burner - Big words but still quite simple. A burner is somewhere in between a 'throw up' and a 'piece.'

Racking – when writers go out to steal paint, from a hardware store or wherever.

Fat Cap – different sized caps determine coverage area of the paint. A fat cap gives more coverage, quicker.

Can silencer – as it sounds. A silencer is a flat, circular piece of plastic you put between the cap and the can that silences the spray. Although it helps with not getting caught, some writers don't like it, however, because the way the spray 'sounds' is all part of the artistic process.

Graffiti sticker – when writers designs stickers based on their work. They can then stick them up wherever they go and won't be prosecuted for it like they would if they painted the design because it's not a permanent piece of work.

Biggest insults in the graffiti world
Lining Out (aka strike) – when a writer draws a line through another writer's work. It's like saying you don't like it. Graffiti artists don't really approve of it, it's considered bad form. A writer might do it when they feel threatened by someone being good, or if someone is on their turf. It's also considered really bad form when a writer doesn't completely cover over the previous piece of work – because it's like they're laying claim to the previous work as well as their own. One graffiti artist told me that once, when they didn't have time to completely cover over the last piece of work, he finished his 'piece' then wrote an apology at the bottom of it saying – 'sorry, ran out of time.'

ACKNOWLEDGEMENTS

Firstly to **all my gorgeous friends** (you know who you are!) who have done nothing but support me and tell me over and over again that I could do this, when everyone else in my life was telling me I couldn't. I love you all to pieces.

To the survivor of Domestic Abuse who shared their story with me. I know it wasn't easy for you but you selflessly did it to help all the other victims of domestic abuse, and those still stuck in abusive, controlling relationships. So for that please accept my massive gratitude as well as acknowledgement of how proud you should be to see how far you have come since you escaped your abusive relationship. Your story I have left until the end.

To **Tim** - who is just one of those genuinely lovely people in life who help complete and utter strangers for no other reason than the fact they are just a good person. You're an amazing counsellor. Thank you for helping me find Kyle, and for writing your piece at the end of this book, helping raise awareness of how young people really cope under trauma and not how we, as adults, like to tell ourselves they are coping.

To **Kyle** - a super, talented street artist now working as a tattoo artist. Thank you for helping me with my research so that this world I painted, the world of graffiti, could feel authentic. Your work is incredible and I think you have got a true gift - and I'm hoping you might still do that canvas for me one day...

Weirdly, I also need to thank **Boom**, my main character, whose story just rolled into my head and whose presence feels very real to me, like he's almost here with me. Thank you for letting me tell your story - because by telling your story, I believe the world will slowly start to talk more about the horrors of Domestic Abuse and that it will one day finally no longer be a subject that gets brushed under the carpet and never talked about... and that in time there will be a way to help reduce the number of cases.

And last - but not least - my two beautiful kids, **Gorgeous One and Gorgeous Two!** You know that all I've ever wanted since the age of six is to be a writer because I've told you that many times. You also know how old I am now (DON'T tell anyone!!) And, you also know that lots of people have tried to put me down and squash my dreams along the way. So I hope by seeing this book in print, I will have taught you one of life's most valuable lessons. Never let other people tell you that you can't do something. Always, always follow your passion - and if you work hard enough, and are determined enough, there is absolutely no reason why you can't achieve anything you set out to achieve. After all, the world is full of people doing jobs that some people will tell you are impossible to do - Presidents, Astronauts, Singers, Writers, Actors.

So get yourself out there!

And go be what you need to be...

COUNSELLING FOR YOUNG PEOPLE BY TIM SHUKER-YATES

The main reason I offer counselling to young people fits into my reasons for becoming a counsellor in general. There is a part of myself that wanted to understand what my baggage was, what the pivotal and painful moments in my life were. A lot of these events happened in my adolescence and finding out how I felt about this time, why I felt it and coming to terms with that process was so cathartic for me. I now want to offer this to others but catching people when they are yet to embark on their life journey and in time to make more informed decisions can be wonderful. Helping someone change the trajectory of their lives for the better is such an honour.

I first really got involved when I started work as a youth worker. Before that I was involved in creative projects for young people, but the youth work allowed me to get to know groups of adolescents really well and offer support that may be lacking in their life. I loved it!

However, it didn't take long for me to think there was something more I could do, something deeper. Psychotherapy was the obvious next step. We all need that space to reflect on how we are feeling but we live in a society that only welcomes some feelings, such as happiness or those associated with success. But, we all feel all emotions, and we need to acknowledge that it's ok to feel every emotion, including things like anger. We all need safe places to explore our feelings and acknowledgement of all our emotions is important. How we act on them is different, but acknowledgement gives us choice and choice will help free us. Children and young people are no different. For them, it is even more important because they have less life experience, they are more immediate in their outlook and therefore more extreme in their views and behaviour. They need to push, so being in a safe environment really helps.

I've heard it said that kids will bounce back, and actually this can be true! I think kids can be surprisingly resilient to some awful things, but only if they are given a secure, nurturing environment and time from which to think and feel about what has happened. To me, this is what it means to bounce back and ignoring this or impinging upon it is what stops the healthy process. If we don't get the chance to explore the trauma in our lives, it festers and can come out in all sorts of ways, the longer we leave it the harder it is to see. As someone who works with adults too, I see how a thing that a teenager gets to grips with in one session can take years for a person in their 60s to acknowledge.

The character in the book is only one story. What makes my job fascinating is that I see each person's individual story, the novel of their life. It really is a privilege.

Essentially, I would say that if you are worried about someone, talk to them. Communication is everything. Even if it seems too much, by listening you can help them realise they are not alone, and possibly that they can make changes. Counsellors are professional listeners really, so once someone is no longer in danger, which is the most important thing to address first, then they should seek help. Luckily, counselling is easier to find for young people. A large proportion of schools now offer the provision, but also a person's GP will have details of public and private counselling. There are some really amazing charities that offer space for young people and many counsellors and psychotherapists in private practice, which even if you feel you cannot afford, at least get in touch, they may be able to help.

About Tim
Tim is an experienced and qualified psychodynamic counsellor and psychotherapist who has expanded his practice to integrate other useful methods of thinking, such as creative practice. He graduated from the BACP accredited MA/PGDIP contemporary therapeutic counselling course at the university of Hertfordshire and now works regularly in schools, counselling services and in private practice in Cambridgeshire.

Issues with which he has worked include:
Depression, Stress/anxiety (including Panic Attacks), Low Self-Esteem, Low Confidence, Lack of Direction, Bullying, Relationship Issues, Emotional/Physical/Sexual Abuse, Trauma, Issues of Sexuality and Sexual/Gender Identity, Work-Related Issues, Anger, Communication Difficulties, Assertiveness, Bereavement and Loss.

Accreditation and Supervision
Tim is an accredited member of The British Association of Counselling and Psychotherapy (BACP) which is a membership organisation that sets standards for therapeutic practice and provides information for clients, therapists and the general public.

To find out more go to: www.timshukeryates.co.uk

INTERVIEW WITH A VICTIM OF DOMESTIC ABUSE

why is it important for victims of domestic violence to speak out?

It struck me when you asked me to let you interview me, that it's not something that victims of domestic violence go back to. It's really positive that people talk about it, but even when you want to, you don't. It still feels like you don't want to bring it all back up but more people need to do it if they can. There are so many more people it's happening to now that you won't even know it's happening to. I think sharing our stories help us to fully come to terms with what's happened and put our pasts behind us where it belongs. By sharing our experiences I think it helps others trapped in this abusive pattern to connect with the feeling of not being the only one, hopefully seeing there is another life available and that this isn't just what a normal relationship with ups and downs is.

how long were you married to the man who abused you for?

We were married for six years, together for nine. I met him when I was 24 and I was desperate for a family of my own. I was born wanting my own family. And I think my background brought me to being with someone like Mark *(**names have been changed to prevent identification)* because I have always wanted to help people.

do you have any idea how, or why, it all happened?

Mum and dad brought us all up to love everybody unconditionally and there were no clear boundaries around saying no. I'm one of four and we have all ended up in caring professions, so we all have this drive to care for others. Having been brought up in such a loving family I almost felt guilty about people who didn't grow up in such a positive, loving environment. When I met Mark, he was fiery, headstrong… nothing like anybody I had ever met before. It was exciting. He wasn't afraid of confrontation. He would speak up for people as well. If there was any bullying in town, he would go up and sort it out. So the confrontation was there from the beginning, but when I first got to know him, I thought it was in a really good way. That's probably why I was so attracted to him because he was so different to me. I always found it hard saying no to people but he wasn't afraid to just say what he thought. I knew he had a son and that was a draw to me because I love children. Mark was making out he was a wonderful dad and that was very attractive to me. He smoked weed openly and he did cocaine every so often but never in front, or around, his son. I didn't see it as a red flag back then but for him I think he used to smoke weed to suppress his anger. Pretty soon he told me his best friend had killed himself, and that he had lost two friends in a motorcycle accident, so there was a lot of trauma he was telling me about and that was a way of covering up his behaviour because abusers often paint themselves as a victim. I became his comforter and maybe he subconsciously wanted to get me into that position as a means of control. I was open and loving and had no boundaries. I think that is why we were drawn together as we both were able to fulfil our 'roles' of victim (Mark) and rescuer (me). Another red flag looking back was that he didn't really have any friends and he also had a difficult relationship with his family. He told me his mum had only found out she was pregnant with him quite far along and that her dad had wanted her to have an abortion, so there was also all these underlying issues in the family. He had grown up in another part of the country and then moved down here, so that was always the way he explained why he had no friends. Looking back, the inability to be able to make, and retain, friends coupled with strained family relationships should have been a sign to me that he had a history of relationship issues. But coming from parents who would write to people on death row, I came at it from the viewpoint that this is ok, no-one is perfect or has had a perfect life. When the violence began Mark had never shown any confrontation towards me at the beginning. I just saw him as someone needing love and then I met his son and formed a very close relationship with him and that completed everything for me. At first his temper wasn't directed at me. He would see something happening that he thought was wrong and would go up and have a go at someone for it. The one thing he couldn't stand was bullying and now, looking back, I think that was because he was a bully himself and couldn't accept it. We spent many nights talking about his feelings. This reinforced the message to me that he was a wounded person I needed to help and codependency began. And this in a way was reinforcing me allowing him to do stuff and it being ok. I think everyone should look at codependent relationships. It is very easy to get into one.

how the violence began

It must have been about nine or ten months into our relationship when he became physically abusive towards me. He had his own home at the time but he would spend quite a lot of time at mine. In the end he had to move in with me because he had lost his job and had to rent his flat out to pay the mortgage, so him and his son moved in with me eight months before our wedding. He was struggling because his dad had been diagnosed with quite a serious illness and so his cannabis use had increased. The morning after our wedding his home had been repossessed but he wasn't even bothered, it was like he didn't care because he had me then. His violence started off with him shouting at me and smashing objects in the house. It would just be about anything, just normal arguments. At first I would shout back my point of view but it became pretty clear he was unable to listen or accept another person's point of view and thought he was right all of the time so I stopped speaking out as it felt like I was hitting a brick wall. It started with his shouting and slamming doors, which I just blamed on him having had alcohol or taken drugs. He also had a very high sex drive and that was often the cause of an argument because soon his demands didn't match mine and I found I was afraid to say no. At that point though the violence was only pushing. He would grab my arm and push me out of the way. The first time he hit me I remember he punched me, it made me realise it wasn't because he was drunk or on drugs, he just did it. We were out in his work van at night and it was dark. He saw some traffic cones on some council land that he wanted. I was telling him they weren't his but he went to get them anyway. When he was getting them someone was shouting out of their flat at him, telling him to leave them there, so they ended up having an argument. I was in the van worried. I was shouting from the window, shouting "Mark, you need to get back in the van." Eventually he got back into the van but the anger he had with the man was turned on me. He was really angry because

I had used his name when I was calling him back into the van, so he was telling me if the police came looking for him later it would be my fault as I had given away his name. I was just flabbergasted as I hadn't done anything wrong. He was ranting all the way back about how stupid I was and how it would all be my fault if the police found out. Once we got back I said I needed some space and went to walk into our bedroom but he grabbed me by the arm, swinging me round to face him and punched me in the face, just under the right eye. It just felt numb and unreal. I didn't even feel any pain, I think because I was so pumped up with adrenaline anyway because he had turned all his anger with the man on me when we were driving home in the van. I felt it was my fault for getting him more wound up. As soon as he had hit me, everything just slowed down. It felt unreal and because it felt unreal, it was easier to forget. It suddenly hit me then that he wasn't drinking, he wasn't on drugs, he had just punched me. But I had been with him for nearly a year by then so I believed that I loved him and started coming up with excuses. It was beyond confusing so in many ways I think my mind shut down so I didn't keep thinking about it. Straight away he said, "Oh my God, I don't know what happened". I told him I needed space and I just went into the bedroom and hid under the duvet. The next day I was too scared to look in the mirror.

why I hid what happened

My reaction straight away was I wanted to hide it and forget it happened because your natural reaction is you don't want to believe that someone you love - and who loves you - would do something like that. Even though in my head I knew it was out of order, I wanted to forget it because I couldn't comprehend that someone who loved me would do that to me. The next morning his sister popped round and I pretended I was ill. I literally went into cover up mode and all I focused on was how I could cover my black eye. I covered it with makeup and had a story of falling in the hen run if anyone asked. Carrying on as if it never happened made the shame and disbelief go away and it felt good to escape the truth of the situation. I also didn't say anything because I was scared about what would happen to us, and his son, if I said something.

the abuser plays the victim

When someone is violent, they immediately go into victim mode. 'I am such an idiot, how could I do this to you?' and I just wanted to hide under the duvet. Mark was so apologetic that day, bringing me cups of tea and showering me with attention. It was always the same after that. After every violent outbreak he would be the one that couldn't cope and I would be the coping one and I always believed him when he said it would never happen again because I wanted with all of my heart to believe it.

violence always creeps in gradually

Before Mark started punching me in the face, he started with wrist grabbing and pushing and shoving. It's important to look at violence as a gradual thing and then the violence becomes extreme - but by that time you have no self-esteem because you know you have put yourself through this and chosen to stay.

why I carried on as though nothing had happened

Carrying on as if nothing had happened made the shock and disbelief go away. It made me feel good to escape the truth of the situation. It started out as infrequent, maybe once every few months, so that time in between would make you feel like it would never happen again. If it had happened every day at the beginning of the relationship I would like to hope I had enough self-esteem at that point to have gotten out of the relationship. But because it was gradual and infrequent at first it was easier to forgive and try to forget. When I knew things had got really bad after one argument, I curled myself up on the kitchen floor to protect myself from being hit but he just ended up kicking me in the back and legs instead. And I just thought he knows I am scared of him and he is still trying to hurt me, knowing I am scared.

why I didn't leave

In between the violence, we had wonderful family moments and with his promise of change, I wanted to believe the violence would stop. We even had marriage counselling and the police were involved at one point. And the violent incidents would only happen when we didn't have his son staying with us, so it was like I was living two lives. We would have lovely family times but when his son went to his mum's, I would think, 'shit it's going to happen now'. And each time the violence kept getting a bit worse. I felt trapped by my own lies that I had concocted to cover up what was happening and I was scared of what he would do if I left as he frequently threatened suicide.

marriage didn't make a difference

I remember getting married and things were just getting worse. I thought getting married would make it better, but it just got worse. He beat me up on our honeymoon and my denial was getting deeper. Things escalated. And it was always around sex. I had this idea that I had to please my husband, but I couldn't keep up with his sex drive. The arguments were more frequent but I didn't know what to do.

did anyone else ever witness it?

No. Our dog was the only person in the whole world who witnessed all of it. He would be cowering in the corner and when it was all over he would come over and lick me and that would make me cry, and then he would lick my tears away.

One time the police got involved

One time I ran out of the house because he was smashing things. It was after him kicking me, because I knew me being scared wouldn't stop him. I didn't have any shoes on. I ran down to the park, I ran to the phone box and before I even knew what I was doing I was calling 999. I was engaged then, so I told them 'my fiance's drunk, he's really angry and he's smashing things in the house and I am worried he might harm our dog'. The police were really good, they were there in two minutes. They were amazing. They said because it was a domestic incident and Mark was drunk I wasn't allowed back to the house. I didn't want to call my mum and dad because I didn't want them to know what had been going on but I had to. I remember telling them that Mark had got really drunk and he was smashing stuff in the house. The police had to interview me once they had driven me to my parent's and asked me, 'has he ever hit you?' and I was saying no. There was a specific questionnaire I had to fill in to assess if I was in danger. I was saying no because I was scared of him losing his son. They asked if he had ever shoved me. And then they asked me if he had ever tried to strangle me or drown me. I knew from what they were asking me that there were different levels of domestic violence and that things could escalate. I lied to them because I was ashamed to say yes. Once they had gone my mum asked me, "sweetheart, has he ever been angry or violent with you?" I answered no and I felt so ashamed I lied to her face. I had the chance to change this and chose not to because it was easier to keep lying to everybody and stay stuck.

how bad did the violence get?

He tried to strangle me on three separate occasions as well as try to drown me in the bath. The first time he tried to strangle me, my survival instinct kicked in and I headbutted him making his nose bleed. Straight after he kept saying he couldn't believe what I had done; deflecting away from the fact he had tried to strangle me. And for the following week or so he twisted it around and made me feel as bad as him. I started to hate who I had become; first a liar and now violent. I didn't recognise myself.

marriage counselling

We went to see a marriage counsellor after a year and the counsellor asked me if Mark had tried to strangle me and I said no. I felt too scared to say how bad the violence had got and was ashamed of myself for getting into this position. I said he had a real temper and sometimes he would push me. Mark would then tell the counsellor how he couldn't control it and then I would have to sit there with him whilst he worked through all his problems with the counsellor. After the counselling finished, everything was fine for about three or four months and it felt like it had helped him and that it was worth it, that marriage was about for better or worse. But then he had a disagreement with his ex about his son and access and the violence towards me started all over again, with denial close behind.

after he'd been violent

After Mark had been violent, he would go into overdrive and be extra loving towards me. He would help me with the housework, make me cups of tea, so between the attacks he would be extra loving. So I spent a lot of time between a state of denial, and fear, which would kick in when his son would go to his mum's, as that was when the violence would always happen at the start. I spent a lot of time trying to work out why it was happening but before I could think of my way out his son would be back and all would be 'well' again.

why victims of domestic abuse don't admit it is going on

For people who are in this situation, it is bliss pretending it isn't happening. You can't comprehend it is happening, the pain is horrendous. the reality of the situation is too much to bear because you know if people find out you will have to face it.

things got worse

After a while, the attacks started getting worse. At first it was every other week, then every few days and then it started to spill into the time Mark's son was staying with us, but his son wouldn't know about it because he was older by that point and would be out with his friends.

how does it feel to live through domestic violence?

If I had to describe domestic violence I would say it is like a black treacle that spreads through your life and covers up any light. You feel like you can't get away from it.

why it happened

Because I didn't have any clear boundaries and I believed that all Mark needed was love, it was very easy for Mark to get under my skin. But if I had have had boundaries and they were broken, there was no time for them to be rebuilt, so as a person I started to feel worthless and that I was not really a person. You turn it onto yourself and then you start to hate yourself because you have lied to people.

when I started to look at it differently

I think for me it was when Mark's son started to grow up, I knew he would grow up and leave one day and I knew things would reach a pint of no return. Mark had tried to drown me and strangle me a couple of other times so I knew things were escalating and reaching dangerous levels. I had started to have suicidal thoughts and kept feeling like I was running out of excuses and there was nowhere to go.

when things finally came to a head

The final straw was when Mark's son was with us one time. I had gone upstairs to be by myself. I had reached such a state of depression and self-loathing because the more I thought about it the more I hated myself. I remember feeling I would rather be dead than feel like this. Mark came to find me and started having a go at me, asking me why I was depressed and telling me I needed to go and see a doctor. I just looked at him and said, "it's you" and when I said it, every bit of me felt relief and shock. He immediately turned into the victim and said it was me that had changed and he no longer recognised me. He started pleading, 'don't leave me'. I felt like I couldn't even stand the sound of his voice any more. My body was completely repulsed by him. I had reached my breaking point. I pushed him off me and told him I needed time apart and that's when he pinned me down on the bed and bit my jaw. I don't know why after everything else he had done before, but there was something about him biting my jaw that was the final straw for me. I called his son upstairs and gave him a really big hug and told him I loved him. I just told him, "whatever happens between me and your dad, I will always love you, this has got nothing to do with you." and that was the last time I saw him. Mark had always threatened he would stop me seeing his son and it was this fear of having to let go of our close relationship that kept me in danger for so long. I remember shutting the front door after Mark left, putting the keys in the lock and then going to tell my mum and dad.

had friends and family ever suspected anything?

Over time, family knew there was something that wasn't quite right but they couldn't put their finger on it. I had lost a lot of weight at that point because it's the only thing I could control. I was running a lot because it was the only time I could go out without Mark badgering me. When I told mum and dad what had been going on, they said I needed to get the police involved but I didn't want Mark's son's life messed up and I was scared with Mark what he would do if I got the police involved.

help I would recommend

I would recommend for anyone who thinks they are in an abusive relationship to look at something called the freedom programme. Domestic violence is such a complex thing, and there are so many different situations, someone might not own a house like I did, or they might have their own children with their abuser. The freedom programme is about recognising the signs of an abusive character. They can be loud and argumentative or quiet and calculating to name but a few and there are different types of control they have over you, like finances for example. The Samaritans were really good too because no-one knew what was going on with me, but they were just able to listen. That really helped because it's no good saying talk to friends as that would involve admitting you had lied to them about everything being fine. And I would say if it is happening to you, get out asap as the longer it goes on, the harder it is to get out.

signs to look out for

I would say to people just listen to your instinct. Your gut instinct is there for a reason. With Mark, my heart was telling me, 'I love this person' and my head was telling me it is too hard to get out of, I have lied to too many people, and I was hearing Mark's voice in my head about how stupid I was. Possessiveness is a sign of controlling, abusive behaviour. And it can be in subtle ways. If I went out with friends, Mark would always text me so I felt like I couldn't do anything without him. He was very needy. He never stopped me going out - I think he realised it was very important for him to let me go out - but he just made going out too hard to maintain.

abusers play the victim

Abusers play the victim a lot so look out for excuses for their behaviour, the poor me scenarios. With Mark he had moved away from the area where he grew up so that was how he excused not having any friends. But the fact he hadn't made any new ones showed he struggled with relationships, so if you struggle with friendships then you are going to struggle with any kind of intimate relationship. Also, look out for sudden anger, which comes out of nowhere over minor things like leaving a light on, or a door unlocked. I think when you see that kind of anger, I honestly believe the violence is inevitable. By me letting Mark push me, I was reinforcing to him it was ok to act like that. He would also slowly chip away at my confidence. If I asked for his help with something, he would say 'you're so stupid', so he was chipping away at my self-esteem and I began not to trust my own judgement. With my close friends he would point out faults in them, to isolate me. Then I would start seeing less and less of my friends. It's inevitable that when people get married, they get on with their own lives, so I think friends just thought it was that. My friends and family have since said they could see I was changing but because I had always kept up a pretence about everything being rosy, I had convinced them there was nothing to worry about. I went from being a very sociable person to someone who just stopped going out or seeing anyone. Any time anyone asked me, it was easy for me to go into denial mode. That was my only comfort if you like because when you are pretending it's not happening, it's amazing what you can convince yourself.

how does someone in an abusive, domestic violence situation leave? and, how do they move on with their lives?

Once you leave, that's when the work starts. The work on yourself is hard, but it is nothing compared to the situation you have been in. When you have lived in a state of fear and worry for so long the key thing is to be kind to yourself. I came out of it feeling like I didn't have any friends because that is what Mark had told me, but gradually I started letting friends back in. It also helps to have a focus of work, to have normality in your life and a routine. My work had always been my stability. Some people have to leave to go to a refuge but for me I had my job and a routine. But if someone doesn't work, they can do things like make sure they wake up and go to sleep at the same time every day. And then it's a case of just doing things bit by bit. And you have to keep reminding yourself that no matter how you feel, anything is better than living like you were. Even if you are living on your own and you feel lonely, it is still better because you are not scared for your life any more. Yes, you still have fears and worries about how you are going to be living your life, but it is important to spend some time on our own, working around creating healthy boundaries because a lot of people pleasers find themselves in abusive relationships. There are also social care support workers, and it is also good knowing that the police are there to help. Know that the police are there to protect you and they will. There is a lot of help there for you but you have to be ready to be truthful and really look at what has happened to you.

moving on

Once you have got out of your situation, you need to focus on love, and the positives of every day. Just getting through each day is a positive. Pets and animals are also really helpful because they live in the moment so they bring you back to the present. When I first got out of it, I couldn't even walk down the high street on my own. But do little bits at a time, don't over challenge yourself, but do little bits every day. I started to notice patterns in my behaviour. For example, when my anxiety got really bad I realised I was either panicking about the future and what was going to happen or the past and what had happened to me; both of which were not my present reality. I realised then I had a choice - I was free to decide and whilst I was 'present', all was ok. I know when people read this, they might think I have heard this shit before, but you really do just need to live every day, and realise you are surrounded by love. There are far more loving people in the world than there are abusive people. There is so much help out there. Look up online to get an idea of what is available to you and take all the help that is offered; don't be ashamed of needing it, you have been through so much. There are forums and even meetings with other people who have been through, or are still in, an abusive relationship. Knowing that you are not alone is so important. It's also about knowing that you have been through the hard bit and that you are an incredibly strong person if you have come through this. Also make self-care a priority, i.e. taking baths, reading a book… taking time to do something you love is all a good place to start. You may not know what you want or love at first, but that's to be expected, so try to see it as an adventure experiment, exploring things that you can do with your freedom! And it's about knowing you are going to go through an emotional rollercoaster. The whole time I was going through this abusive situation, I couldn't cry. I had made myself numb to things as a coping mechanism so when you come out of it you are going to feel emotions you haven't felt for a while and just know, that's ok. It is also important to know it is ok to be angry that this has happened and that anger is not a bad or negative emotion if it is directed in a healthy way. I'd also recommend finding something you love doing just for the sake of it. Just enjoy your freedom and any time you feel down, just remind yourself you are free and you are surrounded by love. It took me a few years before I felt I was ready to be in an intimate relationship but I made a plan of giving myself this time after my divorce to get back to finding 'me' again, with the focus of a brighter future ahead of me.

is there hope at the end of it all? can you go on to live a normal, happy life after something like this?

Everyone who has been in this situation is capable of finding a healthy, loving, happy and balanced relationship and it starts with having that relationship with yourself first and then you attract someone on the same level. I have ended up finding the person I was meant to be with, who I love and adore and who I can disagree with and there is no drama attached. He knows about my past as I felt I wanted to share that with him to give him more understanding about where I am coming from and he fully accepts me for who I am today, scars and all! I am happier than I ever imagined possible and I am thankful for being here to tell my story.

For details on the freedom programme, mentioned above, please go to:
www.freedomprogramme.co.uk

The national domestic abuse helpline is confidential and available 24 hours a day and can be contacted on 0808 2000 247

The Samaritans can be found at:
www.samaritans.org. You can call them on 116 123 or email them at: jo@samaritans.org

ABOUT THE AUTHOR

If you were to ask me why I write, I'd say it's because it fulfils a need in me. Writing gives me the ability to create - and tell - a story. To make people feel something at a real and deep level, and to get people talking.

If you have got this far, thank you for buying my book. Just know that that alone makes me very happy. I hope I have made you laugh, as well as cry, and even though my book does not have the happy ending you may have wanted, I hope I have left you with a sense of hope. Because wherever there is life, there is always hope. Which is where my motto for this book comes from... Don't let your past define you. Or, the slighter ruder version (which I prefer)... Don't let your shit define you.

To follow me, please go to: www.hadleyc.com. You can contact me direct at: hadley@hadleyc.com

Printed in Great Britain
by Amazon